FRATERNAL BONDS

THOMAS DONAHUE

AUTHOR'S NOTE

Fraternal Bonds is a work of fiction. The events in this novel—including all prison scenes—are neither real nor based loosely on factual events. Any similarities between plots, characters, and real persons are unintentional.

ACKNOWLEDGEMENTS

The construction of *Fraternal Bonds* was like the building of a sailboat. I assembled the hull, the deck, and even the rigging, yet the vessel would not, and could not, seem to move. I realized, years later, that it was the generous and unyielding support of others which provided the wind that set it free. Ellen Slingsby—my friend, classmate, and copyeditor—was diligent in using enough red ink to make my original manuscript look like a Civil War battle site. Chris Lambert, Ken Berg, Marcus Torrejon, Kevin McGillicuddy, and Dave Coleman were all instrumental in technological aspects of the project. The long list of sample readers who offered advice (some of which was taken) helped inspire me. Most notably, I thank the late Neena Doherty for her unabashed honesty. Others motivated me unknowingly with a periodic question: "How's that book project coming along?"

My former professor, and friend, Harris Elder, wisely suggested—halfway through the first draft—to switch from a first-person voice to the third-person narrative. It was sound advice. Several members of the BPD—who requested anonymity—were kind enough to give me insight into various angles of investigation. My friend and classmate Geri Calos gave the novel a meticulous last look before submission. Thank you to my Kappa Delta Phi fraternity brothers who gave me the necessary push to *write a novel* at one of the many weddings we shared together. A special message for the crew at The Pitchers Mound, as well as all my North Adams connections: you rock.

My West Roxbury neighborhood families are awesome—the salt of the earth. Our parents allowed kids to be kids while always instilling the need for love and responsibility. Part of the novel takes place on Meredith Street, a small connector between Clement Avenue and Kenneth Street where I raised Cain as a kid. Four of my childhood friends departed too soon; I will always remember them.

My friends and colleagues at the Suffolk County Sheriff's Department were a big part of this story. We labor—mentally and emotionally—in a world that is seemingly surreal. Television shows, Hollywood films, and even books can't replicate the palpable uncertainty of what the next tour of duty may bring. Many correctional stories, and feelings, are permanently concealed behind cement walls, never eligible for parole.

Last, yet never least, is my family, both near and extended. Without the support of my parents, siblings, wife, and kids, I do not think I would have been successful at any venture in life. They are, in short, the glue which holds me together. Although this work is an act of fiction, one fact is unavoidable. The title *Fraternal Bonds* reflects accurately the importance I place on my personal relationships. My protagonist, Mr. Stephen Nicholson, knowingly avoids the straight road because he is flawed by an overload of sentiment and emotion. He is not unlike several people in my life.

—T.D.

"Boys, tomorrow will be the jury of the judgment you exercise today."

- Joe Donahue, circa 1988

PROLOGUE

I'm rather ambivalent. I've been warehousing bad memories for a dozen years. The memories aren't secretive—far from it, in fact. Yet I have not spoken freely about them.

Until now.

Internalizing negativity is a dangerous game. So, it's time to unravel my mind and "set myself free," as people like to say. That phrase is cliché; I'll find out if it holds true, but I guess the future shall dictate its authenticity.

Perhaps my cleansing began this morning when I wept at Mickey O'Sullivan's funeral. The tears were traitorous, though, because they streamed not from a river of sorrow but rather pity. Nevertheless, the patronizing drops were God's way of reminding me I'm human. Funerals have become commonplace lately. Mickey was not the exception. He was the rule.

Crying for Mickey was important because it gave finality to a series of incidents that took place back in 1999. You remember that year, right? It was the year Prince sang about in the early '80s, the year Roger became a Yankee, and the year all major software companies scammed billions of dollars from consumers with the infamous Y2K-proofing of computers. On a personal note, I didn't have much happening. I only hunted around Massachusetts for a serial killer and almost lost my corrections job trying to help Mickey O'Sullivan out of a prison drug-dealing racket. Oh yeah, I also fell in love for the first time at age thirty. Other than that, it was a boring year.

Okay, I'm being sarcastic. It's my worst trait, or so says Peachy. Sarcasm is the cheapest form of wit, she reminds me, and I'm guilty of frequently drinking from that reservoir. These are my mom's words, mind you, not mine. Peachy is my mother, but I rarely call her Mom. Everyone calls her Peachy, and my dad goes by Eamon. I'm no exception—that's what I call them. That's what my brother Matty calls them, too, and it's what my kid brother, David, used to call them. They are more than a mom and dad to me; they are my brain trust, the coveted counsel I seek when in need of guidance.

Mickey can't escape my mind. You see, he took his life six days ago. He didn't do it by any conventional method, either. No, that would have been too easy for Mickey. This sick bastard took the cake, as far as suicides are concerned. Some might say it was a fitting, or not-so-fitting, end to a sad life. What did he do? He somehow gained access to a radio station tower on the Route 128 beltway in Needham. Everyone in Metro Boston knows the Needham towers, a comforting beacon upon return home from a long trip. They are also extremely high.

The Norfolk county coroner estimated Mickey's fall at four to five hundred feet. It's almost implausible, if you knew Mickey. He was fifty pounds overweight, had a permanently disfigured leg, battled wind gusts of fifty mph, and had an autopsy BAC of 0.09, which is technically a legal state of intoxication in the commonwealth. The alcohol factor was never released to family or friends; the family never made an inquiry. I know this to be true because the coroner is a friend of mine. I read the autopsy report.

I envision Mickey swaying back and forth on the ladder at two hundred feet. The wind was snapping, his hands were aching, and he was assuredly out of breath and sweating profusely. Yet he climbed higher. He climbed with purpose, demonstrating that his need to die outweighed his will to live. I wonder where exactly Mickey determined he had climbed to the appropriate height that guaranteed death and avoided continuation of life. Is rung number one hundred the Mason-Dixon line of tower-jumpers?

Do you want to know the real kicker, the ultimate in melodrama? He made a cell call before imitating Greg Louganis. I didn't have to be told this by the Needham cops, or snoop around for cellular phone records. I know this because the shitbag called me.

I apologize for the vulgarity. It's unbecoming, and Peachy frequently corrects me when I curse. She doesn't mind the soft swears, but the bad words she won't tolerate. She used to say, "Your brother would expel you from his class if he heard that devil talk." You see, Matty is an English professor by trade, and Peachy acts like he never committed sin before. Maybe it's middle child syndrome; maybe it's just me.

Anyway, I was at home on my couch watching an ESPN special on the success of Boston sports teams when Mickey called. That's right; the blubbering jerk called me to apologize for his actions of the past. He could've called his parents; his sister, Jacqueline; his dream girl, Jo Jo; or even his damn bookie. No, he felt the pressing need to call me, as if I hadn't swallowed enough fuc—excuse me, I almost dropped an f-bomb. What I'm trying to say is that I've ingested my fair share of Catholic guilt over the years, and then Mickey found a way to rub salt in old wounds. Of course, I thought the whole jump-from-the-tower act was a joke until I realized the incessant whipping sound in the background could be nothing other than a strong New England wind.

I did my best to coax him down, to play the role of hero—a nonsense tag I got years ago. But the truth is I couldn't help Mickey. Maybe no one could. I'm still pretty freaked out. I don't consider myself a typical person. I've witnessed and experienced too much craziness. I harbor no delusional thoughts that I enabled Mickey to jump, but I know this—the Good Samaritans won't be knocking down my door to offer me a volunteer position on the suicide hotline. Pardon me—there I go with the sarcasm.

The phone conversation seems like it happened years ago, though it hasn't been a week. Mickey rambled on and on about my kid brother, David. They had been best friends as kids, and Mickey was present when he died.

Yes, the plot thickens early.

My mind is racing as reality sets in. David's dead, and now so is Mickey. Kid brother has been dead well over twenty years, a full generation. The year 1987 remains embedded in memory. Remember 1987? Wow. What a year. The Celtics were in the finals, long hair was in style, Motley Crue rocked, and IROCs were the speed car of choice. But it was a bad year for me. It was the year a girl I thought I could've loved was savagely murdered. Her name was Laiken, and you'll soon know all about her. More importantly, it was the year God came calling for a sixteen-year-old soon-to-be junior at Catholic Memorial High School. His name was David Nicholson, and yes, he was the aforementioned kid brother.

My breakfast looks and smells delicious. I'm sitting alone in a booth at a diner next to the bowling alley on Centre Street in West Roxbury, Massachusetts. Some of you may be familiar with it. The irony is that I'm very hungry, yet I can't eat. Not right now. My emotions have turned from sadness to guilt to anger. Too many of my colleagues have died in the last couple of years; too many guys in their twenties, thirties, and early forties.

My full-time occupation is correction officer at the Boston House. Technically, my title is deputy sheriff, but the title and patch on my shirt will never get me on an episode of *Cops*. You see, I work *inside* the joint. It's where the convicted bad guys roam uncontested in packs and you're expected to maintain some semblance of order. And it ain't like television, either. We don't walk around with billy clubs or cans of mace. We have radios, pens, and each other. That's it.

There's been an Irish Curse at the Boston House over the last few years. We've lost ten officers, and nine of them had Irish blood in their veins. That doesn't mean they were from the Emerald Isle, or even had an Irish last name. It just means they were at least part Irish. Massachusetts has a high percentage of Irish Americans, but this statistic is still a bit alarming. The Irish Curse typically refers to a deficiency in size of the male reproductive organ, but in this case, it's worse. The Boston House has become death personified.

You know all about correction officers. It's the profession everyone in America badmouths at some time or another, but to your face they say crap like, *That's a tough job, I don't know how you guys do it, that must be really dangerous, they don't pay you guys enough, make sure you're safe.*

Whatever.

In any event, I've decided it's time to talk about 1999. Open up my soul, air everything out—you know, that sort of thing. It'll probably make me feel better. Mickey O'Sullivan and his antics would have typically been headline news, as far as my interests are concerned. But Mickey actually took a back seat.

It's time for me to talk about the Olympian.

Mirrors canvas the walls in the eatery. I stare into a large mirror to my right and I see the Olympian—at least, it looks like him, anyway. Who knows, maybe it is me? I remember high school psychology class; Freud divided the human psyche into three parts, the id, ego, and superego. Some people favor one part over the others. The Olympian favored the id; the Olympian is a serial killer.

The Olympian killed and I'll never know why. Maybe it's best if I don't know. Nevertheless, it's time for the story to be told because it is—for lack of a better phrase—a story worth telling.

I invite you all into my time machine. You will travel to Hoosac Mills in western Massachusetts and meet Laiken Barnes, William Jonathan Barnes, Josef Kieler, and the brothers of Kappa Chi Omicron. You will get a taste of corrections with my friends and foes at the Boston House. I will introduce you to my family. As in most stories, both real and fictional, there is a special connection between man and woman. Oh yes, reader—you shall meet Melanie, my dear, sweet Melanie.

You will soon discover that my professional life is not limited to corrections. I am, in fact, a licensed private investigator. That, my dear readers, is what put me on to the Olympian. That is what started the whole mess. But that is the past, and there is no better time to discuss the past than the present. Now is that time.

I feel better already. I start eating, and the food is delicious, as I knew it would be, as it always is. The story will be told, but I cannot tell it myself. I recuse myself from a first-person account because I could never be objective. It wouldn't be fair to you, the reader.

I can breathe easier now because I am ready to reflect. I actually want—and need—to talk about the things that I bottled up for so many years. I'll start with David. I remember him at different stages of his life. It's all part of the continual healing process. You must realize, one never completely recovers from the loss of a young family member. It's like losing a limb. Life continues and you make the most of it, but you are never whole again. Not totally. Don't take my word on this, either. Ask around; others will attest.

When I close my eyes, I revisit David's trick-or-treating phase of the late '70s, his growth spurt of 1984, and yes, the day God took his hand in—you know when—1987. I've coped with that year enough. In the next couple of pages you'll be taken to 1987 because of necessity, but the bigger picture in my tale deals with the more immediate past. It's time to travel back to 1999, to the watershed moment of my life. It was the year I learned how to love, and remembered how to cry.

1.

C_ollege towns seldom sleep. Christmas break offers a rest and summer session is merely a nap. But there is no true hibernation. Like clockwork, college kids roll into town each September. They are young, vibrant, and in most cases, eager to learn. They bring money to the town and fresh thoughts to the classroom. They are idealistic—the future of America. Regardless of gender, race, or creed, they all share one common trait: attitude.

One such town exists in the upper left corner of Massachusetts. It's well over a hundred miles from Boston, yet only minutes away from New York and Vermont. The people work hard and return smiles. They pay taxes and don't complain. They go to high school sporting events and town meetings. They aren't afraid to cheer or jeer. They worship each Sunday; attendance, however, is determined not by a church mandate, but rather their strong belief in God.

Some of the unspoken town rules are simple. Buy a man a beer and he buys you one back. Insult a man's girl and get a punch in the mouth. No frills, no thrills. What you see is what you get. Locals are called Millers. It's a nice place to live.

Welcome to Hoosac Mills.

Hoosac Mills is a twin-engine town. Taconic State College employs almost six hundred people, either directly or indirectly. Its existence is vital, yet it is not the sole source of major employment. While all laud the college with respect to education and job opportunity, its place in the town's economic climate is clearly defined. Taconic State College is queen of the

1

land, but Hoosac Electric is king. Yes, the mighty Hoosac Electric Plant—kingdom on the river—employs over fifteen hundred Berkshire County residents. Some skilled jobs at Hoosac Electric require advanced engineering degrees and years of experience. Most jobs are on the assembly line. With the exception of the bean counters, all jobs are dangerous. Dozens have been severely injured in electrical accidents over the years; four have died. There are some certainties: the conveyor belts never stop, and the incessant demand for production continues. *Efficiency.* That is the word majority owner William Jonathan Barnes preaches. Barnes is controversial—loathed by many, loved by some. Regardless of opinion, all employees refer to him behind his back by the same name: King Billy.

* * *

High above Hoosac Mills a young man's legs dangled from a ledge. His wide eyes stared into the valley. The lights were bright in the city. Oh yes, with a population exceeding twenty thousand, Hoosac Mills actually is a city. It's complete with a mayor, city council, school committee, and even a council on aging. By Boston standards such a population warrants township, but not in sparsely populated Berkshire County. Either designation is acceptable to a Miller. They don't mind being referred to as a town as long as you play by the Berkshire rules, not the Boston rules. Unlike Boston, life in the Berkshires moves at a slower pace.

Rules are delineated, and the young man ruminating on the ledge knew them. In fact he had grown to despise rules—not the Boston or Berkshire rules, but rules in general. He was unhappy with the regimentation of society.

Rules are for followers. Rules are for the mentally and emotionally inept. Rules are for sissies.

He had become embittered with women. The anger didn't stem from their pretty faces or curved bodies per se, but instead the resulting effect these attributes had on men. Great looks complemented by sensuality transferred into power. He didn't loathe women who exuded this scent, but rather those who abused its power. He understood its hypnotic abilities, its omnipresence, and its destructive whip. It was an invisible force that had ruined families and even sparked war between nations. Fathers, uncles, and big brothers had warned young men over generations about its danger. The advice was always the same: *Don't think with your little head,* or

2

Get your mind out of the gutter. Many men heard the advice, yet few heeded it. They fell prey not because they were weak, but rather vulnerable. They could not withstand the proverbial power of pussy.

Yes, he was frustrated. He contemplated his actions. He looked into the valley, seeking guidance. The valley lights flickered but offer no counsel. He drew from the flask, which, ironically, was gift from *her.*

The flask was emptied. He stood atop the ledge. It was a long drop, maybe two hundred feet. The wind blew. It would be easy to jump, painless not in body but in mind. He considered it. So much had happened in the last couple of years. He reflected. A month ago a drug dealer was shot seven times in the torso and lived to tell about it. Last year a beautiful woman, a teacher and a mom, lost her life in a voluntary space mission. Good versus evil, right versus wrong. He couldn't possibly weigh the world's scale of justice. It should be called the scale of injustice. Billy Joel's lyrics resonated: *Only the good die young.*

He dropped the flask. The initials on it read BB, short for *Boston Boy,* a ridiculous nickname used only by her. He checked the time. Yes, he could still pull it off. It was the decision of a lifetime, literally. Yes, he would proceed. Life's tipping point had arrived.

* * *

Boston Boy was anonymous. He moved slowly from room to room, sipping his beverage. He was at a Halloween party at the Kappa Chi Omicron frat house. It took only three minutes to find her. Once he saw her, his emotions raged. Any thoughts of abandoning mission were quickly disposed.

He rested against a wall and observed the party. The party itself seemed to observe his intended mark. *Interesting.* It was so damn interesting how a young woman captivated so many. The results of his visual survey were obvious.

All eyes watched Laiken Barnes. There was little to dispute. She was beautiful and smart, the envy of the girls and the obsession of the boys. She was a local girl—a Miller.

Laiken was King Billy's daughter.

Her costume of choice would soon be the talk of campus. She was Catwoman—dressed in a sleek black outfit that was skintight, accentuating her curvy figure.

Bose speakers pumped Van Halen lyrics into the crowded basement. It was a special party, occurring once each semester. The décor was odd—sheets of tin foil clung to the cement walls, and flashing green light bulbs illuminated the cavernous rooms. Even the booze was different. In lieu of beer kegs the fraternity served a dangerous combination of cheap vodka, lime rickey, sherbet, and ice. It was called Green Machine. The sweet taste belied its potency, though, and many Taconic State College students referred to Green Machine as an aphrodisiac.

Laiken eased through the party. She marveled at the costumes: Elvis Presley, Elton John, Cyndi Lauper, and Adolf Hitler were just some of the impersonators milling about. All had drinks in hand and hidden thoughts of lust. After all, this was college, not high school. In college, post-adolescents grew into adults and the most important lesson was a course called life. Sexual education was an unspoken requirement and almost all were willing to participate. Laiken Barnes was no exception.

She sipped her drink, catching a group of freshmen boys ogling her. She leered at them, blowing a kiss before issuing a seductive purr. Embarrassed, the boys moved to another room. She was Laiken Barnes, most sought-after girl on campus. She knew it. Not one to be smitten by the pretty boys or campus jocks, Laiken dated whomever she liked, whenever she liked. She was confident without being haughty, a gray-area attribute that made her likable. The thrill of sexual pleasure, however, was a game to her.

Some boys were actual (though temporary) love interests, and others were merely conquests, prey. Prey—such a callous word, yet it was fitting. Some boys misread Laiken's attraction to them. They became obsessed while she remained detached and impersonal after a night of ecstasy.

Boston Boy breathed heavily. Laiken walked past him. She suddenly stopped and looked right at him. She stared into his mask. He was draped in costume, replete with mask, black cape, and prop. Something was oddly familiar about his stance. Curious, she took an aggressive step forward. Twelve inches separated their faces. "Hello there, stranger," Laiken said. "Do I know you?"

"I believe you do, Miss Laiken," he replied.

Laiken grinned. "What a pleasant surprise, Boston Boy. I've missed you."

"That's good. I suggest we reacquaint without delay."

"You mean right now?" Laiken asked. "Green Machine just started."

Boston Boy smiled. "Don't fret," he said. "We'll only be gone for a moment. Meet me outside in ten minutes."

Laiken was excited. "Are you sure you'll be able to handle me, Boston Boy?"

"What do you think?" he asked.

"I should hope so."

Boston Boy raised a finger to his lips and whispered, "Not a word to a soul."

"Okay."

Laiken briefly roamed the cellar, drinking Green Machine and chatting with friends. True to her word, she didn't mention Boston Boy to anyone and reported outside as directed. She immediately spotted him at the corner, leaning against his car. Laiken was excited—no, she was enthralled because she knew that the next few moments would be sexually invigorating. With little delay they were driving down the street. Both were unmasked. "Nice to see you in the flesh," she said.

"And I can't wait to get you in the flesh," he replied. "Any objections to revisiting one of our old rendezvous points, my lady?"

Laiken gazed. She loved everything about him—his presence, his confidence, his intelligence, his speech, and his body. She loved all these things yet she didn't love *him*. She lusted for him. "No, I have no objections," she said. Laiken deftly maneuvered her hand under his costume and unfastened his trousers. She established direct eye contact with him before licking her lips. "And I'm no lady." The car moved slowly—one head visible—until they came to a halt in a dirt parking lot.

They were in a relatively isolated location near the entrance of the Hoosac Tunnel. It was Halloween night but the Berkshire air was warm. It was Indian summer. "I have a blanket. Let's lie underneath the stars," he said.

"Are you a closet romantic, Boston Boy?"

"Perhaps so," he said.

They attacked each other without delay. He was careful, utilizing latex. He heard the distant rumbling of an approaching train, then peered at his watch.

Right on time.

In a matter of moments they both climaxed. He withdrew and carefully placed the condom in a paper bag, unaware his fluid had leaked. The train approached rapidly. He reached under a corner of the blanket and retrieved a shiny instrument.

Bushes and the dark sky precluded the conductor from a good view of the parking lot. It was a freight train, filled with heavy cargo and over a quarter of a mile in length. The nearest residences were within earshot. Boston Boy rolled atop Laiken, staring into her with blank eyes—dead man's eyes.

"What are you doing?" she asked. He simply smiled—an evil grin—and she didn't notice the knife in his left hand.

"To hell with you and your kind," he said flatly as he raised his hand above his head. Now Laiken could see clearly. She was frightened, confused, and paralyzed.

"No!"

The train ran its course, taking its load while drowning the piercing screams of Laiken Barnes. The man, the one Laiken called Boston Boy, now moved with alacrity. He had no choice. He fetched his bag from his vehicle—his kit—and began his cleanup. Laiken's eyes, without the slightest hint of life, stared at him. "You got what you deserved," he said. He approached the dead girl. It was time for a present. A tear fell from his eye, though it was not on Laiken's account. He donned plastic gloves and clasped a gold chain around her neck. He muttered a name to himself and departed. Time was now his enemy.

* * *

At eleven-thirty the party was still rocking. Boston Boy reappeared in the basement. This time was different, though. He was greeted with open arms, seemingly a fresh face to all. The excitement of the kill pumped his blood and swelled his muscles. Young girls cast lascivious looks.

By one-thirty the party had waned. A beautiful sophomore had been watching him. She was drunk when she approached him—tentative. He returned her signals, and small talk quickly led to an invitation back to her room. He located the fraternity treasurer, the only sober person in the basement, and overtly shook his hand goodbye on the way out the door.

They talked and kissed en route to her room. The young girl had no intentions of sleeping with him. It was a prudent decision on her part. They lay on her bed, kissing and clutching. He mockingly teased her.

"You're such a bad boy," she said flirtatiously. Her name was Carmen—young, pretty, trustworthy, and naïve. "So bad, so bad," she said again. He smiled sincerely. He laughed on the inside: *if she only knew.*

Her name was Carmen—alibi girl.

* * *

At five in the morning another freight train rolled through town. Three bakeries warmed their ovens, paperboys turned off alarm clocks, and two street cleaners negotiated the barren roads before the snowy weather came. White smoke billowed from the Hoosac Electric chimneys. Birds chirped, but not loudly enough to disturb anyone. High on a residential hill stood an impressive home with a wealthy man. The man was awake, standing on his balcony and looking down upon the town. He was a man of stature. Regardless of the day he wakened early, because he was regimented. He was a man who not only created rules, but modified them when and where he deemed necessary. He was William Jonathan Barnes, and Hoosac Mills was his town. The town wakened early and so did he. He was King Billy, and that's how he liked it.

Because college towns seldom sleep.

2.

Boston, Massachusetts
February, 1999

Prisons never sleep. This opinion is not unanimous, however, because the Inmate Guidebook disagrees. It's a thick sheaf of prison rules and regulations etched in black and white, leaving little room for interpretation. Inmates are told when to rise, eat, bathe, go to class, play basketball, et cetera...page fifty-one actually states, "*All cell lights and/or illuminating devices shall be turned off by midnight each evening. No exceptions.*" The Inmate Guidebook is powerful. Its presence is legendary at internal inmate disciplinary sessions. Seemingly every time an inmate sensibly pleads his case at a hearing, a quick swipe of the hand finds a page that refutes his testimony. The Inmate Guidebook is strict. It lacks mercy. It is punitive.

Yet it lies. The Inmate Guidebook lies because it is decidedly prejudiced. It is inanimate, not speaking the *whole* truth. Juries convict and judges imprison, but no book of rules on God's earth can shackle a man's dreams, fears, regrets, promises, or even hope. These are human factors, invisible emotions that don't apply to common law, canon law, or any law. A man's mind is his personal highway—free to roam at any speed at any time. A man's mind may never be subjugated by the criminal justice system.

One such prison with rules and wishful hopes exists in Shawmut County, Massachusetts. It is a place misunderstood by many because twenty-foot walls preclude invitation to objective eyes. Some sordid reports of its activity hold water, some are prevarications, and in either case, most are embellished. Certain facts cannot be disputed. The prison's inmate and officer racial composition are unfortunate yet telling barometers of Boston's street life and political front. Wayward minorities land behind secured walls, while politically connected whites land secure jobs in blue. It's just how it is. The recidivism rate nears seventy-five percent. The math is simple: 25 percent of the inmates "find the light," while the majority can't be helped or don't want help. Society calls them the incorrigibles.

The inmates are urban—streetwise and tough—reared by the reality of abject poverty, not the privileged hand of opulence. They are cunning, intimidating, and shun authority. Childhoods are branded by abuse: physical, sexual, mental, and psychological. Addiction is rampant. Oddly enough, some actually prefer being in jail; it's safer than the street. The *real* truth—the truth that uppity white folks won't discuss at the dinner table—is that most inmates would have seen a different fate had they grown up on a tree-lined street with a two-car garage and a dog named Satin. Two-parent households are uncommon to the average inmate, and even a conservative social worker will admit that the average convict didn't have a chance coming out of the gate.

Rules are rules nonetheless. When a man or woman commits a crime, they must face judgment day. The saying is old: "If you're gonna do the crime, be prepared to do the time." If that's the case, put life on hold for a stretch, sacrifice all liberties, and adopt the inmate code of conduct. A not-so-hospitable residence awaits.

Welcome to the Boston House.

* * *

Sean Connery was dying. He was on his back, aged and sweaty, clutching his rosary beads and religiously reciting one word: "penitent." Harrison Ford played the hero, the prodigal son who was the only person capable of saving his father. The prison audience of 175 was held captive, rooting for Indiana Jones to find the Holy Grail and save the day. This audience paid attention. They were incarcerated, knowing privileges at the Boston House aren't guaranteed. When a good movie is screened, all seats are filled.

A mock Irish American reunion was being held at the 6-Block correction officer's panel. Stephen Nicholson was the Lead Dog, prison jargon for officer-in-charge. Even though Mickey O'Sullivan and Billy Malley were assigned each night to 6-Block, seniority prevailed in the event that the assigned Lead Dog was on a day off. Such was the case tonight.

The unit was big, shaped in a horseshoe with sixty-eight cells, two tiers, and a sealed-off recreation deck. There were blind spots. The seating arrangement resembled that of a 1950s theatre in a border state. The whites sat to the left, Hispanics in the middle, and the blacks—the largest population—sat to the right. The few Asians in the crowd found a niche in the white section. Like all societies, there is a caste system at the Boston House. Social misfits of all orders sat up front. The unit was quiet and all eyes were glued to the two big-screen televisions, replete with digital imaging, DVD, VCR, cable TV movie stations, and surround sound.

Inmate Renzo DiLorenzo was the exception. He sat in the crowd but wasn't watching the movie. After all, he knew plenty about movies. Renzo was nearing the end of a two-year sentence for aggravated battery on a nerdy low-budget Hollywood producer. In Boston, local unions have an unusually strong influence in all feature film productions. Sometimes their influence extends past the law; sometimes their influence gets people hurt. Renzo was a freelance enforcer, a man who, in street language, was considered *capable*. That street reputation carried into prison. Renzo was the unanimously chosen Caesar of 6-Block, that is, the top dog of the white boys. Yes, Renzo knew about movies but didn't give a damn about Indiana Jones.

Renzo eyed Roscoe McFarland. Roscoe was the proverbial black sheep of a well-to-do family from the Point in South Boston. Deemed an underachiever, Roscoe was unmarried and worked as a courier in downtown Boston. A late weekend night behind the wheel of his Toyota had yielded two drastic results: two months in the hospital for a female passenger, and six months behind bars at the Boston House for Roscoe. He was thirty but had the physique of a lanky teenager. Roscoe was passive and aloof, not wanting trouble in his maiden prison bid.

Trouble follows bad habits. Incarcerated men and women aren't permitted personal effects from home. Photographs of family and friends enter via US mail and must be preapproved by prison staff. Items such as food, toiletries, undergarments, and Walkmans may be purchased in the inmate canteen. There is one personal possession, however, which does not discriminate against race, gender, or social class. Not even the most diligent correction officer can prevent its entry. It follows its victim like a shadow. It can't be seen, touched, or smelled. It's the perpetual eight-hundred-pound gorilla on the back of many people—addiction. Yes, Roscoe now served prison time because of a one-night battle he'd lost with alcohol, but no, he was not an alcoholic.

Gambling was Roscoe McFarland's vice. A recent slump in the college basketball ranks had indebted Roscoe to the prison bookmaker, Mr. Renzo DiLorenzo. In prison, all debts must be paid in full; there are few exceptions. Insolvency was Roscoe's quandary; his canteen account was dry and no one from home was willing to help. He was in prison, in debt, and on his own.

Roscoe was awed by Indiana Jones. He vicariously injected himself into the hero's role. Maybe he could, ever so briefly, stave off his seemingly unsolvable problems. He didn't want to think about his limited options: a stint in the safe haven protective custody unit or an unscheduled trip to the hospital. As the movie neared its end, Roscoe clapped loudly. His life had been a failure; now he sought just a moment of solace. He even managed a smile when Indiana Jones prevailed.

The imminent future was unavoidable. Roscoe wasn't a tough guy. Yet he was smart enough to differentiate between society rules and prison rules. Conflict resolution in the real world might mean counseling, intervention, or mediation. In prison, conflicts were resolved with beatings. The credits rolled and Roscoe rose with a sea of prisoners. Noise levels increased as inmates returned to their cells for the night. One last look at Indiana Jones and Roscoe marveled, "That's a hero."

Roscoe inched toward his cell near the end of the unit, far away from the safety of the officer's panel. The unit lights slowly gained power. Roscoe sighed. He didn't see himself ever returning to prison. He also didn't see Renzo DiLorenzo emerge from behind a concrete stanchion. Roscoe only felt what would later be described as an enormous elbow to the side of his face. Blood would come, oh yes, but not until the impact of the blow caused Roscoe to spin and fall flat on his face. His nose was shattered; his left orbital socket was ruptured. Inmates scurried, locking themselves in before accusatory eyes placed them near the assault. There was an exception, though. Inmate Squeaky Tubbs was always game for a good show. He loved the violence, and even some of the drama that came with it. Squeaky watched Renzo carefully. It was his moment to do what he did best: collect information.

Renzo didn't scamper; it wasn't his style. In fact he delivered a merciless kick to the semiconscious Roscoe's head before callously sauntering away. Leaning against a nearby wall stood correction officer Mickey O'Sullivan. He began his patrol slightly before the film ended and, to his chagrin, witnessed the entire act. Renzo considered the moment. He locked his steely eyes with O'Sullivan, and then raised his left index finger to his nose. "Shhhhh," he whispered.

Sweat glistened on Mickey's forehead. In the blink of an eye Renzo vanished. O'Sullivan called to his partners, alerting them to the crisis before radioing for assistance. He tended to Roscoe McFarland, the fallen inmate, while Nicholson and Malley secured inmates in their cells. Roscoe's eyes were shut, his body twitched, and irregular heavy breathing produced what could best be described as snorting sounds. He was in trouble.

Mickey O'Sullivan reflected. Roscoe McFarland was a respectful inmate, a guy whose street transgressions were no worse than many of his friends', let alone himself. In fact, Mickey had recently gotten to know Roscoe. Mickey gave him a cleaning job that reduced his sentence by three days a month. He liked Roscoe, a guy who just didn't seem to belong in prison. Funny, Mickey didn't seem to fit in the prison, either. Mickey knew Roscoe was a delinquent gambler. Mickey also knew Roscoe owed Renzo DiLorenzo.

Mickey neared panic, fighting to control his nerves. Prison, addiction, gambling, and Renzo were all bad words. He knew the feeling of being indebted.

Mickey O'Sullivan knew what it was like to squirm at Renzo's glare.

Roscoe's knees lifted off the ground and his feet flailed. The unit sally port door opened and emergency response officers flooded the unit. Two nurses hurried to the injured inmate. Mickey cleared way, keeping his eyes on Roscoe.

I guess you could say we're kindred spirits, buddy.

Assisting personnel secured all cell doors. The nurses signaled for an ambulance. It was a new night in the urban prison, but the same story. Violence was the king. It's just the way it was.

Officer Stephen Nicholson pulled Mickey aside. "You okay, buddy?" Mickey was sweating and his hands were trembling. His face reddened.

"Yeah, Stephen, I'm fine. Thanks."

Nicholson was savvy. It didn't take much analysis to know that Mickey was troubled. "Hey Mick, you were close by when this thing went down. What did you see?"

Mickey, sweating feverishly, paused for moment. He thought of good times: Christmas, tailgating at Foxboro, late nights with Jo-Jo, summer weekends at the Cape, and old Parkway Little League games with his best friend, David Nicholson. The last thing Mickey needed was more trouble, as in Renzo breathing down his neck.

Mickey respected Stephen Nicholson—always did, and always would. In fact, he loved the entire Nicholson family. There was a lot of history. That's why Mickey couldn't look Stephen in the eye.

"Didn't see nothing," he said.

* * *

Nicholson didn't leave 6-Block that night. He opted for an easy overtime shift from eleven at night to seven in the morning. At time-and-a-half, it was easy money. He stared at the unit clock: 2:30 a.m. His only partner was at lunch, probably toying with dumbbells in the staff weight room.

Nicholson surveyed the unit. Two cells on the second tier had lights on, and of course, everyone knew that lights must be out by midnight.

Cell thirty-five was part of the handle to the "horseshoe," located directly above the officer's panel. Stephen ascended the nearby stairwell and approached the steel door, fitted with an eight-by-twenty-four-inch window. It was a two-man cell. One inmate appeared to be asleep on the top bunk. A blanket covered half his face. He was snoring.

The other inmate wasn't sleeping. The soles of his feet were pressed against the cell door and he performed rapid-fire pushups. He breathed with precision. Sweat glistened on his shirtless, muscular back. A tattoo of crossing flags—American and Italian—occupied a healthy portion of his right shoulder blade. Beneath the flags, in the spot usually reserved for a surname, was etched Eastie.

The pushups continued. Stephen lost count after seventy, and he had arrived during the exercise. Finally he tapped on the glass. Renzo DiLorenzo sprang to his feet, as if on cue.

He spun at the door and was almost nose-to-nose with Nicholson. A steel door and thick pane of glass, however, served as a divide to the twelve-inch gap. "Good evening, Officer Nicholson," Renzo said quickly.

The room suddenly darkened. Renzo seemingly vanished. Nicholson never said a word.

The other handle to the horseshoe was cell sixty-eight, directly across from Renzo's cell. The fastest way to cell sixty-eight was to descend the nearby stairwell, walk across the common area, and ascend the far stairwell. Stephen didn't do that, though. Count time wasn't for another half hour, yet he opted to take the walk around the horseshoe. He needed time to think.

Stephen didn't like working 6-Block because of cell sixty-eight. He avoided the unit whenever possible. But this was business. He made his way to the door and looked. A hulking man with his back to Stephen was seated at his desk, thoughtfully writing with his left hand. A New American Bible lay to his right and charcoal sketches of what appeared to be Stations of the Cross were taped to the wall.

Only the penitent man shall pass.

Stephen lightly kneed the door. Anthony Marconi—known in prison as Marconi Beach—rose and slowly approached the door. He examined Stephen, speechless. Marconi Beach was well over six feet and about 285 pounds of solid muscle, save a baby spare tire around the waist. At thirty-three, his hardened face had never recovered from its long bout with acne. Like Renzo, Marconi was nearing the end of a two-year stint. His schizophrenic girlfriend had alleged abuse, calling 9-1-1. A rookie cop, in his first solo shift, had arrived at Marconi's North End condominium. The girlfriend screamed bloody murder. She was unscathed but demanded action. The indecisive cop told Marconi he was under arrest. The normally passive Marconi still to this day couldn't remember knocking out the rookie with a straight left to the jaw.

One punch and nearly two years later, Marconi now stared at correction officer Stephen Nicholson.

A minute passed. Neither man spoke. Finally Marconi lifted his notebook and showed the cover. It was his personal memoir, entitled *Prison Tiers*. Nicholson's smile was a show of approval. Marconi then scribbled on a pad of paper. It read: "Peachy? Eamon? Matthew?"

Stephen gave a simple nod. *They're all doing well, friend.*

Marconi's inquiry was about Stephen's family. He knew all about Stephen's mom, dad, and brother. He should have—he'd lived with the

Nicholsons in 1985 and 1986. Marconi's mom, Margarita, had been a best friend of Stephen's mom, Peachy. They had worked together since the two women were both twenty-two years old. In 1985, Margarita lost her battle with breast cancer. His father, Anthony, Sr., was a volatile alcoholic. Young Anthony, attending community college, needed a safe place to stay. He was an only child. The Nicholson family provided that haven for two years until Anthony, Jr. could establish himself on solid ground.

Anthony, Jr. blossomed under the Nicholson roof. His hard study in the community college classroom earned him a scholarship to Bentley College. He also developed an everlasting bond with the Nicholson boys, Irish American guys from West Roxbury, which was a world apart from his Italian American upbringing in the North End. The Nicholson brothers poked fun at Anthony's North End dialect, and Anthony teased the Nicholsons for eating pasta sauce—not gravy—from a jar. Anthony would later succeed in the business world, and all was fine until his freakish encounter with the rookie cop. Although they only saw each other a few times each year, before incarceration, Anthony Marconi was considered family in the Nicholson household on Meredith Street.

Department protocol dictated that Stephen report his relationship with Anthony Marconi. He didn't do that. Some deputy superintendent at Boston House would have invariably dubbed it a conflict of interest and transferred Anthony to another prison in the commonwealth. Anthony wanted to do his time at the Boston House, so Stephen never said anything. Only a few of Stephen's closest friends knew the extent of his relationship with Marconi.

Now Anthony Marconi stood before him. He scribbled on the pad again.

I am un-free, Stephen.

Stephen could do little to help. Marconi's face was blank with emotion. He suddenly pressed his left palm against the glass. Stephen stared at the big palm. Stephen met the glass with his right hand and nodded. "Lights out, brother."

At 3:40 a.m. Stephen rubbed his eyes at the officer's panel. A Jeffrey Shaara book about the American Revolution rested on his knees. It was a great read, but not an antidote to fatigue. His partner sat motionless watching an old Robert Mitchum movie. All lights were out, just like page fifty-one of the Inmate Guidebook stipulated.

An eerie feeling overcame Stephen. He felt a burning hole in his back. Instinctively he spun and looked up to cell thirty-five. A shadowy figure stood in the doorway, staring down. Stephen returned the stare, speechless, until the figure disappeared moments later. Nicholson tried to go back to his book.

Who the hell does Renzo think he is?

The gentle giant in cell sixty-eight, Marconi Beach, also stood at his door. He had witnessed the quick visual exchange between Renzo and Stephen. Yes, Marconi knew all about the tough guy in cell thirty-five—and wasn't impressed.

Marconi Beach maintained his focus. Each night he analyzed his life, questioning mistakes of the past and planning goals for the future. Imminent release would bring positive change. For years he had been one of the good guys. A second lease on life approached.

There was a quandary, though. Marconi sensed that something was brewing with Renzo. Marconi's street and prison IQ said so. Renzo was cunning and calculating; he didn't get into stare-downs like that with correction officers just for fun. It wasn't his style.

Renzo had watched Stephen. No—Renzo had *flexed* to Stephen. There was a difference, but it didn't go unnoticed.

The watcher had been watched.

Time didn't matter. Renzo would get his just desserts. He would learn that at the Boston House, all parties are vulnerable, and even the unit Caesar must beware.

Because prisons never sleep.

3.

William Jonathan Barnes studied the report. It was a comprehensive background check covering everything from W2 filings to favorite desserts to unfavorable quotes from ex-girlfriends. Private Investigator Parvis Pipp didn't disappoint Barnes. Pipp's disheveled physical appearance—tattered clothing and mangled hair—had been an initial concern, but Barnes was a businessman who catered to results. He enjoyed the irony: private eye investigating private eye. He liked what he read.

The subject held a degree in criminal justice. More importantly, his chosen profession in the prison world complemented his street smarts. This was essential. In 1997, his combined income was a bit over eighty-five thousand dollars; a subsequent analysis—ascertained through unethical means—detailed a well-managed investment portfolio. The subject wasn't physically imposing but he exercised religiously. All reports stated he could fight well. His best weapons, though, were his quick wit and tongue.

Virtues such as loyalty and honor appeared more than once. So did the mention of late nights. Barnes turned to the last section of Pipp's work. He found the information particularly informative. It was labeled *Family History*.

Barnes read and reread intently. Yes, Parvis Pipp performed exceptionally well. The subject increasingly fascinated Barnes. The intrigue, oddly, developed into commiseration. Barnes picked up his ale glass and walked onto the second-floor balcony. The biting Berkshire wind didn't budge him. Young Laiken had been dead twelve years, the longest dozen years of his life. Old age would invariably get the best of him if he didn't find the truth. Now was the time. Barnes returned to his desk and stared at the subject's photograph.

Good-looking kid. I see why he caught Laiken's eye.

The grandfather clock in the foyer tolled twelve times. Barnes went for his phone and dialed. It answered on the third ring. "The Library, we're open until two o'clock." Barnes immediately recognized Josef Kieler's voice.

"Good evening, Josef."

After a short pause, he said, "Nice to hear from you, William. What would you like me to do?" Josef Kieler was one of a handful of Millers who addressed William Jonathan Barnes by his first name.

"Arrange a meeting with Stephen Nicholson," Barnes said. "It's time."

* * *

Mister MaGoo's Tavern was a popular West Roxbury watering hole on Centre Street. It was primer night, also known as Thirsty Thursday. The bar swelled with a fine blend of all walks of life: blue collars, yuppie white collars, and even a mix of gray collars. The tavern was close enough to Holy Name church to ward off demons, and close enough to District 5 police station to keep out the drug dealers. Mister MaGoo's also had something envied by some suburban taverns: a two o'clock liquor permit.

Stephen Nicholson sat near the dartboard with his correctional brethren. They were embroiled in a nonsensical debate about favoritism in the workplace. It was the same old routine. The redundant rhetoric could have been recorded five years earlier: *"O'Connor, you're a ball suck…O'Brien, stay out of the captain's office…McNeil, when's the last time you worked population?"*

Stephen watched people instead. Love seemed to be in the air. He snickered as he watched thirty-something-year-old guys chase twenty-one-year-old girls while a couple of guys in their twenties made their moves on two divorcees.

Stephen's eyes found Mickey O'Sullivan. Mickey swayed on a stool across the bar. He was alternating between a Bud Light bottle and a drink that looked like a gin and tonic. Two empty shot glasses sat in front of him. Stephen approached. Mickey's eyes were bloodshot. He was drunk but still keen to perception. He knew Stephen's immediate presence was an act of concern.

Mickey gulped from his gin and tonic. "I've been meaning to talk to you."

"Okay, what's up?"

"I have problems, Stephen."

Stephen smiled. "Everyone has problems, Mickey."

20

"No, you don't understand, man…I have *problems*."

Stephen offered a sympathetic nod while casually scanning the immediate area. It was crowded but also very loud. No one was eavesdropping. "Try me," he said.

"I saw Renzo DiLorenzo bang out that Southie kid and I couldn't do shit about it," Mickey said.

"Really?" Stephen mused. "Why not, Mickey?"

"I like gambling, Stephen."

"I know that, Mick." Stephen paused, yet Mickey didn't respond. "How deep?"

"The Falcons porked me, man," Mickey said. "They porked me real good."

Stephen knew it wasn't good. Why had he bet against John Elway and the defending champs? "I asked how deep, Mick."

"Would you believe fifty-five hundred?"

Stephen wasn't demonstrative. He paused, then gave a simple nod. "That's a lot of cash, Mick," Stephen said. "How does Renzo factor into this equation?"

"He's the prison enforcer for my bookie."

"Stop with the games, Mickey. Give it up. Who's your bookie?"

"Lucky Giannessimo," Mickey said.

Stephen nodded. "Lucky is a maggot."

"Now the catch," Mickey said. His speech improved as he gained clarity. "Lucky is pressuring me to bring…contraband into the prison."

Stephen's eyebrows came together. "You lugging?"

"No, I haven't brought anything in, but they're pressuring me," Mickey said "They're pressuring me *real bad*, man."

"What type of pressure, Mickey?"

A final gulp drained Mickey's drink. "Renzo collects debts for Lucky on the street—and inside the Boston House. Renzo has mentioned my sister's name—even said 'it would be a shame if anything happened to that fine piece of pussy.'"

"That a direct quote?" Stephen asked.

"Yeah."

"Did Renzo mention Jacqueline by name?"

"Yeah."

"What kind of drugs we talking here, Mickey?"

Mickey wouldn't establish eye contact. He stared at the floor. "Heroin," he said.

Stephen's blood boiled. "Have you done it yet?"

"No, but these dudes are sweating me."

"You must have said something to Lucky."

Mickey found the nerve to look at Stephen. "Lucky said that if I can't pay the consequences, then I shouldn't play the game."

Stephen leaned back and sipped a Michelob Light. He looked at Mickey O'Sullivan. No—he looked *into* Mickey O'Sullivan. Stephen was searching. He was trying to find the wiry kid he'd known many years ago—ice cream on his face, dirt on his hands, and constantly hunting for his brother David at the Nicholson family front door. What happened to that Mickey? Where was the kid who could hit a baseball a country mile but couldn't catch a routine popup? How about the mischievous fifth-grader who got suspended from school with David for dealing bottle rockets and firecrackers?

Stephen looked deep and hard at Mickey, trying his best turn back time and reinvent Mickey's innocence. His eyes wouldn't deceive him, though; it just wasn't there. Gone was the teenage boy who'd once breathed air into Stephen's brother's lungs in an attempt to save his life.

The Ghost of Christmas Past couldn't deliver a miracle. The old Mickey O'Sullivan was dead. He was never to be reincarnated because he couldn't be reincarnated. Reality set in. Stephen instead saw a pathetic, portly guy in his late twenties with a gambling problem and zero self-confidence. He saw a target, a professional victim who gave meaning to the word prey and a full-course meal to predators like Lucky Giannessimo and Renzo DiLorenzo.

The situation necessitated swift action; otherwise, smoke would lead to fire. Stephen analyzed the delicate matter. Dealing with Lucky Giannessimo was the first step. Yes, the problem was correctable. Stephen looked at Mickey. "I'll take care of everything," he said.

Mickey breathed a sigh of relief and stared to the floor again. "You know, Stephen, I really appreciate…"

When Mickey looked up moments later, he realized no one was there.

* * *

Hanover Street in the North End is a tourist trap. It's the main thoroughfare that cuts through Boston's oldest residential neighborhood. Notwithstanding the influx of new Boston blood, the neighborhood is still quite rich in Italian culture. Parking is bad all the time, and even worse when out-of-state plates congest the streets while staring at road atlases.

Stephen got lucky. He slipped his black Jeep into a tiny spot just as an old guy from New Jersey sped away. Waiting on the curb was Josef Kieler. Josef looked like a poster boy for middle-aged dads. He wore khaki pants, brown penny loafers, and a button-down shirt he'd probably ordered from an L.L. Bean catalogue. He was a tad less than six feet with a nondescript face. Perhaps he weighed 190 pounds. Josef looked American—not handsome, not ugly. His second-best characteristic was a thick head of manageable brown hair.

Stephen followed Josef without conversation half a block and made a right onto Parmenter Street. Within seconds they stood outside Pagliuca's, a cozy Italian ristorante.

"Nice to see you, handsome," Josef said. Then he smiled. Yes, in the Mills—as it's often called—Josef Kieler's smile is legendary. Josef's smile is the proverbial cherry-on-top to his disarming presence. He uses the smile to gain allies and deter foes. It's his number-one trait.

"No, sir, the pleasure is mine," Stephen said.

Josef was owner of The Library, a college restaurant and bar in Hoosac Mills. He was Stephen's boss at Taconic State; more importantly, he was an uncle figure. Josef was a typical Miller, a man who respected family, hard work, and loyalty. A curious phone call from Josef had lured Stephen to the North End. Josef was vague about the meeting, not mentioning any names or intended purpose. Stephen didn't give it too much thought. He always liked the North End, and besides, he hadn't seen Josef in almost two years.

The ristorante was small; it offered authentic North End ambience and genuine Italian food. Two men rose as Josef and Stephen approached their table. The man clearly in charge was an austere-looking gentleman. First impressions implied a man of authority. He was tailored in a dark pinstriped European suit, an expensive but not flashy Rolex, brown Italian leather shoes, and manicured fingernails. Maybe sixty years old, he was the athletic type who played racquetball or squash on a regular basis. The gentleman smiled and extended a handshake. It was firm.

"Thank you for coming on such hasty notice, Stephen."

"No problem."

"Can I order you a beer or mixed drink?" the gentleman asked.

"A Michelob Light would be fine."

The waiter was not in earshot of the conversation. Stephen was certain. Yet the waiter appeared quickly for the drink order. He also established eye contact with the gentleman who called the meeting. This man had *presence*.

"You're probably wondering who I am," the gentleman said.

Stephen knew his exact identity. "You look familiar."

"I am William Jonathan Barnes," he said.

"A pleasure to meet you, sir."

"The man to my right is Simeon Kolotov," Barnes said. "He is my personal assistant."

Stephen and Simeon shook hands. Simeon was a rugged-looking fellow with husky shoulders, a boxed Slavic skull with a protracted jaw, wrinkled skin, and a wide nose that had been broken several times. "Nice to meet you," Stephen said. Simeon did not reply.

They all sat at Barnes' instruction. Stephen stared at Barnes with a hint of awe. After all, this was The William Jonathan Barnes: multimillionaire, electrical plant owner, and financier. He was the big cheese. He was Laiken Barnes' father.

He was King Billy.

"What can I do for you, Mr. Barnes?"

"In due time, Stephen," Barnes said. "Let's get acquainted."

The waiter arrived. Ample entrees for four filled the table. Refills of drinks were served. Stephen had chicken over fettuccini alfredo. "I hope you don't mind me taking the liberty of ordering for you," Barnes said.

Stephen looked at Barnes, then grinned. "Not at all, sir. It's my favorite Italian dish."

"How is your private investigation business?" Barnes asked.

"Supplemental income," Stephen said. "It keeps me busy, puts money in my pocket, and keeps me out of trouble."

"Describe the challenges of working for the sheriff's department."

The question was innocuous by all accounts. Yet it was open-ended, of course. Barnes was clearly a man who enjoyed provoking thought. If he sought a yes or no answer, then he would frame the question as such. Stephen's eyes shifted toward the front door. An ex-inmate entered, woman in arm, and quickly spotted Stephen. The ex-inmate offered an ever so subtle head nod; Stephen countered. It was a respectful, mutual acknowledgment. No one else in the restaurant was privy.

Barnes' question—and its answers—exploded in Stephen's mind. A correction officer's job was a giant cycle of contradictions: Don't take your job home with you, but always be willing to vent...Never kiss ass to the boss, yet don't forget to attend the department's functions..."Eight hours is eight hours" in any position, but no one wants to work the block...Treat the inmates fairly yet never be called a caseworker...Report misconduct immediately, but do not challenge the blue line of corrections called *The Culture*...Fear the wrath of the sheriff's punitive hand, yet secretly relish the suspensions of others...Never use excessive force, but you'd better not be a pussy...Avoid undue familiarity with coworkers of the opposite sex, yet dream of sinking your vampire fangs into a prison nurse...Always work in complete unity, but 7-3 hates 3-11 and 3-11 hates 7-3 and neither pays attention to 11-7...Never reveal personal information, yet some inmates are more compassionate than officers...

Stephen reached for his beer. Less than two seconds had expired. He freed his mind of the contradictions. He focused now on the positive gravitational pull which helped him maintain his sanity at the Boston House: Locker room pranks...Extended lunches...drunken fights after work (at times with each other, of course)...fundraisers for brothers and sisters in need...bonding among racial and ethnic groups...the speedy response—always—to an "officer down" call...staff caricature cartoons...errant radio piracy..."choir practice" after a 3-11 shift...moral support...group Red Sox and Patriots games—always a bad idea...officer weddings...officer funerals, where the eulogies honored the men or women who'd worn the badge with unabashed pride—and honor...

He balanced his thoughts on the correctional scale of justice. It tipped to the right.

Yes, Stephen liked his job.

He locked eyes with Barnes. His beer bottle returned to the table. Only three seconds had ticked off the clock. "The job has its pros and cons, sir."

Barnes smiled. He sensed—correctly—greater depth to Stephen's eight-word reply. "I see," he said. He wasn't satisfied. "Give me a word which connects both officer and convict."

"Emotion," Stephen said. "Actually, it is a failure to harness emotion."

"Could you elaborate?"

"One moment you're up—happy-go-lucky—the next moment you're in a fit of anger," Stephen said. "The pendulum swings swiftly and without warning. But it doesn't have to be bliss or melancholy, either. It's everything. All kinds of traits and characteristics apply to everyday prison feelings: happy, sad, mad, invigorated, eager, indolent, intense, brave, compassionate, empathetic, ignorant, naïve, and even sadistic."

Barnes smiled. "You speak quickly."

"So I've been told."

The conversation slowed. Drinking was limited. Neither Josef nor Simeon spoke for twenty minutes. Stephen grew antsy. He hadn't fought traffic in the North End to profile inmates and his coworkers. Everyone passed on dessert and opted for coffee.

The table went silent. Barnes broke the ice. "Stephen, it is my understanding you were a friend and one-time interest of my daughter, Laiken. Is that not correct?"

Barnes had lived in America many years but still retained his British accent and phraseology. "Yes, sir," Stephen said. "Laiken was my friend. The Taconic kids were saddened by her death—including me."

"I'm glad you feel that way, Stephen," Barnes said. "I've been told you're a sentimentalist."

Stephen looked at Josef. "May I ask whom you heard this from?"

"Multiple persons, actually," Barnes answered. "I shall disclose right now that I paid top dollar for an extensive background check on you."

Stephen laughed. "Are you talking about that guy with the cheesy mustache that wears those god-awful sunglasses that look like blue-blocker knockoffs? The same guy who drives the midnight blue Explorer?"

"Yes, I am," Barnes said. "I assume you were privy to his presence."

"How could I have missed him?" Stephen said. "He looked like he just lost a Magnum P.I. look-alike contest."

"I understand," Barnes said.

Stephen raised his left hand in front of his face. "My wrist has recently healed. I fractured it while breaking up a fight on the job; I was out of work for ten weeks. I figured your guy was a city investigator."

"Quite the contrary," Barnes said.

"Then why was he checking me out?"

"I want you to find Laiken's killer," Barnes said flatly.

Stephen was shocked. He'd assumed Barnes wanted him for insurance fraud or internal wrongdoing purposes. Any investigator from western Mass could adequately perform those tasks, even Parvis Pipp. A murder investigation? That sounded preposterous. "You're putting me on," Stephen said.

"Not at all," Barnes answered. "I'm quite serious. Mr. Parvis Pipp was quite detailed in his summation report of you. I was impressed in more ways than one. I select you."

"I'm a ham-and-egger, Mr. Barnes," Stephen said. "You know this much already."

"Don't minimize your value," Barnes said.

"Mr. Barnes, I catch truants, wealthy kids smoking pot, and then, if I'm really lucky, I'll get an assignment in which my subject is a stripper. That has actually happened. The biggest case on my resume is tracking a runaway rich kid to California. And I did that by simply chasing credit card receipts."

Barnes smiled. He was aware of his dashing looks and inexplicable charm that seemed to hypnotize anyone he lobbied. Conversely, he was a wicked businessman who'd put many a man in the unemployment line. The charmer stared at Stephen. "You were present at the 1987 Halloween party. You are a brother of Kappa Chi Omicron fraternity," Barnes said. "All primary suspects, less the reprehensible P.J. McClaren, were brothers in your order. You know them all quite well. You are, I could say, an insider."

Stephen wanted to laugh. He didn't. "Okay, Mr. Barnes," he said. "Let's say that I take this case—and I'm not saying I will. Point number one is I don't have the foggiest idea how to begin a murder investigation because (a) I've never done it before, and (b) I'm not qualified."

"So say you," Barnes answered.

"And another thing is that I don't think any of my fraternity brothers could have done that to your daughter. But even if they did, and I could prove it, what makes you think I'd give them up?"

"Your family history," Barnes said.

"Excuse me?" Stephen asked. He leaned forward. "What do you know about my family history?"

Barnes reveled. It was show time. "Both your parents are first-generation Irish Americans. They are honest, hardworking people who are civic-minded and follow the teachings of Christ. You are practicing Roman Catholics. Your father, Eamon, was reared in Charlestown. His sons call him Townie. He has worked at Gillette for thirty-seven years and is currently an evening shift assembly line manager." Barnes paused, gauging Stephen.

"Go on," Stephen said.

"Your mother, Peachy, is endeared to all members of your extended family. She assumed the role of family matriarch when your maternal grandmother died in 1995. She grew up poor, dirt poor I shall say, in Jamaica Plain, affectionately called JP. She is a registered nurse in the oncology ward at Massachusetts General Hospital.

"Your brother Matthew is an interesting fellow. He has a unique combination of brains and brawn. He graduated Taconic State before you arrived on campus. He is large, bigger than you, adept with his fists and even more so with his intellect. He boxed extensively at a gymnasium in Roslindale Square, not far from your home. He teaches English literature at a community college on Route 9."

Barnes went quiet. Stephen wasn't pleased, but he waited for Barnes to continue. It didn't happen.

You're baiting me, you son of a bitch, aren't you?

Stephen anticipated the train crash but couldn't help himself. "What else?"

Barnes' eyes filled to the brink of tears. He was quite an actor when he wanted to be. It was now Barnes who leaned forward. He lowered his voice. "Stephen, I wasn't the only person devastated by family tragedy in 1987." No answer. "In June, 1987, your brother David, three years your junior, was killed while driving your sedan without a license on Beech Street in Roslindale. Two passengers—a Mickey O'Sullivan and Amanda McMasters—escaped with minor injuries, but your brother didn't survive the night.

"All police and insurance reports blame the intoxicated operator of the other vehicle who struck your car. That was also the opinion of neighbors who served as first responders. My reports tell me you have assigned yourself blame for David's death. You believe you failed in protecting your brother while your parents were away." Barnes paused. A breath couldn't be heard around the table. "Stephen, you too know what it's like to pick up a rose from the coffin."

Stephen was somber. "You found neighborhood guys who gave up that info for money?"

Barnes the actor gave a sympathetic life lesson. "You'd be surprised to learn how many people will speak freely for money." Stephen stared at the floor. Josef was embarrassed; his eyes wandered. Simeon was void of emotion. He couldn't care less about Stephen Nicholson or his scarred family past. "That's what separates you from the rest," Barnes said. "I too have been riddled by guilt over Laiken's death. My dear wife has been dead six months. I have waited a long time for closure."

The jury was out on Barnes. Was he victim or villain? Barnes was one hundred percent professional, adept at striking the right chords to get what he wanted. He sat idle, playing the victim role to a T. He was a man simply seeking answers to personal tragedy, right? Damn, this guy was good, real good. How many people had he screwed on his way to the top?

Stephen's post-college life flashed before him: prison, private investigations, gymnasium workouts, splintered relationships, and not much else. He hadn't been challenged—truly challenged—in years. He was single, thirty years old, and in truth had nothing to lose. After all, his Kappa brothers never could have committed such a heinous crime, could they?

Don't give yourself too much time to think.

"I'll do it," Stephen said.

Barnes was pleased. "Excellent," he said. "I'm familiar with your fee system. I will pay an additional twenty-five percent to your normal rate, which shall include travel time."

"That's an impressive offer," Stephen said.

Barnes didn't miss a beat. "At the time most convenient for you I will reserve a suite in your name at the Berkshire Inn. You will have its full access until the investigation is completed."

"There's a matter of logistics we need to discuss," Stephen said. "Next week I'm on vacation. I planned a trip to Gettysburg, but I'll cancel. I can juggle my schedule so that I can be in the Mills three or four days a week."

"Whatever it takes," Barnes said.

"What about Hoosac Mills Police?" Stephen asked.

"Good question," Barnes said. "Unsolved murder investigations are never closed."

"I know."

"The case has been given new life. The mayor and police chief have promised me a fresh investigation with a new detective," Barnes said.

"Who's that?"

"Miss Melanie Leary. A charming young woman, if I may say. You're to work in an unofficial capacity with Miss Leary. Again, the chief will be aware of your presence and you will be afforded full latitude, so long as you don't overextend the purview of your license."

The coffee cups were empty. Barnes glanced at Simeon and Josef. "I'd like a moment alone with Stephen."

They obliged. Barnes the actor retired for the night. His gaze and words couldn't have been more direct. "Provide me with the name of my daughter's killer and I'll give you an additional fifty thousand dollars, cash."

"You don't play around, do you Mr. Barnes?"

Barnes nodded. "Since my daughter's death, Stephen, I'm afraid I haven't had the temperament for games."

"We have a deal."

"Excellent. When you report to Hoosac Mills, I will furnish you with any and all paperwork that applies to the case. I believe five thousand dollars in expense money should be enough to elicit information. If you need more, just ask."

The two men stood, Barnes gave Stephen a firm handshake, left $250 cash on the table, and quickly made his way to a waiting Lincoln Navigator.

Stephen watched the taillights disappear. It was just like he'd imagined: a Godfather offer.

* * *

Frankie Kohan and Matthew Nicholson jumped into Stephen's Jeep in front of the Boston House. It was 11:15 p.m. Dinner and business with Barnes was over. Now Stephen had other important matters to resolve.

Frankie and Matthew, Stephen's brother, were bored and gladly answered Stephen's call for backup. Frankie looked at Stephen. "I talked to Alexia for about an hour today."

"You and Ms. Martinez talking for sixty minutes? That's a long stretch—even for two girls," Stephen said.

Frankie chuckled. "That's because she talked about you for an hour."

Stephen looked at Frankie. "Now, now, Francis. You know we're just friends."

Frankie wasn't a believer. "Whatever you say, Romeo. And she's so damned possessive when she refers to you. It's always 'my Stephen' this and 'my Stephen' that."

Matthew chimed in. "Stephen was outmatched in that relationship anyway. She's probably shacking up with a New York Giant by now."

"Yeah, yeah, yeah," Stephen answered. "Let's just concentrate on our business at hand, tough guys."

They crossed Melnea Cass Boulevard, went right on Albany, left on Plympton, right on Harrison, then left on East Berkley. A quick turn into an alleyway and Stephen parked the Jeep next to a brick apartment building. Stephen looked at Frankie and Matthew. "We're straight on this, right?"

"We got your back," Frankie said. Matthew smiled.

Stephen entered the side door of The McGrath Principle tavern. It was a South End bar familiar to politicians and blue-collar workers across the city. At any given moment, an off-duty employee of Boston Police, Boston Fire, the *Boston Herald*, or the Boston House held down a stool and cooled off with a drink. Tonight, there was a moderate crowd that would probably double after one a.m. Beer taps of Bass and Guinness flowed and music boomed from the jukebox. Stephen greeted two off-duty Boston cops and a *Herald* worker at the bar. He got a Bud bottle. A contingent of Irish immigrants gathered at the dartboard. They were loud, smoking, and drinking heavily. It didn't matter, though, because every one of them would be up at the crack of dawn, hammering nails and slapping on coats of primer paint in the suburbs while their American counterparts caught shuteye.

Lucky Giannessimo, predictably, leaned against the far wall next to the jukebox, working on a Bacardi and Coke. He had a unique look. He was about six-three and sinewy, no more than 190 pounds. He was of mixed European heritage, with olive skin and long black hair worn in a ponytail. He was forty years old. Lucky was sipping from his drink when Stephen approached. "What's up, Lucky?"

Lucky flashed his trademark gold tooth. "Just chillin'. What's up with you, Nicholson?"

"Business. Need to discuss something with you."

Lucky spread his arms, smiling again. He had a gentle, non-confrontational exterior—a classic used car salesman. "Whatever you need, babe."

"I want to settle the business you have with Mickey O'Sullivan," Stephen said. "I want your boy Renzo off his back, and I don't want you taking any more action from him."

Lucky scanned the bar, probing for eavesdroppers. "Let's talk about this outside."

They walked out the side door and went left, entering a small courtyard area that abutted the L-shaped alley. "That's some serious shit you're coming with, Nicholson," Lucky said.

"I didn't come here to talk shit," Stephen said evenly. "Mickey owes fifty-five hundred dollars. I'm giving you four thousand right now. He'll be busting ass on overtime to make good on the fifteen hundred."

"I don't discriminate against money, Nicholson," Lucky said. "I'll take the four grand, but I don't know nothing about this shit with Renzo."

Stephen stepped toward Lucky. "I ain't playing, dickhead. Keep your boy Renzo off Mickey's back or there'll be some major fuckin' problems in your life."

Lucky laughed. "You're a real trip, Nicholson. Damn—you Irish boys are funny. You come to the South End and threaten me?"

"Forget the threats, Lucky, it's a guarantee," Stephen said. "You hold no cards. You're a scumbag who deals drugs and takes numbers."

Lucky pulled a switchblade from his back pocket. He flipped it open and held it in his right hand. "Where's that guarantee now, Nicholson?"

Stephen saw the blade clearly. He didn't move. Lights went on in one of the upstairs apartments. A curious young woman stared into the courtyard.

"I ain't Mickey," Stephen said.

"And I ain't someone to be fuckin' with, Nicholson."

Stephen smiled widely. Lucky was perplexed. Suddenly he felt a circular piece of cold metal pressed against the back of his head. It was a Sig Sauer nine-millimeter, fully loaded and properly registered. "Don't think about moving, dickface," Frankie Kohan said. He had been concealed behind a nearby Dumpster. He quickly took Lucky's knife and slowly placed it in his own pocket. "Now, like Stephen said, you're gonna call off your dog, Renzo. Is that understood?"

Lucky didn't answer. Frankie pressed the gun harder against Lucky's skull with his right hand while pulling him in tight with his left. "I can't hear you, numb nuts. What did you say?"

"Fair enough," Lucky said. "But I want my four grand now, and the kid better make good on the difference…real soon."

Frankie released Lucky. He walked toward Stephen with the gun pointed to the ground. He enjoyed the moment immensely.

Stephen stepped forward. "This is a reverse stickup, Lucky. We have the gun but we're giving you the money." He tossed Lucky a zipped bank bag. "Like I said, there's four grand."

Lucky glared at Frankie. "I'll remember this, Jew boy."

Frankie beamed. "I'll be ready, Gentile."

Stephen and Frankie stepped into the Jeep. Lucky held money in one hand and gave the middle finger to the Jeep with his other. The Jeep wasn't offended. Lucky never noticed the big guy who quietly appeared from behind a corner. Lucky finally turned and was surprised to be face-to-face with Matthew Nicholson. The two men were three feet apart. "Back off, dude," Lucky said. "You look like Nicholson."

Matthew smiled, then delivered a right jab and straight left to Lucky's chin. Lucky was laid on his back, semiconscious. The woman in the upstairs apartment bore witness. Matthew leaned down, nearing Lucky's face. Lucky was dazed but looked into Matthew's eyes. Matthew raised his left index finger to his nose and whispered, "Sshhhh."

The black Jeep with the three men soon disappeared from the South End. Lucky rolled onto his stomach. Blood oozed down his throat, and he vomited. Finally he straightened up. The apartment light went out. He walked off the pain.

Lucky was a reprehensible man. He was morally bankrupt and ethically insolvent. But men like Lucky were a reality, the bane of Stephen and Frankie's profession. He was the crooked bastard often portrayed in the movies and written about in the newspapers. He was more than just a scumbag who dealt drugs and took numbers.

Lucky Giannessimo was a correction officer at the Boston House.

4.

Thursday night represented passage. Only Stephen didn't know it. It marked the beginning of his vacation. It marked the beginning of the Laiken Barnes investigation. Precluding personal feelings from interfering in his work was a must; the looming investigation posed a challenge. The long-planned vacation trip to Pennsylvania was delayed. The dead men of Gettysburg weren't going anywhere. They would have to wait.

Stephen departed early from the Boston House. Traffic reports on WBZ radio gave an all-clear sign on the Massachusetts State Turnpike. It's a straight shot through southern Mass, starting in Boston and extending past Pittsfield into New York. Affectionately called the Pike, it begins only about a mile from the Boston House. It was Stephen's easiest route; it was also the route he didn't take. He opted for Route 2, the old meandering state highway that travels west along Massachusetts' northern ridges.

Route 2 was a voice for central and western Massachusetts. It began in Boston and ran through towns like Fitchburg, Gardner, Orange, Erving, Greenfield, and Charlemont. These blue-collar towns were products of the nineteenth-century railroad. The Massachusetts economic think tanks of the time believed a connection to the Erie Canal and Great Lakes would translate into unlimited prosperity. It never happened.

Undulating hills and an unusually bright moon comprised the scenery. The Jeep dominated the rolling hills. Stephen loved the ride, and loved the hills. After all, the hills signified nature, which signified serenity, and both signified a change from the norm. Yes, the hills made a quiet statement—they were anti-Boston.

It's a bit weird, actually. The extreme parochialism of Metropolitan Boston can be compared only to New York, or perhaps Chicago and

Philly. Most Bostonians think life doesn't exist outside the I-495 beltway. The belief is prevalent. The belief is ignorant. In fact, the Great Blue Hill in Canton is the only "mountain" known to Bostonians. It has an elevation of less than a thousand feet and its reservation is home to miles of hiking trails in Canton, Milton, and Quincy. Why explore western Mass when you can go to the Great Blue Hill, right? But parochialism is a disease, not a state of mind. The same people who parade atop the Great Blue Hill once a year with their beach blankets and Yogi Bear picnic baskets probably don't know the significance of the soil on which they stand. Massachusetts is a Native American tribal name; it translates, literally, to "the great hill."

At midnight Stephen was on the Mohawk Trail section of Route 2, an exceptionally curvy path decorated with signs for Falling Rock and Bovine Crossing. Eddie Vedder, the frontman for Pearl Jam, helped pass the time. Vedder sang about a kid named Jeremy with a gun. Stephen thought about Mickey, Lucky, and Renzo. He couldn't help it; his mind was always in high speed. A high school counselor had once labeled Stephen's continuous racing thoughts as a deficiency. That was her opinion.

On the surface, Mickey O'Sullivan's problem was solved. Money was paid, and Mickey swore to quit gambling. But Stephen realized Lucky and Renzo were professional predators. Lucky was simply an inmate with a badge. That was why Frankie Kohan had taken the extreme measure of holding a gun to his head, and that was why Matthew had practically punched him out of his shoes.

The message needed to be clear. Lucky and Renzo didn't work on State Street with shirts and ties. They didn't respond to niceties like "I'd appreciate if you stop harassing my friend." They'd laugh in your face. They were street guys, thugs. That was why a not-so-subtle hint was then delivered to Renzo. His fiancé, Babee Bendini, lost her visiting privileges for three months when she gave Renzo a mouth-to-mouth kiss at the conclusion of a visit. It was indeed an infraction, though most of the time it was punished with a verbal warning. One of Renzo's canteen slips got "accidentally misplaced" so he was unable to purchase toiletries and snacks for a week.

These would be crushing blows to a typical inmate, but Renzo wasn't a typical inmate. He was a Caesar—when he needed toiletries or snacks, he took them from the weak. Lucky Giannessimo would most certainly surmise the source, and promptly inform Renzo.

These actions were calculating. It was uncharted territory for Stephen. But extreme necessity sometimes calls for extreme measures, and Mickey O'Sullivan—the kid from the neighborhood—needed help. Stephen's dad, the townie, was always inculcating life lessons with clichés: *choose your battles wisely*; *see the forest for the trees*; *know when to hold 'em and know when to fold 'em*. The clichés were considered and weighed. A ruling was made. Stephen, the self-appointed magistrate, decided that an overt message had to be delivered to Renzo.

Don't fuck with my boy.

Besides, Renzo wasn't exactly a poster child for rehabilitation. Prison isn't the real world; it's a place where few are reformed and many languish in their own private fires, such as Mickey O'Sullivan and Roscoe McFarland. But prison fires aren't put out with water because they're nearly impossible to extinguish. The only way to make a prison fire go away is to kill it with another fire, only yours must be a different-color flame, and always greater in intensity.

Prison thoughts disappeared when the Jeep made its descent into the Hoosac Mills valley. Lights flickered. Stephen's heart skipped a beat as memories invaded him: fraternity brothers, girls, friends, parties, and the classroom. Well, a little bit of classroom. There was something missing, though. It was the obvious.

The Jeep streaked past Cumberland Farms convenience store. Stephen fought with the memories. He wanted to keep it pleasant. He wanted to remain objective; he didn't want to think about *her* too much. But that was silly, wasn't it? That's why he was here. Stephen's mind was his best friend; conversely, it was his worst enemy. He had to say the name aloud, but didn't want to. He struggled. He was weakening.

Stop being a pussy. You've come here for a reason. Go ahead, just say it.

"All right," he said aloud. Of course, he was alone in the Jeep. "I'm here to see about Laiken Barnes…Laiken Barnes the campus looker, Laiken Barnes the coquette, Laiken Barnes the Miller."

Sweat dripped from Stephen's forehead. Eddie Vedder no longer sang. The Jeep was quiet. It didn't respond to Stephen's spoken thoughts. Anxiety was setting in. He neutralized it by rolling down the window. The cold Berkshire air was an antidote. He pulled into the parking lot of the Berkshire Inn, found a spot, and turned off the ignition. He leaned his head back, closed his eyes, and listened to a late-night cargo train rumble by. Stephen then stepped out of the Jeep and looked around, surveying the surrounding mountains from the valley. He looked up to a high point in town, the area where she'd grown up. He found the house and noted incredulously that her bedroom light was on. Stephen was sure it was her room. It must have been a light bulb with a twelve-year life span. Why was the light on? Stephen closed his eyes. Again, memories couldn't escape him.

Laiken Barnes, the dead rich princess.

Stephen snapped out of it. He stood still, two bags in hand. Damn—mind freezes and fugues were happening on a regular basis. Something was up—they were occurring more than usual. He'd consult his doctor. Maybe.

Stephen started toward the inn's entrance and stopped. He had the intuitive feeling he was being watched. He looked to the train tracks. Bingo. It wasn't paranoia or imagination. Under the bridge, wearing his patented gray trench coat and Stetson hat from the Salvation Army, and tilting ever so slightly from the effects of alcohol, stood the Can Man. His weathered shopping cart filled with its bounty of beer bottles and cans remained idle next to him. Rusty carts invariably squeak, yet Stephen heard no noise. That meant Can Man had been spying. It was dark, and he stood a hundred feet away, but it was unmistakably him. *How long were you watching me, Can Man?*

Every town has a can man. But in Hoosac Mills, Can Man was legendary. No one knew his real name or age. No one knew his origin. He simply appeared in Hoosac Mills one day in the early '80s, but nobody knew exactly when. Not much was known for fact about Can Man. Popular myth said he was a Williams College intellectual who'd flipped his lid. He had no reputation for violence. He was supposedly well read and never forgot a face. He also was privy to all town gossip—because he listened.

Rumor also maintained he slept inside the Hoosac Tunnel. Learning any information about the Can Man, though, was nearly impossible because he rarely spoke. In fact, Stephen had never heard him speak. He mostly grunted. The Can Man cashed in his daily take and bought liquor and food from the supermarket. That was his simple routine. On occasion college kids teased him when he retrieved treasures later than nine in the morning. Usually he was never seen. That built the mystique.

Stephen and Can Man faced each other. Neither man moved. Stephen looked for a bottle of booze nearby. He couldn't see one; it was probably concealed in his trench coat. The hobo kept his stare, then raised his hand and pointed toward Stephen.

"Obviously, I have no empties," Stephen said.

Can Man continued to point. He stared deep into Stephen, as if he recognized him. Then he started to grunt, or chortle. No, it was closer to a laugh, but not a laugh as most people know it. It had the same effect, though. His noises were deep, meaningful, as if he had been savoring it for years. Can Man doubled over, holding his knees. Stephen was puzzled. *Why are you laughing at me, Can Man?*

A deep, baritone voice came unexpectedly. "Why did you return?" the Can Man asked. Stephen was startled. He couldn't believe that Can Man had actually spoken. Something had changed though, and Stephen didn't like it—he sensed it, yet couldn't accurately define it.

Moments later, he came to the realization. After Can Man had spoken, his face evened and he stopped laughing. He simply strode away.

* * *

Detective Melanie Leary was stunning. Only she didn't know it. It took Stephen about thirty seconds to reach that conclusion. Melanie was his age, about thirty. Her shiny hair was dark—and long. He assumed it was long because she pinned it in the back. She had high cheekbones that were lightly sprinkled with freckles. Stephen guessed her to be a first- or second-generation Irish American. He tried not to spy at her physique through the office window. He was unsuccessful. Melanie was about five-six and weighed somewhere in the 125-pound range. Solid. She wore no wedding ring.

Stephen waited and watched from a wooden bench in the police station lobby. He *presumed* the beautiful woman pacing the floor and talking on the portable phone was Melanie. They'd yet to meet, but a clue, by way of a nameplate with Detective Melanie Leary inscribed on it, was affixed to the open door. The woman he believed to be Melanie Leary bent over to retrieve paperwork from a filing cabinet. Stephen again tried not to stare but couldn't help himself. He was, after all, a guy—and there was something to be said about an attractive woman police officer. All men know it, but it's tough to define. Maybe it's the raw combination of sex and power.

Stephen turned his attention to the outside. It looked like rain, again. His mind, idle for only a moment, was about to drift to Mickey O'Sullivan when his sixth sense told him he had company. He spun his head and Melanie was now three feet away, bordering the threshold of the unwritten personal space barrier. Damn, she was quick, and silent. "Stephen Nicholson?"

He stood. They were face-to-face. "Yes, ma'am."

"Melanie Leary," she said, extending her hand. "Please, come to my office."

Stephen inventoried the office: a neat wooden desk with pictures of little kids, a compact Dell laptop, a black leather swivel chair, early twentieth-century oaken filing cabinets, and maps of Hoosac Mills and Massachusetts on neutral, tan walls. They sat on opposites sides of the desk.

Melanie pulled two manila folders from a drawer. One was thicker than the other. She opened the smaller folder. "Stephen Nicholson, born in August, 1968, at the Lying Inn hospital in Boston...five feet, eleven inches tall, fluctuates between one hundred seventy and one hundred eighty-five pounds...long-limbed with a muscular build...gray eyes, brown hair with a military-style haircut...served in the Navy Reserve yet not an overseas vet...honorably discharged in 1996...full-time—what is it?—deputy sheriff...clean work record...played all organized Parkway sports growing up...graduated Catholic Memorial before attending and graduating from State...middle boy of three...recently suffered a broken bone while exercising force on the job at the Boston House...and part-time private investigator." Melanie closed the small personnel folder and looked at Stephen. "Never been married and presumably is without children."

Stephen laughed.

"You're not five-eleven," she said.

"Excuse me?"

"Moments ago I stood toe-to-toe with you. I'm telling you that on a tall day you're five-ten-and-a-half."

Damn, she's good.

"I'm starting to get a kick out of you Millers," Stephen said.

"Why is that?"

"My last two encounters were filled with min-biographies...of me," Stephen said. "Did Mr. Barnes' investigator give you the same information, Miss Leary?"

"It's Melanie," she said. "There are two things you need to know up front. First, I'm not a Miller. I'm a Springfield girl. Second, I don't get my information from drunks like Parvis Pipp."

"Is that so?" Stephen asked. "Then where did you get the information?"

Melanie smiled. "I'm a detective, Mr. Nicholson," she said. "I detect things."

"Call me Stephen."

"Then Stephen it is."

"Anything else you want to add?"

"Yes, now that you mention it," Melanie said, "You're much better-looking in person."

Stephen blushed—a rarity. She paused. He paused. They both laughed.

Melanie's comment, if read on paper, could only be perceived as flirtatious; in reality, it wasn't the case. It was spoken in a matter-of-fact sense, as if delivered by a third-person voiceover. It was a nice icebreaker.

Melanie then opened the thick manila folder. It produced a pack of papers and series of photographs. She spread them in front of Stephen. She was no longer smiling. "We need to get something straight," Melanie said.

"What's that?"

"You're here in front of me because the mayor said so."

Stephen said nothing. He already knew this to be true. Melanie waited. An odd moment of silence grew to half a minute. Melanie finally spoke. "If shit hits the fan during this investigation, it's my career. This is a side business for you. You have to remember that."

"Fair enough," Stephen said.

"I'm a reasonable person, Stephen," she said. "You have an insider view of some potential suspects, and I want to acknowledge that right now." Melanie hesitated. Stephen didn't reply. "I'm charged with acting in the best interest of the victim, as well as the best interest of the city. That being the case, if you can help me catch Laiken's killer, I'd be most grateful. I just needed to define the parameters."

Melanie wanted Stephen to speak. He didn't.

"Don't expect the members of this department to welcome you with open arms."

"I understand that," he said. "The fact that I hold a private license, and the fact that I'm a screw, and the fact that I'm a Boston boy pretty much sums it up."

Melanie absorbed Stephen's self-analysis. She smiled. "Yeah, that's about right." She slid the folder toward Stephen. "Right now I want your immediate thoughts."

There were over eighty photographs in the stack. Forty were black-and-white, and forty were color. Sizes of the photos ranged from three-by-five to eleven-by-fourteen. The pictures detailed the murder scene, covering everything from various angles of Laiken Barnes' body, nearby tire marks, broken brush, the access road entrance, the nearby train tracks, and some clear shots of the Hoosac Tunnel west portal. A separate envelope contained forty-eight aerial view photographs taken at a hundred, two hundred, five hundred, and a thousand feet.

The two reviewed established facts. The murder had taken place on Halloween night 1987 between the hours of 10:00 p.m. and 1:00 a.m. That was confirmed by the medical examiner. The body was discovered partially clothed. No forced vaginal entry was proven and no semen was recovered at the scene. That did not, however, rule out the possibility that consensual sex may have occurred. It was not, by the medical examiner's account, a rape.

The murder itself was vicious. Thirty-three stab wounds, all by a single-edge serrated knife, were documented to the victim's torso. Defensive cuts and bruises lined both forearms. No stab wounds or bruises were recorded on the victim's face or below the waist. Ostensibly, the perpetrator left no traces of blood, hair, or skin samples under the victim's fingernails.

The victim suffered major damage to all internal organs. Two perforated and subsequent collapsed lungs proved to be the technical cause of death. The victim, Laiken Barnes, stopped breathing before she bled out. The case was officially, and rightfully, ruled a murder.

The unknown subject, also shortened to un-sub, was projected to be a physically strong male at or above two hundred pounds. He was left-handed and wore size twelve Nike sneakers. They were trendy Air Jordans that half the kids in America had sported in 1987. The vehicle believed to have been driven by the un-sub also appeared ordinary. Casts from the tire marks revealed a popular Goodyear pattern for fifteen-inch rims. Twenty-one million such tires were on American roads in 1987. The width between front tires, and length from front to back tires, matched the frames to several sedans engineered by General Motors. The most noticeable match was that of an early 1980s Oldsmobile Cutlass. It also matched two convertible models. Again, millions of these vehicles were on the road.

State Police and Hoosac Mills Police had unsuccessfully linked any potential suspect to the vehicle or tire type. In truth, there were no real suspects in the death of Laiken Barnes. No arrests were ever made.

Stephen picked up an old photo. Some of them clearly had not been packaged with the others. The corners were slightly curled and they were starting to feel grainy. He looked at Melanie. "Twelve years is a long time."

"Especially in a working-class town like the Mills," she said. "Someone should have come forward by now. What do you think?"

"She's as dead now as she was on Halloween, 1987."

"Not the answer I was looking for," she said.

Stephen grinned. "Fair enough," he said. "The truth, Melanie, is I don't know what the hell to think right now. I'm just—excuse me, we're just beginning."

"Instinct tells me she left the party with her killer," Melanie said. "Most likely it was someone familiar with the layout of the house and basement so they could move with relative anonymity."

Stephen paused. She was testing him early—no problem. "You think it was one of my Kappa brothers?"

"I never said that," she said.

"You didn't answer my question."

"The odds say yes, it most likely was a member of your frat."

"I respect your honesty," Stephen said. "Of course it makes sense. All the guys and I used to hypothesize, but in all scenarios it was an outsider sneaking into the costume party and stealing her away."

"I need to deal with some disclosure issues," Melanie said.

"Okay, go ahead," Stephen said.

"I'm aware that Detective Kenny Rocek interviewed you, and I am aware that you were...*intimate* with the victim at one point."

"It became common knowledge," Stephen said.

Melanie considered Stephen's words. The physical relationship between Stephen and Laiken was indeed documented, but how forthright had Stephen been twelve years earlier?

Melanie stared at the folder. "We'll have to reexamine anyone known to have slept with her."

"Understandable," Stephen said. "Is Rocek still working?"

"No, he retired two years ago. But he trained me as a detective. I owe a lot to him," she said. There was a palpable silence. Melanie's intuition was activated. "I take it you're not president of Kenny's fan club?"

"I don't like or dislike him," Stephen said. "I'll say this—he doesn't like college kids, and he doesn't like Boston guys."

Melanie laughed. "You're correct on both accounts. Don't worry about Kenny. He's a sweetheart under his rogue exterior. He still lives in town and we'll both be talking to him later."

They stared at each other. "Let's have a quick exchange, if you're willing," Melanie said.

"Go."

"Laiken Barnes—good kid or bad kid?"

"Good kid," he said without hesitation.

"Promiscuous?"

"Absolutely. She made her way around, specializing in Kappa guys." Stephen offered a conciliatory smile. "Present company included."

"Did you like her?"

"Yes," he said. "I thought she was cool, sexual, and even lustful…but I knew she wasn't the type you could, or should, fall in love with."

"Did you?"

"Did I what?"

"Did you fall in love with her?"

Melanie wasn't recording his answers. She asked, and listened. Stephen seemed to search for words. They didn't come. Melanie changed her approach. "When was the last time you hooked up with her before she died?"

"You mean before she was murdered," Stephen corrected.

"Okay, before she was murdered," she said.

Stephen hedged. "I can't remember," he lied.

"Rocek's file says you had female companionship the night she was murdered," Melanie said flatly.

Again, Stephen recognized the way Melanie couched her statements and questions. She was definitely a cop. "Rocek is correct," Stephen said.

"Tell me about the party itself," she said. Melanie scanned her notes. "You guys called it Green Machine. What's that?"

"We held it twice a year, once on Halloween and again on St. Patty's. We lined the walls with tin foil and put in flashing green bulbs. It's unbelievable."

"Beer?"

"No way," Stephen said. "It's an iced vodka drink—a knockout concoction."

"What time did you arrive that night?"

"Early—probably around five o'clock—but I had a lot on my mind."

"What do you mean?" Melanie asked.

"For starters, I was on the party committee, which meant I was one of the guys responsible for setting up," Stephen said. "Then I had to worry about getting my costume ready."

"What did you go as?"

"I'll show you a picture."

"Okay…what else?" Melanie said.

Stephen thought about it. Here it was, 1999, and he was trying to recall a 1987 frat party. "I was looking out for my brother Matthew and my friends from home," he said.

"Your brother?"

"Yes, Matthew. Matty graduated Taconic the year before I arrived on campus, and no, he wasn't a brother in my fraternity."

"Did Matthew know Laiken Barnes?" Melanie asked.

Stephen thought for a moment. "You mean did he know her before she was murdered?"

"Yes, did he know her?"

"Come to think of it, I don't really know," Stephen said. "He definitely knew all about her after she was murdered, that's for certain. All of Berkshire County knew about her then."

Melanie flipped forward a few pages in her notebook. "Change of subject," she said. "We need to talk about a few of your frat brothers known to have slept with Laiken. Let's start with…"

An overweight desk sergeant named Pluplenski entered the office unannounced and rummaged through one of the file cabinets. Conversation stopped. This was a common routine. Pluplenski's belly drooped over his garrison belt and old coffee stains spattered his blue uniform shirt. He mumbled a few sentences to Melanie. Stephen couldn't understand, but Melanie was fluent in Plupenski-speak. She addressed his issues and then answered a phone call. Five minutes passed. Melanie looked to Stephen, refreshed, and gave a smile that would send chills to any breathing man. "I have to run right now—it's a domestic battery issue—but I'll call you later. I'll need your numbers."

Melanie stood and extended her hand again. Stephen took it. "Are you prepared to catch a killer with me, Stephen Nicholson?"

I've known you for one hour, Melanie, and I'd sail the seven seas with you.

"We shall see," Stephen said.

Melanie pointed to a crate of files next to the office entrance. "See that paperwork?" she asked.

"What about it?"

"Consider it your homework," she said.

"Yes, ma'am."

They walked from the office. Melanie turned to him. "I hope you're not biting off more than you can chew," she said.

Stephen stopped and looked her in the eye. "Clearly you've never worked at the Boston House."

5.

Laiken Barnes' photo never made it to the cover of a milk carton. Instead, milk crates replete with files, photos, and newspaper clippings, all concerning Laiken, sat on the floor of Stephen's hotel suite. He filled the dead time by studying. Stephen read it all: police reports, partygoer witness statements, alibis, criminal records of potential suspects, character references, opinions from family members, and even a glimpse of the autopsy report.

One name appeared often. Detective Kenneth A. Rocek's signature was attached to most of the documents. Rocek—pronounced *Row-check*—had opened a special file that listed the names of all boys who had "experienced intimacy" with Laiken. Stephen snickered.

Why not just call it the Bang Boy list, Rocek?

Stephen Nicholson's brief fling with Laiken was officially documented as "meaningless," and "not of the romantic nature." Those were Stephen's words—but were they true? Rocek, pressing anyone for a confession, asked loaded questions that seemed self-incriminating. In Stephen's mind, the fling with Laiken had been more than physical—but he didn't tell that to Rocek in 1987, and wouldn't tell Melanie now.

Stephen glared at the crime scene photographs with disbelief. Laiken had not been innocent in the purest sense, but she was a genuine good kid. Yet someone had butchered her for no obvious reason.

A young state police detective named McMurtry also had been assigned to the case. It was normal procedure for state police to lead homicide investigations in smaller cities and towns. An exception was made in the Laiken Barnes murder. McMurtry had been new to homicide. The then-veteran Rocek, already trained in homicide by state and Boston police, boasted four murder convictions under his belt. Rocek had been the lead dog. In police circles, it was "Rocek's case" that was never solved.

The old detective had used a bully approach when he spoke to Stephen days after Laiken's death. Rocek used words like *conspiracy* and *obstruction of justice* to frighten all the college kids. Stephen wasn't impressed then, and didn't know what to expect now. Speaking to Rocek, however, was a must.

Stephen fished for Melanie's business card in his wallet. He stopped before extracting the card. He'd studied it yesterday; he remembered the number. As he reached for the telephone, it rang. "Meet me at Kenny Rocek's in two hours at 14 Liberation Street," Melanie said.

"Okay," Stephen answered. "But—" She hung up.

Liberation Street was on the hill adjacent the city hospital. It was a typical nineteenth-century road lined with oak trees and impressive colonial homes. Rocek's two-story colonial was failing. A missing gutter was the least of its problems. Chips of blue paint were permanently soiled into the lawn and the front porch would fail inspection by even a corrupt building inspector. Stephen approached the door quickly and rapped. It opened quickly.

"Melanie just called me," a graying older man said. "Something important came up. Said she had a family emergency. She canceled. You can call her tomorrow."

Stephen stood on the porch, looking at Rocek.

Damn, retirement has not been good to him. Put down the bottle.

"Good afternoon, Detective. I'm Stephen Nicholson."

"Melanie told me who you are," Rocek answered. "You have a private license but you're a C.O. at the Boston House."

"Yes, sir."

"Barnes hired you, huh?"

"That's correct," Stephen said. "You and I spoke for a couple of hours—but that was twelve years ago."

Rocek scratched his head. "Yeah, yeah, Nicholson. I remember you now. All you Kappa boys are either micks or wops, but you didn't have no niggers or spics in that frat, did you?"

He's still half-drunk from last night.

"No, sir," Stephen said. "But back in the day a couple of my boys could throw down with two hands and hang from the rim. Does that count?"

Rocek was perplexed. Again he scratched his head.

Stephen remained on the porch, waiting for Rocek's move. Was the meeting postponed, or was it on? Stale booze seeped through Rocek's pores.

"Wouldn't mind sharing a beer with you, Detective, if you aren't too busy."

Rocek looked quizzically at Stephen. "What time you got, son?"

Stephen looked at his watch: 11:35 a.m. "It's noontime, Detective."

"Well, that changes everything," Rocek answered. "Come on in."

Rocek quickly found two cold bottles of beer. They sat opposite each other in the front parlor in matching sitting chairs that had been uphol-stered back when quality mattered. The chairs were over fifty years old.

The living room was plastered with framed police certificates and pho-tographs of Rocek and other men in blue. A lifelong bachelor, Rocek had made police work his life, and he missed it dearly. The room smelled of a retired cop.

Rocek sipped from the bottle. Stephen matched him. "What do you want to know, son?"

"Your general thoughts on the case," Stephen said.

"There ain't that much to it, kid. None of the college boy leads worked out because no one can finger any person leaving the party with her. All you boys who played in her sandbox had sufficient alibis, too. We had no hard leads, just suppositions. And suppositions mean shit in front of grand juries. Yeah, it had to be a drifter that did her."

Stephen liked the euphemism—*played in her sandbox.*

Rocek stared at Stephen. "So you're a private eye, are you, Nicholson?"

"Side business," Stephen said. "Pays me decent cash and I get to be my own boss."

Rocek laughed. "So a screw-turned-gumshoe is gonna come up here from Boston and solve this case?"

"I never said that."

"I know you're from Boston," Rocek said.

Stephen shrugged. "So what?"

"You're an Irish kid. What neighborhood?"

"I'm a West Roxbury guy."

"Roxbury," Rocek said. "Jesus, Mary, and Joseph—you're from Roxbury?"

Stephen wouldn't give Rocek the satisfaction of differentiating the diametrical neighborhoods of Roxbury and West Roxbury; instead; he catered to Rocek's unabashed bigotry. "I'm from what some people call White Roxbury."

"So maybe a ghetto boy will solve this case," he said.

Rocek's state of mind was tenuous. Stephen wanted to capitalize. "Why do you say it was a drifter, Detective? Laiken was last seen in the fraternity house, so common sense would dictate that it was someone at the party."

"No way," Rocek said. "All of you kids had sufficient alibis, Nicholson. Speaking of which, you damn kids are lucky you all don't have AIDS the way you all fucked around like bunny rabbits. And besides, back in the '80s the kids at Taconic weren't carrying knives. No way—it had to be an outsider."

Rocek was obstinate by nature. Stephen opted for a different approach. "Don't you find it odd, Detective, that everyone remembers seeing Laiken at the party, yet not one soul identified her leaving with anyone?"

"I think she left the party alone and met him outside. She got into his car, drove near the train tracks, and probably smoked marijuana. He wanted to fool around, she said no, and then he did her."

"You're shitting me, aren't you?" Stephen asked.

"Nicholson, this is how these murders happen. The girl was a whore, so the guy assumed he'd get lucky, but then she got cold feet and said no. They were both probably drunk and high, and he knifed her spontaneously."

"But Detective, if you claim that it was a drifter, or an outsider, how would he know that she was a whore, as you say?"

Rocek gave a condescending laugh. "Son, any bitch who leaves a party with a guy that she just met is a whore. Besides, only five of you Kappa boys were lefties at the time, and you all had decent alibis. The perp was a lefty, if you haven't forgotten." They were silent for a moment. Rocek went to the kitchen for round two.

Rocek sat down and rambled aimlessly about the case. A hint of a slur was becoming apparent. He cited William Barnes' name several times; the references were not spoken in deference. Rocek resented the pressure that Barnes had applied in the beginning of the investigation. He had performed his job to the best of his capabilities, and there was no physical evidence or eyewitness to arrest any suspect. It was Barnes' wife, Theresa, who basically called off the investigation four years later. She had become emotionally distraught since her daughter's death, and the ongoing probe exacerbated her anguish. That was why William Jonathan Barnes didn't pursue the issue until after his wife's death.

Round two graduated to round three. The beer flowed. Rocek's eyes were floating. Stephen wanted to push a button or two. "Detective, you seemed to limit your scope of suspects to left-handed individuals. Don't you think that's an exclusive group, sir?"

Rocek looked puzzled. "What are you trying to say, Nicholson?"

Stephen was respectful but confident. It was common knowledge that 90 percent of the population was right-handed, a very inclusive group. If the murder of Laiken Barnes had been a crime of passion, as Rocek suggested, then it would be most likely that the killer had used his dominant hand. People do what is natural to them in situations of spontaneity, including acts of rage. The autopsy revealed multiple stab wounds committed by a left-handed attacker. Stephen didn't dispute this fact, but he offered a different angle.

If the crime *was not* spontaneous, Stephen hypothesized, then the killer could have utilized his strength. By intentionally using a weaker hand, a perp may effectively thwart an investigation. That would make it a crime of premeditation, something that had never been considered. Stephen reasoned that an intelligent, strong man easily could have overpowered a skinny girl like Laiken and effectively murdered her with a weaker hand. Rocek's mouth was ajar when Stephen finished.

"That's your crackerjack theory? That she was really killed by a righty, and he covered up suspicion by doing her with his left?"

"No, Detective, that is not my theory," Stephen said. "It is simply another thought. Excluding ninety percent of the population may be wrong, sir. I understand probabilities and statistics, and systematically narrowing evidence to a certain suspect. If you watch the Discovery Channel for a week you'll learn that much. I just don't want to rule out *everyone* based on the strength of a left or right hand. Remember, Laiken only weighed about a buck fifteen."

"How about you, Nicholson? Are you a lefty or a righty?"

"I'm a righty," Stephen said. "You already knew that."

"So did they teach you that kind of horseshit thinking at prison guard school, Nicholson? That broad was a whore, and you know it."

Stephen's eyebrows rose ever so slightly. "Really?"

"You know it, Nicholson. She probably decided to tease some guy, but she didn't give it up for whatever reason, and then got herself knifed. That's what happened."

Rocek was a curmudgeon. A debate was out of the question. Rocek was a narrow-minded, stubborn pessimist who lived in a black-and-white world. He was inflexible, never to be receptive to new ideas or methods. Kenny Rocek was sixty-seven years old. He wasn't changing for anybody.

Stephen rose from his chair. "Thank you for the drinks," he said.

"Anytime, kid. Just remember to listen to Melanie. She'll show you what time it is around these parts. This ain't Boston and this ain't the Boston House."

"You don't have to remind me of that."

"And another thing—Melanie ain't a bad detective…for a broad." Rocek laughed aloud as he walked Stephen to the door. "Anything else you need, son, just let me know and I'll be happy to help you."

"I'll be sure to call on you," Stephen said. Telling Rocek what he really felt would be unwise. It was his first day on the case—a cold case. He needed friends, not enemies. Stephen would stay clear of Rocek and let Melanie deal with him. He drove away, keeping an eye on Rocek in the rearview mirror as he stood on the porch finishing his beer. Stephen's first interview had come with resistance and netted zero results, but that was okay. It wasn't the first time Stephen walked into a dead end, and it wouldn't be the last.

6.

Melanie answered her phone on the first ring. "Good morning."

"Strategy time, Melanie," Stephen said.

"I'm sorry about yesterday," Melanie said. "There was a minor family disaster, and I had to pick up a few pieces. I'll reschedule with Kenny."

"I talked to him for over an hour," Stephen said. "He serves a pretty cold beer."

"Are you serious? Did you really speak to Kenny without me? That's not what I wanted."

"No one told me not to talk to him without you there."

"Whatever," she said. "What's the big strategy?"

"We're going to the scene of the crime, so to speak. There's a Kappa party tonight and I think it'd be pretty cool if you experience what it was like—kind of—on the night of the murder."

"Okay, that's fine," she said. "Any thoughts on eating beforehand?"

"I'll make eight o'clock reservations at The Caboose," Stephen said.

"You're on."

Stephen was seated at a window table when the lady detective strolled in. Then again, all the accommodations were window tables. The Caboose was a moderately pricey restaurant that catered to the Mills' upper middle class. It was framed in a long, rectangular wooden building that obviously befitted its name. The interior was rich with railroad history decor, and the wait staff all wore black-and-white attire that somehow matched the railway theme.

All eyes watched Melanie Leary. She looked different—not like a cop, but rather a sexy young college professor. At work she dressed professionally. Now her appearance was more personal. She wasn't cute, or even pretty. She was beautiful. Her dark hair swung freely below her shoulders. She wore a tight maroon sweater that would look foolish on other women, but not on her. Denim jeans fitted her backside well. One sight of Melanie would be enough to make a magazine-cover beauty run to the bathroom to regurgitate. But Melanie had more than natural beauty. She had the *wow factor*—sex appeal.

Stephen contained his ogling. She sat, looking at him. He wore khaki pants and a long-sleeved plaid Perry Ellis shirt. "I like your shirt," she said.

"Thanks," he said. "You look okay yourself."

"Tell me about your meeting with Kenny." she said. Stephen recounted the event, including the consumed beers and racist slurs. Melanie absorbed the information, nodded several times, and then said, "Kenny can be a real dickhead when he wants to be."

Stephen laughed. "Tell me how you really feel."

"Stephen, I've been a cop for ten years," she said. "I call it like I see it."

"How much did you interface with Rocek about this case?"

"Interface?" she asked. "Are you serious, Stephen? Do you really talk like that?"

"Sometimes," he said.

There had to be a first time, and this was it. Stephen grinned at Melanie, but it wasn't a typical grin. There was something in his eyes that won the grin a particular name: a Nicholson shit-eating grin.

"You're unbelievable," she said. "I can only imagine the horseshit you get into at the Boston House."

"You don't want to know the nonsense that goes on at the Boston House."

"I came here five years ago from Wilbraham. I was a patrolman for two years before I made detective. Kenny broke me in before he retired. We never discussed this case."

"Seriously, you guys never talked about Laiken Barnes?"

"Tough to explain," she said. "It's a pink polka-dotted elephant—everyone in the Mills knows it's there but won't talk about it...until now."

"What do you think of Rocek?" Stephen asked.

Melanie made a funny face and almost laughed. "I like him," she said, "but he's not the most polished person I've ever known. He has a heart, believe it or not. You have to know what makes him tick."

"And what's that?"

"Police work and booze, in no particular order."

The waitress came, took orders, and departed. The food was secondary. The conversation flowed. "Rocek wasn't very responsive to me," Stephen said. "But then again, I work in a prison. Someone acting like an ignoramus, à la Rocek, is second nature to me."

"You shouldn't have met with him alone."

"You should have averted a family crisis," he said. She smiled. The food came—chicken and vegetables for both. She looked at Stephen. "No more speaking to Hoosac cops without me present."

"Fair enough," he said.

"You say you're from Springfield," Stephen said.

"Yes," she said, "What of it?"

"Red Sox or Yankees?"

"Please, Stephen," Melanie said. "I probably went to more Sox games in high school with my father than you have in your life."

"Get outta town with that talk," he said.

And that was it. The discussion began with baseball, moved to football, and continuously bounced around. Everything was up for grabs: the Barnes case, professional sports, prison life, private investigation licensing procedures, knitting, reading, and even family talk—a little. They chatted and chatted, not missing a beat. Chemistry was born.

Soon it was nine-thirty. There was a party to attend.

They casually approached the large Victorian duplex on Mohawk Street. Stephen hadn't been there since attending an alumni weekend three years earlier. Stephen and Melanie were significantly older than the college seniors; it was obvious they weren't students. As they descended the stairwell into the basement, the fraternity president, Peter Donnelly, recognized Melanie as a Hoosac Mills police officer. "Oh shit," he muttered.

Stephen appreciated the moment. Many times in the past he had stood in a similar predicament. Unexpectedly, he extended his hand to the fraternity president, giving him the ritual handshake. "Long time no see, Peter. I'm glad to see you've risen through the ranks and have assumed the king's chair. Congratulations."

The younger man squinted, then recognized the older Kappa brother. "Stephen Nicholson, what the hell are you doing here? You guys scared the shit out of me. I thought I was getting pinched…again." Stephen introduced Melanie to the fraternity president, briefly explaining the nature of their visit. He told Peter that he would be in town for a while off and on, so the boys could expect to see him around.

They milled about the party. It was a symmetrical basement; a stairwell from the upstairs divided the two large rooms, and a flimsy wooden partition split the two small rooms. At capacity, the cellar could occupy two hundred people. On this night it was jammed, the number probably exceeding capacity. "How many exits are there?" Melanie asked.

"Only one, the way we came in. It's a fire hazard, I know. There's a door upstairs in the kitchen that we—excuse me, the fraternity—keeps locked so no one sneaks in. The brothers who live here have a key for it." Stephen spoke as if he were still an active member. Melanie now led Stephen around the party. Curious eyes followed them.

"Detective Leary, what are you doing here? It's nice to see you," a young girl said. She was a junior named Emily, and she was obviously drunk. Melanie had helped her with a restraining order last year against her abusive ex-boyfriend. Melanie smiled at Emily.

"I'm here on police business—undercover work, Emily," Melanie covertly whispered. The girl blushed, thanked Melanie again, and walked away.

Several younger fraternity brothers, aware of Stephen's Kappa Chi Omicron legacy, came to speak with him out of deference. Stephen and Melanie declined several offers of keg beer. Stephen reminded the young students that his presence would be common in the coming weeks—or months. He broke from the group, now leading Melanie around the basement.

"You said it was a costume party the night Laiken died, right?" Melanie asked.

"Correct," Stephen said. "The Halloween Green Machine is costume; the St. Patrick's Day party is not."

"So it would be fair to infer that a person in costume—with a concealed face—could have left with Laiken undetected?"

"Absolutely—no doubt about it. Green Machine parties are absolute chaos. College kids are used to drinking keg beer, not vodka. You can't taste the alcohol in a Green Machine and the next thing you know you're smashed. So your inference is fair."

Melanie was curious about the infamous Green Machine. "What exactly is in this drink, anyway?"

"The secret formula?" he asked.

"Yeah, what is it?'

"A tub and a half of green sherbet, half a gallon of lime rickey, three gallons of hot water, three gallons of cold water, a case of cheap vodka and ice."

"You're kidding me, right? You people actually mix that together and drink it?"

"We like to refer to it as the nectar of the gods."

"But we figured that Laiken had left the party no later than ten o'clock. The party started at nine o'clock that night. That's only one hour of drinking," Melanie said.

"Melanie, did you just hear the drink I described? You've never had a Green Machine. After two of them you're shitfaced. Anything could have happened by ten o'clock."

Melanie shrugged. "Just a thought," she said. She surveyed the thick crowd, watching the amorous advances the college kids were already starting to make to one another. Twice more Melanie and Stephen refused drinks. She shook her head and looked at Stephen. "It doesn't make sense."

"What doesn't make sense?"

Melanie hesitated. "Why are you grinning again?"

"Don't you sense everyone staring at us?"

"Of course," she said, "I'm a city detective and you're a frat brother."

"It's not that," he said.

"Then what are you talking about?"

"Melanie, it's hysterical. They're sizing us up."

"Meaning what?"

"They think we're a couple, and the Kappa boys are trying to slip us drinks to help my cause."

"Thanks for the college-boy libido overview."

"I'm just saying. That's what they are thinking," Stephen said.

"Great. Anyway, this whole damn thing, it just doesn't add up. A college party, with all college kids, and suddenly a vicious murder that goes unexplained. And nobody remembers anything? I don't like it. I'm sorry, but there's just something rotten about this whole story. Too many people were at that party for no one to see anything. Somebody knows something, Stephen, and they aren't speaking."

He pondered a moment. "Okay, there were very few defensive injuries," he began, "so by all signs it appears as though she was not brought to the tracks area by force. Agreed?"

"Yeah. That's about right."

"Then maybe they left separately," Stephen said. "Did Rocek ever explore that possibility? It makes sense—happens all the time at college parties. A girl and a guy want to hook up but want to keep it on the quiet tip. Maybe she didn't want to be seen leaving with this guy, for whatever reason. They stagger their departures by a few minutes and presto, nobody knows anything. It's a clean getaway."

"You're speaking from experience, Nicholson?"

Stephen smirked. "Empirical observation."

Melanie shook her head. "That theory is our worst-case scenario. Let's hope that they left together, and then we'll find someone who'll talk."

"Let's get out of here before I start funneling beers," Stephen said.

"Then I might have to arrest you for aiding and abetting alcohol distribution to minors," she said.

* * *

The forecast early in the week called for snow all day Saturday and Sunday in the Berkshires. New Englanders, however, know better than to rely on the cheery predictions of meteorologists. A fifty-degree sun beat down on Stephen and Melanie as they stood in the dirt lot, the site of Laiken's murder. They referenced the crime scene photographs and pinpointed the spot where her body was found.

"Her body wasn't hidden," Melanie said, "so our perp made no active attempt to conceal it."

Stephen agreed, flipping through the written report. "According to Rocek, he discovered her body at three forty-five Sunday morning—or Saturday night, whichever you prefer. That's kind of a weird time for Rocek to be working as a detective, isn't it, Melanie?"

"No, I believe he was working overtime," she responded.

"Working overtime as a detective or as a patrolman?"

"As a patrolman. Is there something wrong with that?"

Nicholson shrugged. "So the detectives and the patrolmen are in the same union in Hoosac Mills?"

"Yes we are," she answered.

"Pissa," he said. "You have a collective bargaining agreement that allows detectives to take patrolman overtime, but the street cop can't moonlight as a detective? What a joke."

Melanie sighed; the question was rhetorical. They examined the scene for close to an hour. They were trying to reenact the moves of the murderer. Did he panic? Was he startled by anything? Why didn't he hide Laiken's body? Where was the murder weapon? The murder weapon, or lack thereof, was what bothered Melanie.

"Murderers dispose of their weapons quickly. He got rid of his weapon, but what did he do with it?" she asked. The dirt lot was small. It was large enough to serve as a romantic rendezvous for teenagers in their cars, but too small to adequately hide a knife. The train tracks were only forty feet away. Stephen gestured to the right, to the entrance of the Hoosac Tunnel.

"You think he might have ditched the weapon inside the tunnel?" she asked with curiosity.

"Why not?"

Stephen grabbed two flashlights from his Jeep, and they wasted no time delving into the dark, cylindrical passage. Part of Rocek's case file had noted that the tunnel had been searched up to two hundred yards. Nothing had been found.

The Hoosac Tunnel was a landmark in Western Massachusetts. It had been an engineering milestone, racing four-and-three-quarter miles through Hoosac Mountain. The tunnel was old—ground was first broken in 1851—and after multiple delays it was completed in 1873.

It was the longest railroad tunnel of its day, connecting Boston to Western Massachusetts, and outward to New York, the Erie Canal, and the Great Lakes. What a feat it had been, and it came at the price of almost two hundred lives. These many deaths, of course, were said to haunt the tunnel to this very day. It was beautiful and eerie at the same time. In Hoosac Mills, passing through the tunnel was a necessary rite of passage for all kids.

The western portal of the tunnel stood only three hundred feet from the lot. They approached it cautiously. The entrance was imposing, having been built with solid granite. Two sets of tracks once raced under Hoosac Mountain, but now there was only one. Passenger trains hadn't gone through the tunnel since the 1950s, and now usage was limited to a few freight trains a day.

They crept inward. Stephen's light focused on the left, Melanie's on the right. They looked for anything as they moved, mostly finding beer cans, old tires, and empty cigarette packs. The tunnel seemed to stretch forever, never hinting a light at the end.

Melanie became squeamish. "Did you come through here before?"

"Of course I did. It was about ten years ago and I did it with a group of four or five. It was a good time," he said with an evil laugh.

"Stephen, don't scare me! I don't like these types of places. We're not going to find anything in here, you know."

He shrugged and they moved along. Trickles of water echoed throughout the tunnel. "Don't even tell me that you and your friends were sober when you came through here," Melanie said.

"Maybe, maybe not," he said. "I'd bet a million bucks Rocek dogged the tunnel search."

"What do you mean?"

"The right kind of search, I mean—seal it off and delay train activity. Then come in with high-powered mobile lighting and search the place, metal detectors and all, until exhaustion."

The tunnel was adjacent to the murder scene. It seemed almost too convenient a place to dispose of evidence. "There's a damn good chance our guy dropped his knife in here. It simply makes sense."

"Where?"

"Keep looking in the crevices on the walls with the light. You never know—we might just get lucky and hit the jackpot."

They had walked about a mile and Melanie was getting fidgety. Noises bounced off the walls, giving her a little scare. Stephen jokingly turned off his light and began to groan. "Stop it, Stephen, stop it now!" she barked. He laughed and turned his light back on.

They retreated toward the entrance and discussed a plan of action. They agreed it would be important to "get to know" Laiken Barnes. They would talk to her family and friends, and ask even the impolite questions, if necessary. They needed to know everything. Stephen had known her, but he was an outsider from Boston. They wanted input from the people she'd grown up with—the people of Hoosac Mills. Melanie knew that time could heal old wounds, and any person with knowledge of Laiken's murder might be willing to talk about it twelve years later.

A pinprick of light was dim in their view. "I keep forgetting you're not from Hoosac Mills," Stephen said.

"I think I told you I grew up in Springfield," she said. "What's up?"

"The way you talk. You don't have a true Western Mass accent. I can tell someone from the Mills or Pittsfield area, and you don't have that Berkshire twang."

Melanie was curious, and perhaps a bit defensive. "Then what kind of twang do I have, Mr. Western Mass elocution?"

"Almost Connecticut, but not really. You kind of have a news anchor non-accent, if you know what I mean. A lot of yuppies around Boston talk like that, so don't worry about it. I'm used to it." Stephen was pushing Melanie's buttons, and her defense quickly turned to offense.

"You should talk. You're a guy who tries not to speak with a Boston accent but it comes out anyway. Sometimes it sounds funny," she said.

"So I've been told. But I stand by these words: people from Boston and Jamestown, Virginia, don't need to justify the way they talk."

"Why is that?" Melanie asked.

"We were here first," he said. "We don't have accents. Everyone else does."

Melanie shot him a wink. "Touché, my friend," she said. "Now what do you say we go catch ourselves a bad guy?"

"As the saying goes, 'I'm in like Flynn.'"

7.

The boy clung to his mother's leg. His mother was speaking to a strange man. The four-year-old child didn't understand the man's questions, though he seemed to be polite. The child's innate sixth sense, however, felt a palpable discomfort from his mother.

"How about old flames that Laiken tried to keep secret?" Stephen asked.

"I'm sorry, Mr. Nicholson, but I just don't think I can help you. I'm not privy to anything that you're looking for. I wish you luck, I really do."

"Anyone ever abuse her?"

"No, not really….look, I don't have anything to say."

"How about Laiken's relationship with her parents?"

The woman took a soft step toward Stephen. "I wasn't clear enough," the woman said. "Laiken was my friend. What happened to her was the worst thing I've ever seen in the Mills."

The woman went quiet. Stephen didn't move; he waited. Finally she said, "Look, Mr. Nicholson, it's been over ten years. That's a long time. I'd like to remember Laiken for all the good times we had. The questions you ask make me think of death. Now if you will excuse me, I have to feed my son. Again, I wish you luck. Have a good day."

Stephen thanked her and walked away. The afternoon was not boding well. The woman's name was Tara McLeish. Tara had been Laiken's close childhood friend. Yet she was reluctant to speak to Stephen about the murder, or offer insight into Laiken's life. Tara's name was added to what Stephen would come to call the List of Unwilling. Amy McCann, Meghan Popovic, and Melissa Reinshurst weren't any help either. Stephen sat in his Jeep, miffed, wondering how Laiken's friends could be so uncooperative.

He thought about Kitty Genovese, the New York girl who'd been murdered outside her crowded apartment building. Her cries for help were heard by many but aided by none. "What a funny world," Stephen said to himself as he drove away. There was a long list of people to interview, and Stephen prayed that his future meetings would at least offer something to concentrate on. Melanie was speaking with some of Laiken's other friends. Maybe she could net better results.

The Library was crowded for the luncheon special. Stephen sat with Josef Kieler, explaining his problem while eating meatloaf and mashed potatoes. Josef called for his head waitress. Kelli Brunansky appeared quickly. She was an attractive forty-year-old mother of three boys. She was happily married. Kelli was a lifelong resident of Hoosac Mills—and Laiken Barnes' childhood babysitter. She sat with Stephen.

Kelli and Laiken had grown up in the same neighborhood. Kelli was also nine years older than Laiken—half a generation. Kelli was about fourteen when she first babysat for the young Barnes girl. Stephen wanted to know anything and everything about her. "A good kid," Kelli began. "She was always smiling and always a little mischievous, but not in a bad way."

"How about boys—during her high school days?" Stephen asked.

Kelli hesitated. "Well, I'd have to say that she caught the eye of the boys since she was a teenager. She was a pretty little thing as a kid. She was always flirting." Kelli laughed as she searched for memories about Laiken. "The boys used to wrestle over who would take her out on dates, and she loved it. She was a character."

"What about high school?" Stephen asked again.

"You gotta remember, Stephen, I was a lot older than Laiken. I got married when I was twenty-one and started having babies, so I couldn't watch her anymore. But I know she went out with P.J. McClaren for a long time, and he was very jealous." Kelli carefully looked around. "Don't quote me on this, Stephen," she said in a low voice, "but he was abusive, and that's why she dumped him. That isn't exactly a secret, but I have a lot to lose and don't want my name tied to it."

"You have my word. Where can I talk to P.J.?"

"He hangs out at the Eight Ball Hall."

"You're a lady, Kelli," Stephen said. "Thank you very much." He quietly said goodbye to Josef and slipped out of The Library. When Kelli removed Stephen's luncheon plate, she found a hundred-dollar bill.

In truth, Stephen already knew about P.J. McClaren. He had been Laiken's high school boyfriend, and his name was mentioned multiple times in the case file.

At nine o'clock that night, Stephen and Melanie walked into the Eight Ball Hall. The rectangular barroom was dank, and its drop ceiling did nothing to deaden the pasty taste of cigarettes. Framed mirrors with motorcycle emblems—the kind won playing carnival games—lined the walls. The tables and bench seats were bolted to the hardwood floor, which was permanently stained by alcohol. There were no windows. The most appealing characteristic of the establishment was the four pool tables, all being used. Stephen approached the bar. "What'll it be, young lady?" he asked Melanie.

"Coors Light, and don't call me young because I'm older than you. Don't forget, Nicholson, I have all the goods on you."

"And I'm not interested in the goods on you," he said. He quickly exchanged money with the barkeep for two Coors Lights. They drank while scanning the bar.

"How many of the seventy-five people in here know you're a cop?"

"Ninety percent," she said. "And they think you're either a cop or my guy."

"Anything but the latter," he said with a smirk. He pointed to a lengthy list of banned patrons that hung behind the bar. The Eight Ball Hall was a tough joint. Its name was frequently mentioned in the same sentence as drugs and fights. Stephen motioned to the rear of the bar. "There's your boy, Melanie. He's the big dude with the denim jacket, cheesy mustache, and gold chain. Let's go."

"Remember, Stephen, I'm a cop in this town," Melanie said quietly. "Of course I know who he is."

P.J. McClaren was a big man—six-four, 230 pounds. He was mostly muscle, a truck driver with a tough guy reputation. His schedule was routine: the gym after work and the barrooms at night. At the bars he scored women and fights, whichever came first. Tonight he was socializing with a beautiful, busty twenty-one-year-old girl clad in tight jeans and a half-shirt.

They approached. P.J. recognized the female detective and allowed her a curt nod.

"Mind if we have a quick word with you, P.J.?"

"No problem at all, Detective Leary. Anything to help the police," he said sarcastically. "Who's he?" P.J. seemed to recognize Stephen, but couldn't quite place him.

"I'm Wink Dinkerson," he said as he extended his hand. McClaren reluctantly took Stephen's hand, giving him a firm shake.

Melanie tried to keep a straight face; they were here on business. "He's Stephen Nicholson, and he's with me." The jukebox blared, the pool balls cracked, but all patron eyes were aware of Melanie and Stephen's presence. It wasn't the first time a cop had come to Eight Ball Hall to ask questions. "We've reopened Laiken's murder investigation."

P.J. had an uncomfortable look to him. "What's that got to do with me? I already told that old raccoon Rocek that I don't know nothing. I was at home the night she got herself killed."

"Got herself killed," Melanie repeated. "What do you mean by that? I was always under the impression that someone stabbed her. You must know something we don't."

P.J. wasn't at ease; he took a long pull from his Bud bottle. The ditsy girl remained naïve to the conversation. "You both probably know what Laiken was like," P.J. said quietly. "She was a filthy whore who ran around on me."

Stephen saw an opening. "Sounds like a motive, wouldn't you say, P.J.?"

McClaren darted an evil look at Stephen and tensed his body. "What's your name, boy? Nicklaus? Nicholson? I know you from somewhere, don't I? You best watch your fuckin' mouth. Don't come into my bar and talk shit, you understand that?"

"Just calling it like I see it, pal. I gather you're probably sensitive underneath your rogue exterior, P.J." Stephen spoke quickly, and McClaren didn't detect the sarcasm in his voice.

Melanie wanted to stay on course. "P.J., you maintain you were at home on the night of Laiken's murder. Is that right?"

"Yeah, it is. I was home all night—Halloween night at that. My momma vouched for me; we passed out candy and played cards all night. My papa was home too—getting shitfaced like he always used to do." Several patrons eavesdropped. McClaren and several of his friends had served time in the Berkshire County House of Correction; none were inclined to speak with cops. People monitored McClaren's words.

"Did any kids vouch for you passing out candy on Halloween night?" Melanie asked.

McClaren didn't hesitate. "No, because your boy Rocek never asked nobody. But you two should know that. Just ask that old drunk about our interview. He tried to squeeze me. I laughed at him. I told him to go find one of the Kappa boy punks. They killed her."

Melanie was surprised. "Pretty heavy comments, Patrick," she said. Melanie called him by his first name just to get a reaction.

"Just telling it like I see it, Melanie," he responded with a smirk. "Like I said…anything to help the police."

"When was the last time you were intimate with Laiken before her murder, P.J.?"

He hesitated. "Not quite sure, now. Maybe a month or so, I don't know. What do your notes tell you? It was the frat boys that did her, that's the only thing I know."

Melanie gave a sympathetic nod and waited. Then she said, "Anything you want to add, P.J.?"

"I loved that girl, Miss Leary, I really did. But those frat boys ruined her. She wasn't a bad kid at all in high school. But as soon as she went to State, it was all over. The old man wanted to send her to Williams, but no, she wouldn't listen. She went to State and started hanging around those Boston idiots and that was it. Next thing I know she dumped me and was doing all of them. And if I ever find out which one killed her, I'll kill him. And you can quote me on that if you like." P.J. became quiet; the situation had oddly reversed itself. Melanie actually felt awkward, like she just broke open his heart and reintroduced old pain. "Are you all set with me now, Miss Leary?" Melanie nodded. P.J. and his busty door prize quickly headed for the exit. P.J. was looking for instant sexual gratification. He would not be disappointed.

Stephen's peripheral vision caught the oncoming drunk. It was Harold Canniff, a short, unkempt fellow with a pockmarked face and bushy red hair. Harold was known to all Millers. Tonight he wore his usual uniform of the day: dirty dungarees and a plain navy blue sweatshirt. He brushed up against Stephen. Harold was more than just buzzed, he was plastered, but no drink was in his hand. He swayed in his sneakers but somehow managed to keep his eyes glued on Melanie. "Lookin' mighty fine tonight, Detective Leary," he said. His words were markedly slurred.

"You've had too much, Harold. Call it a night," Melanie said.

Harold simply stared. "Mighty fine…mighty fine…delicious, even…."

Harold was positioned to Stephen's right. Stephen adjusted his feet to a forty-five-degree angle with his right foot forward. He coolly set his beer on a table and calmly held his hands together near his belt buckle. No one in the bar could possibly see Stephen's heels rise slightly from the floor.

"Roll out, Harold," Stephen said.

An immense man—over four hundred pounds—positioned himself directly behind Harold Canniff. The giant's back faced Stephen. He wasn't part of the conversation but he provided complete concealment to on-lookers.

Harold disregarded Stephen's words. He stared at Melanie. "Say, Detective Leary, I was wondering…"

"I told you to *roll out*," Stephen said.

Drunken Harold looked at Stephen. "Ain't talking to you, stranger," he said. "Just want to ask the lady a question."

Melanie sighed. "What is it this time, Harold?"

"I been wondering how you maintain the hair on that beautiful-looking pussy of—"

The question was never completed. Stephen kept his hands low, turned his hips and body to the right, and delivered a sharp left hook to Harold's right side. Stephen's hands immediately retreated. He picked up his beer but did not take a sip. Harold gasped and stumbled to his left, slouching into an empty chair. Harold held his side and breathed heavily. He made no plea for help. The giant man, sipping from his beer bottle, had provided visual cover. No one in the in the barroom had witnessed the punch.

Stephen slid three paces toward Harold. He spoke slowly. "Disrespect the lady again and it'll be more than one body shot, dickhead."

Melanie seethed. She squeezed Stephen's elbow, released it, and then motioned him to follow her toward the door. She stopped suddenly at the exit and looked directly at him. "Wait here," she said. Stephen didn't want Melanie dealing with Harold by herself. He followed instead. Melanie sensed his presence. She paused in mid-step, turned, and glared at Stephen. There were three seconds of silence. Stephen nodded and returned to the doorway—and watched.

Melanie walked casually toward Harold. A beer had somehow found its way into his hand, but he still slouched in the chair. Melanie removed her glasses, leaned in close, and whispered, "Can you hear me, Harold?"

"Yes, ma'am," he said. Spittle and beer leaked from his mouth. His eyes wandered.

"Look at me, Harold." She was less than a foot away. He obeyed. "Do you want me to answer your question?"

Harold's eyes drifted again. "Please leave me alone," he said.

"Shut the fuck up, Harold," she said. Melanie gently placed her right index finger on Harold's chin, disregarding the spittle, and straightened his head. "Look at me," she commanded.

He obeyed. Melanie lowered her voice. No person in the crowded bar could possibly hear her words, except the discredited Harold Canniff. "It's a landing strip."

Harold fidgeted. "I'm sorry I disrespected you, ma'am."

Melanie maintained her gaze—her command—of Harold Canniff. "Short as a putting green."

Harold no longer felt the pain of Stephen's punch. He neared panic mode. "I promise I'll never disrespect…"

"Shut up, I said." Harold went quiet. Melanie leaned even closer. "I hope you enjoyed the image, Harold, because you'll never see it in your lifetime." Melanie stood upright, met Stephen at the door, and disappeared from Eight Ball Hall.

Melanie handled the unmarked, midnight blue Crown Victoria like a pro. Her turns were precise, and the passenger—Stephen Nicholson—could barely feel the vehicle slow to a halt when it pulled in front of the inn. The two-minute car ride had been silent.

Melanie turned to Stephen. "I need to be clear about something," she said.

He sensed what was coming.

"Are there women correctional officers at the Boston House, Stephen?"

"Yes," he said, "about forty to forty-five."

"That's a big number," Melanie said. "Do the inmates ever ask them for blowjobs or make inappropriate remarks about their bodies—such as Harold did to me tonight?"

"Sometimes, but to be fair, it's a small percentage of guys who do that."

"Okay, Stephen. So what do you do about it?"

"What do you mean, what do I do?"

"Do you punch every inmate who disrespects a female officer?"

"Of course I don't," he said. "I'd be fired in a second."

"So what exactly do you do?" Melanie asked.

Stephen hedged. He knew he was in a pickle but he was obligated to answer. "The officer in question writes the disciplinary report," he said.

"Why don't you—Deputy Nicholson—write the report?"

"Because I let them handle their own dirty laundry."

Melanie leaned toward Stephen. She did not remove her glasses. "I've been a police officer for ten years, Stephen. I also happen to be two years older than you—to the day, mind you. Let me pose this: Was tonight the first time in my career that some jackass made a sexually inappropriate remark to me?"

Stephen leaned against the passenger door. "No, I know it wasn't. I just reacted...."

Melanie interjected. "I know why you did what you did," she said. "But you need to understand that I must handle business in Hoosac Mills."

Stephen nodded, but said nothing. The silence was loud.

Finally Melanie continued. "You knew P.J. McClaren. You spotted him right away. You never mentioned that you knew him."

Stephen put up his hand. "I never said I knew him. I just happened to know who he was. There's a difference." Melanie's facial expression spoke loudly. "Okay, okay," Stephen said. "There was a situation with P.J. in the Eight Ball during my senior year."

"Now you have my attention," she said.

"A bunch of us—Kappa guys, that is—were shooting pool on a Saturday afternoon when P.J. made a scene."

"What happened?"

"The same rhetoric he just spit out," Stephen said. "He blamed my frat for killing his girl. He went on and on, and then he got a little too close to me."

"You fight him?" Melanie asked.

"Not exactly," he said.

"Stephen, it's either a yes or no answer. Did you fight him?"

"I pushed him. Then when he started to move on me, he got knocked out clean with one punch."

"By someone else?"

"Yes, my brother Matthew."

"Your brother? Didn't you tell me that he's a teacher?"

"Yeah, but Matty's the total package. He's quick-witted, smart, big, strong, and he can fight like a mofo."

"Really?" Melanie asked. She was a bit surprised, and, if her body language signs were correct, intrigued.

"Yes, really," Stephen said. "You're an NHL fan, right?"

"Yeah, you know that."

"Okay. Summer hockey—I want to say 1992 or '93—Matthew fought Chris Nilan."

"Knuckles Nilan?"

"Yep," he said. "I think Chris was done professionally but still played summer leagues."

"How did Matthew fare?"

"He lost," Stephen said. "Knuckles didn't even want the fight, and it wasn't on the ice."

"What?"

"It was outside of the Hunan Pagoda, a Chinese restaurant next to the rink."

"Good stuff," Melanie said.

"Matthew landed about three solid shots but Knuckles definitely landed six or seven."

Melanie laughed. These were the fun stories in life that have long shelf lives. She enjoyed the brief sidebar. "So McClaren recognized you but couldn't quite place you," Melanie said.

"Exactly." Stephen smiled. "Did you notice when I pointed to the Eight Ball's banned list?"

"What about it?"

"The names Matthew and Stephen Nicholson both appear on it. I legitimately earned my banned status tonight. Speaking of which…did I put you in the jackpot by punching that idiot?"

Melanie faced Stephen. "I don't think anyone noticed," she said. "But as a precautionary move, I'll detail a report on what Harold said to me, and if he decides to press charges for battery, I'll go after him for lewd and lascivious."

Stephen shook his head. "He won't say anything." He opened the passenger door. He stepped from the Crown Vic, placed his left hand on the window jamb, and stopped before slamming the door shut. "I gotta ask you something," he said.

"Go ahead."

Stephen looked at Melanie. "What did you whisper to Harold?"

"I answered his question," Melanie deadpanned.

Stephen's heart skipped a beat. His eyes resisted a pressing urge to look at Melanie's belt buckle. "Okay," he said.

"I'll call you before ten," she said.

Stephen closed the door. He walked fluidly into the main entrance of the inn. Melanie watched. Stephen's gait was casual yet confident. His long arms swung in sync; his fingertips nearly reached his knees. *He punched pretty fast,* she thought.

Melanie had spoken words that had to be spoken, yet there was something about this thirty-year-old from Boston that she liked. He was handsome, but not in a pretty boy kind of way. No, that wasn't it, was it? Melanie didn't drive away until he disappeared into the lounge entrance. Sometimes when Melanie drove she didn't listen to the radio. She listened to her thoughts.

Thank you for sticking up for me, Stephen Nicholson.

8.

Cheshire Avenue is known as the money zone in Hoosac Mills. The small city has a population of twenty-two thousand people, but the majority are working class. Like most urban areas, though, there are affluent neighborhoods. Business owners and professors mostly occupy the early-twentieth-century homes on the beautiful tree-lined street.

The exterior of William Jonathan Barnes' home was comforting to the eye; it was impressive in size and presence, sitting atop a sculpted green lawn and outshining its sister Victorians. A high, wrought-iron gate surrounding the premises suggested a degree of privacy. The brass door knocker echoed loudly. A distinguished older man answered immediately. "How may I help you today, sir?" the man asked with a strong British accent.

"Good afternoon, sir, my name is Stephen Nicholson. I'm currently working for Mr. Barnes."

The butler nodded. "Yes, yes, Mr. Nicholson, do come in, sir. I should have recognized you by the description given me by Mr. Barnes. My name is Bernard, and I have been instructed to accommodate any of your requests. Mr. Barnes is not here today, sir, as he is tending to some business matters in New York."

The butler was genuine, displaying an air of professionalism not common in Stephen's world. Stephen thought words such as hospitality, courtesy, and generosity had been replaced with avarice, selfishness, and cynicism. Yes, Stephen liked Bernard the butler. He stood inside the foyer and marveled at the décor of the miniature mansion. Replica works by Vermeer and Picasso graced the walls. Persian rugs clung to the hardwood floors and various sculpture pieces stood in all corners. The home was pristine and the furniture appeared to have been untouched in years. Yet there was no visible dust.

"Bernard, I was wondering if I could take a look at some of Laiken's old things, if Mr. and Mrs. Barnes saved them."

Bernard gestured Stephen toward the stairwell. "Most certainly, sir," he said. "Laiken's room has remained intact since 1987." They ascended the stairwell and Bernard led Stephen down the hallway into Laiken's room. "Should you need anything, sir, I am at your service. I shall return momentarily with some iced water and coffee. Will that suffice?"

Stephen nodded. "Bernard," he said before the butler departed the room, "did Detective Rocek return everything he took from here?"

The butler answered immediately. "Detective Rocek never called on this bedroom or home, sir. If my memory serves, however, her college apartment was inspected. But I do not know what came of those effects, sir."

"Bernard, please call me Stephen."

"Yes, sir," Bernard said automatically.

Stephen was fresh to the case, and certainly green to a murder investigation, but he found it incredible that Rocek hadn't searched Laiken's childhood bedroom. It should have been an obligatory search. The majority of murder victims knew their assailant, so it was reasonable that a clue to the case could be in this room. Rocek had been negligent in his duties.

The bedroom was that of an ordinary teenaged girl. Rays of light beamed through the double-hung windows. The curtains were drawn back. Stephen looked down into the city. The home was on the high ground in Hoosac Mills. How appropriate, he thought. William Jonathan Barnes was a multimillionaire. He controlled the lives of many people in Berkshire County, so it was only natural that his house—his castle—sat above the working class. Stephen viewed everything: church steeples, the business district, Hoosac Electric, the college, his hotel, and most of the single-family homes.

The queen-sized bed was covered with an expensive spread. The oak headboard was carved with a beautiful floral design and looked over one hundred years old. Guilt swept suddenly through Stephen. He wondered how many boys Laiken had taken to this very spot. Had her executioner ever been here? Had he made promises to her that he'd never kept? Had he told Laiken that he loved her, and if so, had he meant it? What about Laiken? Had she seduced him like the siren she was? Had she clawed at his clothing, groaned aloud, and nibbled behind his ear—as Stephen knew she'd been wont to do?

Yes, Stephen had known Laiken in the intimate sense. It all came back to him. He had been one of her prey. Prey—such a callous word—but that's exactly what Laiken's lovers were. She was the controller. That was the difference between Laiken and so many other girls.

He entered the walk-in closet. Extravagant garments and footwear filled the small room. Stephen could only remember Laiken wearing tight jeans and tight shirts, never anything elegant. Long dresses and blouses, the kind bought at Saks Fifth Avenue, filled the racks. These were undoubtedly the clothes she'd worn when she accompanied her parents to expensive restaurants or galas. The closet spoke for Laiken's hidden side—the rich girl, the side unseen by many.

He searched every pocket and every shoe he could find. He rummaged through bureau and desk drawers, which were still filled with old clothing, notes, and pictures. The pictures revealed nothing extraordinary. He looked everywhere for anything, even knocking on panels in search of secret compartments that didn't exist. After ninety minutes he sat on the bed.

A glimmer of light flashed in his face. The sun had changed direction and was now shining on a gold chain inside her open jewelry box. He picked up the box. It contained chains, necklaces, bracelets, earrings, and various trinkets. The chain Stephen held was different from the rest. It was gold; everything else was silver. There were twenty-five pieces in total. Stephen stared at the gold chain. It was affixed with a pendant of Mary the Blessed Mother. Stephen found this strange, so he called out to Bernard. The butler responded immediately. Stephen questioned him.

"Yes, sir, I do find that piece of jewelry a bit odd. Miss Laiken was allergic to gold; I know that for certain. I don't know where it came from. Mrs. Barnes would have been able to help you with your question, I'm afraid."

Something bothered Stephen about this chain. After five minutes he figured it out. "Bernard, what was Laiken's mother's maiden name?"

"It was Felton, sir."

"Was she too from Great Britain?"

"Indeed, sir. She grew up in the same Manchester neighborhood as I. We were acquaintances as children, sir. That is how I was able to attain employment with Mr. Barnes many years ago. He, of course, is from London."

"Are the Barneses Protestant?"

"Yes. They are Episcopalian, as am I," he said.

Stephen knew that Bernard was curious, but guys like Bernard set parameters on professionalism. He fed Bernard's curiosity. "It's nothing big," he said. "The pendant on the chain is called the Miraculous Medal. Are you familiar with it?" Bernard nodded. "Good. It's a Christian religious symbol, but usually something worn by Catholics. Not always, of course, but I just had to ask so I'd know for sure. Thank you."

Stephen secured the chain in a paper bag. It had probably been a gift. It had to be, right? Laiken had been allergic to gold. She wasn't a Catholic, either, but he didn't want to give that fact too much thought.

He moved to Laiken's bookcase. An encyclopedia set, hardcover high school texts, and a wide range of novels covered the shelves. Laiken had been an avid reader, something Stephen didn't know before. She seemed to have had a fascination with Stephen King and Dean Koontz. But it was a book on the third shelf that caught Stephen's eye. He picked it up—Hoosac Mills High School, Class of 1985.

He flipped through the pages, revisiting the 1980s. Stephen smiled at the trendy hairdos. The guys had either bushy hair or mullets, and all the girls had the big MTV-style perms. Stephen, too, was a product of the 1980s. It was a decade when video games, punk rock, and Camaros were the craze. Stephen reflected his own high school days, the time of innocence. He'd attended an all-boys Catholic school. Unfortunately, girls like Laiken Barnes weren't roaming the hallways.

Laiken's popularity was evident from the many parting notes written all over the yearbook by fellow classmates and teachers. Words and phrases like "Good Luck" and "I love you" were plastered page after page. There were 135 kids in her graduating class. Laiken's picture appeared on the first page of the Senior Section.

Stephen was frozen.

He stared into the face of the eighteen-year-old senior. Laiken's blonde hair dangled above her shoulders, and the yearbook paper still absorbed her beautiful blue eyes. Laiken's eyes projected sharply from the page and seemingly looked into Stephen, regardless of how he positioned the yearbook. She was a vampiress. Stephen was drawn to her—still. He was spooked. He wondered who had taken this photograph. Did impure thoughts race through the photographer's mind when he stilled the lens? Was it a student, or was it a sexually deprived social studies teacher? *Who captured you on film, Laiken?* His eyes drifted to her high school parting shots underneath the photograph.

Laiken Anne Barnes

24 Cheshire Street, Hoosac Mills
Cheerleading, Key Club, Honor Society, Drama Club
Thanks: PJ, RG, TW, AW, CW, NC, SS, LP, WR, AT, MC, etc.
Remember when: Bermuda '84, Jr. Prom hangover,
spelunking the tunnel with the crew, Congrats BB—good luck
with Scrooge, chemistry experiments, babysitting for Mr.
Fisch, Fenway Park trip, "Do you really have a butler?",
partying on Mohawk Street
Here I come Taconic State! Watch out!
Thanks, Mom and Dad! I love you!
Ciao!.......................L.A.B.

Stephen stared at the memoir. The reference to the Hoosac Tunnel jumped off the page. Laiken had been murdered near the west portal entrance, a place very familiar to Hoosac Mills kids. It was a rite of passage for Hoosac Mills teenagers to descend into the bowels of Hoosac Mountain and complete the nearly five-mile march.

He looked to the photograph. He caught himself ogling. Guilt overwhelmed him; after all, she was deceased. Did his lust for a dead girl somehow make him a necrophile? "Who did this to you, Laiken?" Stephen turned, realizing he was speaking to himself. The butler was gone. He collected items from the bedroom, including the yearbook, and bagged them.

After thanking Bernard, Stephen left the house and maneuvered into the backyard. The yard also afforded a clear view of the city. Stephen squinted and located the train tracks. He followed the tracks until a hill blocked his view of the Hoosac Tunnel entrance.

Spelunking the tunnel with the crew.

Had Laiken's words been an omen? He didn't classify himself as superstitious, but an eerie feeling arose. A crisp Berkshire wind, whistling through the trees, froze his body.

A dozen years had passed since Laiken's death—a long time. Stephen reflected on the things that Laiken had missed in those years. Germany now had only one Olympic hockey team, "USSR" was just letters in the alphabet, scud missiles had killed American troops, and the dot-com was king. Stephen was ruffled thinking about the lapse of time. Where did the time go?

Ronald Reagan was president when you were murdered, Laiken.

Stephen was distraught. Someone knew something but they weren't talking. Maybe one of his fraternity brothers could make a startling revelation? He checked the date on his pager and nodded. A fraternity alumni party was only nights away—and he intended on getting some answers.

9.

Stephen's Jeep cruised the curves of Centre Street. His judgment, in terms of traffic signal interpretation, was sketchy at best. "Stephen, yellow means stop, it doesn't mean speed up," Melanie said. She rode shotgun.

"I don't necessarily disagree with your assessment," he said.

"What does that mean?"

He looked at her, then smiled. "You may have a point."

At Park Street he made a left, passed the Knights of Columbus and the Irish Social Club of Boston. He crossed a century-old bridge that sat thirty feet above the commuter rail train tracks before making a left on Clement Avenue. He glanced into the rearview mirror before coming to a complete stop at the intersection of Clement and Stratford Street. He pointed up Stratford. "That's where I'm buying my Daddy Vic when I make real money," he said.

"What's a Daddy Vic?"

He gestured to the large homes that lined the street. "A big Victorian—wraparound porches, three floors of living space, the whole nine yards." He accelerated, then made a quick right on Meredith Street. The street was narrow; one-sided parking was permitted on the even numbers only. An open space was available in front of 30 Meredith. Stephen pointed. "That's the Baby Vic where I grew up."

Melanie laughed. "Baby Vic?"

"It's not quite as big as the ones on Stratford, but I love it just the same. Come on, I'll give you the grand tour. I'll even show you my old bedroom—it still has all the ping pong trophies I won from the Boys Club and YMCA."

Stephen's mother greeted them at the door. She was thin-framed but in excellent physical condition. Barely a wrinkle showed on her face, and her black hair was the same shade as Melanie's. Contact lenses showcased her bright blue eyes. Introductions were made. "Nice to meet you, Melanie. Stephen has said lovely things about you," she said.

Melanie looked to Stephen, then smiled. "Nice to meet you, Mrs. Nicholson."

"It's Peachy."

"Then Peachy it is," Melanie answered.

Two men appeared suddenly. The older gentleman appeared to be around sixty. He was about six feet tall and had a barrel chest. He wore a buttoned-down plaid shirt and dungarees with no belt. His hands were big—rough, weathered, Irish hands. His angular face smiled when he was introduced to the young lady. He didn't shake Melanie's hand; he politely nodded. "I'm Eamon Nicholson," he said. "Welcome to our home."

Melanie smiled at Eamon. He immediately reminded her of her own dad—a gentleman, a hard worker, a man who truly welcomed strangers into his home. The other man appeared to be in his mid-thirties. A quick study revealed him to be a larger version of Stephen. Melanie knew who it was: Matthew Nicholson. Matthew was probably six-two and definitely weighed over two hundred pounds. It was muscle, though. His shoulders were wide, his chest was well developed, and he had a small waist. He wore blue jeans and a cardigan sweater that accentuated his physique. Matthew and Stephen's faces were quite similar.

Melanie's mind wandered. Was Matthew better looking than Stephen? "Nice to meet you, Melanie," Matthew said.

"The pleasure is mine," she answered. They shook hands. Matthew smiled warmly. A chill—perhaps derived from Matthew's initial stage presence—rippled through Melanie's body.

Damn—he's a charmer, she thought.

Soon they were seated at the dinner table. The first floor of the baby Victorian was wide open. Only one wall separated the designated areas of the kitchen, sitting room, parlor, and dining table. The women each had a glass of red wine; the men sipped from Michelob Light bottles. Peachy brought out dinner: baked stuffed chicken, garlic mashed potatoes, broccoli, and cranberry sauce. There was no salad. Everyone loaded their plates; Melanie showed no hesitation. After Eamon said grace, all took part in the meal.

"This is excellent, Peachy," Melanie said.

"You're welcome, dear," Peachy said. "I'm sure you're no stranger to this type of dish."

"Not at all," Melanie said. "In fact, if you're willing to part with your garlic mashed recipe, I'll take it."

Peachy smiled. "I'll write it down and you can have it before you leave."

A question-and-answer session ensued: Tell us about Springfield. Did you go to parochial school? What do your parents do? How many brothers and sisters do you have? Nieces? Nephews? What county does your family come from? Do you like Boston? It was typical Irish American banter—talk sometimes just for the sake of talking. Melanie was part of the culture; she understood. Although this type of free speak was acceptable within the parameters of cultural conversation, certain lines weren't crossed. Melanie was over thirty. She wore no engagement or wedding ring. Questions were not asked—it wouldn't be appropriate. She fired questions back at Eamon and Peachy. She was particularly fascinated with Peachy's profession as an oncology nurse.

Melanie turned to Matthew. "You teach English?"

Matthew smiled and gestured toward Stephen. "Yes, at a community college west of Boston. It's my job to nurture the incorrigible minds of eighteen-year-old versions of my brother."

"You wouldn't want me in your class," Stephen said. "I'd make you look bad—and you're too pretty to look bad."

"And you're not pretty enough," Matthew said. "The junior girls wouldn't even look at you."

Stephen rolled up the left sleeve of his polo shirt. He straightened and flexed his arm. His triceps muscles popped out. "You're kidding, right? I'm ripped up like a bad report card."

Matthew snickered and looked at Melanie. "He meant to say that he's ripped up like a fat chick's phone number."

Back-and-forth barbs followed. Melanie liked it. Eamon and Peachy paid no attention. Why should they? All the lines were delivered with speed and wit, but neither brother truly crossed the line. It was a loose, fun family. Finally, Matthew took aim at Melanie. "Tell me about being a detective," he said.

"It's not as glamorous as one might think," she said.

"And how might a typical person think?" Matthew asked.

"That I'm in hot pursuit of suspects all day and night. It isn't like that—there are more phone calls, door-to-door interviews, and written reports than you could possibly imagine."

"Do you like it?" Matthew queried.

"I love it," she said.

All eyes and ears were tuned to the conversation. Matthew spoke. "I love teaching because I think I can direct the future of our youth. But why do you love being a detective?"

Melanie was puzzled. "You say it like it's a bad thing."

"It's not a bad thing, Melanie," Matthew said. "In fact, it's a necessary thing."

"Only necessary?"

"It's a profession that's predicated on counter-punching. The police, and their various extensions—such as detectives—perform the necessary duty of clearing carnage, assigning blame, and effecting arrests that culminate in felons being placed behind brick walls. But the felons invariably are released prematurely and breed the development of words such as recidivism."

"So if I'm a counter-puncher, what are you?"

Matthew smiled. "I'm a puncher, Melanie. I navigate the minds of the youth and set them on the proper path...so they never have to deal with you."

Melanie raised her glass of wine—and smiled. "Duly noted."

The table went quiet for a moment. Eamon studied Melanie. She was beautiful, of course, but she seemed smart, and had a bit of moxie. He liked her. Peachy's thoughts were more direct.

She'd be a great girl for Stephen.

Eamon's curiosity was piqued about the cold case. "This whole thing is about the millionaire's kid that got murdered, right?"

"Yes, her name was Laiken Barnes," Melanie said.

Eamon looked at both Melanie and Stephen. "Be careful," he said, then continued with his meal. Melanie looked at Matthew and Stephen.

"The Townie has spoken," said Matthew.

"What's that mean?" asked Melanie.

"It means that plenty of people won't like talking to you about this case. People in working-class neighborhoods don't like drumming up the past. Expect closed doors and challenges."

Eamon looked up from his dinner plate and gave his eldest son a tacit signal with his eyes that he agreed with the assessment.

"Did you know Laiken?" Melanie asked Matthew.

Matthew smiled. "I knew Mr. Barnes," he answered. "I interviewed him in September of my senior year for the school newspaper. Laiken was a freshman."

"But did you know her?"

Again Matthew smiled. "I was a senior. I wouldn't have known a freshman if I had tripped over one."

Dessert stopped the conversation. Homemade apple pie found its way onto all the plates. Melanie wasn't shy. She even matched the Nicholson sons by accepting a second piece. "Maybe I should visit Meredith Street more often," she said to Peachy.

"You're always welcome, dear," Peachy said.

They finished with coffee and pleasant conversation. Melanie sensed comfort in this house. No—it wasn't a house, it was a home. She liked the ambience; hopefully, she thought, she could visit Peachy and Eamon again.

Stephen and Melanie had plans, of course. Melanie thanked the Nicholsons for the meal and, more importantly, the company. Peachy gave her a hug. On the way out the door, Melanie stopped and pointed to a family photograph on the wall. "What year?" she asked Stephen.

"Nineteen eight-six," Peachy answered as she approached from behind.

In the photo, Eamon stood back right, Matthew was in the middle, and Peachy was back left. Two younger boys took a knee in the center.

"That's my youngest, David, kneeling next to Stephen," Peachy said.

Melanie knew plenty of personal information about Stephen—including things that hadn't been discussed. She stared at the photo, studying it. She turned to Peachy. "Your son David was a handsome boy," she said.

"Yes, he was," Peachy replied. Melanie's statement indicated an implied knowledge of family tragedy. Peachy looked toward Stephen. "Sometimes accidents happen."

Stephen didn't look at his mother; he immediately opened the door. Before there was a reply, Peachy hugged Melanie again. Stephen was halfway down the steps. "Stephen…?" Peachy called.

He turned, looking his mother in the eyes. "Yes?"

"I love you the world, honey."

He hesitated, thought about the statement, then nodded. "I love you too."

Melanie watched the exchange intently as she moved toward Stephen's Jeep. She reached for the handle to the passenger door. A quick-moving hand came from nowhere. The door was swung open with force and speed. "Thank you for visiting our home," Matthew said. He stood about a foot from Melanie. She looked up at him.

"No, thank you," she said. "You were all most gracious."

Melanie experienced an awkward moment. She didn't know whether to give Stephen's brother a thank-you hug or not.

"Stop being a geek," Stephen said to Matthew as he climbed into the Jeep. Melanie turned to Stephen and laughed.

"Stephen, your brother is displaying manners. Maybe you can learn something. Isn't that right, Matthew?" But when Melanie turned around, Matthew was gone. He'd disappeared as quickly as he had arrived.

Stephen looked at Melanie and they began to drive away. "Seriously, is he not one of the biggest geeks you've ever met?"

Melanie mockingly slapped Stephen's knee. "Stop it. He's your brother."

* * *

In twenty minutes they were on Boylston Street. It was function time: the annual Kappa Chi Omicron fund raiser for the Special Olympics. It was held, as usual, at the Beantown Hotel. Each year, the fraternity's alumni association sponsored a gala that raised more than ten thousand dollars. It was a worthy cause, a good party, and a chance for old acquaintances to reunite for drinks and stories. Stephen was always game.

Stephen and Melanie walked into the reception room. Stephen paused—time seemed frozen. He saw the same faces he had known well for a dozen years. In this room there was a certain type of comfort zone that was difficult to define. Some guys might have gone years without seeing one another, but in an instant, conversation picked up like no one missed a beat. Stephen surveyed the crowd. Everyone looked good. College had been a tumultuous experience, causing internal damage that Stephen had once thought irreparable. But now everyone was in the working world, and the guys were all complemented by beautiful wives or girlfriends at their side. He approached the bar. Slaps to the back came from all angles.

Stephen's entire crew was there: Munsing, O'Brien, Fababiano, Ponce, Creedon, and more. Salutations were made; drinks were passed around. Melanie looked stunning in a strapless tan dress, with diamond-studded earrings and her hair swinging free. Preparation at the Nicholson house had taken her only ten minutes, and Stephen was already receiving the proverbial nod of approval from his fraternity brothers.

The drinks flowed for the first two hours. Everybody had rented rooms, so words like *restriction* and *moderation* weren't applicable. As expected, the old stories came buzzing out, and certain fraternity brothers covered their wives' ears when their names surfaced in scandalous stories.

It was funny. The guys, perceiving Melanie to be Stephen's date, showed him no mercy. More than once she mockingly raised her eyebrows at Stephen. They made their way onto the balcony.

Boston is an old town, and its skyline is moderate compared to other cities of its size. Melanie had attended New England University, not far from the hotel, so she was well acquainted with the city. Stephen pointed out various landmarks. "Stephen," she said, "I lived here for almost five years. I'm not clueless. Are you going to be giving the duck tours next?" They laughed like teenagers. Then, sensing company, they simultaneously refrained from their antics, realizing they were supposed to be here for business.

Billy Munsing joined them on the balcony. He was single, and he had come without a date. "So tell me," Billy said, "what's the story between you two?"

Stephen hesitated, laughed, then orchestrated a straight face. "What would you say if I told you that Melanie is a Hoosac Mills detective, and I'm assisting her on the Laiken Barnes murder?"

Billy's face was deadpan. "You're what?"

"I didn't stutter," Stephen said. "King Billy hired me a couple of weeks ago, and I'm kind of teaming up with Melanie—unofficially—and we're gonna try to solve this case. We need help, Billy."

Billy Munsing was one of Stephen's best friends. They had pledged together as freshmen, growing tight through the years and withholding no secrets. They used to joke that if either decided to run for office, a two-minute phone call to any news reporter would sabotage their political career.

"Stephen, I thought that murder was placed in the cold case drawer—unsolved forever," Billy said. Stephen didn't answer.

"Quite the contrary," Melanie said. "Billy, we're looking for any direction we can get right now…from anyone. Can you tell us anything?" The mood on the balcony had spun one hundred eighty degrees.

Billy felt like he was being interrogated. "Excuse me, Melanie, do you mind if I speak to Stephen alone for a minute?"

She nodded and disappeared from the balcony. "Kid," Billy said to Stephen. "Are you shitting me or what? You're really doing this?"

Stephen nodded, then sipped from his beer.

"Do you think one of us guys did her?"

"My instincts say no, but after reviewing the big-ass file in detail, nothing would shock me."

"No shit," Munsing said.

"The facts are the facts," Stephen said. "Laiken got murdered after one of our parties. She used to fuck around with half the fraternity, present company included. We need to start somewhere, brother."

Billy's discomfort showed. He repeatedly took quick sips from his drink while running his left hand through his hair. Stephen noted Billy's anxiety; it made him curious. Billy raised the level of his nervousness. "Am I one of your suspects, Stephen?"

Stephen laughed. "Dude, are you paranoid? You're not my suspect. Technically, however, you'd be considered a suspect because you fooled around with Laiken. But if that's the early barometer, I'm a suspect as well. Right?" he asked rhetorically. Billy finally breathed easier. He was probably just caught off guard. "I'm gonna speak to all the guys here tonight, Billy. You're simply the first. Is there anything you remember about this case that didn't come up twelve years ago?"

Billy relaxed. "Rocek said that some drifter killed her, you remember."

"Until recently, I guess I believed that bullshit," Stephen said. "Doesn't make sense, buddy. By all accounts, Laiken departed from

Green Machine on her own volition, and probably met her guy." Stephen's face changed. He was stone-cold serious. "Billy, it had to be a college guy. Was there anyone who banged around with Laiken that I don't know about?"

Billy didn't expect the question; he waffled before speaking. "Are you for real? Are you *really* working on this murder, Stephen? You ain't yanking my chain?"

"No, I'm not, my friend."

Billy drained his drink. "We're boys," he said. "You know that, right? You're one of my legitimate best friends in the world, Stephen. I trust you like a blood brother."

"The feeling is mutual."

"Then you didn't hear this from me. Agreed?"

Stephen winked—an implicit agreement of his secrecy. The balcony was wide; none of its fifteen occupants were listening. But Billy moved to within a whisper's length, ensuring privacy. Billy was tall, four inches taller than Stephen, but now his proximity made him look gigantic. Stephen smelled expensive gin on Billy's breath. "Your big brother used to bang her all the time."

"Matthew?" Stephen said.

Billy laughed. "No—your *other* big brother."

Stephen immediately noted the correction. Billy was speaking about Stephen's fraternity "big brother."

Jimmy Petrilli.

Munsing continued, "Jimmy's room was next to mine the semester of the murder. We lived on the second floor but his room was closest to the stairwell. He was a sneaky bastard, I've got to hand it to him. Laiken used to scoot up the steps and slide into his room without anyone seeing her. Scandalous, very scandalous, but I knew. You remember him moving out of the fraternity house the following semester?"

Stephen vaguely remembered, but went along with Billy. "Go on, buddy."

"They thought they had everyone fooled. But I saw her leaving his room early in the morning more than once. No one knew anything about it, except for me. He didn't even know that I knew. All of this happened right before she was murdered, Stephen. I never said a word to anyone, and as far as Rocek knew, there wasn't a documented history between the two."

Stephen thought about the case file. Petrilli's name was only mentioned as a resident of the house. He looked at Billy. "I need another drink, brother."

They rejoined Melanie and a large group around the bar. There were more than forty Kappa Chi Omicron brothers in attendance, ranging in age from twenty-three to forty-three. Jimmy Petrilli was not among them. Stephen made his rounds. He introduced Melanie and made his business intentions known. The Kappa guys were intrigued, asking many questions but offering little in return. Perhaps Stephen had hit the jackpot with the first spin of the wheel—with Billy Munsing. Time would tell.

The hotel served liquor until two in the morning, and about twenty couples had reserved rooms for the evening. They partied like old times, and after midnight even Melanie picked it up a notch.

At two-thirty the party was over. The coming Monday would be a good day for the Special Olympics—they would be eleven thousand dollars richer. It was a good night.

Stephen and Melanie slept in adjacent rooms on the twentieth floor. Stephen fumbled for his access card. "Nicholson, do you want to come in for a nightcap?" Melanie asked.

Stephen turned and looked into Melanie's glassy eyes. She was buzzed. She was beautiful. Everything inside him said yes. His mouth said differently. "I'll have to check with the rain on that later, Melanie."

She laughed. "Does that mean you'll take a rain check?"

"That's what I said—only I said it in Nicholson speak."

"Okay. If you change your mind, just knock on the wall. Goodnight, Stephen." She disappeared into her room.

Stephen undressed and climbed under the covers. He flipped on the television. He stared at the idiot box but wasn't paying attention. Instead he cursed himself for choking on what appeared to be an empty-net goal with a beautiful woman. The problem? Stephen was adept at self-analysis. It would have been an unwise decision, prompted by booze. They were working together, and he would certainly jeopardize this case—his first big case—if they started fooling around. Besides, maybe she just wanted company for another drink. Maybe not. Regardless of her intention, he knew he would have attempted some type of stunt if he'd gone into her room. Naturally, Nicholson out-thought the matter.

Maybe when the case was over…

He envisioned her walking around the room wearing boxer shorts and an extra-large sweatshirt that said Nantucket, with the cuffs rolled back. Melanie seemed like a perfect woman, but business was business, and they had to work together. He closed his eyes and his thoughts changed—for the worse.

The conversation on the balcony disturbed him. His attention now turned to Jimmy Petrilli. A fraternity big brother was an older member who guided a fraternity recruit through the difficult pledging program. Jimmy had been Stephen's big brother, his lifejacket, and he would forever be grateful to him for serving as a role model. Stephen would have to speak to Jimmy about Laiken Barnes' murder; he didn't want to. There wasn't exactly a delicate way to broach the subject. He had a few days to think about it, but it wouldn't matter. He drifted to sleep—and dreamed.

It's great to see you, Jimmy. How have you been? Excellent. How's your mom and your sisters? Good, very good, give them my best. Is work in the business world okay? It is? That's fantastic. Who, me? Oh, I'm just swell, thanks. My brother? Yeah, Matthew's great—teaching at the junior college and still making money hand over fist with his investments. What's that? My parents? They're doing awesome, thanks for asking. I'll be sure to tell all of them that you're asking for them. Yeah, yeah, I will, I won't forget….Oh yeah, there's just one small thing I forgot to mention, Jimmy. After you were done fucking Laiken, did you shove a knife into her body thirty-three times?

His eyes opened. The small alarm clock ticked next to him but he couldn't see it. The television somehow had turned off. The blinds were closed; it was dark. In thirty seconds the closet light was on and his sweaty hand opened the snack bar refrigerator. He delicately slid out a can of Heineken. The beer cost six dollars, but he didn't care.

This drink was on Barnes.

10.

Certain aromas are indigenous to college campuses in September: anxiety, anticipation, determination, and, of course, the omnipresence of sex. Young men and women return from summer break with bronzed bodies and recharged cerebral batteries. They are quite anxious to resume academic pursuits. The impending nocturnal pleasures are all part of the college plan—it's one of those things that college recruiters imply, yet never state, during an admission screening.

It was only Wednesday yet the crowd was deep. College life in September represents a new beginning for some, but for most it's a reunion with old acquaintances. And UMass isn't any old school. It's a city unto itself, boasting close to twenty thousand undergraduates.

Heroes was the bar—a sports bar actually, one of the trendy drinking sites developing on the East Coast. Jerseys, banners, and emblems of all major college and professional sports teams draped the walls, many of them autographed by local legends. At six o'clock more than one hundred students flocked into the bar, ordering pitchers of beer as quickly as the barkeeps could pour them.

In the corner sat a man, ostensibly an anonymous student like the rest. He was tanned and sported a dark gray T-shirt, dungaree shorts, and a pair of penny loafers—no socks. His goatee was maintained and his Boston Breakers cap of the defunct USFL was turned backward. On his muscular right bicep, half-visible under the sleeve, was a tattoo of a green leprechaun spinning a basketball on one hand while leaning on a cane with the other. The man was handsome. Covert stares abounded.

The bar was cool and the air conditioners revved loudly, competing with the volume of the television sets. The man was watching a baseball game. The soon-to-be Cy Young Award–winner, rogue and adroit, hurled away for the Sox.

Within thirty minutes two pretty coeds sat at his table. Classes had just begun and their workload had yet to build. They were sophomores, forever free of the freshman label, and they wanted to celebrate their new, liberated status. The man bought them a round of drinks. "Beautiful girls usually have names; I take it you ladies are no exception to the rule," he said with a smile. They giggled and looked at each other. They were both petite and had brown hair and brown eyes.

"I'm Mary and she's Laura," one of them said. He introduced himself. They looked alike, and he innocently chatted away with them for about thirty minutes, buying a couple of rounds in the process. As they spoke his eyes wandered, frequently locking stares with another woman at the bar. The young girls were nice—too nice—thereby eliminating them from his purpose. Through body language he made it clear he wasn't interested in either of them. Laura looked at her watch and realized they were late for a rendezvous with friends at another bar. It was their cue to leave. They thanked him for the drinks and left.

He closed his eyes for a moment, thinking about his mission. He had been quite careless the last time. What a mistake it had been to select a woman known to him; he was smarter than that and he would not repeat the error of his ways. He laughed to himself, thinking about the Polish detective. What a buffoon the cop had been. Rocek the dolt. And the state cop had fared no better, much to his pleasure. But he too had been reckless, and he was lucky that a legitimate investigator had not been given the case.

His newfound prudence was not just a philosophy, for he had recently exercised sound judgment. Phase two of his mission produced an unexpected quandary in July. He had found the perfect whore, an expendable abomination of flesh and bones that would have served his reasoning well. But he ran into a snafu. He erred by not altering his appearance well enough, and two couples in the bar recognized him, approaching his table for conversation. Introductions had been made, thus ending the evening's mission. Disappointment rained, but he brushed it off, knowing that he would never make that mistake again. It was a new day, and he impelled himself to complete phase two if all went according to plan.

He stared into the green eyes of a lustful woman. She had been sitting at the bar, ogling him while he sat with the young girls. She was voluptuous. Sex oozed from her pores. She was only fifteen feet away.

"Mind if I join you?" she asked.

"By all means, please do. The pleasure would be mine."

She quickly slid into a chair opposite him. "What happened to the Ingalls sisters? Did they get frightened and run back home to their little house on the prairie?" she asked while seductively playing with her straw. He slowly sipped his beer.

"They're nice kids; I sent them home to do their homework so I could meet a real woman. It appears as though my wish has been expedited."

"Is that right? What else did you tell them?"

"I advised them not to speak with strange men in bars."

"How paternal of you," she said. "You've got nice arms. Is that a new tattoo?"

"Yes, I went down to Newport a few weeks ago," he said. "Are you a student here?"

"Nope, I deal software for a company out of Newark. It's not the most glamorous job, but I get to travel around a bit, meet new people, and if I work real hard I can make some decent commissions." She paused, sipping from her gin and tonic. "And yourself, are you a non-trad?"

"Negative. Ironically enough, we share similar interests. I wholesale computer parts for a company in Waltham, north of Boston. I've been here the last two days rubbing elbows with the chief buyer for the university."

"Fascinating. But to be quite honest, neither one of us is working, so I'd just as soon not talk business. I believe introductions are in order. I'm Darlene, and it's a pleasure to meet you…?"

"Chuckie," he said.

They sat for an hour, talking and drinking. Darlene did most of the drinking, though; the man didn't want to lose control. He switched to iced water. The waitress walked by and noticed Darlene's hand touching the man's bare knee underneath the table. She grinned, knowing how the game was played.

Any inhibition Darlene had harbored was gone. "I got myself a room, Chuckie. Do you want to come back for a drink?" He smiled. "But you might be taking a chance. You never know, I could be a psycho chick that'll tie you up and rape you," she said laughingly.

"Maybe I could be so lucky. How do you know that I won't put you to sleep…permanently!" he said in a scary voice as he wiggled his fingers in Vincent Price fashion. Darlene, playing along, gasped aloud and covered her mouth with her two hands.

"Come on, let's get out of here," he said. She obliged.

Darlene was staying at the Rin Tin Inn, two miles away, and Chuckie insisted that she was too drunk to drive. They took his car, a late-model two-door Ford. He wasn't drunk, which was important. He had to keep a clear head, and the three beers in his system didn't affect him adversely. They actually had a calming effect.

"Lucid minds win ballgames," he said.

"What?"

"I said lucid minds win ball games. If you maintain focus you can accomplish anything. Something a coach told me once." His statement didn't apply to the setting, but he cast her a sly grin anyhow. She reached over and squeezed between his legs.

"Just be sure to keep your little head lucid for me, Chuckie, and you'll win all night."

He drove steadily, passing the Rin Tin Inn and heading south. "Where are we going?" Darlene asked.

"A change of plans. I rented a log cabin a few miles from here, in Adams Falls. It's cozy—even a little romantic. What do you think?" he asked with a mischievous grin. She responded favorably.

"Whatever tickles your pickle, cutie."

He looked in the rearview mirror, assessing himself. Never in his life had he worn a goatee, nor dyed his hair jet black. The dye and baseball cap would detract any positive identification, as would the leprechaun tattoo on his arm, which would simply rinse off with soap and water. He had made a clean departure.

The sedan entered Adams Falls and soon turned off the small state highway into a complex named Beaver Brook Woods. Labor Day had passed, and the vacationing families had all packed up and gone home.

It was school time again. The compound sat on a thousand acres, furnished with two hundred log cabins, two lakes, and a private hunting ground. Although the camping ground flourished on weekends until Columbus Day, it was nearly barren during the week. Few families resided there this evening.

The man was careful, having rented his bungalow through the mail using a fake name and paying with a supermarket-chain money order. The log cabin was isolated, by request, and nobody was within earshot. It was considered a private cabin, and he had paid double the normal rate of eighty dollars a night. He had spoken on the telephone with an elderly woman named Sarah before his arrival, and she had been kind enough to leave the key in the outhouse, as he had politely requested. No one at Beaver Brook Woods ever laid an eye on him.

The inside of the cabin was less than modest. A fireplace in the middle of the rear wall was the highlight of the twelve-by-fifteen-foot room. A king-sized bed with springs resembling slinkies squeaked in the corner, and an old refrigerator hummed next to the miniature sink. He opened the refrigerator and pulled out a six-pack of Budweiser and a bottle of peppermint schnapps.

"How'd you know I like schnapps?" Darlene asked.

"I didn't. Now take a swig—or are you afraid to party with a *real* man?" Darlene didn't need coaxing, and she dented the bottled with three large gulps. Chuckie drank from his bottle of beer as he stood by the fireplace. Darlene didn't waste any time. "Come on over here—to cum— Chuckie." He approached her as she sat on the rickety bed. Darlene was drunk and horny. She fidgeted with his trousers in an effort to satiate her sexual appetite.

"Hold one moment, Darlene. Why don't you give me something beautiful to look at? Slip out of those clothes." She smiled and stood, losing her blouse and pants without hesitation. Darlene was a pretty woman complemented by a curvy physique. He motioned her to bend over onto the bed, and she willingly obeyed, seemingly happy to assume a subservient role.

He finished Darlene's task of unfastening his belt and unzipped his fly as loudly as he could, and her submissive position precluded her from seeing his true intentions. The blade to the flip knife had already eased its way out of his back pocket, and his left arm was fixed at a ninety-degree angle.

Time slowed. Nineteen eighty-seven had been his last—and first—kill. He had waited and waited to send another message to the whores of the world. They were family-wreckers, and although his actions were small in number, they would be heard by many. The whores would learn about him soon enough.

The Barnes kill had excited him, and he initially had yearned for more. But he was educated, unlike some of the other mission-oriented types he had often read about. Perseverance would be the key to his success. He had decided, with much forethought, that he would deliver his message every fourth year. Patience was his strength. He would never be caught.

Four years was a long time, but it was worth it. He had given this particular job meticulous planning. It would not fail.

Thoughts adrift, he waited too long and Darlene spun her head around. The alcohol had invaded her bloodstream, and she wasn't sure whether her eyes deceived her. Reality set in, and she saw the blade before the man regained his focus. She swung her right hand wildly into his face, immediately spouting blood from his nose. The backhand was delivered with a snap. Chuckie stumbled backward, disoriented.

Darlene sprung to her feet and shoved past him. As a natural reaction he stood, holding his nose to stop the bleeding, but quickly recovered when he realized she was escaping. The knife fell to the floor and took an unfavorable bounce under the bed. He'd lost his advantage. The mistake could be costly. His shorts were never meant to come off, but the physical commotion had dropped them below his hips.

The naked woman fled the cabin, screaming wildly as she raced into the woods to escape her would-be killer. Sobriety had supplanted her alcohol buzz; she literally ran for her life. Her voice pierced the air, but to no avail. Chuckie had paid handsomely for their seclusion. The nearest cabin, unattended, was half a mile away. He bounced from the cabin in pursuit, laughing at her shrieking voice. Go ahead, he challenged. *Scream, scream, scream.*

The knife had been retrieved. He moved steadily, neither running nor walking. The September sun fell from eyesight; it was getting dark. Darlene wasn't visible, but Chuckie could hear shrieks as they hiked deeper into the forest. She moved erratically and her naked body was cut and scratched by the sharp thorns of brush.

Darlene's mind was clear, but an inebriated body penalized her. Alcohol limited mobility and detracted from one's motor skills. She tripped over a stump, breaking her right ankle. She bellowed in pain. It was a beacon for her location, where she was now immobile.

Darlene tried to calm herself, but it was impossible. Fear pervaded her mind. Where was he? Did he become frightened and run away? She hoped so; there was no sign of this crazed man named Chuckie who had seemed so nice. She stood up and limped into some thick bushes, trying to conceal herself. The broken ankle would prevent flight, but did he know of the injury? She would wait him out in hopes of a failed search.

All was quiet. The bushes had further scraped her body and drops of her blood decorated the surrounding brush. She closed her eyes and prayed that he was gone. Hearing became her focus. Birds chirped in the tree limbs. Twigs crackled nearby. She prayed, hoping it was a squirrel.

There would be no such luck. When she opened her eyes he was there. He stood over her, armed with an evil grin and a knife. "Feeble and weak," he said. "You people use your bodies to feed selfish pleasures yet never think of the ramifications." She stared at him, petrified and confused. Tears streamed down her cheeks. "You are a vicious stockbroker, selling your body for gratuitous gain. Your type is evil personified, spreading disease and infecting the minds of our youth. No one will miss your sorry soul…save the tramp who bore you."

Darlene tried to scream but her vocal cords failed her. She wanted to reach out to him. She wanted to plead. She wanted him to know that she was a good person, complete with ethics, values, and morals. This was what she wanted to say, but couldn't. Instead, she seemingly capitulated to his assessment. "I'm sorry," she said.

He grinned—the most evil grin New England would see in four years. "You should have considered your predicament before you decided to sleep with me so easily."

"But…"

He was quick. The blade moved swiftly, and within sixty seconds Darlene would have her last breath. Her voice crackled with a raspy cough, a sign that blood had coagulated in her air pipe.

Chuckie stood over Darlene's lifeless body. He condemned her. From his front left pocket he removed a pair of latex gloves. Mistakes had been made four years earlier. Corrections were now in order. He would leave no fingerprints. He leaned over Darlene's body and fastened the chain. It was his going-away present, a reminder to all that he had been here. Chuckie laughed, knowing that no one would ever understand its meaning. The gold chain glittered in the early moonlight. He walked back toward the cabin to clean the blood. He breathed easily now. As he walked back to the cabin he felt the bodily fluid in his crotch. A faint odor of bleach filled the air. He knew what it was. He smiled.

Justice was served.

11.

Melanie loathed paperwork. Her small office seemed to shrink the longer she worked at anything remotely involving pens, papers, memos, and signatures. The work was tedious; it was the necessary angle of police work not shown on network TV. But sometimes even the most humdrum tasks provided a good lead.

Melanie spoke on the telephone with an assistant district attorney from Hampshire County. She was seeking background information on a guy charged with domestic battery. The accused man had grown up in Amherst and relocated to Hoosac Mills. Of course, he'd taken his propensity for violence with him. Melanie would be providing courtroom testimony against him, so she wanted any intangible information computers didn't provide.

The ADA, Bobbie Thomas, was cooperative and assiduous to detail. Bobbie was a former Springfield police officer; she and Melanie had met in 1994 at a police seminar. They held mutual respect for one another, and made it a point to chat at least two to three times a year. Bobbie assisted Melanie with the domestic case before the discussion branched off. Melanie picked Bobbie's brain. She explained the Laiken Barnes case in detail. With sixteen years of law enforcement experience, Bobbie was efficient and respected by all. The discussion started innocently, but it soon took a sharp twist.

"Melanie, we have an old case that sounds damn close to that one, honey. It happened in 1990 or 1991, before I came to this office—in Amherst or Adams Falls, I think."

"Do you have access to the file?" Melanie asked.

"Of course I do. Tell you what, give me about an hour or so and I'll call you back. Okay?"

"I'll be waiting."

In fifty minutes Melanie answered her phone on the first ring. There was no greeting. "It was a young female victim by the name of Darlene Hughes," Bobbie said. "A left-handed assailant in a secluded camping area stabbed her. No one has ever been charged."

Melanie's curiosity was piqued. "Tell me everything you've got."

Bobbie quickly obliged. She explained that the victim had engaged in conversation and drinks with a guy at a bar and had left with him on her own volition. The best descriptions came from a waitress and two college girls, but the sketches were middling at best. The suspect had black hair and unknown eye color, sported a goatee, and wore a baseball hat of an unknown sports team. Facial features weren't precise. He had been described as physically fit, handsome, and identified with what was believed to be a Boston Celtics tattoo on his right bicep.

Blood was the only major evidence recovered from the murder scene. It was found in a cabin believed to be rented by the perpetrator. The killer mistakenly thought he had cleaned the scene of his blood—type A positive. In haste, however, he had missed a speck on the wall. It was clearly different from the type O of the victim. The only name linked to the subject, given via telephone to the campground manager, was William Sikes. No address was listed, and there were only three people in the general area with that name. One was thirteen years old, and the others were senior citizens. There had been no suspects.

"Are you sure it was a Celtics tattoo?" Melanie asked.

"I don't know," Bobbie said. "I'm only reading from the file. But that's what it says."

"Good. We'll obviously try to use that as a match for any potential suspects. And just to be on the safe side, I'll check out places in Massachusetts that perform laser surgery for removals," Melanie said. "Another thing, Bobbie—you didn't say anything about latents."

"Guy was a pro, Melanie. Not a damn fingerprint in the place. Either he wiped it cleaner than an Army latrine, or he wore gloves. The only prints were those of the victim."

"Skin under her nails?"

"Nothing," Bobbie said. "No defensive injuries on her hands or wrists, either."

"Pubic?"

"No male pubic hairs recovered."

"How about evidence from the cabin or surrounding campsite area?"

"Several female pubic hairs were recovered from the cabin mattress. They were attributed to the victim, Darlene Hughes."

"Okay…"

"A large sample of female pubic samples was also discovered underneath the bed, but they were attributed to a woman who'd rented the cabin with her boyfriend two weeks prior to the murder."

"Noted," Melanie said. "What's the reputation of the medical examiner's office in Hampshire?"

"Top notch," Bobbie replied. "Guy named Arthur Woodwin performed the Hughes autopsy."

"Woodwind? Like the instrument?"

"No. Woodwin, as in W-O-O-D-W-I-N. Believe me, Melanie, he's more than proficient. The perp in this case is a player, that's for sure. He's no dummy."

"Okay—how about the vehicle? Any eyewitness accounts? Tread marks?" Melanie asked.

"Unfortunately, it's no and no. The only thing we know is that the design on the tire marks was fifteen-inch Firestones."

"How popular?"

"I knew you'd ask. Thousands and thousands," Bobbie said with sardonic police humor.

"I see. But I still can't believe they had nothing to work with; after all, you did have eyewitnesses of the guy. Did they interview anyone? Have you ever reinitiated the case?"

"I've never touched it, to be perfectly honest with you. God knows how busy we've been. But no, there have never been any solid suspects. They dragged in the usual sex offenders for some routine questioning, but they all had airtight alibis. They have blood evidence, Melanie, which is huge, but there was never a solid enough perp to seek a DNA sample." The file was new to Bobbie; she was learning about the case as she spoke to Melanie. Then something jumped off the page. "Hold one second. One odd thing of note was that they think he placed a chain around her neck *after* he killed her."

The reference to the chain sent a shock through Melanie. "Postmortem? Go on."

"The chain also had no fingerprints. Not even a partial, not even the victim's. It looked brand new, and the pathologist said that blood was clotted on the chain, but there wasn't any spraying on it like there should have been. I'm paraphrasing of course, but this is what he wrote."

"What does that mean, about clotting on the chain?" Melanie asked.

"The perp cut her jugular when he sliced her throat. The pathologist said that blood sprayed everywhere like a fire extinguisher. The perp was definitely covered in blood, and he would have had to change clothes after the murder. But no clothes were recovered."

"Was it a gold chain, Bobbie?" Melanie asked.

"Yes, it was."

"What would you say, Bobbie, if I told you that my victim was found wearing a gold chain that no one can account for?"

"Coincidence. Most women wear gold of some sort, including me."

Melanie waited for a moment. "How about if I said that my victim was allergic to gold?" The silence on the other end was palpable.

"I'd say that we might have something. We'll have to find out where it was bought and if we have a match."

"You've identified your chain?" Melanie asked.

"Yes, they did." Bobbie explained that certain jewelers in Massachusetts inscribed their jewelry for antitheft purposes. The inscriptions were small but effective. Bobbie flipped through the case file and found the material relating to the chain. "The chain worn by Darlene Hughes was purchased in May of 1991 at the Jewelers Building in downtown Boston. It was bought at Simo Brothers for the price of four hundred ninety dollars. The name of the purchaser was listed as a Mr. Jerry Cruncher."

"Jerry Cruncher?" Melanie questioned. "That sounds like an odd name."

"They're sure it's an alias," Bobbie concurred. "I'll speak to the ADA who handled the case today, ask him a few questions. This perp appears to use pseudonyms. They couldn't find any person with that name, or derivative of the name, living anywhere in New England. It says that the proprietor didn't remember anything either. Why don't you get an ID right away on your chain, Melanie, and call me back. And more importantly, what do you have for physical evidence from your crime scene?"

"We still have her old bloodied clothing with two hair samples, but that's it," Melanie replied.

"Was it run for DNA?"

"No, it wasn't. But if you have blood from your case, and we have clothing and hair from ours…what do you think?"

"It's definitely worth a shot. We might be able to link the murders. Have your evidence shipped to the state police lab in Sudbury, ASAP, and I'll do the same."

"I definitely will. Listen, Bobbie, you've been more than helpful already. Let's plan on getting together later this week."

Melanie hung up and went to the evidence storeroom. In less than two minutes she found the chain that Stephen had taken from Laiken's room. She dusted the chain for latent prints, but it only came up with one set of prints, those belonging to Stephen Nicholson. The microscope, however, would reap more fruitful results. At last, Melanie thought, they had caught some sort of break.

* * *

Stephen dreaded Mondays. His vacation, although not a vacation at all, was over. He had anticipated a refreshing three-night visit in Gettysburg, site of the greatest battle ever fought on American soil. The Civil War intrigued him, and he also set his sights on the Shenandoah Valley, of Virginia, a blood-soaked ground separating the Blue Ridge and Allegheny Mountains. But now he found himself immersed in a murder investigation, and all thoughts of touring the historical fields of America were put on hold.

Stephen hadn't been gone ten days from the Boston House, but he'd missed plenty. The prison had a unique flair for spontaneity. Two of his friends on the three-to-eleven shift had executed their duties admirably, one successfully performing the Heimlich maneuver on a choking inmate, and the other brazenly risking his life by running into an inflamed cell to search for potentially trapped inmates. The cell had been empty, but the twenty-one-year-old correction officer hadn't known that. After being treated for smoke inhalation at City Hospital, he was sent back to work. He hadn't acted in hope of a commendation or a newspaper headline; he'd acted because it was his duty. He gained the respect of peers, and in a prison, that was all that really mattered.

It was too easy for the public to disparage correction officers. Why wouldn't they? The perception of the profession had always been less than favorable. The great Samuel Clemens once remarked that the dregs of society could best be found at the changing of the guard at any prison in America. But Mark Twain was wrong—dead wrong. The prison walls at the Boston House held two purposes: keep the bad guys in, and keep the public out. It was the latter which presented the problem. Hollywood accounts of barbaric prison guards beating helpless inmates were easy to believe. There was no national spokesman for correction officers, someone who could paint a more accurate picture.

The *real* correction officers—the anonymous majority—went home to their loving families after work. But they would be forever unknown to millions of Americans. These officers performed their jobs quietly, disregarding the nasty stigma cast by the few black eyes of the profession. And although unheralded, their honorable duty was a testament to public safety. Every day they waged a different war. Sometimes it was physical, most of the time is was mental, and every day they were awash in a sea of negativity. In prison, love was put on hold in favor of pessimism, sarcasm, and cynicism. Not taking the job home was a daunting task, sometimes impossible. The job was difficult, but true to the saying, somebody had to do it. The good guys never got the recognition or respect they deserved. That was a fact and it would never change—and sometimes Stephen just couldn't understand that.

Too often it was a bad apple that sat in the forefront of Stephen's mind. Now it was his neighborhood boy, Mickey O'Sullivan, who was the ignominious black eye. He was one of the 5 percent—he was one of the bad correction officers. It had been less than two weeks, but it appeared as if Mickey had escaped the hold of Renzo DiLorenzo. Only time would tell. No fellow correction officers—save Frankie Kohan—were privy to Mickey's precarious situation, and Stephen wanted to keep it that way. But unfortunately, there were no secrets in jail.

Stephen ate dinner with Frankie. He apprised him of the Barnes case in detail, knowing that his services could be called on at any time. Frankie had been busy, working a loss prevention case for a shoe store in Roslindale Square. The private eye business was actually boring, yet consistent. When businesses inexplicably experience inventory loss, it's usually an inside job. And Frankie was diligent enough to hide a video camera monitoring the store's rear entrance. It took only three nights to capture incriminating footage of an employee heisting boxes of shoes and sneakers into a sport utility vehicle.

Frankie listened intently as Stephen detailed the new twist on the Barnes case. Stephen was thorough, as expected. Frankie stared at his friend. "Stephen, you know what this sounds like from my vantage point, don't you?"

Stephen shrugged, a bit perplexed.

"No stranger killed that girl, buddy," Frankie said.

"What?"

"One of your boys did her, Stephen."

Stephen winced. Why did so many people say "did her" in reference to a murder? "Ain't the case, buddy—no way. It may have been someone at the party, I agree, but it could have been anyone. I'm thinking that maybe her ex-boyfriend P.J. McClaren might have done it. He struck me as a jealous bastard. He could easily have snuck into that party in a good costume, taken her out, and offed her."

Frankie exhaled lightly—and theatrically. "Okay, let me put it to you like this—and try to remain objective. When a wife is found shot or bludgeoned to death inside the family home, who did it? The husband or the boogeyman?"

Stephen laughed. "Apples and oranges, my friend."

"When are you going to question your pal, the guy from the South Shore."

"Jimmy Petrilli?"

"Yeah, when are you gonna go down and talk to him. Tomorrow?"

"Hmmm. Touchy subject," Stephen said. "But it's the inevitable. Sometime this week, I hope. Melanie may come out to Boston this week so we can talk to a few of the fellas. I think I'd feel a little better if she was with me."

Frankie's eyebrows rose. "You like her."

"Strictly business," Stephen said. "Of course I like her, but I'm not trying to crawl into her pants like some swinging dick that just climbed out of a submarine and hasn't been laid in four months…like some people I know."

Frankie laughed. "Duly noted."

The clock soon struck eleven, but Stephen didn't go home. He stood on the recreation deck on the ninth floor gazing into the night. It was a beautiful skyline, average in comparison to other metropolitan cities, but the Atlantic Ocean seemed to bring a special twinkle that illuminated the Boston sky. He was pulling an overtime shift. William Jonathan Barnes was paying him handsomely, but he still wanted to work. Stephen had a sizable nest egg, but it was earmarked for a house. He wanted big rooms and a backyard, just like the normal people. Buying the house would be easy. Making it a home with a beautiful wife and children would be the difficult part.

His dream home was a large Victorian on Stratford Street, but he knew it was becoming unattainable. West Roxbury was almost unaffordable for a working-class guy. Real estate was booming, and neighborhood folks were being forced out. Yuppies with large bankrolls were invading the city and there was nothing native Bostonians could do to prevent it. Maybe Stephen could buy a duplex on Clement Avenue and rent out a unit to supplement his mortgage. He would explore his options; but in the meantime, all of the hot real estate in Boston was selling to outsiders. All of the new landlords, however, pronounced their R's.

Stephen's mind was a raceway. Unyielding thoughts of Laiken Barnes came next. Why couldn't she have stayed with just one guy? She was so beautiful, so damn beautiful.

I could have been the one. I would have protected her.

But it never could have been. She was too flirtatious. *No, that's the wrong word—too soft. Tell it like it is.*

Okay, she was a slut.

He admonished himself, trying to clear Laiken from his mind. His judgment couldn't be impeded by ancient feelings of lust. Think of something good, he thought. Okay, how about David? Yes, kid brother David— young, impressionable, innocent. Dead at such a young age and nothing he could do about it. Lazarus was one for scripture. Brother David was dead forever, never to rise again. The recreation deck was quiet, yet Stephen's mind was loud. He could still hear David's last words—a prediction—as if it were yesterday: "Celtics in seven."

His pager startled him. It was a segue he needed. He pulled out his cellular phone, violating department policy, and called Melanie. She surprised him. "I think our guy may have committed more than one murder," she said in a rush.

"Whoa, sister, slow down. One step at a time."

"We need to start talking to some of your frat boys because this just got interesting, Stephen. I spoke with an ADA today and I'm fired up. I paged you earlier but you never called me back. I suggest we start tomorrow by speaking with Jimmy Petrilli."

"Would you care to fill me in on what you're babbling about, please?"

Melanie apologized, and explained her telephone conversation with Bobbie Thomas. Melanie, always efficient, had reconfirmed with Kenny Rocek that the gold chain had been found on Laiken Barnes' body and returned to the family after her autopsy. The microscope produced an identification number, FF90191, and Melanie had tracked it to a jeweler in downtown Boston. The name of the jeweler was Faldo & Faldo, a family-owned dealer located two floors above Simo Brothers.

It was more than a coincidence. Melanie knew it. Both jewelers kept precise records and recorded the names of customers with purchases of more than three hundred dollars. A person named Jerry Cruncher had purchased a gold chain in 1991 at Simo Brothers, but that had produced nothing. Now Melanie had been given the name John Dawkins as the buyer of Laiken Barnes' chain. Tomorrow she and Stephen would pursue the lead.

"Melanie, it's only eleven-thirty right now. If you leave by midnight you can make it to the Boston House by two o'clock. We'll have all day tomorrow to take care of business. I'll give you my keys and you can stay at my place. I'll give you the directions, it's easy."

"Aren't you scheduled three-to-eleven tomorrow night?"

"I've got five hundred hours on the books. I'll bang in sick," he said.

"Okay, but I probably won't make it to the prison until three in the morning."

"That's fine. Just make sure you bring photographs of everyone Rocek interviewed so we can show them to the people at the jewelry stores. Hopefully it'll be the same workers, but don't expect it. It's been a long time."

"I know," Melanie agreed. "We'd better hope that our guy is a frequent customer at the Jeweler's Building, or otherwise we're out of luck."

"Okay, I'll see you in the morning. And Melanie—you've done well, Melanie."

* * *

They drove to Forest Hills station from Stephen's apartment and took the Orange Line train into Boston. It was only ten o'clock in the morning and they were both exhausted. There were two Jewelers Buildings on Washington Street in downtown Boston; one was near the Corner Eateries and the other was next to McDonalds. The building next to Mickey D's was their target. They ascended in a cramped elevator. "Nothing like a Mickey D's coffee to start the day, huh, kid?" Stephen said. Melanie looked at him and made a face, too tired to reply, having gotten only four hours of sleep. They got off on the ninth floor and looked around. The Jewelers Building had a weird room-numbering pattern without any sequential order. They found Faldo & Faldo.

A bookish man about forty years old was behind the counter. Melanie introduced herself, showing credentials. It was Anthony Faldo Jr., the same man who'd confirmed the gold chain purchase from 1987. He was polite and precise, immediately retrieving the purchase register for the year 1987. The buyer had given his name as John Dawkins and purchased the gold chain in September, 1987. He'd paid cash and hadn't been required to sign anything. The man had been asked for his mailing address for business purposes, but had evidently declined.

Detective Bobbie Thomas had faxed Melanie a copy of the case file, including a police composite sketch from the Darlene Hughes murder. Anthony simply shook his head after examining it. It was a somewhat generic sketch, complemented by a disguise, and would have matched many physically fit Caucasian men. He leafed through photographs of Laiken's ex-boyfriends and Kappa Chi Omicron guys. Again, he could identify no one. With permission, Melanie borrowed the purchase register with the promise of a safe return.

On the seventh floor they spoke with Simo Brothers about the 1991 purchase of a gold chain, netting the same results. Chris Simo was accommodating, closely examining all photographs and providing Melanie with a dated computer printout. The name of the buyer was listed as Jerry Cruncher. He'd also failed to submit a mailing address. In 1993, all written purchase orders had been transcribed into a new computer system, and some information was lost. The only fact known was that he paid cash.

Melanie and Stephen combed the building. Starting on the top floor, they showed the composite sketch to the owners of each jewelry store. It was a long day. None of the owners recognized the man in the composite sketch. One female clerk on the fourth floor, however, jokingly remarked that the composite sketch looked like Stephen. "Gee, thanks, that's all I need," he said. Melanie laughed, admitting there was a resemblance to her new friend.

With time to burn they strolled the area known as Downtown Crossing; it was loaded with businesses ranging from department store chains to record stores and bagel shops. They loitered on the corner, eating pretzels and talking. The conversation drifted away from the case, touching on politics and Boston sports. They were also people-watching. Professionals scurried by, weaving between truant teenage skateboarders, panhandlers, and self-ordained preachers. Stephen called downtown a freak show.

"Yo, Nicholson, what up, baby? How you doing, man?" It was Ray-Ray, an ex-inmate who had served five years at the Boston House. Ray-Ray would be a con for the rest of his short life, but he had always treated Stephen with respect.

"I'm doin' all right, Money. You just stay out of trouble, okay?" Stephen said as he bumped closed fists with the ex-con. Ray-Ray quickly moved along, intent on working his next scam.

"Did you just call him *Money*?" an incredulous Melanie asked.

"He's an ex-mate." Stephen laughed as Melanie shook her head. "It's prison slang, that's all." Downtown was the most congested area in the city, bustling with tourists and unguarded pocketbooks, thus making it a reservoir of ex-inmates. They wasted two hours walking around, and their comfort level got to the point where an objective eye would have labeled them a couple. They weren't, but they possessed a certain chemistry that facilitated their job. Hopefully it would pay off.

At six-thirty Stephen's Jeep rolled into Weymouth—East Weymouth, to be precise. The people of suburban Weymouth were territorial, like Bostonians. Each section of town staked its pride. Jimmy Petrilli had grown up in East Weymouth and now owned a renovated Victorian on Putnam Street, not far from Jackson Square. Weymouth was a working-class, predominantly Irish enclave. The residents, lifers and third-generation emigrants from the Boston neighborhoods of Dorchester and South Boston, soon would be voting the town government to city status. It was a blue-collar town. Its people were proud.

Stephen had given Jimmy a courtesy call, so they were expected. He opened the door after the first knock. Jimmy looked great, boasting a manu-factured tan and a body that was no stranger to the gym. Stephen hadn't seen Jimmy in two years; he was happy to see his big brother's smile. Jimmy greet-ed Stephen with the "secret" Kappa Chi Omicron handshake and a brotherly hug. After introductions, Jimmy brought out drinks and chips for his guests. They relaxed on his expensive leather living room set. No one drank alcohol.

Pledging a fraternity was a stressful plight, and it was a big brother's job to maintain a semblance of order in the mind of a distressed pledge. Stephen was forever indebted to Jimmy for his support. That was why this particular visit was difficult.

Jimmy Petrilli had grown up with his mother and two younger sis-ters, both of whom had visited Taconic State and attended some wild Kappa parties. They were cute girls. His father had been dead since the '70s, and oddly enough, Jimmy had never once spoken of him. Jimmy, by default, had become the patriarch of his family. He had done an honorable job. Both of his sisters were proud when he walked them down the aisle.

Melanie had run a computer check on all of the boys initially inter-viewed by Rocek after the murder. Jimmy was an honest citizen and, save for a heavy foot on the accelerator, he had no police record. In fact, there was a notation star next to his name indicating preferential consideration for police officer, should he decide to take the examination. On paper, he was pristine. He worked outside sales for a high-tech corporation on Route 128, and his salary had recently climbed into the six-figure ranks.

They drank tonic water and exchanged niceties. Stephen updated him on his life's endeavors, and Jimmy was genuinely pleased that his little brother was doing well. He also knew the real reason for his visit. The conversation bordered on awkward after fifteen minutes, so Melanie got the ball rolling. "Jimmy, why didn't you tell Detective Rocek that you and Laiken were seeing each other?"

Petrilli didn't flinch. "First of all, you're making an assumption that I *was* seeing her, Melanie. Why would you suggest that?"

Melanie smiled politely. "Because someone told us you were seeing her, and we deem that person credible."

Jimmy chuckled, shaking his head and looking at Melanie. The look held for five seconds. Jimmy was a handsome guy who was forever in the business of using his charm to his advantage. What he failed to consider was the fact Melanie had been intimate with men just as handsome. She wasn't impressed by the charm routine.

"Who might that person be?" he asked.

Melanie shook her head. "You know I can't tell you that, Jimmy."

"Stephen?"

He too shook his head. He felt like a traitor, but he reminded himself that this was business. "We can't give up our source, Jimmy, you should understand that. We're asking a bunch of people questions about this murder, so don't think you're the only one. This ain't the Senate Hearings with Joe McCarthy, buddy. Just tell us about you and Laiken, and we'll be out of here. I promise."

Jimmy nodded, respecting Stephen's situation. "I didn't say anything, Stephen, because I didn't think it was any of Rocek's business, that's why. Laiken and I were seeing each other for a while, but it was our own little secret. You remember Taconic. If you kiss one girl up there, everyone east of the Mississippi River finds out about it." Stephen was quiet; Jimmy spoke the truth.

Melanie interjected. "But you lied about it, Jimmy. I read all the reports. It's one thing not to volunteer information, but it's another thing to lie. The truth of the matter is you had sexual relations with her."

She'd pushed his buttons and it worked. Jimmy maddened. "Am I supposed to report all girls that I've banged directly to you, Melanie? It's a pretty high number. Do you want to know about my new girlfriend? She's got fakies, a bellybutton ring, and a razor-thin mohawk, if you catch my drift. She looks dynamite in a thong."

Melanie didn't flinch. "I don't care how many lucky women you've bedded, Jimmy. I just care about the ones who get stabbed to death near the west portal of the Hoosac Tunnel."

Jimmy turned to Stephen, only to be met with shrugging shoulders. The climate in the room heated. No one spoke for a minute. Stephen broke the silence.

"Do you understand why we're here, Jimmy?"

"Of course I do, Stephen. And by the way, does Melanie know that you got it on with Laiken? And *that* didn't surface until *after* she died. How come no one knew about you two, Stephen?"

Stephen steadied his eyes at Jimmy. "Maybe for the same reasons as you, pal. But I came clean with Rocek because I didn't want any perceptions of impropriety. I had nothing to hide, Jimmy. What's your excuse?"

"I already told you: it was nobody's business but mine."

Again, there was an uncomfortable silence, and Melanie feared the conversation was going nowhere—fast. "Jimmy, how were you and Laiken getting along at the time of her death?" she asked. She'd lowered her voice, an implicit sign that she didn't want to engage in a confrontational debate. It was her attempt at defusing the situation and it seemed to work. Jimmy breathed easier, collecting himself.

"Look, I said I know why you're here, okay? I really do. I didn't kill that girl; I actually fell in love with her, to be honest. That statement alone could incriminate me, but now I have nothing to hide." Jimmy paused for about twenty seconds and his face soon found its way into his hands. "I was crushed by her death, and nobody knew it; I couldn't tell anyone. Back then, if I ever knew who killed her, I would have killed them in a heartbeat."

Jimmy appeared sincere. He continued. "There was something about Laiken. It's hard to explain. Stephen knows, just ask him." Melanie looked to Stephen but he was silent. "She was a great kid and she was gorgeous. That's a scary combo. But she'd never commit to one guy, even though each guy thought that he could be the one to tame her. She had a guy's mentality when it came to relationships. I'll never know what would've or could've happened between us."

"I appreciate your candor," Melanie said. "Ever been to Amherst or Adams Falls?"

Jimmy looked up, a bit confused. "UMass Amherst?"

"Yeah, Jimmy, ever been there?"

"I've been there a bunch of times, as a matter of fact. Both business and pleasure. Why do you ask?"

"Just curious. When's the last time you were there?"

Jimmy didn't know where Melanie was leading. "Probably last fall. I work outside sales, so I've been everywhere around New England in the last ten years."

"Have you ever had a drink in an Amherst bar named Heroes, or camped at a site called Beaver Brook Woods in Adams Falls?"

Jimmy reddened, feeling betrayed by an unwarranted line of questioning. "I think I've had enough of this bullshit. Stephen, you've absolutely got to be shitting me. I told you what I knew, spilled my heart out for God's sake, and now this broad starts asking me crazy questions about some other case."

Melanie was calm. "Jimmy, who said I was asking you questions about another case? I never said that."

Jimmy walked to the door and opened it, motioning them out with his left hand. They passed Jimmy without uttering a word. No eye contact was made. Jimmy slammed the door behind them; it echoed throughout the neighborhood.

They rode in silence to Stephen's apartment, picking up a pizza in Kubli Square. They made small talk. Melanie sensed Stephen's anger. She couldn't blame him. A twelve-year bond had just been compromised—forever. He didn't want to talk about it; there would be time later for that discussion. It was approaching eight-thirty. "Stay here tonight," Stephen said.

"I can't. I've got to get back to the Mills."

"Melanie, it's late, what's the rush? Do you have a date or something?"

She avoided the question as she scooted into the bathroom. She came out five minutes later, flipping shut her cellular phone.

"Melanie, you can use my phone if you're gonna call somebody—even long distance. I'm not a cheap bastard. You really do have a date, don't you?"

"I wouldn't necessarily call it a date. It's this guy who keeps asking me out, and I've been blowing him off for a month. I finally said yes, so I'm going to meet him tonight for a drink when I get back."

Stephen shot her a funny look. It was a mediocre job of containing his jealousy. "At eleven-thirty or midnight? On a school night?" he said mockingly.

"Let's just say that he works your kind of hours, Stephen."

"Don't tell me he's a cop?" Melanie shook her head. "He better not be a C.O., Melanie." She gave a nonchalant shrug. Stephen was theatrical in his staged disappointment.

"You're killing me," he said. "Okay, I'll break this dude down easily: he works at the Berkshire House of Correction in Pittsfield, three to eleven, he's between the ages of twenty-seven and thirty, he dresses well, is good-looking, and is a muscle head."

Melanie was astonished. "Stephen Nicholson, how on earth did you know that?

"Instinct," he said.

"And what's wrong with correction officers, Mr. Nicholson? You were a C.O. the last time I checked."

He was having a tough time keeping a straight face. "I love C.O.'s. Some of my best friends are screws; I just wouldn't want one going out with my sister, if you know what I mean."

"I appreciate your concern, Stephen, and I will keep that in mind," she said. She picked up her Diet Coke bottle and toasted him. The day had been long. They both enjoyed the moment. Melanie tilted her head back and stared up at the ceiling. Stephen watched. Her beautiful hair dangled inches above the floor. "If you told me ten years ago that I'd be divorced at thirty-two I would have screamed," she said.

"You were married?"

"For a little over four years, to be technical," she said. "We separated after twenty-seven months."

A knot formed in Stephen's stomach. "You're a catch, Melanie. At least I think so. How did this guy possibly let you get away?"

"Marriage changes some relationships, I guess," she said

"So what happened, if you don't mind my asking?" Stephen wasn't inhibited; Melanie willingly opened the door.

"Well, the obvious was that we were cops together, and that just didn't work out—same department, same shift. It was uncomfortable when we got into fights because we had to work together more than half the time. But to be totally honest, it was deeper than that."

"In what ways?"

"Passion," she said. "We lost the flare we'd had for a two-year period. It's as if I woke up one day and it was gone…like a thief in the night."

Stephen assessed the situation. "You ran out of wine," he said matter-of-factly.

"I what?"

"I mean the two of you—you ran out of wine. You know what I mean."

"Actually, Stephen, I don't know. Enlighten me."

"It's an old saying—I'm surprised that you've never heard it before. It's biblical, from the book of John. It's about Jesus and the Virgin Mary attending a wedding."

Melanie laughed. "You're a lunatic," she said.

"No, I'm serious, Melanie," he said, deadpan. "You're a Catholic, so listen up. Do you remember from religion class, or Mass, the story about Jesus turning water into wine?" She nodded. "That's it. Jesus and Mary attended a wedding, in Cana of Galilee, and they ran out of wine at the reception. Jesus told the waiters to fill up the empty jugs with water and bring them back to him. He turned the water into wine, and basically everyone at the reception got tanked, though they don't word it like that in the gospel."

"Are you some sort of Bible thumper that I don't know about?"

"No," he said. "But I went to a Catholic high school. Remember?"

"Okay. So what's the moral of the gospel?"

"It's been said that married couples should maintain the wine—figuratively—between them, and always keep it bountiful. If the wine runs out, then the marriage dries up. That's where the term Pre-Cana comes from for soon-to-be married couples."

Melanie was inquisitive. She stared at Stephen, yet she didn't even realize it. "So you're saying that Peter and I ran out of wine."

"No—that's, in essence, what you said."

"You know what really sucks?" Melanie said.

"What?"

"I'm really not saddened by losing him. It sounds awful. I guess I still love him in some regard, but not like *that* anymore."

Stephen took his eyes off of Melanie. The sudden patter of rain danced on the roof. Drops of water crawled down the windows that fronted Washington Street. Each droplet of rain took a different route down the panes of glass. "That's because you never loved him the world."

Melanie sat up. "What did you just say?"

"You never loved him the world."

Melanie squared her shoulders and faced Stephen. "Your mother said that to you—'love you the world.' I've never heard it before. What does it mean?"

Stephen kept Melanie's stare. "It means that your love for someone is bigger than anything and knows no boundaries."

"Unconditional love," she said.

"It's unconditional love on steroids," he answered.

Melanie smiled. "Love you the world," she repeated. "Who made that line up?"

Stephen smiled. "My brother David," he said. "When he was a little kid, my maternal grandmother would say, 'How much do you love me?' Then she'd say, 'Do you love me the whole wide world?' David was cute, and he'd abbreviate his answer by opening up his arms and yelling, 'I love you the world.'"

"That is phenomenal," Melanie said. "I love it."

"It's a Nicholson thing," he said.

There was quiet moment. "I told you about Peter," Melanie said. "Has any woman ever loved you the world, Stephen?"

Stephen followed the zigzag pattern of a rain droplet. It streaked recklessly down the glass, as if it were drunk. He thought about Christine Costigan, a Roslindale girl who grew up one neighborhood away. He'd loved her many years before, when he was a teen. He thought about Alexia Martinez from New York—the sexy bombshell who lived just too far away. And yes, the name Laiken Barnes actually bounced around in his mind. He looked at Melanie. "No woman has ever said that to me."

Melanie watched Stephen. She liked his profile as he looked out the window.

You ran out of wine....You didn't love him the world.

Melanie was intrigued. No question. She stood, put her jacket on, and walked toward him. "I'll call you tomorrow," she said.

"Talk tomorrow," he said.

"I hope the prison is treating you okay."

"I got some things going on but it's all under control. I handled it," he said.

"You're a good man," she said. Melanie leaned over and kissed him on the cheek. When she kissed him, she unknowingly squeezed his right arm.

12.

Page ten of the Inmate Guidebook lists all conduct violations. Rule #32 is clearly defined: "Horseplay is not permitted at any time. Horseplay shall be defined as rough, boisterous physical contact between two or more inmates." The problem with horseplay is its frequency; besides, it's a misdemeanor infraction inmates typically have overturned at disciplinary hearing sessions. Thus, the rule against horseplay is seldom enforced.

Mickey O'Sullivan wasn't comfortable enforcing any violation. It was one of his many deficiencies as a correction officer. The white guys at the end of the unit were engaged in horseplay—no, they were all-out roughhousing. Grappling, throws, and punches to the chest were clearly visible. The inmates laughed; they were having their own version of WWF Smack-Down.

Mickey stepped from the officer's panel and put himself in direct view of the inmates, ninety feet away. None looked. He yelled two times in their direction, trying to compete with the growing decibel level of 6-Block. No one responded. Mickey looked for his partners. Malley was still in the staff bathroom. On the top tier, working as a fill-in and much to Mickey's chagrin, was Lucky Giannessimo. Lucky played his typical games. He harassed the no-name inmates by citing them for trivial infractions such as loose T-shirts, unmade beds, and possession of perishable food items, yet he'd never confront the real problem, the unit bullies. Lucky was also in direct view of the roughhousing inmates. He took no action.

Mickey sweated profusely. He sipped from his water bottle and stole another look at the bathroom—no sign of Malley. Leading to the end of the unit were two parallel rows of tables. Four inmates sat at each table, playing cards, dominoes, writing letters, or just talking. Mickey reluctantly walked between the rows. All eyes watched. He made no attempt to deafen the sound of jingling keys, the universal sign of a correction officer's approach. No one at the end of the unit reacted; no one cared. Inmate Shawn Blighe looked to the top tier. Lucky Giannessimo gently stroked his hair with his left hand; Blighe nodded. The signal was given.

In truth, Lucky didn't dislike Mickey. But it wasn't about liking or disliking. It was about business, making money. Lucky was immoral and unethical—the ideal businessman. He would overcome obstacles to gain full control of Mickey, the fish on a hook. Stephen Nicholson—protector of the weak—was an obstacle. How comical. Nicholson was naïve to think Mickey would stop gambling. Mickey was a gambling addict. Period. Lucky scoffed at Nicholson and his threats. Neither Nicholson nor the Jew could stem the invading tide. Mickey initially made good on his debt, paying a thousand. But as the saying went, a junkie is a junkie is a junkie.

Mickey was now eight thousand in the red with no apparent method of paying. He was in dire straits. He couldn't crawl back to Stephen. Lucky relished his newfound leverage. Using Mickey to mule drugs was now a can't-miss scenario. He could net six thousand dollars a month with little risk. What could Mickey do, tell on him? Lucky had Mickey right where he wanted him—behind the eight ball.

Mickey inched closer; the inmates grew louder. "Guys, cut the shit, will ya?" he managed. The door to cell twenty flew open. It should have been locked but wasn't. A forceful push from behind, followed by a shove from the side, and Mickey was quickly in harm's way. He stood deep inside cell twenty. Terrified, he reached for his radio. It wasn't there; an inmate had clipped it off his utility belt. Mickey moved toward the door but was quickly sealed off by an inmate.

It was the unit Caesar, Renzo DiLorenzo.

Renzo grabbed Mickey by the throat with his right and gave him a vicious slap across the face with his left, stunning him. Next he squeezed Mickey's balls, tight. "Still ain't paying the piper, eh, bitch? You best listen good. You *will* bring our shit in after your days off, or one of my boys on the street *will* pay a visit to your cute little sister, Jacqueline. She works at

Pizzeria Uno in Dedham, doesn't she, Mickey?" The slap stung but it was fear that paralyzed.

Mickey soiled his pants. His knees buckled; Renzo held him up. The radio was passed into the cell and attached to Mickey's belt. Renzo got within inches of Mickey's face. "Go back to your desk, bitch, and act like nothing happened." Urine trickled down Mickey's leg. A wet spot formed in the crotch of his black polyester pants. Inmates seemed to evaporate as Mickey slowly walked back to the officer's panel with a pronounced slouch. The card and domino games continued but something was different.

No eyes watched.

Mickey sat at the panel, shell-shocked. An irreparable crime had taken place. Pain in the face was only temporary. Renzo had slapped the manhood out of Mickey. In prison, masculinity outweighed everything; it was priceless. Once taken, it couldn't be returned. Mickey absorbed the moment. Renzo had actually threatened his kid sister. He couldn't believe it. What a bastard.

The bathroom door opened and Malley approached. "Whew," he said, "that's the last time I eat prison food." Mickey said nothing. The right side of his face was red. "What the hell happened to you?"

Mickey stared at Malley—the good kid who would offer help to anybody. "I get hives," Mickey said. "I just popped a couple of Benadryls. Should clear up in a few minutes."

Lucky slithered on the top tier, angled away from the officer's desk. Mickey looked up, caught Lucky's eyes. Inmates surreptitiously watched. Malley was the only person in the unit not privy to what happened.

Lucky blew Mickey a kiss.

* * *

Inmate Marconi Beach was inside his cell during the correctional emasculation of Mickey O'Sullivan. He refused recreation period. Instead, he paced the room with an unopened letter from the parole board. It was true that his sentence was nearing its end, but Marconi wanted his freedom as soon as possible. Many inmates avoided parole; instead they completed what was called a "straight wrap." This simply meant that recidivist inmates quietly accepted their station in life as career criminals and preferred to serve their full court sentences without being subjected to urine testing or other stipulations contingent upon early release.

He walked to the window and stared through the vertical slats which protected the thick, paned glass. Marconi Beach's cell—sixty-eight—was positioned so he could see to the north. He was unable to see his neighborhood. He did, however, get a wide view of the Boston skyline and the ever-changing expressway which led home.

The North End.

He opened the letter and quickly unfolded the two creases. It was only one sheet of paper—his instincts screamed *not good*.

Marconi Beach's instincts were correct. It was a form letter with additives. *The board has unanimously voted to deny parole at this time.*

He placed the sheet down and picked up his prison memoirs, *Prison Tiers*. Thus far he filled three notebooks. The assistant director of education at the Boston House guessed Marconi's memoirs to be at fifty-five thousand words. It was quality stuff. Both teacher and student believed that another ten thousand words would seal a book deal based on his experiences. He looked at the parole rejection sheet.

…violently battered a peace officer…failed to render first aid…has not fulfilled obligatory participation in anger management courses…potential threat to his former girlfriend…

He walked to the cell door and peered out the window. Some type of unofficial commotion had ensued. His street smarts said so. Marconi watched Mickey O'Sullivan circle the panel while pawing at his red face. Officer Giannessimo was making eye contact with Renzo. Roscoe McFarland scampered to the safety of a chair adjacent the officer's panel. The young officer—Malley—appeared oblivious to an obvious injustice.

Marconi eyed Mickey. He remembered perfectly who Mickey O'Sullivan was from the mid-'80s. He was David Nicholson's best pal. The irony, though, was that Mickey—a young man at the time of Marconi's Meredith Street residence—did not remember him. Stephen said nothing. It was better that way. But what Marconi did know was that the best friend of a Nicholson son—dead or alive—needed help. Yes, Marconi Beach decided that somehow he would hold court with Stephen and find a resolve to free Mickey O'Sullivan from the grasp of the vaunted Renzo DiLorenzo.

Unlike 170-odd inmates, Marconi Beach did not fear the 6-Block Caesar.

* * *

Jo-Jo LaFleur couldn't stop Mickey from shaking. She was Mickey's ex-girlfriend, and more importantly, his best friend. It was her duty to help. Mickey sipped from a can of Bud Light on Jo-Jo's couch. It was 1:10 a.m. She listened sympathetically to Mickey's dilemma. Jo-Jo was a dental hygienist; she had an apartment on Dean Street in Norwood and a fat stack of bills. There was no money to give. She listened, counseled. Jo-Jo was the stabilizing influence in Mickey's life. "Gotta get him, gotta get him, gotta get that mothafucka," Mickey said quietly, rocking in Jo-Jo's arms.

Jo-Jo rubbed Mickey's head. "Shhhhh, baby, it's all right," she said. "Things will work out. Don't worry."

His pitiful life flashed before him. He was an underachiever, the black sheep in the family photograph. His older brother was a chiropractor and his sister, Jacqueline, was working her way through pharmaceutical school. What would be next—a drug shakedown of his kid sister? Here he was, the gambling degenerate and would-be corrupt correction officer, relying on Stephen and crying to Jo-Jo. The time of dependency was over—as were the days of being a follower.

Mickey realized the gravity of his dilemma. He could effect action, handle things himself for a change. Stephen couldn't know about this. He sprang up, dried his eyes, and looked at Jo-Jo. She was his world, his everything. One day he would get his act together and win back her heart. He would meet her at the end of the aisle. Mickey leaned down and kissed Jo-Jo on the lips. "I love you," he said.

Jo-Jo feared the worst. "Mickey, NO!" she said. "You're not going anywhere."

It was too late. In fifteen minutes Mickey was at home in West Roxbury. He pulled open the sock drawer. He wasn't searching for Argyles. The Smith & Wesson .40 caliber automatic had never looked so big. It was nickel-plated, bought used for two hundred dollars. Mickey was licensed but rarely carried. He was a good shot.

It was 2:25 a.m. Hidden eyes watched Lucky Giannessimo roll out of The McGrath Principle tavern along with two men. They talked briefly in the alleyway. The men appeared to be associates of Lucky's, possibly on his payroll. Lucky hopped into his El Dorado and sped in the direction of Mass Ave. His friends boarded a Bronco and drove toward the expressway.

The streets were quiet. Within minutes Lucky took a right on Magazine Street and made a series of quick turns. He stopped in front of an infamous Roxbury after-hours joint called Bobby Moe's. Lucky stayed in the car, listening to a classic Marley number. The windows were down to air out the stench of marijuana. Lucky wasn't in a rush; Bobby Moe's didn't have a closing time. Bobby Moe's also didn't have a liquor permit. Lucky took the keys out of the ignition and suddenly felt a presence at his window. He turned and looked into the barrel of an automatic. He immediately recognized the chubby fingers that gripped the gun. "Good evening, Mickey," Lucky said. He smiled as wide as he could. "How was work tonight?"

Mickey was incredulous. The son of a bitch had a gun in his face and was cracking smartass jokes with a smile. "You think I'm a coward, don't you?" Mickey asked.

"I know you are," Lucky said. Mickey gripped the gun with two hands and stepped back, pointing the weapon at Lucky's head. "You don't got the balls to pull the trigger, kid," Lucky said.

"You don't think?"

"No, I don't think."

Mickey was frozen. He wanted to shoot the bastard but he couldn't. At the same time he didn't want to let him off the hook. Lucky's smile widened. The flashing gold tooth sickened Mickey. "You son of a bitch," Mickey said. He debated. It didn't matter, though. A swift kick came from nowhere, freeing the gun from Mickey's hand. It was one of Lucky's boys from The McGrath Principle tavern. Mickey instinctively rubbed his injured right hand instead of going for the gun. It was a costly error. Thug number two spun Mickey against the El Dorado and punched him in the jaw. A follow-up knee to the groin effectively removed the weak possibility of retaliation. Mickey was having a bad night. It was about to worsen.

Lucky stepped out of the car, laughing. He grabbed Mickey by the hair and pulled him close to his face. "I want you to think of your beautiful sister, Jacqueline. Now then…the word of the day is amnesia. Repeat that," Lucky said. Mickey said nothing. Lucky pulled harder.

"Okay, okay," Mickey said, "The word of the day is amnesia."

12

Lucky gave him a patronizing slap on the back of the head. "Good boy," he said. Lucky looked at thug number two. "Give him a reason to remember us."

Thug number two stuck his Browning .32 caliber automatic on the fleshy meat of Mickey's left leg and pulled the trigger. The shot echoed throughout the streets—not an uncommon sound in the inner city. Mickey bellowed in pain, falling to the ground. Lucky pocketed Mickey's gun. He and the thugs jumped into their respective cars and fled. Mickey writhed in pain, turning pale white as he rolled around the sidewalk. He passed out before the EMTs arrived. When he awoke in the Boston City Hospital emergency room, his memory had mysteriously faded. The attending physician was adamant in his questioning: "Who did this to you?"

Mickey thought about his beautiful little sister. He was equally adamant. "I was with a hooker," he said. "The pimp shot me."

13.

Evidence from the Barnes and Hughes murders was sent to the state police laboratories in Sudbury for DNA examination. It would take time. Technicians who tested DNA were professional and precise, but they were inundated with a heavy workload. Cold cases just weren't a top priority. Melanie and Bobbie, in the meantime, would have to demonstrate patience.

They had compared files and notes ranging from eyewitness accounts, or lack thereof, to autopsy results and methods of killing. Both killers had been left-handed—or at least, as Stephen had noted, had used their left hand to kill. Both killers seemed to be physically strong, as were most, and the sneakers worn by both perpetrators were similar, differing by half a size. That point, however, could easily be discounted. Men frequently wore different types of sneakers; they didn't generally stick to one brand. A Converse size twelve wasn't the same as a Nike size twelve. Some brands ran big, others small.

The notion of disguise was obvious. The Amherst killer wore a cap, glasses, and a goatee. The Hoosac Mills killer had the luxury of "hiding in plain sight" because the victim was attending a costume party. Barnes' clothes were old and tattered, and the only hope of linking the murders would be with DNA. Melanie and Bobbie kept their fingers crossed.

Stephen worked double shifts all week but Melanie apprised him of all details. Frankie Kohan was unsuccessful in attempting to chase down the name John Dawkins. During college, Frankie had worked in the university library, so he was skilled at cataloguing and research. There were five men named John Dawkins in Massachusetts. None was a suitable suspect. The names were a mystery. Jerry Cruncher, William Sikes, and John Dawkins were unknowns for now—pseudonyms in search of a true identity. Patience would have to be a virtue; after all, it was a cold case, and up until now no one had attempted to track Laiken's killer.

Melanie couldn't wait to slide out of her stiff professional attire. She slipped on an oversized sweatshirt and a pair of hospital pants and sat on her recliner. She sipped a light beer. She worked long hours and her mind begged for relaxation. She thought about her ex-husband. Maybe Stephen was right. Maybe they just run out of wine. The date with the Pittsfield correction officer had been a bust, which only made her feel worse. She drained the beer and got another from the refrigerator. She stared at the big-screen television, clicker in hand, and channel-surfed. She searched for something positive on the idiot box.

There was nothing. She wasn't interested in the repetitive negativity of late-night news. She picked up a stack of papers that Bernard the butler had dropped off at the station. It was a collection of Laiken's personal effects that he'd found in the basement of the Barnes family home. As exhausted as she was, Melanie couldn't sleep. She randomly selected letters and cards to read, an invasive way of getting to know the victim.

Love notes and cards from P.J. McClaren dominated the bag. The tough guy P.J. was a softy at heart, writing things like, "You are my sunshine, my only sunshine, don't ever let me go." Melanie smirked, thinking how embarrassed P.J. would have been if his friends had seen his sensitive side. She continued to pick through the pile. An American flag served as the background for a group of elementary school pictures of the 1970s. Melanie smiled as she looked at the transitory photographs of Laiken; she had gone from a toothless ponytailed girl in the second grade to a budding prepubescent beauty in the eighth grade. Melanie shifted her weight on the sofa, and the light from the floor lamp shone directly on Laiken's eighth-grade photo, illuminating it. Laiken had been beautiful.

Melanie read letter after letter, spying on Laiken's past in an attempt to secure any new information. What a shame it was, for Melanie knew that posterity was the real purpose for old photos and letters—not police investigations. It was getting late. Melanie rubbed her eyes and read a handwritten letter to Laiken from an unknown friend. After pausing half a minute, she read it again.

September 29

Laiken,

How are you, honey? I broke up with Billy just like I said I would the first week I got back. Sorry it's taken so long to write, but it's been crazy! It was kind of tough, but like you said, it was for the best. I cried a lot, but I'll get over it. I hope!

Two cute guys (one is from Chicopee) have already asked me out, can you believe it? I'm not sure what I'm going to do, though, we'll see, and I'll keep you posted. Billy would probably freak out. But I already heard that he's been fuckin around. He scooped a girl that I thought I was friends with. We took Intro to History together two years ago and became somewhat close, and now the bitch is blowin Billy! We'll see about that...

So what's new in the Mills, babe? Anything? You'd better fill me in or I'll kill you. Is PJ still following you around like a retarded little puppy dog? Tell him to get over it and grow up if he is. I bet that he's not too excited to see the Kappa boys return to school, is he? Speaking of which, how are your boys doing? I'd love to get back there early before Thanksgiving to go to one of the parties, but I don't know if my 'rents can afford to fly me home. Maybe you can steal the Hoosac helicopter. Promise the pilot I'll show him a good time for the flight home. Ha ha! I sure ain't gonna drive again! I learned my lesson from that! I'll let you know.

Have you seen your Boston Boy lately? I hope so, for your sake! You'd better hook up with him, because a good tongue like that should never go to waste, honey! Who knows, maybe the three of us can get to–

gether again over the Christmas break when I come home. It would be déjà vu! But we would have to get real drunk again, that's for sure. Give him a big kiss for me, will you? Have fun this semester, but don't get into too much trouble. Tell your mom and dad I said hi, and w/b as soon as you can. I love you and miss you very much. Give Bernard a kiss for me, but make sure he doesn't pop a bona!

Yours dearly-always, Renee

The letter fell from Melanie's fingertips. Who was Renee? She wasn't on any lists of names that were in the case file. Yet it was clear she was a close friend who must be interviewed. And who was this Boston Boy? The tone of the letter intimated strong sexual content, but the name didn't ring a bell. Stephen was a Kappa brother, and he was from Boston. Hopefully he could shed light on these newfound mysteries.

Melanie had worked all day on an empty stomach, as was frequent in her career. Two beers turned to three, and she swayed a bit as she walked to her bedroom. Melanie felt lonely, going to bed by herself—again. She was ashamed of her loneliness, wondering when her Mr. Right would come into her life. Or had he already come? No, she shouldn't think foolish thoughts, but the beers had taken their effect. Her mind wandered.

She wondered what Stephen was doing right now. Though tired and buzzed, she still couldn't sleep. In need of company, she called Stephen at home. He was asleep, but picked up the receiver just as the answering machine turned on. "Who's Boston Boy?" she blurted out.

His voice was raspy and she repeated the question. The conversation could have waited until morning, and it was evident she was looking for an excuse to call. He was confused.

"I don't know what the hell you're talking about, Melanie." It would take him a couple of minutes to clear his head. He detected a slur in her voice. "Melanie, do you have any more beers in the fridge?" he finally asked.

"Yes, I do."

"Then go grab one more and slug it down. It's the perfect sleeping pill, trust me. I'll talk to you tomorrow." Melanie felt like a little girl, having just been admonished by her big brother.

"Okay, Stephen, sorry for waking you up. Are you mad at me?"

"No, Melanie, but I'm more tired than a porn star after a long day of retakes." Ever so tired, Stephen still managed a bit of wit.

"Sorry. Pleasant dreams, Stephen."

"You too."

She followed his instructions, draining another beer in front of the television and then climbing underneath the covers of her bed. She would have a sound sleep that night, and the dreams would come. When she awoke in the morning, she had a smile on her face.

* * *

Most police officers say that domestic issues are the worst part of the job. Detectives dread them because so many times battered women refuse to press charges or testify against their abusers. Hoosac Mills was no different than any other small city, and unfortunately Melanie had experience with these cases. Two women had just refused to press charges against their abusive husbands. Melanie wasn't supposed to take the job personally, but it was difficult not to. She sulked, hoping the next police responses to the women's homes wouldn't be for homicide.

It was too early in the day for Melanie to be glum; she needed something to give her a boost. The door to her office was ajar, and a pretty woman knocked softly and stared into the room. "Detective Leary, right?" she asked hesitantly. The woman looked familiar, but Melanie couldn't place her.

"Yes, I'm Melanie Leary, please come in. And you are?" she asked, extending her hand.

"I'm Desprise Johnston. I am an RN at Taconic Medical Center. We've met before." Melanie nodded with familiarity and offered the woman a seat.

"I didn't recognize you out of your nursing uniform, Desprise."

"Don't worry about it. I hear that a lot," the nurse replied. Desprise was a confident and cheery woman.

"Desprise—that's a pretty name, I like that. What can I do for you today?" The nurse looked around, making sure that no one was listening. "Don't worry, you're in a police station," Melanie said in attempt to allay Desprise's nerves. "Fire away—it's okay."

"Well, it kind of pertains to the investigation you're doing now."

Melanie was a busy detective; she probably had twenty-five active cases. She looked at Desprise, trying to register what case she was talking about. It finally came to her. "You're referring to the nurse at Taconic and her abusive boyfriend? That case?" Desprise shook her head and again looked around. She rose from her chair and closed the office door. Melanie was fully alert; Desprise had certainly captured her undivided attention.

"No, Detective Leary," she said. "I mean the Laiken Barnes murder from 1987."

Melanie nodded. "Yes, that case has resurfaced," she said. Melanie stood and retrieved two bottles of cold water from her dormitory-style refrigerator. She untwisted the cap on one bottle and handed it to Desprise. She then took a seat. The task took twenty seconds. It was Melanie's attempt at appearing nonchalant; meanwhile, the wheels in her mind spun wildly. "What do you recollect about the Barnes murder, Desprise?" Melanie asked.

Semantics matter. That was one of many things Detective Kenny Rocek had instilled into Melanie. When questioning or simply speaking to a witness, the importance of the spoken word wasn't centered on *what* was being said, but rather *how* it was said.

Clearly Desprise came with information. That appeared to be fact. Yet Melanie didn't want to rush to the point; after all, Desprise initiated the meeting. Melanie's question, however, was innocuous. It could have been directed at anyone who was a 1987 college student or city resident in Hoosac Mills. It was neutral speech; it was disarming.

"I know a little something, I guess. I was working the graveyard shift at the hospital on the night they brought Laiken in."

"You were a nurse back then?" Melanie interrupted. "How old are you, Desprise?"

"I'm thirty-one now, but I was only nineteen at the time of the murder. I was studying for my LPN, so I was actually in training. For all intents and purposes, I was performing regular LPN duties."

Melanie nodded. She didn't reach for a pen and paper or a recording device. "So what can you tell me about that night? Take your time."

Desprise sat upright in the chair opposite Melanie. She closed her eyes, trying to recreate the scene in her mind. "Laiken was dead when they brought her in, that I'm positive about. There was no coroner in Berkshire County that night." Melanie gave a puzzled look. Desprise elaborated. "What I mean is, they couldn't find him."

"Where was he?" Melanie asked.

"I don't know precisely where he was, but I overheard a couple of veteran nurses saying that he was out drunk somewhere. Laiken had to be officially pronounced dead, and they brought her to the ER so a doctor could do it. EMTs can't pronounce, and neither can nurses."

"I'm following," Melanie said.

"Well, the body has to be completely naked, and the intern tells *me* to take all her clothes off," Desprise said. "I know this girl, for Christ's sake. I wasn't good friends with her, but it was Laiken Barnes, and they're making me take all her clothes off."

"Her dead body, in a sense, was a crime scene," Melanie said. "Was Detective Rocek present?"

"He was in the hospital, but he wasn't in the room with me at the time. I don't know why he wasn't there and I don't know if he was supposed to be there. I just remember that I was alone."

"What did you do?" Melanie asked.

"I didn't have a choice. I did what I was told. Laiken's torso was bloodied; it was, to this day, the goriest thing I've ever seen in my life."

"I'm sorry," Melanie said.

"Thank you," Desprise answered. "Then I roll down her black one-piece suit all the way—she had gone to a college party as Catwoman, I guess—and then I saw it." She stopped, partly to collect herself, and partly to make Melanie elicit the information from her.

"What did you see, Desprise?"

"Semen," she said. "Laiken wasn't wearing underwear, and there was smudged semen in her pubic hairs."

This was news to Melanie; the autopsy report and case file never mentioned seminal fluid. That was a fact that wouldn't have been overlooked. "Are you *sure* it was semen, Desprise?"

The nurse leaned forward. "Detective…"

"Call me Melanie, please."

"Melanie, I may have been nineteen at the time, but I wasn't peddling Girl Scout cookies. It was cum, and I'm telling you right now it was cum," she said with authority.

"What next?" Melanie asked.

"I notified my nursing supervisor, Mrs. Bonjowski."

"What did Mrs. Bonjowski tell you?"

"She told me to stand by, and then, after about ten minutes, she came back and told me to shave all of Laiken's pubic hair, place it into a vial, and label it."

Melanie was incredulous. She leaned forward. "She fuckin' what?"

Desprise was no longer nineteen. She was a composed woman, a professional registered nurse who had experienced much since the Halloween murder of 1987. She actually smiled. "That's why I'm here, Melanie."

"That is insane!" Melanie said. "You had no business performing such a task. This DNA evidence—wherever it is now—would get tossed out of court in less than a minute."

"I know that."

"Did Detective Rocek give these instructions to Mrs. Bonjowski?"

"I don't know," Desprise said. "I would assume he did, but I don't know."

"What did you do with the vial?"

"I gave it to Detective Rocek."

"I want you to remember clearly, Desprise. Was Detective Rocek in the room when you collected the semen specimen?"

Desprise didn't hesitate. "No, he wasn't. He came in afterward. He was acting weird. He made several remarks that I wasn't wearing gloves and that my bare hands could compromise any evidence on the body."

"Did you wear gloves?"

"No," Desprise said. "The latex glove box was empty, she was already dead, and there wasn't any blood in her pubic region."

"How did you shave her?"

"Cordless razor, like at a barber shop."

"What did you do with the razor?"

"I don't remember."

"Then what did Detective Rocek do?"

"He asked me to leave the scene. He was mad at me for touching Laiken's body with my bare hands. How should I have known? I still can't believe they made me do that."

"I have news for you, Desprise. A lot of procedural policies were violated. It wasn't your fault."

"The detective certainly made it appear as if I did something wrong, Melanie. I have never felt so wrong about something in my life. That's why I'm here."

"You did do the right thing, Desprise. Did you tell anyone else about this?"

"Only Mrs. Jespers. She's a veteran nurse and my mother's closest friend. She's retiring next year. But she told me to keep my mouth shut and mind my own business. So I did."

"And this is the first time you've ever spoken about this? Why?"

Desprise locked eyes with Melanie. "Because someone butchered Laiken, that's why. And my gut feeling tells me that the detective didn't do a damn thing with the evidence I gave him. I've lived here my whole life, and I know that's the Lord's truth. I've never liked that old guy; I think he's as crooked as the day is long. I might as well have thrown that vial into the Deerfield River for all he cared." She paused, sipping water. "I came here to you, Melanie, because I think you care."

"Thank you," Melanie said with a smile.

Desprise hedged for a moment. "Nobody in the Mills wants to talk about this case."

"What do you mean?"

Desprise shrugged. "It's a bad mojo. They want the past to be the past."

"Then why are you here?"

"I'm not like everybody."

"That's a good thing."

"Another thing," she said. "No one's gonna say anything to that Boston guy, either. He used to go to school here years ago."

Melanie involuntarily chuckled. It broke up the seriousness of the discussion. "You know him?" she asked.

"No," Desprise answered, "but a few of my friends do. They say he's pretty funny. I saw him down The Library a couple of weeks ago. I guess he used to work there. He's cute, actually—nice body. Good kid, too, they say, but no one will say much to a Boston guy."

"Well, Desprise, you've already helped me—exponentially."

"Will I get in trouble with Detective Rocek? He belongs to the same veterans organization as my father. I don't want to make waves for my dad."

"Don't worry about it, Desprise. I may have to call you back, though, to talk with you some more. Would that be okay?" Desprise nodded. The women rose and shook hands. Desprise, now clear of conscience, left the police station.

Melanie leaned back in her chair. She stared at the ceiling; it offered no answers. The integrity of her mentor, Kenny Rocek, was being challenged. She would have to address him—delicately. Melanie didn't look forward to the conversation. She exhaled. "Say it ain't so, Kenny, say it ain't so." The words came out clear, but no one answered.

14.

Stephen skipped out of work early, knowing that a two-and-a-half hour trip lay ahead. Days and nights were mixing together; he'd been without a full day off for three weeks. Nothing made sense to him anymore. Jimmy Petrilli couldn't have been responsible for Laiken's death, could he? He'd acted rather defensively earlier in the week, and the Kappa Chi Omicron rumor mill was already talking about Stephen and Melanie's visit. Stephen too was becoming defensive, fending off three phone calls from frat brothers. He insisted that it was merely a routine question-and-answer visit. Stephen made sure it was known that other fraternity guys would be interviewed as well. Were people getting nervous? For a moment he thought that this murder really could be a nasty Kappa Chi Omicron cover-up, a secret he wasn't made privy to twelve years earlier.

He parked the Jeep in the pub's lot, entering The Library twenty minutes before midnight and quickly located a table of young Kappa brothers. They welcomed the alumnus with open arms, and their hospitality was reciprocated with generosity. Stephen paid for every pitcher of beer. The active fraternity brothers were good kids—not unlike Stephen's gang, only ten years younger.

By twelve-thirty the topic of conversation shifted from Stephen's college war stories to his current investigation. He was selective with the information he disseminated, speaking in enough generality as to not compromise the case, but with enough public information to satisfy their palates. The beer tasted good, as it always did.

Stephen felt as if he had never left Hoosac Mills.

* * *

Sergeant Tony Petrowski was a twenty-nine-year veteran of the HMPD; he was a paternal type admired and respected by all of the city's badges. He entered Melanie's office at five past nine. "This just in—I believe it's what you've been waiting for, hon." He dropped the computer printouts on her desk. Melanie thanked the sergeant. She picked up the sheets of paper. It was examination time.

The computer system at the HMPD wasn't exactly antiquated, but it had recently been in a funk, refusing to download certain programs and requests. After meeting with Bobbie Thomas and agreeing that the Laiken Barnes and Darlene Hughes murders might be connected, they decided to seek assistance from FICA.

Felonious Information for Criminal Apprehension was an upstart computer law-enforcement tool now being used in the six New England states. It was an offshoot of the FBI's VICAP system, which was used by federal agents to collate criminal data and seek comparisons among dated crimes. Designed by FBI criminal profilers, VICAP had been used successfully to track down serial rapists, serial killers, and other social deviants. Melanie hoped that FICA could reap the same rewards. She meticulously read the report, and her attention zoomed in on the summary page.

F I C A
Felonious Information for Criminal Apprehension

Connecticut   Maine   Massachusetts   Rhode Island   New Hampshire   Vermont

Request #9900212
Hoosac Mills Police Department, Hoosac Mills, Massachusetts, 01247
Page 14 of 14

Attn: Sgt. Petrowski

There are 7 cases which meet the criteria of your submission for crimes committed between January 1985 to present in the following states: Connecticut, Maine, Massachusetts, Rhode Island, New Hampshire, Vermont.

Name	SS#	DOB	DOD	Place of Death
Barnes, Laiken Anne	016-TW-1063	4/3/67	11/1/87	Hoosac Mills, MA
Barron, Amy Lynne	015-RV-1468	1/3/60	2/27/90	Providence, RI
Hartlett, Joan Marie	015-WH-4815	10/6/72	4/11/93	Hartford, CT
Hughes, Darlene	016-EF-2084	5/20/66	9/7/91	Amherst, MA
Manders, Michele T.	014-KV-4983	11/30/72	7/21/96	Portland, ME
Stevens, Georgia Ann	012-RP-2852	6/7/71	1/24/99	Bangor, ME
Rivera, Alicia Ana	015-YQ-4925	10/10/71	8/31/95	Wellfleet, MA

Melanie couldn't remove her eyes from the list—a very short list. She marveled at modern technology. Hundreds of women had been stabbed, some superficially and some to life's end, but now a computer could actually link the commonality of crimes. FICA wasn't an absolute power, Melanie understood, but it was a new technology weapon that could help whittle down the suspect field to find a common link between murders. Her eyes bulged at the sight of Darlene Hughes' name.

She paged Stephen. There was much to discuss; she needed to see him. They hadn't interacted in almost a week, less the telephone. It was busier than the last couple of weeks, that was certain, and now they finally had solid ground.

Stephen called, and soon arrived at her office. Melanie slid him a copy of the handwritten letter from Renee to Laiken. He read it quickly and put it down, shrugging and giving Melanie a questioning look. "Read it again, Stephen, and take your time. Read *between* the lines, and tell me if you're thinking the same thing I am."

He obeyed, and after a moment a smirk came to his face. "I think I'm reading this correctly," he said. "Our new friend, Renee, implies that a little ménage à trois took place with this guy Boston Boy."

"That's right," she said with a nod. "But who is this Renee character, and who's Boston Boy?"

"I've heard of a lot of nicknames at Taconic State, but Boston Boy isn't one of them. People from Western Mass will refer to you as a Boston boy, but they don't usually call you that."

"Well, we need to find a last name for our new friend, Renee, and have a talk with her. And then maybe she'll tell us who Boston Boy is so we can speak with him. The funny thing is that the name Renee isn't included in any of the lists I was given by Kenny."

"Does that surprise you?" Stephen said sarcastically. Melanie shook her head. She then apprised Stephen of her surprise meeting with Desprise Johnston. Stephen's brows furrowed as he quietly listened. He let the story settle inside before he spoke.

"I've read all the reports, Melanie, as have you. The autopsy protocol said nothing about sexual penetration or contact, consensual or forced. Am I correct?" She nodded. "Do you believe this girl...what's her name?"

"Desprise Johnston."

"Does Desprise Johnston have any credibility? Do you think that there was semen on Laiken's body? Do you believe that this girl shaved her, gave it to Rocek, and then nothing came of it?" Stephen's questions were semi-rhetorical, but he was trying to create an accurate picture of what they could be dealing with. "Melanie, if you believe her, then this could put a different twist on everything."

Melanie left the office momentarily and returned with two cups of coffee. She paced the small room for a moment before resuming her seat. Finally she spoke. "I believe Desprise. As much as I don't want to, I do."

Stephen opened up his hands. "So when are we going to speak to Kenny Rocek?"

"Correction," Melanie replied, "when am *I* going to speak with Kenny Rocek, and the answer is ASAP."

"Why can't I go?"

"He doesn't like you, Stephen, that's why. Think about it. You know what, don't think about it. Common sense can dictate here. It's better if I speak to him alone because I'm sure he has some type of logical explanation."

Stephen stared at his detective friend, thinking of some type of advice to give. "Listen, call that…curmudgeon on it right away. Go for the jugular and gauge his reaction. He's a seasoned pro, but most times people with something to hide give themselves up without even knowing it."

"Is that a correction officer tactic for best eliciting top-secret information?" He laughed. Melanie gave him a copy of the FICA printout. "Skip to the last page, and you can read the rest later."

He scanned the material. "You can't be serious. This computer linked all of these murdered girls together?" Stephen was unfamiliar with the program. Melanie explained. The computer simply collated data fed into it by an operator. There were hundreds of different crime categories but Melanie had chosen just a few: female stab victim; female homicide stab victim; high probability of left-handed assailant; perpetrator shoe size 11, 12, 13; perpetrator classified as physically strong; personal inventory of homicide victim.

The results of the search could be altered greatly with the simple adjustment of one category. FICA was an aid in solving crimes, not a method of actually solving crimes. In the past, many law enforcement officers had extrapolated data from VICAP and used it to successfully apprehend suspects. But it was supplementary, and Melanie reminded Stephen of that.

"So what do we do with these names here?" he asked.

She gave him a sickening smile. "Real simple, Mr. Private Detective from Boston. We research all the murders on that list. We read case files, autopsy protocols, talk to detectives, talk to family members, and cross-reference everything about the victims. We check employee records, school records, credit card records, ex-boyfriends, and anything else you can think of."

"In hopes of finding one common link?"

"Exactly," Melanie said. "It ain't pretty—it's painstaking, actually—but it can be damn effective. If we find nothing, then we can expand our category base on the FICA program."

Stephen was legitimately impressed, but he eschewed research work whenever possible. "Okay, it appears as though my pal Frankie is going to be busy for the next couple of weeks. He's the balls at these types of things."

"Then get him on it," she said. Melanie looked at her watch. "Time to call on Kenny. You can call Mr. Barnes in regard to our new friend, Renee."

"Will do, boss," he replied.

"Hey, Stephen, I have other business to tend to today, so I won't see you this afternoon." She hesitated for a moment. "Can I tempt you with a home-cooked meal tonight…say around eight o'clock?"

"Yeah," he said with a grin. "But just don't try anything funny on me, that's all."

She appreciated his humor, and overtly crossed her fingers in front of him. "I promise I won't."

* * *

The Library was crowded. Yet the multimillionaire, seated with his loyal servant—and the young Boston private investigator—somehow never looked out of place. William Jonathan Barnes could appear relaxed anywhere. Barnes agreed to meet Stephen on short notice; the lunch crowd at The Library was a comfortable blend of college kids and city DPW workers. He looked at Stephen. "Her last name is Gleeson," Barnes said. "She is the most splendid woman."

A college girl worked the grill while Josef took orders, waited tables, and tended bar. Simeon sat quietly. Stephen surreptitiously eyed Simeon, taking inventory. Barnes' driver was unique; he was aloof by all appearances, yet exuded a threatening mystique.

Stephen updated Barnes on the progress of the case, omitting nothing. He would use any piece of information or advice he could get, and he would seek assistance from Barnes whenever possible. Barnes was a good listener, but never passed on an opportunity to speak. "She was Laiken's best friend, almost inseparable at times. They went the full route together, from kindergarten to high school graduation. Laiken, of course, was the salutatorian."

"Do you know her well?" Stephen asked.

"Yes, I do, as a matter of fact," Barnes answered.

"How come Detective Rocek never interviewed Renee after Laiken's death?"

"I guess you'd have to speak with the detective. Why do you ask?"

"I need to know, it may be important. Could you postulate, Mr. Barnes?"

"I guess I could. Let me see…Renee attended university in South Carolina, and that's where she was on Halloween night. She flew home for the wake and funeral, and then went back to school shortly thereafter." Barnes started to reminisce, and he actually had to stop for a moment to collect himself. "As I stated, Renee is a beautiful woman. She was devastated by Laiken's death. She stayed down South after graduation and married a boy she met in her senior year."

Stephen was impressed. His dad could barely remember the names of neighborhood kids, yet Barnes' memory served with unblemished clarity. "But you say that she was Laiken's best friend, and yet Rocek never questioned her. Doesn't that sound odd?"

Barnes was a reasonable man; part of his success could be attributed to objective analysis. Pragmatic thinking aided problem solving. He listened to Stephen's thoughts, surveyed them, and offered a hint of a smile. "Yes, Stephen, now that you mention it, it does sound foolhardy not to have spoken with Renee. I must say that the practicality of her input never entered my mind. But that is why, young man, I have hired you. I want answers. I want the truth. When your service with me is finished, I want definitive answers, not theories."

Stephen paused. "Did you ever hear your daughter refer to someone as Boston Boy?"

Barnes thought about the question and looked to Simeon, who merely shrugged. "No," he replied. Barnes spoke about his daughter, reliving memories of his only child. She had been a wild child, but a good girl at heart. She would often crank the stereo and lounge around the house dressed in her dad's clothing, much to his dismay. He once admonished her for those petty things. Now they were the fond memories he missed most. She was the apple of his eye, his baby girl, and some villain had taken her away. It's said that time heals all wounds, but the love for a child is unconditional, and neither Father Time nor millions of dollars prevented the tears from flowing when he sat alone in his house at night.

It had been twelve years since Laiken's murder, and less than a year since his beloved wife had succumbed to illness. He was truly alone now.

He sought justice—that was, *his* brand of justice. "Renee comes home every August to see her parents, and she always fancies a visit with me. I adore her and her children, and there is nothing in God's world I wouldn't do for them. If it is her telephone number you want, that is no problem. I will furnish you with her number and address within the hour, if you deem it necessary."

Stephen nodded. Barnes and Simeon rose to leave just as the door opened. It was P.J. McClaren and another man. They looked drunk. P.J. scowled at Barnes; the animosity between the two was no secret in Hoosac Mills. P.J. and his friend stood near the bar. When Barnes and Simeon passed, P.J. made a dribbling sound with his lips. In prison, the gesture was called a flat tire. But this wasn't the prison, and it soon became evident that Simeon was more than the driver for William Jonathan Barnes.

Simeon was quick. The next thing Stephen saw was Simeon's hand attached to McClaren's waist. A closer glance revealed that Simeon was holding a barely visible snub-nosed .38 caliber revolver. The muzzle barrel touched McClaren's shirt. Simeon leaned close to P.J., whispering inaudible words. In a moment, the gun disappeared faster than it had arrived. No other patron saw the gun. Simeon and Barnes slipped out of The Library. P.J. fell onto his stool. His skin was the color of copy paper. In truth Simeon could be arrested and charged with assault, but it would never happen. William Jonathan Barnes employed hundreds of Hoosac Mills residents, and the ramifications of a townsperson crossing his path would be costly. Besides, P.J. McClaren was a known loser, and the townsfolk in the bar actually found it entertaining. The handful of college kids in the bar never saw a thing; they didn't know the principals, so their attention was glued to the television.

Stephen waited a moment before leaving. Initially he didn't want to rub salt in McClaren's wound, but the temptation was too great.

"Hey, P.J., do you remember the movie *Rain Man?*" Stephen asked. "Well, Kmart's right down the street. Why don't you have your friend shoot down and buy you a new pair of underwear, because I suspect you just drew some mud, big boy."

P.J. heard Stephen, but he was still too shaken to speak.

* * *

The retired detective greeted Melanie with a warm smile. He invited her in and gave her a cup of coffee. Kenny Rocek, though having a rogue and chauvinistic reputation, always had a special thing for Melanie Leary. Maybe it was a sexual attraction. That seemed to be the most logical explanation, the one generally accepted by the Hoosac Mills cops, but the truth was that Melanie had good instincts and common sense. And there was more.

Rocek, working an overtime shift, had been given the unenviable task of training Melanie when she first arrived at Hoosac Mills. She was new to the men of Hoosac Mills, and although she was a lateral transfer from Wilbraham, she still had to prove herself to the HMPD veterans. In any uniformed job, the new faces have to prove themselves quickly. No one wants to be branded a coward or a rat. Melanie's rite of passage came on her third night of patrol for the HMPD.

She and Rocek responded to a dispute at Eight Ball Hall. It was a typical bar fight with broken bottles and bloodshed. Upon arrival Rocek identified the two street thugs, both intoxicated from liquor and punch-drunk from fisticuffs. Rocek handcuffed the first drunk without incident. But the second hooligan was resistant. He mistakenly misused the King's English by calling Melanie by a name for female genitalia, using a term that was inappropriate even by slang standards. It was a costly mistake. Melanie didn't hesitate. Her right fist connected on the drunk's jaw, knocking him to the floor. The partying patrons gasped, but the emotion was one of thrill. She handcuffed the man and dragged him to the cruiser, his mouth swollen and his ego shattered.

Who was this new girl in town?

Rocek had stood motionless as Melanie proved her deftness and courage. He stared at her with delight, knowing they would get along just fine. In his mind, as opinionated and sexist as it was, Melanie had a set of balls. She had heart.

Now they chatted courteously for ten minutes, but Rocek's innate sense told him that it wasn't a social call. "What can I do for you, hon?" he asked. "Do you need advice on the Barnes case?"

"Advice isn't the right word, Kenny," she replied. Melanie was earnest. He didn't overact when she mentioned Desprise Johnston's visit to the police station, but then again, he was a seasoned pro. Melanie recounted her conversation with Desprise, and asked Rocek about the vials Desprise had given him. He answered immediately and casually.

"Yeah, she's a good kid. She was really young back then, just about eighteen or so. She was nervous, acting frightened, but I guess you couldn't blame her because she probably knew Laiken. It was an emotional situation, you can imagine. I dressed her down in front of a lot of people. She was embarrassed, probably doesn't like me to this day."

Melanie nodded. "Did she give you two vials?"

"Absolutely. I gave them to Henry Cummings immediately, but it was all for naught. It wasn't semen, like she said. Henry ran some tests on it and he said it was nothing more than postmortem vaginal fluid and sweat. Weren't nothing on her pubic hairs neither. That kid actually acted out of line. She could have very well compromised real evidence if it was there."

Rocek was speaking so matter-of-factly that Melanie had trouble doubting him. What motive could an experienced detective like Rocek have for concealing evidence? The problem was that she believed Desprise.

"Henry said that it's possible Laiken had sex on the day of her death," he continued, "but it would have been consensual, definitely not forced. There were no apparent signs of bruising or trauma to her pubic region. He examined her entire body for semen and found nothing on her body, in her uterus, or in her stomach."

Melanie was frustrated, yet a feeling of guilt overwhelmed her because she had gone to Rocek's home thinking she could unearth new evidence at his expense. But no startling new evidence existed. Old Kenny held no key to a surprise; if anything, he was guarding a secret. If that was the case, then why? A wave of ambivalence crashed. Melanie was a bit unsure of what to do. She couldn't talk to Henry Cummings. He'd been the Berkshire County medical examiner for almost thirty years and had died of cancer in 1996. Dead men gave no statements. It was a cold case, so she could only work with the facts she had. She had a written autopsy report and the word of a trusted retired cop, and by both accounts there was no semen recovered on the body of Laiken Barnes.

"I need a break, Kenny," Melanie said. "I need something, something tangible."

He nodded in paternal fashion. "You don't need to tell me, honey, I understand. I spent hours and hours on that case and I got nothing. I'll say this much, though. If you ever do finger the guy, you better collar him quickly."

"Why is that?" Melanie asked.

"Because William Barnes will have the guy whacked, that's why," Rocek replied calmly.

Melanie was a bit taken by the comment but she didn't reply; she just nodded in agreement. She stayed for another twenty minutes and talked about current events, his retirement, and her love life, or lack thereof. Then it was time to go. Rocek showed Melanie to the door, giving her a kiss on the cheek. "Remember, Melanie, in this business patience is a virtue, and it is patience that will pay dividends."

She ingested his parting words and left, knowing that there was a difference between understanding words of an adage, and actually adhering to them.

15.

Their wine glasses touched, very gently but with enough contact to elicit the familiar pinging sound. Melanie's pasta and chicken plate, with a touch of Alfredo sauce, was a treat. Traveling intra-state for several weeks had deprived Stephen of mom's home cooking.

They finished dinner, and at his insistence, Stephen washed all dishes. They shared their days and formulated a strategy. Then both agreed not to talk about the case for the remainder of the evening. Stephen retrieved the quart of ice cream he'd brought for dessert.

"What are you trying to do, make me fat?" Melanie asked.

He assessed her curvy figure and overtly double-pumped his eyebrows. "Why, are you afraid your correction officer friend won't call on you?" he snickered. Melanie sighed. "I'm sorry if I touched a nerve," he said sincerely.

"No, believe me, you didn't touch a nerve, but I won't be going out with him again. Trust me."

"Pray tell why. Were you playing goalie?" he asked.

"Goalie—what the hell are you talking about?"

Stephen simulated a hockey goalie waving his hands in front of his pectorals and groin, as if he were blocking oncoming pucks, or, in this instance, a guy's hands. Melanie found the humor—she laughed.

"No, no, it was nothing like that." She laughed again. "Goalie. I've heard a lot of them in my day but never that one. He didn't maul me, it was just his attitude."

"Let me guess. Before the end of the night he told you how many girls he'd been with and how much he can bench-press." Melanie was astonished; Stephen loved it.

"Stephen Nicholson, how in God's name did you know that?" she asked.

"I'm an expert on one thing only: deviant correction officer behavior."

"I've told you about my ex, but how about you, Stephen?"

"Moi?"

"Yes, you," she said. "You have looks and physique. You have personality, charisma, yet no wife on your arm. I know we talked a bit about this before, but I am flabbergasted that you're single. Why is that, Stephen?"

He sat idle, pensive, thinking of a response to a seemingly simple question. "An array of answers, I guess. Afraid to commit, like a lot of guys, is probably one of them. I've lost a few girls—a few good girls—because I'd rather hang out with my brother Matty and the neighborhood gang instead of growing up. That's changing, though, and everyone's getting married, but here I am, still living in the early 'nineties. I can't be a Toys 'R' Us kid my whole life, that's for sure."

Melanie wanted to kiss him. But she didn't—she couldn't. "Let's make a promise," she said. "When this case is over we'll do something together that isn't work related."

Stephen disguised his enthusiasm. "Any place in particular you'd like to go?"

"I've never been to Maine, if you can believe that. I sound like a fool even admitting that, but it's true," she said.

"Aha! The landlocked girl from Springfield has never swum in the cold rivers of Vacationland. I'll tell you what—when we're done I'll take you skinny-dipping in the Penobscot River. How's that sound?"

She smiled and extended her hand, the solidification of a deal between two friends. They had been somewhat serious and Stephen decided to lighten things up. "I've got a good one for you. I talked to Frankie today and he's got some interesting snapshots."

"Pictures of what?"

Stephen began to answer but started laughing. He finally controlled himself. "We got a job last week. A couple that lives near my parents hired us to investigate their teen daughter."

"Why?" Melanie asked.

"Because she's eighteen and her grades have been slipping. She's a senior in high school and she's on the waiting list at a couple of good colleges, so her grades are important for this quarter." He again laughed and Melanie punched him in the arm.

"What, Stephen? Tell me!"

"So Frankie's been following her, which in and of itself is hysterical. Anyway, he knows she's been smoking weed with one of her girlfriends, and that's probably the root of the problem. So he follows this girl to her friend's house outside of Cleary Square, in Hyde Park. They're in the basement smoking pot." Stephen stopped again, holding his stomach from laughter.

"Tell me," Melanie said.

"So Frankie's doing his job, taking the incriminating photographs, and all of a sudden they start going at it." Stephen couldn't stop laughing and it took a moment for his words to register with Melanie.

"You're shitting me," she said as she too began to giggle.

"No. Both of the girls are gorgeous—lipstick lesbians, eighteen-year-old hard-bodies—and thirty-something-year-old limp dick Frankie was watching the whole thing. He could have had a heart attack."

Melanie appreciated the humor. The Barnes case was starting to introduce stress into Stephen's life, and it was obvious to Melanie that he needed a light moment. "So what are you going to do with the pictures? You can't tell the parents that their daughter is gay because that part of your case isn't relevant. The pot is, but her sexuality isn't."

"I ain't snitching, don't worry. But the pictures are a different story." He regained his composure and managed a straight face. "First we'll put the photographs on the Internet, and then we'll sell copies of the originals for five bucks a pop at the Boston House. Those freaks will clamor over each other to buy them, trust me."

Stephen was a quick guy, but not fast enough to stop Melanie's left hand from slapping the top of his head.

* * *

They huddled in Melanie's office. Stephen insisted that Melanie should be the one to telephone Laiken's friend Renee Gleeson. It was a gender issue. He knew that a strange male voice would reap no rewards. The investigation was officially leaving New England; Melanie picked up the phone and dialed long distance—to South Carolina. It was early, but according to Barnes, Renee had three children. She was likely to be home. The answering machine picked up after four rings. Kids sang in the background of the recorded message, but it was interrupted when an adult woman picked up the phone. Stephen closed his eyes and listened to a one-way conversation.

"...of the Hoosac Mills Police Department. Yes, that's right, Leary, Melanie Leary."

One of Stephen's boyhood friends had graduated from the Citadel in South Carolina and his thick Boston accent had been replaced by a slow Southern drawl. Stephen wondered if Renee had maintained her Berkshire twang. He hoped so. Stephen loved the Hoosac Mills tongue. It was more than that, though. Southerners knew their people; did Renee understand she would always be a carpetbagger?

Melanie continued. "No, I'm of no relation. I grew up in Springfield, but I'll tell you all about that later if it's okay. I'd like to ask you a few questions about Laiken Barnes. I understand that Detective Rocek didn't speak with you after Laiken's death. Is that true, Renee?"

Stephen looked out the office window. Two teenaged boys with their mothers were speaking with Sgt. Petrowski. Both boys were bloodied and one was holding his right hand in obvious pain. Stephen surveyed the injury—boxer's fracture. He left the office and bought a soda, or a tonic, as they said in Boston, from the machine. He smiled at the boys—probably friends—as their mothers admonished them in front of the police sergeant. Boys will be boys.

Stephen went outside for air and a gulp of soda, spending the next few minutes people-watching in front of the station. Cars cruised past him, and nosy drivers gawked at the strange man loitering out front. He forgot that he wasn't a student anymore, and any unknown face over the age of twenty-five or so was considered a foreigner. He returned to the office as Melanie finished her conversation with Renee Gleeson. Pictures speak a thousand words, and Melanie's facial expression spoke volumes.

"And you too, Renee. By all means give me a call if you can think of anything. You have my number. Thank you again, Renee. Bye-bye." Melanie gently placed the receiver down, though she wanted to slam it. She stared at Stephen.

"I already know the answer, but...what's up?" he asked.

"I don't like it, Stephen, I don't like it one damn bit. She sounded distant."

"I assume you're speaking figuratively."

"No joking, please."

"Fair enough. Did you ask her about the gold chain?"

"Yes, as a matter of fact I did," Melanie answered, "and she affirmed that Laiken was allergic to gold. She said that P.J. had given her gold before, but it was back when they were sophomores or juniors in high school."

"What'd she say about my pal Kenny Rocek?" Stephen asked.

"That's one of the things I didn't like about the phone call. She said Kenny never contacted her, and she even telephoned him from South Carolina two times to inquire about the investigation and to offer help. He brushed her off, telling her that they had a few leads and they didn't need her help."

Stephen shook his head. "That's bullshit, Melanie. He didn't even ask the victim's best friend what guys she used to dick around with?" He hesitated, aligning his thoughts. "Who's your best female friend in the world, Melanie?"

"My sister, Heather," she replied.

"Okay, besides your sister, who would it be?"

"Tracy O'Connor, but I haven't seen her in two years. She moved to Boulder with her husband."

"But do Heather and Tracy know everything about you? About the guys you've slept with, or the guys you like, the intimate things, girl stuff?"

"Of course they do. I tell Heather and Tracy everything."

"That's my point exactly," Stephen said with a little ire. "Rocek should have grilled Renee Gleeson after that murder. Anyone who's read a damn murder mystery book could tell you that." Stephen took a seat and tossed Melanie a diet soda he'd purchased from the machine. "Okay, now that I've got that off my chest, let's get down to the nitty-gritty."

Melanie nodded in anticipation. "Her letter to Laiken and our mystery friend, Boston Boy?" she asked. He nodded. "That's what I meant about her sounding distant. I read the letter verbatim to her. It was the fair thing to do if I was going to ask her about something she wrote twelve years ago."

"What'd she say?"

Melanie made a sour face. "She basically said nothing, Stephen. She said that Boston Boy was some Taconic State kid Laiken used to fool around with years ago, but that she kept it pretty hush-hush. She said she'd only met him a couple of times, and that she was drinking every time she was around him. She told me she didn't remember his real name."

"Did you ask Renee if he was a Kappa Chi Omicron brother?" Stephen asked.

Melanie sensed the nervousness in his voice, and she was sensitive to his personal involvement in the case. "Yes I did, Stephen. She said she couldn't remember if Boston Boy was a fraternity brother or not. I ran a bunch of Kappa guy names by her, but nothing seemed to ring a bell."

"Two more questions," Stephen began. "Will she look at fraternity/suspect photographs, and did you ask her about any unusual sexual escapades?"

"The answer to your second question is no. This was my first time speaking to the woman, Stephen, so I didn't want to overdo it with personal and intimate questions. The first question is what bothers me."

"Why?" Stephen asked.

"Because she told me not to bother sending down any photographs because it's been so many years and she won't remember him anyhow."

They were quiet, and Stephen mulled his next thoughts. "What about a field trip down to South Carolina?" he asked.

Melanie shook her head. "The chief will never authorize it. Forget it. I'll call her again in a few days."

Stephen held up his hand. "The phone call didn't work today, and it won't work in a few days. To hell with the appropriation of city funds, I don't care. Barnes gave me a bag full of money for expenses, and we'll use it to fly you down there. The guy's got more money than Rockefeller's grandchildren, Melanie, so let's use some of it."

She thought about it for a moment. "We'll see. I won't rule it out. But enough of this, it's time to get busy. Take your FICA sheet and get moving, mister."

Stephen stood at attention and bowed down to Melanie in a deferential fashion. "Whatever you say, your highness."

Melanie escorted Stephen out of the station, giving him a low five for good luck. He and Frankie planned to be busy for the next ten days. They would be researching information from the murders linked together through the FICA criminal database. Bobbie Thomas was handling the Darlene Hughes murder in Amherst, so Stephen and Frankie split the remaining five murders. Frankie would travel to Providence, Hartford, and Wellfleet, while Stephen took the northern route to Portland and Bangor. Unlike Stephen, Frankie didn't yet have a private investigator's license in Massachusetts. Upon receiving the FICA printout, Melanie had wisely contacted all police departments in question and received copies of the murder case files. More importantly, she notified them of Stephen and Frankie's imminent arrivals in the respective towns. This guaranteed cooperation, saving them the headache of snooping around.

Melanie returned to the station. The high school boys involved in the fight had been thrown in adjoining cells. The boys weren't placed under arrest, but their mothers wanted to teach them a lesson, and they asked the desk sergeant to let the boys spend a few hours behind bars to make them sweat. They were normally good kids, so the temporary incarceration was not a cool rite of passage as it was for other teens. Sgt. Petrowski happily obliged the parents' request. She gave the sergeant a friendly thumbs-up before returning to her office and closing the door, something she rarely did.

Melanie cleared her desk, spreading Laiken's case file in front of her. She divided the papers into separate piles, ranging from fraternity brother statements to photographs to autopsy protocols. She glanced over her desk, looking at everything yet concentrating on nothing. She became depressed.

Desprise Johnston had sought her out, insisting she'd swiped semen from Laiken's body. She was adamant about it. Rocek had downplayed it, citing ignorance and youthfulness on Desprise's part. But the nurse seemed honest, too genuine not to believe. Why would Desprise lie? She had no ulterior motive, no axe to grind with anyone. Or did she? Maybe Desprise's credibility should be checked. Hoosac Mills was a small city—it certainly wouldn't be a problem.

Melanie swiveled in her chair, thinking. No, it was a preposterous notion that Desprise had misjudged the sight of semen. She was only nineteen at the time of the murder, but was candid in acknowledging her familiarity with the fluid. And after all, Kenny had admitted to receiving the vials. Yes, she believed Desprise, and by default that meant she doubted Kenny. Why wouldn't Kenny have interviewed Renee Gleeson after the murder? Renee was Laiken's best friend. It didn't make sense—nothing made sense.

Kenny Rocek wasn't the most popular cop in the history of Hoosac Mills, but he was effective, earning multiple awards for valor throughout his distinguished career. He was once an uncle figure to Melanie, and she didn't want to accuse him of having a dirty hand. He wasn't exactly her hero, but her respect for him was measured greatly. "Why didn't you interview Renee, Kenny?" she thought aloud. She was frustrated and slammed her fist onto the desk. "Semen. Damn Kenny, was it cum? Is that what it was? Why did you look the other way, Kenny? Why?" She didn't want to believe it.

Her maternal grandfather suddenly came to mind. He was a native Chicagoan and fanatical baseball lover. Repeatedly cursing the White Sox, or the Black Sox as he said, used to be his passion. Melanie knew all about the great baseball betting scandal of 1919. She spoke aloud again. "What the hell. If Shoeless Joe can throw the World Series, I guess a cop can botch an investigation."

Sitting still like a sculpture, thoughts raced through her mind at lightning speed. It took fifteen minutes, and after much internal waffling she knew what needed to be done. She would request a new set of medical records on Laiken Anne Barnes, new high school and college transcripts, new phone records, and new records of anything she could get her hands on. It was time to begin from ground zero, and she wasn't happy about it.

16.

It was reggae night at the Seaweed Surf Club. Seven nights a week
during the summer, bands from around New England jammed to the
delight of hundreds of tourists. Every night there was a new band:
Groove Street Junction, Medal Heads, Animal Farm, and more. The bar
had a picturesque location, sitting atop a cliff overlooking the North Atlantic.

He arrived alone at quarter to ten, dressed inconspicuously. It wasn't
unusual for patrons to dress to the theme of the band. His dreadlocks,
dark glasses, and tie-dyed shirt were the garb of choice. In fact, he almost
looked like the lead singer of tonight's popular South Shore band, Sun
Roots. At a city bar his attire would alienate him from the crowd, but
that wasn't the case on this evening at the Seaweed Surf Club. Tonight he
looked pedestrian, and that was just how he wanted it.

Scantily clad waitresses roamed around the wooden floor, taking drink
orders and selling shots of hard liquor. He wisely avoided the waitresses;
instead he approached the busy barkeep for the night's drink special, rum
and Coke. He mingled with the crowd, humming and singing a Bob Marley song. He leaned against a wooden support beam in the center of the
floor, swaying back and forth to the music while surreptitiously scouting
the crowd.

The club was packed. He scanned the floor for familiar faces. He was
one hundred miles from home, but he knew that the Seaweed Surf Club
was a popular haven for party-driven folks of Metro Boston. He took a
long route to the men's room, his dark shades concealing his peripheral

sights as he methodically watched the dance floor. After fifteen minutes and an extra lap of the club, he breathed easy. He recognized no one; he was truly a stranger.

The club was populated with pretty young girls, the twenty-something types in grunge who didn't have a care in the world. They were beautiful, oh so beautiful, but as soon as they engaged in conversation, the limited capacity of their intelligence engines was exposed. His eyes wandered in ogling fashion but he quickly regrouped, angered that he'd permitted his veins the consumption of lust. He considered lust—a most forceful emotion.

The man was no virgin, and would take umbrage if someone were to suggest so. He just couldn't accept the senseless offering of flesh for a temporary moment of pleasure. It was lust—the poison apple—that he loathed. Its strength was palpable. He thought of the thousands slain in world history because of advances on or insults to royal women. Lust was an odd emotion, though. It oozed through the mind, unyielding, until it was sated. But the difference was this—at times it created an equally powerful yearning for redemption in those victimized by sinful lust. His experience with lust was vivid, searing.

Smoke permeated the air, another tangible reminder of the young crowd. He resumed his position against the support beam. His section of floor was elevated, giving him a bird's-eye view. He could see all.

Two pretty girls sat at the bar smoking cigarettes and sipping mixed drinks. Both lipped the straw seductively. They were sexy, and he'd immediately spotted them when he entered the club. No doubt lingered as to why they were seated at the bar, and he couldn't believe no libido-driven man had sent them drinks yet. Without warning, one of the women rose and hugged her friend, checked her watch, and scurried away. The abandoned friend leaned back, blew a ring of smoke, and swiveled toward the bartender. She was alone.

The man maintained a relaxed posture and slowly bobbed to the reggae music. He breathed in the music. His innards swelled with adrenaline, his eyes reddened, and his muscles bubbled. But he looked cool, and no one would ever have suspected that a bona fide killer danced among the drunken crowd. In a few minutes the vixen was on her feet, charting a zigzag course through the dance floor en route to the restroom. The floor was laced with mines, though. Men spontaneously began to slam-dance, upsetting anything in their path. Before she could reroute herself, a drunken patron careened into her, sending her headfirst toward a partition. The man was fast, however, and he grabbed her around the waist, protecting her from injury. The slam-dancer was drunk, and he added insult to injury by leering at the pretty woman. She looked up into her guardian's eyes, mortified but grateful. "Thank you very much," she said with an interesting accent. "You saved me, and that jerk didn't even apologize."

"Not a problem. Chivalry is an archaic concept, wouldn't you agree?" His insight struck her as odd, but she couldn't keep her eyes off him. His tilt of a smile and funny way of speaking immediately intrigued her. He wasn't a typical guy at the bar. He seemed different—intelligent—not her typical one-night-stand guy who always flexed his muscles but never his brain. Yet he was also muscular, and handsome. Maybe he was a rare blend of brawn and brains. Yes, he was different from the rest.

"Yeah, I suppose you're right. Guys nowadays just don't know how to treat a lady." He pulled her to her feet, facing her upright. "Are those real dreads?" she asked.

"Perhaps. I guess that's something you'll have to discover on your own, isn't it?" he said as he seductively lowered his sunglasses and locked eyes with her. The pretty woman was instantly mesmerized.

"How about if you let me thank you by buying you a drink or two?" she offered.

"I've a better idea. How about strolling down to the beach for some cold beer?" She paused, staring at the man who sent a pleasurable shrill down her spine. He was quite direct with his proffer. Thoughts of rolling around with him on the beach excited her.

The club deepened with customers, and the two were enveloped in a sweaty crowd. Music and dance movements augmented the free-flowing sexual vibes that now transferred between the two. She moved closer, wedging his knee between her legs and giving him a sensual kiss. It was a provocative gesture, but a common sight nonetheless and unnoticed by all. She squeezed his buttocks and released her lips. "I don't suppose you have a name," she said.

"Most men do," he said with a grin. "Mine is Dick."

She smiled. "How appropriate. I'm Alicia, and it's a pleasure to meet you."

"*El gusto es mio*," he replied.

She wasn't Hispanic, but her childhood tongue was close enough. She understood the message: the pleasure was all his.

He was sweet.

After a trip to the ladies room she was ready to leave. They vanished from the club as anonymously as they had arrived. The man took her hand as they descended the great sand hill toward the beach. The crescent moon emitted enough light to accent small caps of water breaking onshore. They walked west toward Eastham, holding hands and stopping every minute to kiss like teenagers. They traveled more than a quarter of a mile before Alicia finally stopped. "Where's the beer you were talking about? I'm thirsty."

"Patience is a virtue, Alicia," he replied. "Just a little while longer; it'll be worth your wait." He led her between two sand dunes. As he walked he remembered Laiken Barnes and Darlene Hughes. They were filthy whores. He was convinced he had done a service to the world by effecting their disposal.

Intelligent, he was acutely cognizant of his existence. In 1987 and 1991 he'd murdered two women; in 1995 he would answer his call again. He was a murderer, a pernicious criminal who took orders only from himself. The four-year lapses were difficult but purposeful. The thrill to kill was addictive, but to him it was mind over matter. He understood the characteristics, traits, and even principles of serial killing. He was wise, knowing that frequent and senseless killings would only lead to his capture. Killing hiatuses of four years were almost unheard of. He wouldn't get caught.

He could justify his hatred for the whores. Like most serial killers, words like *remorse* didn't exist in that particular sense. But his lack of remorse was limited to the whores; he felt compunction for any transgression he committed against the good people, as he should. The whores rented space in his mind. Too much suffering had been inflicted on the good people by these tramps, and he was taking action.

Alicia was another family-wrecker in his mind—quick to leave the bar with a stranger for her own satiable needs, but unaware of consequences she could face. She was a vampiress, a wicked monster waiting to drain the life from an innocent man. But not tonight—tonight would be different. Tonight he was the stalker, and she the oblivious prey.

A small Styrofoam cooler sat on the sand, and Alicia quickly ripped open the cover, retrieving two canned beers. The cooler had been chilled and the beer was ice cold. Both were quiet as they quenched their thirst after the long walk. Alicia finished her drink and stepped back from the man. "I've got something that you might want to see, Dick," she said seductively. He was quiet, speaking a thousand words with a leer. She was beautiful, very beautiful, and his eyes remained fixed on her body. Alicia was purring like a kitten, and the man's silence and gaze titillated her even more.

A bubble of spittle formed at his lips, but her sensual body was not the catalyst for his thrill. It was the forthcoming kill that excited him. He thought about Laiken Barnes again. How foolish it had been to engage in sexual intercourse that evening. But that was different; it was a new time, a new place, and he was better now, more proficient.

She tossed her articles of clothing at him in an enticing manner. Soon she was naked. Alicia was a true head-turner. She could have posed for Hefner's men's magazine. She had perfectly symmetrical C-cups, a washboard stomach, and a narrow, dark brown landing strip. Impotent men would have risen at her sight. She ran playfully into the water, then turned toward him. "What are you waiting for, Dick…aren't you gonna join me?"

"I'll be right there Alicia, don't you worry, honey," he responded. She was soon submerged in the warm Gulf Stream water while the man quickly removed sand from behind the cooler.

In a matter of thirty seconds he had unearthed a large Gore-Tex bag. It was his buried treasure chest. He removed his clothing, disguise and all. Alicia waded in the water in anticipation. He extracted his weapon from the bag and slowly walked toward the water.

She was ready for him, smiling. "Wow, I guess they really were fake dreadlocks, huh?" He nodded and returned the smile. They stood waist deep, her perky breasts touching his chest and her arms wrapped around his neck. "I've been waiting for you. Where have you been?" she asked teasingly.

He was dexterous, and Alicia never heard the snap of the flip knife. He stared at her. "You people never learn, do you?" he said.

"Huh?" she replied.

Dozens of responses raced through his mind, but he settled on something simple. "You say you've been waiting for me, Alicia? Well, there's an old adage that says be careful what you ask for because you might just get it."

"Dick, I don't understand..."

It was too late. The man snaked his right arm up her torso, pushing her left arm off of his neck and creating an opening. His left hand was quick, slashing her throat from right to left. She was stunned, never to speak again. He squared shoulders with her and stabbed her torso with a dozen thrusts, dropping her limp body into the water.

It happened quickly; the adrenaline rush excited him, giving him a high no drug could possibly induce. The first cut had been exact. Alicia never had a chance to scream. His attack had been fierce, the knife penetrating the body deep enough to pulverize her internal organs. She floated helplessly in the water. Asphyxiation would be the cause of her death, by default. He remembered his gift to her, though, and he temporarily pulled her ashore. He was careful, taking her beneath the armpits and not letting his fingernails touch her.

He went back to the bag and pulled out a bottle of rubbing alcohol, a cloth, latex gloves, and a gold chain. His reasons for the chain were personal, very personal, and he knew the FBI and other agencies could never draw the connection. It would be impossible. Besides, it was none of their damn business.

He would never do anything freakish and take a body part, like some of the psychopaths he'd researched. He equated that practice with cannibalism, and wouldn't take part in that type of inhumanity. Nor would he be foolish enough to take jewelry from the victim. There would be no trophy.

The police didn't overly concern him, either. His kills were spaced apart, and he never gave his real name upon purchase of the jewelry. He doused the cloth with rubbing alcohol and applied it to her lips and tongue. He had kissed her, and didn't want to leave any of his DNA with the girl. He then put on latex gloves and clasped the chain around her neck and left her on the shore. She would be at the mercy of the tide, at the mercy of Mother Nature. If the tide didn't pull her out she would be found in the morning; if it did, she would be dinner for the sharks of the North Atlantic. It didn't matter to him, though. She was dead. His service was complete.

He returned to the bag. His clothes, the knife, the empty beer cans and the cooler were zipped up within a minute. He tied the Gore-Tex bag around his waist and made his way back into the ocean. He passed by

Alicia's lifeless body on the shore without even looking at it, spitting along the way. The sea was calm, like a pane of glass. He was a good swimmer, so his mild buzz didn't hinder the two-hundred-yard swim. A small beacon glared in the night, and he swam toward the light.

The man soon reached the twelve-foot boat. He climbed in, turned off the lantern, and opened a new, smaller Gore-Tex bag that awaited his return. He toweled off and donned a new T-shirt, underwear, and shorts. He pulled anchor and the twenty-five-horsepower engine roared at the first snap of the cord. The few clouds parted from the crescent moon and the Gulf Stream waters sparkled. The small boat was quiet, making a buzzing noise as he cruised into the night, drinking a cold victory beer.

The craft steered west toward Eastham, toward Boston. He laughed as his thoughts turned to his first victim. What did Laiken used to call him? Boston Boy, that was it, she used to call him Boston Boy. At one time he'd liked her, liked her very much. But then she changed, and began sexually accommodating any boy in heat. Laiken was the first of the whores to be disposed of, and he'd known then that more would follow in her wake.

He sipped the refreshing lager. Number three was dead, but he wasn't finished. Number four would be his defining moment, the one most important to him, the ultimate in satisfaction. He could have taken her years before, but he opted to wait. Goose bumps covered his arms, but not due to the chilly air. He relished the thought of cutting her skin—the ultimate reward, and the ultimate revenge. After his next conquest, he would be redeemed.

This time it was personal, and his deep hatred could only grow. The hatred in his mind was pure; it had already manifested, and now it would marinate.

17.

"**S**orry, but he's too short," the ride attendant said. "Why don't you take him on the Galaxy 'cause there ain't no height requirement."

"Come on, pal, show a little heart," Matthew Nicholson said. "He's my littlest brother and he's been dying to go on this roller coaster. It would really make his day." As he spoke, Matthew coolly pulled a five-dollar bill from his pocket and slid it to the attendant. The attendant looked left, looked right, pocketed the five-spot and waived the group through the gate.

"Remember," the attendant yelled to no one in particular, "keep your hands inside and don't try to stand up. Enjoy the Giant Coaster—the greatest roller coaster on earth! Next!"

Eleven-year-old David Nicholson was excited beyond belief. He raced down the wooden platform and secured a spot in the first car. His big brother—his idol—Matthew sat next to him while everyone else from the neighborhood piled into the remaining cars. The roller coaster slowly ascended the chain-driven track ninety-eight feet into the air. As the cars reached the summit, they looked down at the teeming marks eager to spend money.

Paragon Park was on Nantasket Beach in Hull, a virtual Fantasyland to Boston kids. It was the permanent carnival—bigger and better—a place where access to rides, games, cotton candy, and pretzels seemed endless. The carousel was legendary, as was the boardwalk on the beach where musicians played to cheerful crowds.

"Matthew, look at the ocean. You can see Boston!" David yelled. But before Matthew could respond the car raced down the steep track. Matthew's hands were high to the sky—against the rules—while David's were glued to the handlebar. Along with the excitement of the first steep drop came the unnatural feeling of a sinking stomach. The train of cars riveted back and forth, whirling around the curvy tracks. Within one minute the ride was over, and David's dream had been fulfilled.

The large group congregated on the exit platform, high-fiving after the adventurous ride. David Nicholson glistened with excitement. He had not only ridden the Giant Coaster, but he'd brazenly sat in the front seat. He couldn't wait to see his best friend, Mickey, though Mickey might not believe him. Yes, David was happy, and he showed his thanks by suddenly wrapping his arms around Matthew. It was a time of innocence, and at that split second everything in life was pure.

"Stephen, snap out of it, man. Cut the shit with that daydreaming. Come on, Pedro's on the mound right now," Dennis McCarthy said.

Stephen stood in the hallway staring at the family portrait, reminiscing about old times. He looked at Dennis, his lifelong friend and fellow passenger on the roller coaster many years before. "Okay," he said, "I'll be right down. But I can't stay long."

* * *

The basement of the Nicholson family home still resembled a clubhouse. Once a place for late-night parties after closing time, it now served its suited purpose as a television room. But the stolen soda machine humming in the corner was still filled with cold cans that belied the soft-drink labels. Matthew Nicholson deposited three nickels in return for three cold Michelob Light beers, tossing one each to Nicky Pappadoupolous and Dennis McCarthy.

Stephen declined a beer. A road trip was already planned. It was six o'clock, and Matty and the neighborhood guys were watching a Red Sox spring training game. Pedro pitched, and he was in his typical ace form. The guys argued over the starting rotation and manager Jimy Williams' propensity for using all twenty-five players on the roster. "You morons can't manage your checking account," Matthew said. "And now you think you understand the depth and principles of baseball better than Jimy Williams? I don't think so, Moe, Larry and Curly." Matthew was in rare form, and he knew that the guys were just getting him worked up, as they always did. "On second thought," Matthew continued, "I don't want to insult the good Curly Howard by aligning him with you cretins. Make that Moe, Larry, and Shemp."

"Hey, Professor," Stephen replied, "why don't you go back to your little geek classroom and whisper some Charles Dickens into the ears of some nineteen-year-old girls, you freak? It's probably your most potent sexual weapon." Matthew, the associate professor of English literature at Wellesley Community College, was an avid Charles Dickens fan. Stephen often reminded his elder brother that he'd once rejected Celtic playoff tickets in order to complete his thesis on the collective works of Dickens.

"My nineteen-year-old kids could slug a six-pack and still score higher on the SATs than you clowns," Matthew said. The guys mockingly toasted the professor. The kids from Meredith Street, Clement Avenue, and Kenneth Street had grown up, but in their hearts they would always be young. They had formed a camaraderie years before, and it had lasted well into the '90s. The attention turned to Stephen.

"Why the hell do you have to go to Maine, buddy? Do you think that chick's murderer lives up there?" Nicky asked.

"No, you guys may not believe this, but I think our guy might actually be a serial murderer," Stephen replied. "I've got to check out two murders from Maine, and my boy Frankie has to investigate old murders from Rhode Island, Connecticut, and Wellfleet."

"A serial murderer? Are you shitting me? I thought your case was about the Barnes broad from Hoosac Mills," Matthew said. The three men stared at Stephen.

"Don't worry, Matty. And don't get Mom all excited over this, either," Stephen replied. "Things are starting to take shape in this case. It looks like our perp may be a serial killer…legit."

The three men were in awe. "Any suspects?" Dennis asked.

Stephen wavered. These were his best friends from childhood, but he didn't want to say too much. He opted for vagueness. "Unfortunately, one of the guys from my fraternity is a suspect, but that's all I can say. Don't even start with the name game, fellas, because it won't work. Melanie and I are working with a DA from Hampshire County and a young guy from the Staties. It's gonna get interesting, that much I'll say."

The three men knew most of the Kappa brothers, so it was only normal that their curiosity was heightened. All three simultaneously drank beer, waiting for elaboration that wouldn't come. Stephen's cool demeanor surprised them; they'd grown up together and naturally expected Stephen to sing like a canary.

"How in God's name have you connected multiple murders, little brother?" Matthew asked.

"Real simple," he said. "It's the use of modern technology—computers. That's all. Plus some people are starting to talk. We're even awaiting DNA results, so things could get interesting really soon." Stephen noted the time. "Look, boys, I've got to make my move to Bangor. I want to get up there in time to secure a room and have a drink. If I meet any horny Maine girls who are looking to perform some charity sex acts, I'll be sure to call you guys who all are dancing on the fine line of latent homosexuality. Lord knows you geeks have whiffed at the plate enough times in Massachusetts."

"Latent homosexual?" Matthew said. "Melanie would prefer my teeth pulling down her thong, younger brother."

"Ouch."

"That's your comeback—ouch?"

"What am I supposed to do—justify my heterosexuality to you clowns? But now that I think about it, I remember a certain Guns N' Roses concert at the Garden back in 1993." Matthew, Nicky, and Dennis knew what was coming next. "There were what—ten of us? We get invited back to that all-chicks college dorm on the Riverway, and if my memory serves correct, only three of us left the following morning without lipstick smudges and class schedules. But I won't name names."

They all laughed. Stephen gave them all high-fives before leaving.

* * *

Stephen arrived in Bangor after ten o'clock, tired, and went straight to bed. He arose early in the morning, but it would be in vain. He reported to the Bangor police station, met the contact detective Melanie had arranged, and immediately ran into a dead end. The Bangor murder victim, Georgia Ann Stevens, had been killed a couple of months earlier, in January. Bangor police had arrested Georgia's boyfriend only yesterday in connection with her murder. A quick check on the suspect revealed that he had been serving county prison time in October, 1987, and September, 1991, the times of Laiken Barnes and Darlene Hughes murders, respectively.

Portland fared no better, as the victim, Michele T. Manders, had also been killed in a domestic dispute. The murderer was her husband. They were living in California at the time of Laiken's death, and in New York City at the time of Darlene's death. Nevertheless the detectives in both cities were kind enough, as a favor to fellow detective Leary, to give Stephen copies of both murder case files.

Stephen had allotted four to five days for his Maine trip, but after a day and a half he was finished. He returned home empty-handed. He constantly reminded himself that time was on his side. The investigation south of Boston, however, would be more fruitful.

He took a day off from the investigation. He wasn't due to work at the Boston House for three days, so he caught up on sleep. He spoke to Melanie, but nothing of interest had happened in Hoosac Mills over the last several days. It was near noontime when the telephone awoke him.

"We got a match, Stephen, we got a match, I can't believe it!"

Stephen rose from his bed and rubbed his eyes; he had no idea where he was or what time it was. "Slow down, Yosemite Sam, slow down," he said.

Frankie couldn't control his enthusiasm. "Wake up, sleepy head, and get your ass down to Wellfleet. The same guy who killed Laiken and the girl from Amherst murdered Alicia Ana Rivera!"

"Are you sure about that, Frankie?"

"Damn skippy I'm sure about that! He left a gold chain around her neck and I already traced it to the Jewelers Building. I spoke with her mother and two of her childhood friends. They never saw the chain on the girl before the murder. It's the same guy, Stephen."

"What name did the guy give?" Stephen asked.

"No name given—or no name recorded—this time. But it was purchased from the same building. No coincidence, brother."

"Okay, okay, I'm gonna call Melanie right now. Good job, Frankie."

The hot water from the shower cleared his head. He moved quickly, arriving in Wellfleet in three hours. By seven o'clock Melanie arrived; the trip from Hoosac Mills to Wellfleet stretched the extreme breadth of Massachusetts, from the northwest corner to the famous eastern tip of the Bay State.

A Massachusetts state police detective met Melanie and her entourage at the Wellfleet Police Station. Wellfleet was a quaint Cape Cod town with a small force; no detective from the town had been assigned the case, but a competent patrolman sat with the group and took notes. The state detective overseeing the murder investigation had retired a year ago, so detective

Marcus Torres was now the lead man. He gave Melanie copies of all material pertaining to his case, and she reciprocated. Melanie meticulously explained the possible correlation among the three murders, including the involvement of Bobbie Thomas. It was clear that a joint task force was necessary. FBI cooperation would be necessary. The matter of initiating federal help, as the detectives knew, was out of their hands and would be up to their respective superiors.

Marcus Torres was an efficient type, well kempt and bookish. "He's a professional," Marcus said of Alicia's killer. "The bartender and wait staff remember seeing Alicia that evening. She was a regular. But no one saw our un-sub." Marcus read Stephen's and Frankie's faces. "That refers to 'unknown subject.' We've theorized that he met her in the club, put on the quick charm, and left with her. If that's the case he's not only confident but damn good. We may have our work cut out, folks." Marcus showed photographs of Alicia Ana Rivera to the threesome, both personal pictures and murder scene photos. Frankie gasped at the woman's bloody corpse, strewn on the beach and covered with seaweed. Stephen enjoyed a lengthy gaze at a photograph taken of Alicia only days before her death.

"She was beautiful," he said.

"Exactly," Marcus noted. "Our guy is a player, so to speak. Alicia Rivera was on the promiscuous side, but she wouldn't have left with just anyone. How would you physically describe the other two victims?"

"They were both pretty," Melanie said without hesitation.

Marcus nodded. "Why don't we step into the conference room so we can all take a seat."

The next three hours were spent comparing notes and brainstorming. Marcus gave a brief history of Alicia Ana Rivera. She was twenty-three at the time of her death, single, and lived at home with her mother and siblings. Her father, a proud Portuguese fisherman, died when she was ten, leaving his widow with three children to raise. Alicia had never come to terms with her father's death.

She worked at a supermarket in Orleans and spent her free time in the clubs with girlfriends. She hadn't been dating anyone steadily at the time of her death, and none of her ex-boyfriends had histories of violence. She was beautiful yet insecure. Alicia slept around.

On the night of her murder Alicia was with her best friend. But her friend left to meet her boyfriend. The best friend said that no men had approached them while they were at the bar. No one could place Alicia at the beach, and the murderer didn't leave any physical evidence—no blood, no semen, no hair, no fingerprints, nothing. Police theorized that the perpetrator murdered the girl, changed clothes, and retrieved his vehicle in the Seaweed Surf Club parking lot to escape. Their theory was wrong, but then again, they had nothing to work with—until now.

It was late, but Melanie telephoned Bobbie Thomas anyway during a recess. They chatted for fifteen minutes while Stephen and Frankie got to know Marcus. He was a young detective, twenty-nine, a Desert Storm veteran, and up for a challenge. He spread out a map of Massachusetts and highlighted Hoosac Mills, Amherst, and Wellfleet. "Gentlemen, look at this. This guy really works the whole state," he said, noting the fact that the three murders had occurred at the polar ends and the middle of the Commonwealth. "And look at the years—'87, '91, and '95."

Melanie soon joined the conversation. "He's operating in four-year increments," she observed. She stared at Marcus' map, noting the varied murder locations. "There's a word for that—something that occurs every four years."

"Quadrennial," Frankie said automatically.

"Thank you, Frankie. Yes, it's quadrennial." Melanie smiled at Frankie. "Okay, we know that three girls were slain by a left-handed assailant. These deaths occurred in 1987, 1991, and 1995—in a quadrennial sequence. We know all three girls were beautiful, and were known to be promiscuous."

"Be careful with that statement, Melanie," Stephen interjected. Melanie raised her hand.

"This is for our purposes, Stephen. I'm not going to write that down and send it out to the families of the deceased." Stephen nodded. "We know that he's physically strong, has the ability to disguise his looks, and uses crowded alcohol settings to operate. These bars are his comfort zones, the places where he operates successfully. We know that he uses aliases, and we know that he leaves gold chains on his victims' necks. But we don't know why he does that."

Marcus Torres was shaking his head. "Is it random or does he know the victims?" he asked the group.

"That's the unknown variable," Stephen said. "I wouldn't be surprised if he knew Laiken, the first victim. That, of course, is assuming she *was* his first victim. Either way we're going to cross-reference any and every guy these girls knew. Who knows? Maybe we'll get lucky."

They were quiet. "To hell with luck," Melanie said. "We're gonna catch this bastard before he strikes again. Take a look at your calendar. It's 1999. According to the limited information we have, he's due to hit again this year. We won't let that happen."

* * *

Melanie's fingertips were sore. She had been plugging Social Security numbers into her computer for the last hour and a half. Bobbie Thomas and Marcus Torres had been diligent, as expected, and they relayed dozens of names and Social Security numbers to her. It was a TRW file, and its purpose was simple. She simply entered a Social Security number into the system, and it spit out all of the subject's known addresses for the last ten years. It was monotonous, but she was hoping for a little luck. Hoosac Mills, Amherst, and Wellfleet were the sites of the murders, and maybe one name would come up twice, or even three times.

Bobbie Thomas, ADA, was the investigator in the death of Darlene Hughes. Law enforcement was an odd field in some ways, and it didn't really matter that she was a lawyer and Melanie and Marcus were only detectives. Besides, she had been a cop before, and now they were all on the same team. She'd just returned from Newark, New Jersey, the hometown of Darlene Hughes.

Bobbie met with Darlene's parents, both now in their sixties. They'd never recovered from the loss of their youngest child. Darlene was a good girl, they boasted, but she had always been insecure about her appearance. That was foolish, of course, because men always gave Darlene a second look. Mrs. Hughes pulled Bobbie aside and spoke forthrightly; she didn't want her husband's ears to be tainted with any negative comments about his beautiful little girl.

Darlene had, like so many other people, battled weight fluctuations throughout her life. She had always been pretty, but her tendency to put on pounds had made her unsure of herself. Mrs. Hughes knew she couldn't bring Darlene back. But she could cooperate fully by withholding nothing. Like Alicia Ana Rivera, her daughter's lack of confidence had led to promiscuity. It was Darlene's way of asserting herself and searching for love, for respect. She had been wrong in her philosophies, though, dead wrong. Mrs. Hughes gladly provided Bobbie with a list of men her daughter had known; she had given detectives a similar list years ago. Bobbie sympathized and admired Mrs. Hughes for her candor.

Melanie finished her preliminary list of names for the TRW search. There would be more, but for now she alphabetized all completed names and searched, looking for anything that might catch her eye. It was a long process, but halfway through the pile she perked up from her chair. "Oh my God," she said aloud. She paged Stephen, who was in Boston. He called from the South Shore Sports Center, where the neighborhood guys played floor hockey. "You'll never guess what, Stephen."

He could barely hear her due to the echoes. "Speak up, Melanie. What is it?" he asked.

"Guess who lived in Wellfleet for the summers of 1994 and 1995?"

Stephen was stumped. "Let me take a guess—Dick Hurtz and Eileen Dover."

"I'm not playing games," Melanie said. "William R. Munsing, that's who. Can you believe that? He lived in Hoosac Mills in 1987 when Laiken was killed, and he was in Wellfleet when Alicia Rivera was killed. What the hell is up with that, Stephen? Isn't he the same guy who asked to speak with you alone at the party in Boston?"

Melanie continued speaking but Stephen didn't hear her. He stood with the phone at his ear but was in a daze. He was shocked. When he snapped out of it a minute later, he heard Melanie's repetitive voice.

"Stephen, are you there? Stephen?"

"Yes, Melanie, I'm here. I slipped into a blur, my apologies."

She was silent for a moment. "How do you want to handle this?" she asked.

He thought about it a moment. "Let me talk to him first. I'm gonna have to give this some thought. I don't know right now, but I promise I'll call you later, either late tonight or tomorrow."

"Are you okay, Stephen?" Her concern was genuine. He knew it.

"Yeah, I'm okay. I'm sure it's nothing. Billy and Laiken were never an item. He's a pretty boy, not a killer."

Melanie elaborated on her discovery of Munsing's name. She wanted, unnecessarily, to justify her findings to Stephen. "I entered the names of all Kappa brothers who were active in the fall of 1987 into the system. Munsing's name was one of many." He understood. "And I talked to Bobbie. She says the results of the DNA from Laiken's clothes and the blood recovered at Darlene's murder scene will be in tomorrow from the lab in Sudbury. Expect a call from me when I get the results. Okay, Stephen?" He was still in a funk but managed a grunt for acknowledgment. "I'll talk to you later," she said before hanging up.

Stephen was in shock, but Melanie was in pursuit. She switched computer terminals and entered Billy Munsing's Social Security number. She wanted to know everything about the man from Dorchester.

18.

The Eire Pub was well known in Boston. It was where Ronald Reagan had once raised a beer—although many claimed he never took a sip. There had been two Eires—one on Hyde Park Avenue in Roslindale and the other in Adams Corner, Dorchester. Stephen had been to both, but was by no means a regular at either. The tavern in Roslindale had changed owners, and names, so tonight's trip to the Eire Pub could only land him in Dot, the affectionate name for Dorchester. He entered the blue-collar Irish bar and saw Billy Munsing immediately. He was seated at the bar, alone. Billy was his friend. No, Billy was his fraternity brother—closer than a friend.

The visit pained him, but it was necessary. Melanie had researched Billy Munsing. She discovered that, unbeknownst to Stephen, Billy had a sealed juvenile record. Well, nothing in the Commonwealth of Massachusetts was *truly* sealed. Melanie had to cash in a huge favor to cut the red tape protecting Billy's "sealed" record. Stephen was disheartened when Melanie called him. Her words lingered in the air: assault and battery—with a knife.

It was true. The chilling part about it was that it was a female victim, an ex-girlfriend of Billy's. He was fourteen years old when he stabbed a young Dorchester girl named Mary Ann Delaney, his thirteen-year-old former girlfriend. He pled guilty, lowering the charge from attempted murder. Billy served only three months—a prearranged summertime stay—with the Department of Youth Services. His documented reason for stabbing the young girl: "The little tramp kissed another boy."

Stephen was in shock. He knew Billy well, really well, or so he'd thought. But Billy's DYS time had been a secret, a well-kept one. Stephen had known some of Billy's childhood friends somewhat well. They visited

Taconic State many times; they had even toasted drinks with him on Meredith Street. Nary a word was uttered about Billy's past. They were stand-up kids.

Billy handed Stephen a beer and raised his glass. He lifted the beer with his left hand, as he always had.

Billy Munsing was left-handed.

He surveyed his friend—handsome, dark and handsome. Meeting pretty women was never a challenge for Billy; it came naturally. Born of a German father and an Irish mother, his dark Irish countenance was complemented with broad, athletic shoulders and long, muscular arms. Yet there was never a steady girl at his side. Why was that, Billy? Stephen too was a bachelor, but at least he could speak of old flames.

Stephen believed candor would be the best policy. It wasn't exactly successful with Jimmy Petrilli, but it didn't matter. He wasn't going to skirt any issues with Billy Munsing; it wouldn't be fair. "I have a few questions for you, buddy, so I guess I'll start by asking you about your juvenile record that you never told me about," Stephen said.

Billy was a city guy, street smart, and Stephen's tone on the telephone had indicated that this would not be a typical social visit. He expected to answer some personal questions, and he actually gave the hint of a grin. It was a ploy Billy used often, unconsciously, to win the favor of women. But Stephen was no woman, and he expected an answer.

"It wasn't the brethren's business, Stephen. What happened years ago was exactly that—years ago." He spoke with confidence and a trace of remorse.

"But you didn't even tell me."

"I couldn't, Stephen," he said. "Couldn't tell anyone, zilch. People never would have trusted me, especially girls. And I can't argue that I'd blame them." The common sense and matter-of-factness of Billy's reply made Stephen feel stupid. It made clear sense. No one at Taconic State would have trusted Billy if they knew of his lurid past.

"Okay. I have some other questions for you," Stephen said.

"Shoot."

"We've been tight for years, Billy. Wouldn't you agree?"

"You're one of my best friends, Stephen, you know that. Where are you going with this?"

Stephen hedged. This conversation—no, this interview—seemed sur-real to him. He stalled by ordering another round from the barkeep. "So then, if we're such great pals, Billy, how come I didn't know anything about you renting a house down in Wellfleet for two whole summers back in the mid-'nineties? I got no call, no written invite, no nothing."

Billy looked at Stephen, incredulous. "What the fuck does that have to do with the number of cowboys in Montana?"

"I'm curious as to why such a good buddy wouldn't invite me down for a weekend in Wellfleet. I love the Seaweed Surf Club, and I'm sure I would have joined you for a rum-and-Coke and reggae tunes."

Billy shook his head. "Look, Stephen, if you really want to know, it was simply a business deal that I turned a few thousand on. But I still want to know why you give a shit."

"Tell me."

"I rented the place out for three months—June, July, and August—for a lump sum. Then I subleased it for a week at a time to people I know, or friends of friends. I kept the place for the last week of August and still made a substantial profit from the other eleven weeks."

"And you only did this for 1994 and 1995?" Stephen asked.

Billy thought for a moment. "Yeah, that's correct. It got to be a pain in the ass, though. One crew of kids that went down there wrecked the place and was slow in paying me the money to fix it up. I stopped doing it."

"How come I never got the offer to rent?"

Billy rolled his head, giving Stephen another look of disbelief. "Come on, brother. You had your own thing going on in W.R. with your brother and your boys, so who are you shitting? And I still want to know why the fuck you're asking me these questions."

Stephen wouldn't lie. "We think whoever killed Laiken Barnes also murdered a girl in Amherst and a girl in Wellfleet."

They were quiet for half a minute, and Billy's face sank. "You think I did it?"

"No, I don't, Billy," he answered. "I honestly don't know what to think anymore. I don't like the fact you were in Wellfleet when the girl was killed, or that it was you who told me that Petrilli was fooling around with Laiken. It was almost as if you had something to hide and were trying to deflect attention from yourself."

Billy slowly nodded, understanding Stephen's plight. It was an awkward situation, one neither had experienced in their thirteen-year friendship. They had been freshmen together, living on the same dorm floor and sharing the pains and pitfalls of growing up. Stephen and Billy were tight, but now the strength of their relationship was being tested.

"Do you remember how I told you about Jimmy and Laiken?"

"How could I forget?"

"Well, I didn't tell you everything I knew," Billy said. Stephen's face was blank in anticipation. "The real truth is that he knocked her up."

Stephen's eyes narrowed. "Are you yankin' my chain? How the hell do you know that?"

"The same way I found out about them screwing around—I overheard them in his room. That's it. I didn't find out on the quiet tip or anything like that; I simply overheard them talking. He got her pregnant, Stephen, and the next thing I know she's dead." Stephen fell back in his chair, momentarily speechless.

"How certain are you? You'd better be on the mark."

"I ain't lying, brother. It really happened, it's the real deal."

"What the hell did Jimmy do? Did he make her have an abortion?"

"Don't know, I only know he knocked her up."

"King Billy find out about this?"

"No idea, man."

Billy's younger brother, Eric Munsing, suddenly approached the bar. He slapped both Stephen's and Billy's backs. Eric knew Stephen well. He was excited to see him, but after a minute he sensed palpable tension. He offered a few hospitable words, then departed. Stephen was afraid to ask the next question, but he did anyway.

"You think Jimmy murdered her?" The question itself was simple: five words and a question mark. But they both knew it wasn't an easy answer. Billy finished his first beer and swigged from his second; he always could drink with the best of them.

"What's that good-looking girl's name you're working with—Melanie?" he asked. Stephen nodded. "Does she know that I tipped you off to Jimmy?" Stephen shook his head. Billy again pulled from his beer before returning to Stephen. "Yeah, I think he whacked that girl, Stephen. Yeah... I do."

Stephen was in suspended disbelief. "Thanks for your honest opinion."

"Where do you go from here, Stephen?" he asked.

"Melanie tells me that she'll be getting back DNA results from two of the murders to look for a match."

"DNA? What kind of DNA do you guys have?" he asked anxiously.

Stephen hesitated, staring at his friend. "Sorry, kid, I can't tell you. I'd be violating my agreement with Melanie if I talked about something as serious as that," he said. They continued to stare at each other before Billy broke the silence.

"You want me to submit a DNA sample to the cops on account of having a place in Wellfleet?"

"Slow down, Billy. I don't want you to submit anything because I don't think you're guilty. But the Staties or Hoosac Mills may ask you. And they're gonna want to know where you were on the night of the Rivera girl's murder. And if you didn't do it, you might as well." Stephen depersonalized Melanie from the investigation with his word choice.

Billy's body swiveled on the barstool. His mind vacillated in thought. After a moment he said, "If I did nothing wrong then I shouldn't have to give my DNA. It's the principle of the matter. Besides, I may trust you, but I won't trust the Staties. I had my run-in with them when I was a kid. I want nothing to do with those dudes. And Stephen, how the hell am I supposed to remember where I was on the night of that girl's murder? I can't tell you what I had for lunch yesterday."

"But if you didn't do it you have nothing to worry about."

Billy thought about it. "Fuck that. Make them hit me with a court order," he said. Stephen shook his head; he was in no mood to argue. They sat at the bar for another thirty minutes talking in spurts before Stephen got up and left.

As Stephen departed he took his friend by the shoulder, bodies touching, and gave him the fraternity handshake. When Stephen was gone Billy unconsciously rubbed his right hand; his longtime friend had squeezed hard.

* * *

The un-sub couldn't resist temptation. He felt a yearning, a visceral calling to visit her. Her remains would be old, rotten, but those remains would forever mark the inception of his battle against the deadly whores. She would always be special—she was his first.

His internal clock was ticking. He needed reassurance, and his visit to the cemetery gave him the renewal he needed. He was no idiot, this man, and he understood the reality of multiple law enforcement agencies working together. Soon the nosy Feds might become involved, exacerbating his problem. He must move swiftly.

He had been imprudent with the gold chains, he knew. It had been a game, actually—a "catch me if you can" ploy that was not necessary. Perhaps, he mused, it was part of his flawed engineering. He intentionally left evidence which potentially could lead to his demise. Yet he still doubted the aptitude of the investigators. In his mind they just weren't smart enough. But vanity could be a dangerous thing, he reminded himself, as many an intelligent man had been caught before. He thought of change—a change for the better. He would alter his modus operandi for his next mission, the mission he deemed most important. He had already waited twelve years, and revenge was a dish best served cold.

He sat high on the hill: dark, windy, brisk, and eerie. The granite slab looked the same. It could have been erected yesterday. It said her name: Laiken Anne Barnes. Then he said her name. "Laiken Barnes...how are you, dear?" The epitaph indicated she'd lived only twenty years—such a young age in a world of modern technology. But her death had nothing to do with the science of medicine.

He touched the stone, stiff fingers clawing its face. Excitement ebbed through his veins; the four-year hunger for a kill would be over soon, and he would be rewarded for his patience. He remembered an adage from childhood: good things come to those who wait. The criminal experts scoffed at the notion that his type—serial murderer—could actually wait long periods of time between kills. That may be true for the majority, but not for him. He was not a simpleton: disorganized, unkempt, alone, and uneducated. He was intelligent; there was vision in his work. His mission served purpose, and although he was a churchgoer, his actions were not predicated on ecclesiastical beliefs.

Cars zoomed by on Route 7, unable to see his dark shadow cast by moonlight. He produced a flask and sipped liqueur: hot, delicious, rewarding. He leaned against the slab, atop his victim once more. He grimaced—she'd gotten what she deserved.

After sixty minutes he descended the hill to his vehicle. If seen by a familiar face, he would most certainly raise suspicion. He headed east on Route 2, back toward Boston. In a short time he would make similar visits to Amherst and Wellfleet. They were risky yet necessary pilgrimages for his psyche. He was preparing, and 90 percent of the preparation was mental. His excellent physical shape was never a concern.

Whore eradication was his deepest fantasy. Dreams of such genocide were sweet; it would be the ultimate gift to mankind. Such militant views were the exception, though. There was a time when he too had bitten from the apple, as most men do. It was okay, because to err was human, and he had changed. Some would always lust the whore, the man-eating land shark. In time he realized that such reality was beyond his control. One man's utopia was another's hell.

He now accepted his station in life. He couldn't kill all the whores; he would methodically pick his battles. Proficiency had become his best ally; he was calculating, quick, and thorough. His next victim would be his testimony, and he anticipated it like none other. She had, in fact, been the catalyst for his mission, though she was unaware of it. He shifted gears and drove away from Hoosac Mills.

* * *

Miles to the east a beautiful woman, now in her thirties, tucked her youngest into bed. The child had been ill all week—chicken pox—but the dutiful mother had been a loving and responsible mom, as always. The woman went to the kitchen and made a tray of hot chocolate for her husband and two older kids. She joined them in the living room, sharing the large sofa under the warmth of a comforter. The family cuddled together, sipping cocoa and keeping each other warm. They were a classic American family.

They felt safe in the sanctity of their home. A Disney movie played on the big screen. The children's faces were lit up with smiles. The woman was happy; she had made an improbable about-face years before—a virtual one-hundred-eighty-degree turn—and now she appreciated the finer things in life. What she didn't know was that she was now in grave danger.

19.

Melanie made the trek to Stephen's condo. It was nearing one o'clock in the afternoon. They sat in the living room, listening to cars zoom by on Washington Street. "Damn, Stephen, how fast do they go?"

He laughed, noting it was a straight shot for half a mile. "They can get past a buck if they crank it; usually they're hammered at that speed. More than a few cars have crashed and burned on this stretch. It's probably the fastest road in the city, along with Hyde Park Ave and American Legion Highway." Sirens raced by the apartment as they spoke.

"It's like the *Dukes of Hazzard* on this street," she remarked.

"Yeah," he quipped, "and I'm Boss Hog."

They drank soft drinks and tended to business. Much had transpired in the last twenty-four hours and they both knew the case had finally taken palpable form. The DNA evidence from the Darlene Hughes and Laiken Barnes murders matched—Melanie had gotten word from the state police laboratory late last night. The perpetrator had been diligent in the Alicia Ana Rivera murder, however, and left no physical evidence, less the gold chain. He'd purchased the gold chain from the Jewelers Building, at Ashley Engel's, but didn't leave a name. Ashley Engel's only recorded the names of buyers who spent more than one thousand dollars. It was no coincidence, though. It was the same guy. Melanie stared at Stephen. "Okay, so what's this late-breaking news you have for me?"

"According to one of my clandestine sources, it appears as though my fraternal big brother, Jimmy Petrilli, impregnated Laiken Barnes."

Melanie's jaw almost hit the floor. "Munsing tell you this last night?"

He shook his head. Stephen knew Melanie wasn't stupid, but he was obligated to protect his friend. "I ain't being a punk, Melanie. I can't tell you who told me. We have to find out whether it's true, that's all. So do me a solid on this one…please."

She nodded. "I'll be all over that tomorrow when I get home. How about Billy—did he admit that he was at his rental house for the last week in August in 1995?"

"Yes," Stephen said, "but he admitted it without reservation."

They stared at one another for a long time. "Stephen, that means that Billy was physically present in Hoosac Mills in 1987 when Laiken was murdered—at the same party nonetheless—and he was physically present in Wellfleet when Alicia Rivera was killed. He also has served time for stabbing a girl. Now, I know I'm not the female Sammy Spade, but I can safely reason that he's our prime suspect right now. I believe there may be a little deflection on his part right now."

Melanie made sense, but until all avenues were explored, Stephen would remain optimistic that Billy was a victim of circumstance. "Any development on FBI intervention?" he asked.

"Monday, but I think the appropriate word is assistance. It'll still be a joint task force investigation. The guy's a big wheel—name's Milton Glavin. He's both a special agent and a profiler, so when he comes in Monday I'll give him everything I have on the case. I've already faxed him the basics. Bobbie Thomas and Marcus Torres have agreed to come out to the Mills for the meeting."

Stephen opened up his hands. "And moi?"

"Sorry, Stephen," Melanie said with a shrug. "Milton made it perfectly clear that he'd deal only with law enforcement agencies. I told him about you and he was explicit in not dealing with you or Frankie. He doesn't care if I work with you, but he won't entertain anything you have to say."

Stephen gave a mock frown. "I sense a predisposition against sleuths," he said. "Did you tell him I have naked pictures of teenage girls over eighteen, and I'm a deputy sheriff—vested with police powers in Boston, Chelsea, Winthrop, and Revere?"

"Yeah, and he wasn't too impressed."

"Just another roadblock for us lowly correction officers, the smallest fish in the law enforcement food chain—one step below court officers and one rung above shopping mall guards."

"I'd bet you look good in uniform," Melanie said. He winked at her. "To hell with working overtime tonight, Stephen. Barnes is paying you a boatload; come to the seminar with me."

"Can't. I'm working for comp, not money. An eight-hour shift nets me twelve hours of comp. I use the comp time to work on the case. One hand washes the other." She understood.

Tonight Melanie was returning to her alma mater, New England University, for a seminar detailing the traits and characteristics of serial murderers. Most of the folks going would be students, cops, or people fascinated with the subject. Melanie's attendance reasons would be different, though. It was business, and maybe she could learn a thing or two. But was he on the loose? He might be incarcerated already for another crime, or he might be dead. Melanie couldn't afford to think like that, though. She had to assume he was among the crowds, an imminent threat to society.

Stephen put on the stereo; they sat back and relaxed before Stephen left for work. "What time is the seminar?" he asked.

"Eight o'clock."

"So what're you doing between two and seven?" Melanie shrugged. Stephen made a quick phone call in the kitchen, returning moments later. "Do you like window shopping?"

"Yeah, why?"

"I can have Peachy here in thirty minutes. She'll take you up Centre Street to pass some time. Are you interested?"

"Sure, your mom's awesome."

"Settled."

* * *

At seven-forty Melanie walked into Patriot Auditorium, the largest hall at New England University. The school was on Huntington Avenue, abutting the tough inner-city neighborhood of Mission Hill. Melanie walked the halls of her alma mater, reacquainting herself with the campus she loved so much. Various sports plaques and trophies decorated the walls of the proud university. The calendar had changed by a decade for Melanie, but the school was the same. It was she who had changed, leaving school a naïve twenty-two-year-old and blossoming into a respected police detective.

She had contacted her former criminology professor, Dr. Harris. He was all too eager to meet with the beautiful detective, who was—in his opinion—one of his protégés. Nothing pleased the professor more than seeing his students apply their studies to real-life criminal investigations. The professor was not ignorant, though. He knew quite well that common sense, persistence, and the use of informants more than complemented any methodical detective wizardry.

Melanie chatted with Dr. Harris longer than anticipated. At five past eight she entered the packed auditorium only to find a seat in the front row. The guest speaker was Devon Patterson, a retired FBI agent who'd served two decades' time as a behavioral specialist. During his career he had tracked four serial killers throughout the country. He was fiftyish. Devon looked the part of a stereotypical Fed—tall, athletic build, handsome, and well dressed. Five hundred people were hushed as Devon, with all signs of vanity, recounted his career.

Devon told the story of his first capture. He was an excellent public speaker. Melanie was awed with the manner in which Devon hypnotized the crowd. What drew people to these lectures? Why were people so enamored with sadistic tales of calculated horror and wickedness in which man inflicted pain unto fellow human beings? Melanie had seen misery in her tenure as a police officer; she surmised that the public's fascination was predicated on fear. Besides, homicide and debauchery were things that only happened to *other* people. Right?

The man could see her. He too had known about the seminar; he knew a wise man wouldn't forego an opportunity to learn something new, because knowledge was power. His philosophy was simple: once a student, forever a student, and shame on the man who thinks he is beyond new wisdom. He sat in the back row on the aisle seat, nearest to the exit. His disguise was perfect—thick, Coke-bottle glasses, tan gloves, a wig, and a cushioned midriff to cast an appearance of portliness. When Melanie entered the auditorium she unknowingly brushed against him.

Ironic, wasn't it? He smiled.

This Leary woman was different. Intriguing. She seemed the proficient type who wasn't past reproach or self-improvement. He admired self-effacement in a professional, in a person.

Devon Patterson spoke. "…And that is the difference. Those who subscribe to paleopsychology believe our human brains are built on a primitive, animalistic core known as the R-complex. Deep inside we all possess savage-like instincts, like our primate ancestors." Devon's lecture fluctuated between real-life cases and serial-murder philosophies. The man thought Devon was a blowhard. He wasn't impressed by the G-man, storied career or no storied career.

Big deal. Could he catch me? Probably not.

He stared at Melanie. Every so often she canted her head, offering a profile view of her beautiful face and lively hair. What a woman. He respected men and women of the badge. He understood their value; without their indisputably selfless courage and dedication, the streets would swell with anarchy. He was not a ruthless criminal, a thug who preyed on helpless citizens. In fact, he despised the recidivist offenders who populated the prisons—and drained the taxpayers' purses.

And…he truly respected this Leary woman. She wasn't the embodiment of the only thing he hated—the whores. No, Melanie was no whore. She didn't unlock her vault of womanhood at the simple downing of a drink. She was a true woman, a true professional.

Yet a quandary existed nevertheless. Melanie's sense of professionalism had become his impediment. Was she getting too close? Did she have the skill set to connect the proverbial dots? It appeared plausible. A decision had to be made—a business decision, in a sense—on what to do about Melanie. Harming her was not on the itinerary.

But if he had to…

Devon Patterson continued. He spoke with such fluidity that the student newspaper would lavish him the highest accolades in their review. He highlighted famous serial killers such as the Son of Sam and Jeffrey Dahmer, disclosing common traits and characteristics that often linked such deviants.

Much of this was repetitive information for Melanie. Her mind took a side trip. What was *he* thinking? Was he plotting the macabre death of another woman right now? She didn't care for statistics; she wanted to know what motivated the man who had mercilessly butchered Laiken Barnes, Darlene Hughes and Alicia Rivera. Were there others she didn't know about—and more importantly, would there be more?

The man also tuned out his auditory senses. The arrogant Fed became invisible. Now he could only watch Melanie—sweet Melanie. She appeared puzzled, and it was evident that she too was not attentive to the guest speaker. *Why is that, Melanie? Are you thinking about me? I hope so, because I'm thinking about you.* How nice it would be to come home to a woman like Melanie, a lady with pride, self-assurance, integrity, and beauty. Oh yes, the probability wouldn't be unreasonable—on paper. The man was popular, handsome, articulate, and successful by society's standards.

But it could never be. He had his agenda and he could never compromise that agenda for anyone, or anything. His next kill was imminent; he grinned while thinking about her, his next prey. Times changed over the years and people typically made improvements in their lives. It was only natural. His next target, the one he had waited so patiently for, had made those very changes. But the man didn't care, for he believed deep down she was still a venomous whore, a wolf dressed in sheep's clothing. She would be re-dressed.

Devon Patterson fielded questions from the crowd, and his replies were as arrogant as his soliloquy. The man was disgusted by Patterson as he postured at the podium like a Greek god. He was sure that at one time Patterson had been a worthy agent, brash but effective, but now he was an egotistical showman, a well-dressed carnival barker.

Loss of humility was tragic. Patterson couldn't possibly maximize his keenness; pride had consumed center stage.

Patterson spoke of the great stress and danger of tracking serial killers. "To quote my friend and former colleague, Bob Ressler, 'Whoever fights monsters should be careful that, in the process, they do not become a monster themselves. And—'"

A sudden interruption from the back spun heads.

"And remember," the man said loudly as Devon Patterson fell silent, "whenever you look into an abyss, the abyss looks back into you."

The crowd froze. Patterson sought the mystery voice. The students surrounding the man gazed at him, thinking he was odd and funny-looking. The crowd then looked to Patterson, curious for his response.

"I see we have a fan of Robert Ressler. Well, that's not a surprise, seeing that we're all at a serial killing seminar." Patterson played to the audience and they laughed. Robert Ressler was a noted author, and he had been a preeminent FBI serial-killer hunter before retiring. Most in attendance were familiar with Ressler and his works.

"Maybe I'm not a fan of Ressler, Devon. Perhaps I like Nietzsche." The man spoke in reference to Friedrich Nietzsche, the German philosopher and poet who was credited with the theory of fighting monsters and staring into abysses. Patterson was interested by the mystery voice.

"Please stand, my new friend." The man was confident in his disguise and obliged. The lecture hall was filled to capacity. He actually blended in with the nearby standing-room crowd of thirty students. "Now then, young man, do you have anything else you'd like to bless this lovely crowd with this evening?" Patterson said patronizingly, eliciting laughter from the crowd.

The man locked eyes with the ex-Fed from a distance. "You generalize too much," the man said. "You understand the exceptions to the rules, but don't mislead these students. An instructor is supposed to teach all facets of a subject—both tangibles and intangibles. Anything less would be unsuitable."

Patterson was taken aback. "Would you care to elaborate a bit, Mr....?"

"The name's Carlos."

"Good then, Carlos. Please expound on my shortcomings. I'm quite sure the crowd is most interested."

Melanie laughed; she didn't bother turning around because she didn't want to give the idiot the benefit of her attention. Everyone else looked.

"Devon, I understand the concept—and the success rate—of criminal profiling, but you speak to this crowd tonight and lead them to believe that everything is black and white. Just like you wrote in your book, you classify serial murders as if you're talking about the four basic food groups. The law enforcement future sits in this room tonight, and they'll leave here thinking the apprehension of a serial murderer is an x's and o's process. It's not, and you know this. You dispense facts and figures and assume the crowd will drink every word. So far it's working. But I recommend less grandstanding and more reality. Everyone here knows your track record; you've been an adept agent, so there's no reason to expatiate on your career."

Patterson didn't know whether to laugh or frown. Indignant behavior in a lecture hall, rather than on the street, was new to him. All eyes and ears awaited his response. He simply motioned with his hands, a signal for Carlos to continue.

"There are intangibles as to why serial killers do what they do. Some indeed are psychotic," Carlos stressed. "No one disputes that. But there are others who operate out of passion, and are truly driven by what they believe is best for society. They perform a necessary evil."

Patterson was game for a show. "By all means, continue with your enlightenment. I'm sure the audience is mesmerized by your intellect."

The man didn't waver. "Most citizens condone the fight for the extinction of drug dealers, pimps, prostitutes, and junkies. They are a liability to this nation—a clear and present danger to the children of today and tomorrow. But people in this country don't possess the courage of their convictions, and they continuously take a backseat to these dregs of society. So Devon, I am suggesting that some of the so-called serial killers in this country who dispose of these wretches are performing a public service. They should be commended." All were quiet, wanting more. "And Devon, your book reinforces the accepted belief that rape is a violent crime, yet serial murder is a sexual one. Insightful—a thousand clinical psychiatrists and the entire Behavioral Science Unit affirm the notion, but the truth is it's contradictory. So is the thought that the kill serves as a substitute for sex. The reality of it, Devon, is that you truly don't know unless you've been there." Carlos stepped into the aisle. He was watching Melanie.

"Do you speak from experience, Carlos?"

"No, Devon, just speaking hypothetically."

"Incisive but disjointed, if I may say. I admire your knowledge on the subject, though I tend to disagree with your liberal judgment of who deserves to die. I hope that a man such as yourself will never wear a robe in our halls of justice."

Melanie fidgeted. Carlos' voice was recognizable, somehow. Was it a Berkshire accent, or the attempted concealment of it? She spun around. It was too late. The stranger had just turned the corner, exiting the auditorium without much notice from the crowd around him.

Devon Patterson didn't miss a beat. It would take more than a freakily dressed zealot to rattle him. He continued speaking, entertaining more questions and comments from the audience.

An innate sensation pulled Melanie from her chair. She scurried up the aisle in pursuit of the familiar voice. The lobby was empty, save a campus police officer. "Did you see a man just leave, officer?" The cop nodded, pointing toward the street. She rushed through the double doors and hurried to the curb of Huntington Avenue. Cars zoomed by at high rates of speed. Pedestrians scurried along the sidewalk without making eye contact. She scanned left to right.

He was gone, nowhere to be found. How could that be? She'd been right behind him, or so she thought. She collected her thoughts. Where was her common sense? This was just a typical weirdo who attended speeches and protests and public events, yes? Melanie reasoned to herself that it was just her crazy imagination playing tricks. No actual serial killer would dare walk into a seminar littered with cops and speak freely. That would be foolish, like entering the lion's den without a whip. Melanie turned back toward campus.

He watched her. She was sweet, so sweet, and he didn't know how he could release her from his mind. He must, for he couldn't let anything hinder his next quest. It could be his last.

He emerged from the concealment of a parked car and casually strolled down the street toward his vehicle. A hooker approached. She propositioned him. He gave her an icy stare. "Trust, lady of the evening…it's an imprudent gesture to seek my acquaintance."

The hooker's sixth sense pulsated through her veins. She ran away.

20.

The meeting site was moved to the Hampshire County DA's office. The conference room looked like a military strategy center; walls were laced with autopsy photographs, crime scene pictures, and the vague police sketch of the suspect. The sketch was marginal—at best. The girls who had been at Heroes in Amherst hadn't given a good suspect description. Melanie stared at the sketch; it looked neither like Billy Munsing nor Jimmy Petrilli. It didn't look like P.J. McClaren either; in fact, it didn't really resemble any of their preliminary suspects.

Milton Glavin wasn't the stereotypical Fed that Melanie, Bobbie Thomas, and Marcus Torres expected. He was short, five-nine, and weighed about 165 pounds. He was thirty-five—young for a profiler by FBI standards. He dressed like an ordinary businessman who brokered trades for J.P. Morgan. But Milton preferred a relaxed working atmosphere, insisting that professional titles be left behind when they interacted behind closed doors. He didn't want anyone calling him Agent; his name was Milton. He spoke with confidence and zero arrogance.

It was the first meeting of this agency collaboration—this new task force. Milton made it clear that he would handle any and all media questions. The public's right to know was always an important intangible in any serial murder case, but each case was different. At this time he decided on a proactive approach.

"Define 'proactive,' Milton," Melanie said.

"Real simple," he said. "We're gonna bait the un-sub."

Milton explained that many serial killers intensely follow their own stories in the media. It was yet another sadistic way for them to relive their crimes. Using the media was risky, but it had paid dividends in the past for the Bureau. It wasn't uncommon for criminals to inject themselves into investigations, either. The reasons varied: guilty conscience, a need to be caught, sometimes just another vicarious thrill. Milton would leak a story to the major newspapers in Massachusetts, hoping the lure would work.

"Have any persons launched themselves into any of these respective investigations?" Milton asked the group. They all looked at each other, waiting for someone to speak.

Melanie took the lead. "This may be speculation," Melanie said, "but I have grounds to believe that a guy named Billy Munsing—that is, William Munsing—offered the name of a fellow Kappa Chi Omicron fraternity brother in regards to the Laiken Barnes murder. The other frat brother's name is Jimmy Petrilli."

"You know this or you postulate?" Milton asked.

"I strongly suspect it," Melanie said. "A source of mine—Stephen Nicholson, the private investigator—gave me the tip but he didn't attach Billy's name to it. I'm quite sure he's the leak, though."

"Okay, then there's a good start. We'll take a hard look at Munsing."

They compared notes, sifting through lists of the victims' friends, co-workers, employers, and other names they had. They checked credit cards, educational background information, gymnasium and social club histories, sporting interests, and more. They sought a common link, something that could tie all three women together.

Melanie began briefing Milton on Billy Munsing and Jimmy Petrilli before he abruptly stopped her. He would eventually interview all suspects in the case, but not until the completion of his criminal profile. To do so he would first examine all bits of evidence and factual information from the three murders, then create a profile of a would-be suspect. The names themselves—Munsing and Petrilli—were unimportant. It was the personal information about them that he couldn't hear just yet. Milton refused to prejudice his profile with loose pieces of information on any individuals; otherwise he would compromise his objectivity.

At this juncture Milton wanted to form a tight group among the law enforcement agencies, one that would best facilitate the apprehension of the perpetrator. He was neither territorial nor egotistical, not caring who got the collar. Milton was single and loved his job; he only wanted the murderer off the street. Career goals were important to him, but he knew that honest police work was the best conduit to ascension in the ranks.

Other agents he knew were sneaky, playing childish games like pitting cops against cops, just so their polish shined brightest when a case was closed. That was bad business, and Milton Glavin would have none of it.

He spoke with confidence. "All right, people, it's time to give our unknown quantity a name. Any takers?" Milton asked. Melanie, Marcus, and Bobbie looked at each other momentarily and sort of shrugged. "Anyone, anyone?" he asked again.

"Our man kills every four years, right?" Marcus asked.

"So we think. That theory could change," Milton said.

"Why not call him the Olympian?" Marcus suggested. The room was quiet for half a minute; Marcus started feeling foolish, as if he had just said something wrong.

But to his surprise, Milton liked it—and so did the others. "He kills in odd numbered years, but yes, that name would be appropriate. If we link him to more murders that don't fall into a four-year pattern, we'll rename him. But for now, we'll refer to our perpetrator as the Olympian," Milton said.

Milton stressed the fact that all persons involved in the case must be thorough in their work, no exceptions. He cited FBI cases where shoddy investigations had cost them convictions, which was unforgivable. If Milton lost, he'd want the bad guy to beat him; he didn't want ineptitude to be the excuse. He wanted all witnesses re-interviewed. Someone could be withholding information and might not even know it. Melanie thought of Renee Gleeson, Laiken Anne Barnes' friend who lived in South Carolina and had been seemingly uncooperative on the telephone. She mentioned it, and Milton didn't hesitate. "I can have an agent at her doorstep in forty-five minutes."

Melanie shook her head. "No, on second thought, maybe I will go down there. She sounded pretty reluctant to speak to me on the phone before. Don't take this the wrong way, Milton, but I'm a woman and I live in Hoosac Mills. I could probably get more out of her than an FBI agent." Everyone agreed.

"Will Hoosac Mills appropriate the trip? If not, I'll see what I can do," Milton said.

"I don't know," Melanie answered. "But I'm not worried about it. Mr. Barnes will pay for it, no questions asked."

"Good," Milton said. "Get down there this week." He knew that Melanie had other important items to deal with. "I'll have my profile soon, after examining all three murders. Of course I'd liked to expedite it, but I need as much factual information as possible."

They continued for another hour, exchanging ideas. There would be another joint meeting; it would be called at Milton's discretion and all were expected to attend, regardless of their itinerary. Suddenly Milton said, "Birthdays, birthdays. I need birthdays and dates of death of the three victims."

Melanie scrambled through her paperwork. "I've got it right here. You want years or just months and days?"

"Just the months and days," Milton answered.

"Okay, here we go...April 3, November 1...May 20, September 7... October 10 and August 31. That's it, but why did you want those?"

Bobbie and Marcus smiled; they knew. Milton gestured to Bobbie, giving her the floor. "Serial killers are funny ducks. They have a tendency to visit gravesides and locations of their murders. Again, it's their way of reliving the kill."

"Bingo, Bobbie, well said. Melanie just read off two hot dates—April 3, which was just the other day, and May 20."

"What are we gonna do?" Marcus asked.

"Simple," Milton said. "If the investigation is still ongoing next month we'll stake out the grave of...which victim?"

"Darlene Hughes," Melanie said.

"Thank you. We'll stake out Darlene's grave and the location of her murder. Who was the April 3 date?"

"Laiken Barnes."

"Okay, this one may be hot. There's a legitimate possibility that our unsub visited her graveside the other day. After this meeting we'll go to her grave and dust it, look for gifts he may have left."

"I have an appointment with Laiken Barnes' primary care physician in a little while," Melanie said.

"Don't worry about it, I'll take care of it," Milton said. Bobbie Thomas stared at Milton.

"And if it's okay, I'll go with you," she said.

"Deal. Maybe you can show me how things are done in the Bay State."

Before they left the door swung open. It was Devon Patterson. "I heard about the big powwow and didn't want to miss it," he said before shaking hands with Milton, his protégé.

"Pleasure to see you."

"Likewise," Devon said. "You think you'll need the old man to put the uniform back on to help you on this one?"

Milton smiled, excited. "We'll take any help, especially from one of the masters."

Introductions were made. Devon Patterson had just learned about the case and he decided to forego his lecture circuit. Something much bigger loomed. He was offering his services to his most apt pupil of the early 1990s. Milton—the devout student—embraced the moment.

* * *

The grass surrounding the grave was well maintained. Laiken's plot was set high. It overlooked much of Hoosac Mills. The face of the headstone was dry. Milton dusted the top and face of the stone. To his surprise he discovered four streaks—not prints, but streaks—on the left side of the stone. "This is odd," Milton said to Bobbie. "When's the last time it rained in these parts?"

"March was miserable, but it hasn't rained in about ten days."

He continued dusting, concentrating on the left side until he netted results. "Look here, Bobbie, I think we've got something." She stared at the impression and saw it, clear as day. It was a partial left-hand palm print—not pristine, but potential for a match. Bobbie smiled, and suddenly her eyes caught something very small resting on a blade of grass.

"Don't move," she said to Milton. He promptly obeyed as she drew out a pair of tweezers and reached down, retrieving something so small that Milton couldn't see it. She aided his vision and brought it close to his eyes. "What does that look like to you?"

One solid look was all it took. "That's a broken fingernail," he said.

"And what are those?" she asked, pointing to the streaks on the face of the headstone.

"May I postulate?" Milton asked with a grin.

"Please do," she answered.

"I think that our un-sub—the Olympian, if I may—paid a happy birthday visit to Laiken and couldn't keep his murdersome hands off of her headstone. Those streaks are the top of his fingers, and he broke a nail scraping the rock."

"You read my mind. Too bad the smudges are no good," Bobbie said.

"Doesn't matter, we can get DNA off the nail. We'll have to print all groundskeepers and any of Laiken's family and friends who may have visited here recently. We might catch some luck with the partial." He drew in a breath and looked at Bobbie, pleased. "Good catch, counselor." They placed the fingernail in an evidence bag. The spontaneous trip had panned out.

"I thought you said no titles, special agent," Bobbie said sarcastically.

"I lied," he said. "What are you gonna do, call the cops on me?"

* * *

Laiken's medical records had been recovered from a special filing storage facility. Staff members from the medical practice in question—Dr. Wehter & Associates—referred to the records locale as the Dead Files.

Melanie carefully placed Laiken's documented medical history on a large, round table. The paperwork was arranged in clockwork fashion. Gynecology/obstetrics records were placed at 12:01; autopsy reports lay at 11:59. Melanie read carefully. It was typical medical material pertaining to a young girl: vaccinations, tetanus shots, bee stings, a broken bone, acne, pubescent issues, yeast infections, allergies, yearly checkups, etc....A section of Laiken's medical history appeared to have been tampered with. The paper came from Kenny Rocek's file, so it was twelve years old. Under the box labeled *Procedures,* Melanie caught an inconsistency with the black lines. It looked like the copied report had been altered. No, on further thought, the copied report *had* been altered. Someone—specifically Kenny Rocek—may have applied Wite-Out to the medical report. Stephen told her Laiken had gotten pregnant, and now Melanie was doing her homework.

Fifteen minutes later Melanie sat across the table from Dr. Patrice Wehter. She was a charming woman who was the Barnes' family doctor. She received Melanie warmly. William Jonathan Barnes had personally consented to Melanie's medical inquiry.

Dr. Wehter reviewed Melanie's paperwork before Melanie arrived. She made a perfunctory glance at the array of documentation before making deliberate speech. She looked Melanie in the eyes. "On October 13, 1987, I referred Laiken to a family planning agency in Pittsfield to terminate a pregnancy."

"Does Mr. Barnes know this?" Melanie asked.

"Not to my knowledge," Dr. Wehter said. "Laiken wanted confidentiality. Detective Rocek knows, of course."

Melanie's facial expression changed, ever so slightly. Dr. Wehter was quick. Years of treating people bestowed a certain sixth sense. The doctor had detected foul play on the part of Rocek. But a sixth sense was also a gift—and in Melanie Leary she saw a woman who was strong, honest, and righteous.

Laiken Barnes had been dead since 1987, but Dr. Wehter had never stopped caring about her. She gently took Melanie's hand. "Godspeed, young lady," she said. "Do what you must to put an end to this sad chapter in Hoosac Mills history." Melanie thanked Dr. Wehter. She nodded but was too incensed to speak. She took a hard look at Dr. Wehter. The doctor, unlike the corrupt, immoral souls who infected society, was a symbol of everything that was right about the world. The matronly doctor viewed life differently. She operated with virtue and compassion.

It was her duty.

Melanie was livid. She drove to the family planning agency and, despite the initial reluctance of the agency's administrative assistant, received a copy of Laiken's abortion paperwork. The termination procedure had taken place on October 15, 1987, two weeks before Laiken's death. The box entitled *Father* remained blank—forever. She called Stephen at work and told him. She was irate at Rocek, too maddened to speak to him right now. Stephen tried his best to mollify Melanie, but nothing worked. Stephen knew that Rocek was a role model of sorts to Melanie, as ridiculous as that was, so her anger wouldn't subside for a while.

He called his captain and got permission to leave. "Don't talk to Rocek without me, Melanie, please. I'll be there in three hours."

Melanie was relieved. Stephen had been working predominantly in the prison lately. She missed him.

She went home—tired, nauseous, and cranky. She grabbed her mail and took a seat on her recliner. She had a few hours to waste and figured she'd relax until Stephen arrived. A yellow eight-and-a-half-by-eleven envelope caught her eye. It was mailed priority and it was addressed to her: Detective Melanie Leary. She found this very strange. Why not send something to the police station? She opened it. It was a poem, written in sixteen-verse form. The poem was written for Melanie, and unless it was a bad joke, it was the work of the serial murderer, the work of the Olympian. It was typewritten in Roman print, unsigned. Melanie reached into her purse and donned latex gloves.

You are most apt my sweet Melanie
Though your efforts may die in vain

It is I the perpetrator of felonies
And how I pray that your skills do wane

You seek answers to a grisly crime of yore
In which young Stephen did dance that night

Indeed the fresh blood made me yearn for more
And stealing Laiken's breath gave me such delight

Yes it is now the year I am due
I've dreamt an eternity for this next kill

But this time I shall leave you no clue
Oh how number four presents such a thrill

Poor old Rocek could not make the bust
Of the ghastly work that I'd done

You shall give it your best I trust
But when all is over I shall have won

Melanie was mesmerized, frozen on the recliner for the longest minute of her life. Was Milton Glavin prophetic? He had just spoken about criminals injecting themselves into investigations. This was a little different, yes, but for all intents and purposes the Olympian had just knocked on her door.

Instincts took over. Melanie's Glock 22 semiautomatic revolver magically appeared in her hand. The Olympian was clearly a thrill-seeking sociopath. Why wouldn't he want to see the look on her face as she read his poem? A quick glance out the window revealed nothing. A careful search of her apartment, and surrounding grounds, also proved fruitless. But the foundation had been poured. The serial killer—if it were he, or she—had made official contact. Personal safety was now at a premium. The stakes had been raised.

Melanie slid the sheet of paper and its envelope into separate paper bags. Then she reported directly to the crime laboratory at the Hoosac Mills police station. She photographed the envelope and piece of white paper and dusted them for latent prints. One set of prints was found on the white sheet of paper; they belonged to Melanie. The yellow envelope had several sets of prints, but she was already discouraged. She knew that they would ultimately be identified as postal worker prints.

By obligation she should have notified Milton Glavin immediately, but she didn't. She wanted to speak to Rocek, and she wanted to wait for Stephen. This was a delicate matter, so Melanie wanted to proceed with caution. Maybe Kenny Rocek would have a logical explanation. It most likely wouldn't be the case, but she tried to remain optimistic.

Stephen arrived sooner than expected. There wasn't any traffic and he sped the entire ride to Hoosac Mills. They met in Melanie's office. Melanie typed the poem on her computer, saved it, then sealed the papers in an evidence bag. Stephen sat behind Melanie's desk, reading her facsimile of the poem. He was quiet for a minute. Stephen couldn't believe that the murderer would actually goad Melanie. It was an insult, actually, a "catch me if you can" tease. He shook his head when he saw his own name in the poem. Who was it? Was it Jimmy or Billy? He pondered—couldn't be anyone else, could it? "Do you find this a threat?" Melanie thought about it, rereading the verse, *Though your efforts may die in vain.* Was the perp really writing about her effort, or was it a death threat?

"No. I think it is what he says it is—a caveat of things to come. Stephen, it's 1999. This psycho is due to kill, and we both know he means it," Melanie said.

"Just pissa," Stephen said. He paused. "Well…let's get the inevitable over with. It's Kenny time."

Melanie disregarded the doorbell and rapped on Rocek's door. She hit the door hard, harder than Stephen would have expected. It was an emotional knock. Kenny was her mentor; she didn't want to question his integrity and professionalism. He answered the door after twenty seconds with a mixed drink in hand. He smiled at Melanie and barely glanced at Stephen. He reeked of booze. "Come in, dear," he said with a bit of a slur.

He led them into the parlor and disappeared. Rocek came out with two bottles of beer and a glass for Melanie. He poured Melanie's beer for her and tossed Stephen a bottle. Drunks enjoy company. They took a seat at Rocek's insistence.

Rocek had distinguished himself during his police career, more than thirty-five years of public service. Certificates and plaques hung from the walls—everyday reminders. Rocek wasn't stupid; he knew this was a business call, not a personal one. "What can I do for you kids?" He asked the question out of formality. Police intuition already told him why they sat in his living room.

Stephen felt Melanie's nervousness. He remained quiet. Rocek had been her teacher, so he would let her handle everything. Finally, Melanie stated flatly, "Kenny, you put Wite-Out on some of Laiken's medical records. The girl had an abortion two weeks before her death, and you covered up that fact. I already spoke with Dr. Wehter, Laiken's family physician, so I know it's true. Why, Kenny, why?"

The old detective denied nothing. In fact, he said nothing. Instead, he stood and walked to the large double-hung window. He stared into the night. His house was set high—on the opposite side of the city from Barnes—but he too could view the breadth of the small city.

"Times have changed, Melanie," he said after a thirty-second pause. "This city ain't what it once was. All the damn mills have closed. People have up and moved, and all the real men seem to have disappeared." He went quiet for a moment. Melanie and Stephen were silent as the old man ruminated. "You work your ass off for years…breaking up domestics, slapping the shit out of punks selling drugs, helping out the elderly, and giving your heart and soul to the community. And what do you get for it in return?" The question was rhetorical. "I'll tell you what you get. You get a gold badge and a retirement party down the Vets club, and then they tell you not to let the door hit you in the ass."

"You fall in love with the department, but the department doesn't love you back," Stephen said.

Rocek considered Stephen. Maybe the young man did understand the nature of this business after all. "Yeah kid," Rocek said. "It's something like that."

Again there was silence. Stephen thought about some of the men who had retired from the Boston House during his tenure. He weighed Rocek's words, knowing that truer words were never spoken. Melanie said, "Kenny, about Laiken and the abortion?" He turned to her, nodding. He pointed to a large photo album and motioned her to pick it up. Both Stephen and Melanie flipped through old police photographs and articles until Rocek stopped them at an old newspaper article, dated September 6, 1976. They read the article slowly, then reread it. Everything became clearer. Stephen almost swallowed his tongue when he was finished reading. It had taken a few weeks, but now things were making sense.

Officer killed responding to domestic disturbance

By Robert Sullivan—Reporter

A veteran police officer of the Hoosac Mills Police Department was shot and killed yesterday morning after reporting to an alleged domestic dispute on Pinehurst Avenue.

Police Chief Robert P. Umbrowski confirmed yesterday afternoon that patrolman James F. Spillane, 31, was pronounced dead at 11:17 a.m. at Taconic Hospital, due to gunshot wounds sustained to the chest.

Hoosac Mills police have arrested a suspect in the fatal shooting, Thomas R. McDevitt, 32, of Hoosac Mills. He is being held without bail at an undisclosed location.

According to reports from neighbors, a loud verbal disturbance began yesterday at approximately 9:30 a.m. at the two-family residence at 55 Pinehurst Ave. Police records confirmed an anonymous call that reported a "husband and wife dispute." Patrolman Spillane was dispatched to the scene at approximately 9:40 a.m. One neighbor, who would only identify himself as John, said, "Domestic fighting is common in that house," and, "It's a shame that the officer had to lose his life for such a senseless reason."

Police have not yet formally charged McDevitt, who has only minor previous infractions with the law. Chief Umbrowski confirmed that a revolver believed to be the murder weapon was recovered at the scene. The gun is being sent to the Massachusetts State Police Crime Lab in Boston for ballistics testing.

Michael Timberlake, spokesman for the Berkshire County District Attorney's Office, said, "We will diligently oversee the investigation of this case. No rock will remain unturned." Upon further questioning, Timberlake declined, noting the "severity and sensitivity of the case."

McDevitt's wife, Charlene, 27, was in the home at the time of the shooting. She was questioned yesterday by Hoosac Mills police, and it is unclear whether she is considered a suspect. No charges have been filed against her at this time. Hoosac Mills police are not officially commenting on the case, but an inside source said, "It should be an open and shut case against McDevitt (Thomas)."

Officer Spillane is the first Hoosac Mills officer to be killed in the line of duty since July 1, 1955, when Sergeant Peter L. Michelangelo was fatally shot while attempting to halt a bank robbery in progress on Main Street.

Chief Umbrowski summed up the somber mood at the Hoosac Mills police station. "This is a sad day for law enforcement. Jimmy was a great kid, and he will be missed by all. May God bless his wife and children."

Officer Spillane, at age 20, became the youngest recruit in the history of the HMPD when he joined the force in 1965. He was the recipient of two Gold Star awards, given to officers who demonstrate acts of bravery.

Officer Spillane leaves his wife, Rebecca T. (Petrilli) of Weymouth, and four young children ages four to eleven. Funeral plans are pending.

* * *

Stephen and Melanie were in shock. It was the last paragraph that forced Stephen's mouth agape. Rebecca Petrilli of Weymouth was the wife of Officer James Spillane. Rebecca Petrilli was, more importantly, the mother of Jimmy Petrilli.

Melanie recalled war stories that she'd heard from the veteran officers about the heroics of Jimmy Spillane, the brazen officer who was felled in the line duty. She'd passed by his bronze plaque many times, a silhouette memorial affixed to the exterior wall of the police station. The two were quiet and Rocek spoke. "Kid's father was a hell of a cop," Rocek said with affection. "Had balls. Two kids were giving me a rough time down the tracks years ago, giving me a beating. They were shitfaced, and one of them pulled out a blade. Would have used it, too." He stalled for effect. "Jimmy responded to my call for assistance…aced one of them. Clean shoot. Those punks would have done me if he hadn't showed. Kid had balls the way a cop is supposed to have balls. He had heart."

"Hoosac Mills and Weymouth are on polar ends of the state, Kenny. What's the connection with Jimmy Sr. and Rebecca?" Melanie asked.

Rocek explained the background information, and did so fluidly without any traces of slurred speech. Jimmy Spillane and Rebecca Petrilli had both grown up in Weymouth. Jimmy's boyhood dream was to become a police officer. He took the civil service examination after high school, and the only city across the Commonwealth that would hire him was Hoosac Mills. He and Rebecca were newly married high school sweethearts, and they packed up and moved to Hoosac Mills for a new life.

The young couple wasted no time making a big family. They were establishing themselves in Hoosac Mills. Young Jimmy was a rising star in Hoosac Mills, loved by the townsfolk and his fellow officers. He worked long hours, though, and the time away from his family created marital problems, serious marital problems. "I broke that kid in, damn it, and I warned him about the fooling around, I warned him."

The two hung on to each of Rocek's words, anticipating his next sentence. "But he didn't listen. He started screwing around with that little tramp, Charlene." Rocek's eyes were glazed, and it now appeared as if it were he who stared into the abyss.

"So what happened?" Melanie asked.

"Becky Spillane found out about it, of course. She packed up the kids and moved back to Weymouth, to her mother's house. She filed for divorce and took back her own name just to piss Jimmy off."

"And?" Stephen baited.

"And Jimmy continued to screw around with the home-wrecker Charlene, the bitch who was married herself. This was going on for a while, and naturally Charlene's husband, Tommy—another loser—finds out about it.

"So Tommy starts whacking Charlene around one morning and a neighbor calls it in. Jimmy happens to be on duty so he responds." Rocek stopped for a minute; it was obvious that the next part of the story was difficult for him. "Jimmy wasn't ten feet through the door when McDevitt lit him up—fuckin' aced Jimmy before he could even break leather." Stephen and Melanie unconsciously bowed their heads. "The papers said he died two hours after the shooting—bullshit. I was on scene ten minutes later and he was as dead as a doornail."

The connection had been made. Rocek had nothing else to hide. Jimmy Jr. had been shamed by his father's exploits. He resented his father for delving into the waters of infidelity and letting another woman break up his family. It was a disgrace for young Jimmy, a disgrace so deep that it resulted in him, along with his younger siblings, changing his name to Petrilli.

It was not the city of Hoosac Mills he resented, though. He had grown up there, spending his first eleven years in the valley. He actually had an affinity for Hoosac Mills, and still loved his dad's former partner and friend, Uncle Kenny.

He had eagerly returned to Hoosac Mills for college, but intentionally shielded his past from his Metro Boston friends. As far as they knew he was simply Jimmy Petrilli from Weymouth. Why wouldn't he be? He played football and hockey for Weymouth North High School and had the varsity jackets to prove it. Besides, he even had the Boston accent, just like the other kids. Were there Hoosac Mills students—Millers—who knew of Jimmy's past? Yes, a few, but the sensitivity and facts surrounding his troubled past made it a forbidden subject. The Hoosac Mills kids were solid.

"The abortion, Kenny?" Melanie finally asked. Rocek didn't falter.

"The kid knocked her up. She had more money than Rockefeller, but she said it was his responsibility to pay for it. He was a little short at the time so he came to me. I gave him the money and a couple of weeks later she was dead."

"He had no reservations about going to you?" Stephen asked.

"He called me uncle," Rocek answered. "He had demons with his old man, not with me. I always looked out for him while he was up here. Why the hell you think, Nicholson, that half of your frat wasn't locked up every weekend you were raising hell? It was because of Jimmy, and you morons didn't even know it."

It was now Melanie's turn to ask the inevitable. "Did Jimmy murder Laiken?"

Rocek smirked, an evil smirk. He got up and went to the kitchen, returning with a fresh mixed drink and two more bottles of beer. He sat down and looked at Melanie.

"Don't know, I never pursued him. I convinced myself he didn't do it, that's all." The two simply stared at the retired detective. Rocek had seemingly aged in the last couple of months, as if he'd known tht this day was coming. "He was my partner's son…he was my partner's son."

Stephen and Melanie rose from their chairs. The visit had been a success, though bittersweet. Stephen was heartbroken; Melanie could feel the pain in his body as he quietly walked from Rocek's house. The irony was that Stephen felt for Kenny Rocek. He understood the unwritten codes among men in blue. But Rocek had gone too far; he'd crossed the line between protecting your own and upholding the law. He'd hindered an investigation, and perhaps harbored a murderer.

Melanie turned to Rocek before closing the door. He stood in the hallway, a defeated and disgraced man. "I'm sorry, Melanie" were the only words she heard before she left.

Back in her office she sat alone in the dark, speaking softly on the telephone to another law enforcement officer. She read the poem, repeating it three times and promising to make copies. She relayed the day's events. It was a difficult phone call to make, knowing that her professional career would never be the same. But she was obligated, for she was a sworn police officer.

It was her duty.

* * *

The pizza delivery van rolled to a stop in front of the Victorian house on Putnam Street. It had been converted into three condominium units, one on each floor, with a community basement. The deliveryman approached the porch, ringing the bell to the first-floor unit. An unexpected woman came to the door. She must have been a new girlfriend. "What do you want?" she asked through the door.

"Pizza delivery for Petrilli," the man said as he looked at the box. "A large pepperoni and black olive."

"We didn't order any pizza, you must have the wrong person," she said as she called for Jimmy. The deliveryman shrugged and simply waited on the porch. Thirty seconds later Jimmy Petrilli opened the door, remaining inside the hallway. Jimmy was well built but was wearing only a pair of shorts.

"What's up, guy? We didn't order anything," he said.

"It's already paid for, mister," the deliveryman said. "I'm just delivering it to you. Your name Petrilli?" Jimmy nodded. "Look, I don't ask no questions. They pay me to drop off pizzas and subs, that's all. It don't bother me none if you don't want it. I can give it to one of my buddies."

Petrilli gave an innocent shrug. "What the hell. I suppose we'll take it, thanks."

The policeman-deliveryman was a professional. He maintained a distance of about four feet between him and Petrilli. He didn't move, and Petrilli reached out to take the pizza box. It couldn't have worked any better. When Petrilli extended his arms past the doorjamb, a handcuff was slapped on one wrist. The policeman-deliveryman, knowing his role, stepped back as one of his partners snapped on the other handcuff before Petrilli could react. The pizza box fell to the porch, and suddenly two Boston Branch FBI agents, along with two Weymouth police officers, were atop Petrilli. The four officers had been quietly waiting on the porch, inches from the "deliveryman" but unseen by Petrilli.

Petrilli fought the best he could, but to no avail. Already handcuffed, there were too many men on him. He was confused, and his new girlfriend woke the neighborhood with her shrieks and yelps. After three minutes he was placed in an unmarked sedan, ready to be transported to Western Massachusetts. A strange, well-dressed man in a suit sat next to the driver. He looked over his shoulder. "Nice to meet you, Jimmy. My name is Special Agent Glavin, I'm with the Federal Bureau of Investigation. You have the right to remain silent…"

* * *

Stephen stood on the suite balcony. He was depressed and wanted to be alone; Melanie understood. He breathed in the cool Berkshire air. There was something special, something different, about the Berkshires at night. He loved the small mountain range. It had always been popular with tourists from New York and eastern Massachusetts. He never appreciated its beauty while here at school. He was too busy playing his own nocturnal games with his Kappa Chi Omicron gang. He had missed out.

Damn you, Jimmy, he thought. How could he do something so dastardly, so wicked? Stephen would try to sleep, try his best to separate his mind from this nightmare.

But sleep would not happen. He took a beer from the refrigerator and went back onto the balcony. He didn't know that as he stood on the balcony, a retired detective also stood on his porch. The old man was shamed. He had committed an irrevocable crime, a malfeasance of duty and neglect that he couldn't live with.

He had not given his honest effort; in fact, he had initiated a conspiracy, a cover-up. The bottle of gin was at his feet. He wouldn't dress in uniform, like some of the old disgraced Marines had done. And he wouldn't further embarrass himself by answering questions from law enforcement types half his age. He had already served as judge, jury, and defendant.

Now he would assume the role of executioner.

Yes, Stephen loved the dark Berkshire night. It was beautiful, and the stars seemed to flicker brighter than in Boston. He stood at the rail, motionless. Suddenly there was a distant noise. It echoed throughout the valley of Hoosac Mills—a bang. The city was funny that way; it was burrowed beneath the mountain range and sometimes provided an acoustic musical show. Every sound, from Mother Nature to manmade, reverberated throughout the land.

But Stephen didn't pay much attention to the noise.

21.

A woman waited in the Boston House parking lot. It was 2:10 p.m. Stephen parked his Jeep and saw her walking in his direction. She looked familiar but he couldn't place her. She wore casual tan pants with a white spring jacket. Her hair was up and she wore glasses. Dried streaks of mascara covered her cheeks. Stephen finally recognized her. It was Jo-Jo LaFleur, Mickey's girlfriend—or was it ex-girlfriend? He couldn't remember. "What's wrong, Jo-Jo?" Stephen asked.

Jo-Jo straightened her posture, composed herself. "You deserve to know the whole truth about what happened to Mickey."

Stephen paused. "Climb in my Jeep."

Jo-Jo told Stephen everything. He simply nodded as she spoke. Stephen wasn't naïve; he never believed Mickey's cockamamie explanation of the shooting. Jo-Jo wasn't just relaying information. She was pleading for help. Mickey was in so deep that maybe it didn't matter. Besides, Stephen had already come to Mickey's aid—and he never learned his lesson.

Stephen didn't judge Mickey. He could have, but didn't. Instead he remembered an old photograph. It was a team picture of the Roslindale Youth Hockey Squirt All-Stars. Mickey and his brother David were on the team. Mickey's helmet was two sizes too big, and both of David's front teeth were missing. No kid wore a face mask. It was a classic photo.

"Jo-Jo," he said.

"Yes, Stephen."

"Mickey is David's best friend. I'll take care of everything. I promise."

Jo-Jo considered Stephen's tense. Shouldn't it be "*was* his best friend"? She leaned over and hugged Stephen, kissing him on the cheek. "Thank you so much. You're a handsome and beautiful man. I knew I could count on you."

Stephen squeezed Jo-Jo hard. All bets were off. It was time to play hardball.

* * *

The Boston House was a hideaway. Odd as it sounded, it was true. Stephen was glad to be out of Hoosac Mills; too much bad news had bled from there lately. Jimmy Petrilli was being held without bail at the Berkshire County House of Correction on unspecified charges. Was it murder or conspiracy to commit murder? It had to be—couldn't be anything else. The one thing he did know was that the Feds were calling the shots. Tonight he wished it all away, hoping that the problem would somehow work itself out. After all, the notion of Jimmy Petrilli being a murderer was foolish, wasn't it? But what Stephen didn't realize was that bad news tends to come in droves, and things were about to worsen.

After work Stephen and Frankie collaborated. They had to devise a logical Mickey-O'Sullivan-fix-it-plan and needed a perfect think tank location to register their thoughts.

Mister MaGoo's.

Two Bud Light bottles, joined together like Siamese twins, slid down the long, wet bar and stopped directly in front of Stephen and Frankie. It was a scene from a movie or beer commercial. They looked up at the approaching behemoth, Michael Shaughnessy. Frankie smiled. "Ain't ever a college girl shortage in Brighton, so I don't know what brings your raggedy ass to White Roxbury."

Michael returned the smile. He coolly and theatrically placed both palms on the bar, then said, "This is the year of the Red Sox, boys—I can just feel it." Stephen and Frankie responded by also placing their hands on the bar. Michael nodded.

Table talk.

Table talk was an old-school correction officer cue that the impending conversation was serious and, more importantly, off the record. The three men quickly relocated to an empty table near the dartboard. The surround sound speakers blared Guns N' Roses. No one could eavesdrop.

Michael looked at Stephen. "Why didn't you tell me about Mickey?"

It was a reasonable question. Stephen, Frankie, and Michael had all entered the prison business at the same time. Michael was a solid member of Stephen and Frankie's correctional brethren. He was also well over six feet and packed 255 pounds of muscle. In 1989, a tough Latino kid from the Bronx stopped Michael's full ascension to greatness at the Golden Gloves boxing tournament in Lowell. Michael Shaughnessy was inarguably one of the toughest human beings at the Boston House, including inmates.

They sipped their beers. Stephen hesitated. "Anyone else know?"

"Just me," Michael said. "He was at the Sports Depot in Allston the other night. Shitfaced. Bad. He told me."

Stephen nodded. "We tried to handle it on the quiet tip," he said. "I hope you understand."

Michael took another sip. He smiled, knowing he was part of a secret. "Time to play hardball, my friends."

Frankie studied the table yet raised his right index finger. He looked up. "We can end this crap tomorrow, Stephen," he said. "Talk to Eamon. He grew up with Sheriff Lindehan and he can handle it the Charlestown way—on the down low. It would work."

Everyone was silent. No one moved. Finally, Stephen said, "Leave Eamon out of this. Sheriff Lindehan needs to know nothing." Stephen looked directly at Michael. He stood, gazed around, and sat down again. Unknowingly, he cracked his neck. "Renzo's mine," he said.

"Whoa, whoa, whoa!" Frankie stammered. "Not so quickly, handsome."

Stephen remained quiet. Frankie looked at Michael, seeking a tacit sign of agreement. It didn't come. Instead, Michael extended his right arm and grasped Stephen's left bicep. He squeezed, cementing his support and friendship. "I've got your back, kid."

Frankie was incredulous. "You two aren't serious." Neither man replied; neither looked at Frankie. "Are you two for real?"

Stephen said nothing. Michael faced Frankie. "It's a neighborhood thing."

"A neighborhood thing?" Frankie asked. "You two are assholes. Renzo is one of the toughest sons of bitches at the Boston House, and you—Michael—will let Stephen get his ass kicked over some bullshit Boston Zip code game. You should be fighting this dickwad, not Stephen."

"Excuse me, Frankie?" Michael asked.

"You heard me," he said. "You Boston clowns compartmentalize everything between ethnicity and neighborhood. Are you from Southie? Are you from JP? How about Hyde Park? And heaven forbid if you're from Dorchester, what parish are you from? Boston people are the biggest jackasses I've ever known, and me—the New Yorker—I am a bigger jackass because I willingly hang around with you."

Frankie had his A-game going. He was sweating, he was fidgeting, and he was wildly entertaining. They all reached for their beers. Michael scanned both men. "Mickey opened up the other night," he said. "He spoke at length about Stephen's brother—David."

The atmosphere shifted—a seal was broken. David Nicholson's 1987 death was not a secret to Stephen's Boston House friends; instead, it simply wasn't discussed publicly. Frankie Kohan, the unimpeachable best friend of Stephen, was the one prison guy who could mention the name without fear. This was a curveball. Michael turned to Stephen. "Excuse my faux pas," he said. "I should have said, 'This is a family thing.'"

Stephen raised his beer bottle and nodded, approving of Michael's motive. He quickly rose and walked to the men's room. Frankie and Michael sat quietly, acting like a couple that was pissed at each other. Frankie rapidly peeled the Bud Light label from the bottle. Michael eyed the local feline talent. Frankie suddenly slammed the bottle on the table. A few drunkards gazed, yet only temporarily. He leaned across the table. It was almost a whisper. "My family members are either dead or have abandoned me," he said. "The Nicholsons of Meredith Street are the closest thing I got in my life, Michael, to a family of my own." His face was stoic. "Do you understand this?" Michael nodded. "If Stephen gets his ass kicked—and he will—I am gonna be the one explaining this shit to his parents, Eamon and Peachy."

"Stephen's got good feet," Michael said. "Renzo won't be expecting that."

Frankie picked up his Bud Light backup. He took a long haul. "Let's not fool ourselves," he said. "Stephen can fight, but Renzo Caesar he is not."

Stephen returned. His correctional sixth sense identified tension. "We good with this?"

"I don't like it," Frankie said. "Why not have your boy Marconi Beach bang him out—if he's got it in him."

Stephen shook his head. "Leave Anthony out of this," he said. Stephen was the only person at the Boston House who referred to Marconi

Beach by his real first name. "He already approached me, and I made it clear: no, no, no, and no."

Frankie pulled out a black ballpoint pen and scribbled on a napkin. He showed the one word to both men. It read: Lucky.

"Well, I was already thinking….." Stephen began.

"STOP!" Frankie said. Then, for the first time in an eternity, Frankie Kohan smiled. Actually, he beamed. "I've given this some careful thought; I've formulated a devious plan that will deep-six that cocksucker without jeopardizing anyone's job," he said.

Michael motioned for a toast. Soon three Bud Light bottles clanged. Someone had to utter a thought. It was Michael. "To brotherhood," he said.

* * *

At nine-thirty the following evening, inmates Renzo DiLorenzo, Shawn Blighe, and Squeaky Tubbs were still performing their work details in the gym. Renzo pushed a wide broom across the rubber floor while listening to his Walkman radio. Blighe and Squeaky swept behind the pull-out bleachers. It was effortless work, but each month it reduced the inmates' prison sentence by a few days. Michael Shaughnessy, the gymnasium officer, quietly approached Squeaky Tubbs. "All set, Squeak, you can roll out. I got your time sheet covered for a full night."

"I ain't done yet," Squeaky answered.

"Squeak," Shaughnessy said, "I said you're all set."

"No problem, Deputy Shaughnessy," Squeaky said. "I know you got my back." Squeaky headed for the door. His convict's sixth sense smelled something afoot. Why wouldn't he? He was Squeaky Tubbs, professional information collector and connoisseur of prison drama. His suspicions were soon answered. As he pushed his way out the double doors, he stole a quick glance through the gymnasium office window.

Stephen Nicholson appeared from the gymnasium office unannounced. He wore sweatpants and a tank top. In preparation he had stretched and blasted out sets of pushups and crunches. His glistening body was ripped. He walked slowly onto the rubber floor, stopping twenty-five feet from Renzo. Shaughnessy locked the door. Both inmates looked on and smiled. Stephen's sudden appearance was unexpected, but the obvious implications were welcome. The two men, by nature, were carnivores. They smelled blood.

It was show time.

Stephen couldn't believe what he was doing. His career, although turbulent at times, had never led to such a dilemma. He was partaking in the most primitive form of correctional treatment—punitive measure. Or at least he would be attempting. Stephen searched for focus, for cause. He had to fight, didn't he? Mickey O'Sullivan needed help and he was the provider, no matter how unethical the predicament. Besides, this fight wasn't just for Mickey O'Sullivan. It was for all the Mickey O'Sullivans of the world.

The task at hand—from a sheer physical sense—was burdensome. He would need a guardian angel. Perhaps David was watching over him. Stephen winced. *What were you thinking that night, little brother?*

Stephen waffled. Maybe Frankie was right; maybe Michael should take this fight. But no, it wasn't about winning or losing, he knew. It was about principle, courage, and will. What would mom and dad say? He risked losing his job. Dad always said, *Choose your battles wisely, son.*

Yes, this was a fight worth fighting. Stephen took a deep breath and cracked his neck. He crossed the imaginary line—his mind seeped more than halfway into the forest. There was no turning back. Stephen couldn't shake his father's words from his head.

Tomorrow will be the jury of the judgment you exercise today.

Stephen's thoughts were jumbled. *Fight? Don't fight? Can't walk away and maintain dignity.* No, there must be a fitting representation of neighborhood; more importantly, a representation of self. The time gaps closed.

"This gonna be a fair one?" Renzo asked Shaughnessy.

"Yep." In prison, a fair one was an off-the-record fight, be it inmate versus inmate or inmate versus officer. The rules were simple: no weapons allowed, no reports written, and no one goes to the infirmary.

Renzo dropped his broom, gleaming. "One little rich boy from White Roxbury gets into a jam and another runs to bail him out. I'll drop you like a bad habit. I'm from East Boston." Stephen grinned. Boston guys held no reservations of announcing what neighborhood they were from—unsolicited.

"Yeah, you're right," Stephen said. "It's just like *The Outsiders*, Renzo. I'm a sosh and you're a greaser. But you're no Matt Dillon."

"Nicholson, what are you babbling about? You're about as tough as a cupcake." They moved closer, slowly.

"I see they're still teaching similes and metaphors to the orangutans in the GED program," Stephen said. "You still think a synonym is something you put on toast and an antonym is a song sung by a little black bug?"

"Huh?" Renzo replied.

Stephen measured his distance carefully. "And I suppose you think a dutch oven is a stove imported from Holland."

Closer, reaching striking distance.

"Nicholson, what the fuck are you talking..."

Stephen had a quick first step. He advanced, snapping a left back fist that landed on the bridge of Renzo's nose. A combination right-hand punch whizzed by Renzo's jaw, missing by inches. Renzo was stunned. He stepped back several feet. Blood flowed from Renzo's nostrils. In Hollywood fashion, he wiped the blood from his nose—then tasted it. He faced Stephen and smiled. Renzo was Stephen's height but weighed 230—truly a force to be reckoned with. Stephen pursued him, kicking Renzo in the knee with a forceful front kick. This time Renzo's leg failed him. He went to the floor, landing on his butt. Renzo's knee swelled. "Get up, pussy!" Stephen shouted, growing with confidence.

Renzo hobbled to his feet, injured. His mobility now impaired, Renzo would have to be careful. Stephen maintained the momentum, coming in with a left-right combination. The left jab landed on Renzo's eye, but the straight right was parry-blocked. Renzo countered with a left hook to the body and, thankfully for Stephen, just missed a right uppercut to the chin.

Renzo hit with power, forcing Stephen to back off. Stephen's right side would ache in the morning. Neither man could hear the cheers or admonitions coming from their respective corner men, Michael Shaughnessy and Shawn Blighe.

They squared off. With unexpected quickness Stephen snapped a front leg roundhouse kick over Renzo's hands, striking the top of his head. Blood sprayed from Renzo's nose as it was jolted to the side. Stephen's move was risky, but it worked. Renzo backed off, dazed, off balance, and, truthfully, surprised at Stephen's ability. Stephen didn't squander his opportunity; he shifted his stance and gracefully leapt, landing a hopping sidekick into Renzo's midriff. Cracking ribs echoed in the gymnasium. The Caesar was visibly hurt but stayed upright.

Stephen then made a costly mistake, breaking a cardinal rule of pugilism. He came with a lead right—a virtual no-no in the circuits of boxing or even competitive street fighting. This time Renzo anticipated Stephen's punch and reacted appropriately. He leaned left, evading Stephen's right hand, and instantaneously countered with a left hook that landed flush on the face. It was similar to the punch Tommy Morrison hit Donovan Ruddock with. It produced a similar effect. Stephen's knees denied him. He fell on his back.

Stephen squirmed on the floor and Shaughnessy came to him. It was a devastating punch. Now Stephen knew that Renzo DiLorenzo's reputation was warranted. Stephen looked into his friend's face. The gymnasium lights shined—bright, blinding, irritating. Slowly his mind became lucid and within a minute Shaughnessy had Stephen on his feet.

Renzo was hunched over near the bleachers, hands clutching his midsection. Blighe supported him. It appeared Renzo was coughing up blood. It could be internal bleeding—not a good sign. Shaughnessy approached the inmates as Stephen swayed on his feet, punch-drunk. He spoke softly. "That's it Renzo, no more. You leave Mickey O'Sullivan alone or every night you'll have to fight one of us, and I ain't shitting you. That goes for you too, Blighe." Renzo's breathing was labored but he paid attention to Shaughnessy. "I mean it. The only way to make us disappear is to go to IPS, that's it. But seeing that you're running a drug gambit and seeing that you're known stand-up guys… that won't happen, will it?" They were quiet, and finally Renzo nodded.

"Do we understand each other? You leave Mickey alone, we leave you alone. Capiche?" The inmates looked at each other.

"Deal," Renzo said.

"Good. Now, you two go back to your unit." Shaughnessy unlocked the door and the inmates left. He returned to Stephen, holding him upright. His friend was dazed.

Michael Shaughnessy couldn't help but laugh. Stephen had fought well. Drool hung from Stephen's mouth and he could barely respond to questions. It was a non-sanctioned bout, though, so no doctors stood by at ringside. Shaughnessy would have to care for him now. He looked at the sink in the open staff bathroom. It would be a start.

* * *

Stephen sat in the dark on his couch. Shaughnessy had driven him home, thankfully. He never would have made it alone. Stephen alternated an icepack and bottle of Budweiser on his eye. It was swollen and looked like someone painted it black and blue. Tiny blood spots formed underneath the eye.

The room was quiet—no lights, no stereo, and no television. Stephen brooded over what just happened. His mind was a blur. Condensation from the beer bottle dripped through his fingers. He paid it no attention; in fact, he didn't remember getting the beer from the refrigerator. He couldn't account for the three empties on the table, either.

Emotions took over. He was angry with Mickey O'Sullivan; he was angry with the manipulative inmates; he was angry at the system, a system no man could beat. The knockout punch didn't bother him. He'd lost fights before, and besides, he traded blows pretty well with the prison tough guy.

Stephen had earned his red badge of courage.

He and Michael Shaughnessy were confident that Mickey was now absolved from the edict of Renzo DiLorenzo. Stephen panned his living room wall, his eyes stopping on the monthly calendar. He checked his beeper, confirming the date. He stared at the calendar, closing his eyes and trying to wish the date away. He opened his eyes, yet the date wouldn't change. Actually, the date couldn't change.

The shades were up and the moonlight—uninvited—crept inside. He began hyperventilating; it took five minutes to calm down. He picked up the phone and dialed. After four rings a tired voice answered, "Hello."

Stephen was silent, knowing what to say but unable to express it. The raspy voice repeated his greeting, twice. Finally Stephen said, "He was just sixteen, buddy, sixteen. A damn kid, that's all."

The tired voice was confused but recognized the caller. "Stephen, what's the matter?"

"Ain't nothing wrong with me, brother, I'm just kicking back doing my bid, that's all."

Matthew Nicholson was concerned. There was emptiness in his brother's voice and he spoke in prison jargon. "Talk to me, Stephen, what's wrong, buddy?"

Again Stephen was quiet, and the silence was biting. After decided thought he spoke. "Mofos rape, pillage, and burn down the village and get sent away for what—a year, eighteen months, a deuce? Our boy does nothing wrong and he's pushing up daisies at sixteen. It ain't fuckin' right, know what I'm saying?"

There was an abbreviated silence before Matthew spoke. "Stephen…Stephen, are you there, buddy?" It was no use; the phone line went dead.

Stephen grabbed his jacket, leaving the beer and ice. He walked briskly down Washington Street toward Roslindale. The wind was nonexistent but the April air must have dropped the temperature fifteen degrees in the last hour. It was cold. Taxis and passenger vehicles whizzed past him. A Boston police cruiser slowed and took a perfunctory look at Stephen, a late-night stroller. Stephen kept his head down and walked faster. At LaGrange Street he made a left. After a small rise nearing Bellevue Hill, the street made a slow, winding crawl toward Billings Field and Centre Street. It was sleep time for most; only doorway lights shone from the pristine colonials. Residents in these homes, an even mix of white and blue collars, nestled in their beds and dreamt about the future.

Stephen increased his pace, fixated on the past.

His destination was almost two miles away. He crossed Centre and continued on LaGrange. Ten minutes later he crossed the VFW Parkway and made a left. Nerves took over. He soon found himself jumping an old stone wall that was rife with cement fragments. He was at Saint Joseph's, a place he didn't frequent. It was one of the biggest cemeteries in Boston, but Stephen never came alone. He went only on special days, and even then he was always in the safe company of family. Not tonight. Tonight's visit was long overdue. He had to go alone.

Stephen was deliberate in step, carefully walking down the grass lanes separating the headstones. He made every effort to remain unobtrusive in such a sacred place. In three minutes he found his little brother's plot. He looked down at the stone and saw the wrapped flowers. It was April 15—David Nicholson's birthday.

Peachy and Eamon were regular visitors. Finding fresh flowers was no surprise. He looked down at his little brother, not knowing what to say. Suddenly he was stricken with guilt for coming at such a late time. But David wouldn't mind, would he? Of course not. Stephen was his big brother, and he loved him.

Young David had been driving a car he shouldn't have been in, and Stephen had forever punished himself for not stopping him. The guilt had been long-standing among the Nicholson boys, but Stephen had absorbed the lion's share of the blame.

And Barnes had reminded him of that guilt.

Stephen considered William Jonathan Barnes—millionaire on the hill, overlooking his lowly Hoosac Mills subjects who should be grateful for employment. He controlled the mayor, the city council, the school committee, and even the council on aging. Barnes was the man, puller of the purse strings. Barnes decided who worked and who didn't, and did so with little interference. After all, he was William Jonathan Barnes: entrepreneur, philanthropist, and patrician.

Fuck you, King Billy, you officious bastard.

The Brits are known for their candor. At times such matter-of-factness wades into delicate areas, even broaching the sobriety of death. But the rules in America are different, especially in the Catholic community. The times for mourning are clearly delineated: funerals and the traditional waking hours of two to four and seven to nine. Or maybe from four to eight. It is then—and only then—that the unspoken moratorium permits grown men to cry in public. After that window men are expected to be stoical; that's just how it is. Any questionable remark about a family member's dead relative outside of those time lines is an egregious violation of tact.

Barnes was candid when he evaluated Stephen's healing process. The accuracy of his opinion wasn't important. It was the unsolicited manner that mattered. Barnes was injudicious in making such remarks. Stephen weighed Barnes' assessment. The rich man had spoken out of school. Stephen would neither forgive nor forget.

What about your past, Mr. Barnes? Stephen thought. What sordid secrets lie with you? How deep is the river from which your guilt flows? Why did you wait so long to find peace with your daughter's death? Did you do something with Laiken you shouldn't have done, Mr. Barnes? Was that it? Why was Laiken such a wild child, a loose cannon you permitted to attend lowly State, and not the prestigious Williams College? Did she blackmail you? How big are your demons? Were there any private investigators making judgments on how you handled your daughter's death? Was it your fault Laiken died, Mr. Barnes?

Stephen snapped his head back, erasing William Jonathan Barnes from his mind—and feeling shame. He shouldn't have thought such vindictive thoughts. Peachy and Eamon raised him better than that. No, he could no longer hypothesize the reasoning of a wealthy, childless widower; it wasn't his place to do so. Instead he looked down at his brother, reflecting.

The steering wheel had killed David. No seatbelt. Stephen would give anything to turn back the hands of time. He could have stopped him. But H.G. Wells didn't really invent a time machine, did he? It was only fiction. Reality was reality. David was dead—had been dead. Stephen stared at the inscription on the stone. David was just sixteen years old when he died; he was sixteen forever. There was no senior prom, no high school graduation, no college, no career, no wife, and no refrigerator pasted with indecipherable drawings addressed to Daddy.

Stephen closed his eyes again and drifted back through time, to the late 1980s. He remembered the funeral—the going away celebration, as it was often called. Father O'Connell was the priest. He too was a griever; David was once an altar boy. The church was packed on that Friday morning. There wasn't a dry eye in the house, save Stephen. He remembered it vividly. A well-known Catholic hymn penetrated his body, a hymn he'd never forget.

YOU SHALL CROSS THE BARREN DESERT, BUT YOU SHALL NOT DIE OF THIRST
YOU SHALL WANDER FAR IN SAFETY, THOUGH YOU DO NOT KNOW THE WAY

Time slowed. He looked over his shoulder at the outgoing sophomore class of Catholic Memorial High School. They wept loudly for David, one of their own. After all, he was a great kid—charming, athletic, and popular. These wonderful kids had formed a queue outside Gormley Funeral Parlor on both nights of David's wake. Their accolades, delivered individually, were sincere and touched the hearts of the Nicholson family. They would never be forgotten.

The organist leaned on the keys with precision; the attending congregation empathetically mourned the loss of such a young and beautiful boy. The female soloist pierced the mourners.

YOU SHALL SPEAK YOUR WORDS IN FOREIGN LANDS,
AND ALL WILL UNDERSTAND
YOU SHALL SEE THE FACE OF GOD AND LIVE!

His eyes drifted. Peachy's head lolled on Eamon's shoulder and Matthew wept in his hands. Stephen remained frozen, on autopilot. The whole thing was so bizarre—so surreal. A familiar odor and clucking noise made its way around the casket. It was Father O'Connell, swinging the incense boat like a pendulum. Soon his brother was pushed down the aisle. The anonymous pallbearers were crying, but why? They didn't know David. The hymn ran amok, and wouldn't let go.

Father O'Connell gave the final prayers on the very spot where Stephen now stood. The casket was draped with flowers. Each family member, in Irish-Catholic tradition, removed a rose from the casket. With this act a piece of David remained with them forever. Stephen never took a rose.

BE NOT AFRAID, I GO BEFORE YOU ALWAYS
COME FOLLOW ME
AND I WILL GIVE YOU REST!

Stephen awoke from his fugue.

He looked around. It took him a moment to remember where he was and why he was there. His eye now ached. Stephen wiped his face; traces of blood smudged his palm. He looked down at David and smiled. He leaned over and kissed the headstone. "Happy birthday, little brother," he said.

Suddenly a strong hand gripped Stephen's left shoulder. He turned and looked into the eyes of Matthew Nicholson. There was silence for half a minute. Matthew could see the condition of Stephen's face. Finally, Matthew said, "A drunk driver killed him, Stephen. Do you understand this?"

Stephen stared at Matthew but said nothing. "You know that he idolized you, don't you?" Matthew asked.

Stephen continued to stare.

"It's true, Stephen, and you know it," Matthew said. "I may have been the oldest, but the reality was that David always sought your friendship... your approval."

Stephen nodded. He acknowledged Matthew's assessment.

"Stephen...he loved you the world," Matthew said.

Stephen dropped his head. The flood gates opened. Matthew faced his brother and braced him with both hands. After two minutes, Matthew quietly and effortlessly led Stephen away.

The sky was clear, but what could have been a puddle of saline water saturated the ground in front of David's gravestone. It had been a dry dozen years, but Stephen Nicholson's drought was finally over.

The rain fell.

22.

Pittsfield is the largest city in Berkshire County. It lay south of Hoosac Mills, a five-minute drive to New York. A blue-collar city like Hoosac Mills, it boasts a mixed bag of racial and ethnic groups. Home to almost fifty thousand people, it's a metropolis by western Mass standards. Stephen drove his Jeep by Silver Lake and found Second Street, home to the Berkshire County House of Correction.

Melanie had called him earlier with troublesome news. It was a difficult phone call and she stopped several times to cry. Stephen consoled her; he understood the relationship between her and Kenny Rocek, and it was only natural that news of his suicide would be troublesome. The last meeting with Rocek had changed Stephen's feelings about him, though it shouldn't have. Rocek had failed to do his job, and he'd ostensibly concealed the culpability of Jimmy Petrilli.

But that was a different issue. Surprisingly, Stephen had found himself commiserating with Rocek when he sounded off on the inequities and lack of appreciation of his job. Stephen was a correction officer—a prison guard—so he felt Rocek's pain. But Rocek was dead, and Melanie and he were compelled to move on and solve the murder of Laiken Barnes, a murder that Kenny Rocek had neglected.

Stephen entered the prison and reported directly to the visitor registration window. The Boston House was a larger facility, but the logistics and procedures for daily operations were much the same. Stephen had called ahead, advising the correctional staff of his impending visit. Sergeant Holmes greeted him. He was friendly and professional, recording information from Stephen's driver's license, private investigator's license, and deputy sheriff's identification card. Prisons were naturally security-conscious facilities, so Stephen wasn't fazed by the twenty-minute sign-in time.

"Do you have a weapon, Mr. Nicholson?" Sgt. Holmes asked.

"No, sir."

Sgt. Holmes extended Stephen a professional courtesy and personally escorted him to a special accommodation. He led him to a ten-by-ten office, an area usually reserved for lawyer meetings. Stephen was a correction officer, so if any inmates recognized him they would think Jimmy Petrilli was an informant.

Snitches didn't lead healthy lifestyles in prison.

An officer led Jimmy Petrilli into the room. He was bound in leg irons and waist chains, which restricted him from moving his hands above the waist. Stephen was allowed to bring in two cans of soda, and the officer placed a soft drink in front of Petrilli.

"What the fuck do you want?" Petrilli asked.

"Pound sand, Jimmy," Stephen said. "You knocked up Laiken. You plan on sitting there, judging me, and act like that didn't happen? Like that's some piece of inconsequential and circumstantial evidence we're supposed to overlook?" Jimmy was quiet. The two men simply stared at one another.

Finally Jimmy spoke. "Those pricks bundled me on my own porch like I was some kind of pig. They pounded the shit out of me and threw me into an unmarked car like I was a mobster." He too had a black eye and scratches on his face. Jimmy was enraged—veins bulged in his forehead. "If I wasn't chained, Stephen, I'd kick your ass right now, but by the looks of you someone else beat me to the punch." Jimmy's voice rose when he spoke, so the Berkshire County C.O. walked to the window of the room. Stephen waved him off.

"Kenny Rocek ate his gun the other night," Stephen said.

"Fuck Rocek," Jimmy said. "Tell me something I don't know."

"Okay. I have a gut feeling that the FBI is gonna get a court order mandating you to submit a DNA sample." Again Jimmy simply looked at his fraternity brother, not offering a response. "If you're innocent, Jimmy, why not voluntarily submit it?"

"Because my lawyer told me not to. I have a can't-miss lawsuit against a lot of people. Including you."

"Bullshit."

"Bullshit my ass, Stephen. You'll see."

"If you didn't kill her, your DNA will clear you. Don't you get it—or do you have something to hide? But seeing that you knocked her up, I guess the answer is yes."

"I can't!"

"My ass you can't! You can, so kick it in and get yourself out of this jam. This ain't 1930, Jimmy. DNA is the real deal. Unless you have some unknown twin brother who killed her, your DNA will save your ass."

"I didn't kill anyone, Stephen!" Both men's emotions were high and they were sweating.

"You impregnated her, Jimmy. Melanie spoke with Laiken's primary the other day and went to the abortion clinic for verification. We also had a talk with Rocek before he offed himself."

"What'd he tell you?"

"I know that your first two years of Little League were played in Hoosac Mills."

Silence.

"So now you know," Jimmy acquiesced. "But I still didn't kill anyone."

Stephen stood and paced the small room before sitting back down. He spoke softly. "I'd love to think in my heart of hearts you didn't kill Laiken. That's why I'm here. But it isn't looking that way, is it?"

The yelling had ceased and Jimmy leaned back in his chair. He looked at Stephen and shook his head. Stephen Nicholson—his fraternity little brother turned private eye. There was a sick irony that brought a smile to Jimmy's face, but the smile was not one of joy.

Jimmy rolled the dice.

"I had sex with her on the day she was murdered," he said. Stephen nearly fell over.

"Are you shitting me?"

"No. But I didn't kill her, I swear. And I've been trying to tell you, I don't know anything about those broads from Amherst or Wellfleet, either."

"Do you have alibis for those dates in 1991 and 1995?" Stephen asked.

"I think so. That's what my lawyer is doing right now. Laiken and I screwed around on the afternoon of the Green Machine Party, but then we got into a fight. I'm afraid my DNA is on her, Stephen, and that's why I don't want to submit anything."

Stephen hedged. "They found more than one person's DNA on Laiken's clothing, but you didn't hear that from me." The mood shifted 180 degrees; Jimmy nodded in appreciation.

"Thanks," he answered with sincerity. "But my lawyer already knows that." They opened their soda cans and drank.

"So if you had nothing to do with Amherst or Wellfleet, give them your DNA."

Jimmy's wry smile broke into a condescending laugh. "You make it sound so simple. If I test positive for Barnes, they'll fry me for her and act like the other two weren't connected, and you know that. These cocksuckers don't play fair. I'll let my lawyer handle it because he knows what he's doing." A surge of guilt overwhelmed Stephen because he knew it was true. "Now, you better get the hell out of here before you get yourself into trouble. As a matter of fact, does that Milton Glavin guy know you're here?"

Stephen shook his head. Jimmy's DNA theory made sense so Stephen didn't rebut. They looked at each other for another moment but didn't speak. Stephen thought about the poem sent to Melanie but said nothing. The visit was over.

The C.O. on duty led Jimmy back to his cell. As soon as the visiting room cleared, a member of the Berkshire County Internal Affairs Division entered. His orders were short and sweet, and within one minute he was done. It was now an intense hunt for a serial killer, and the rules were being bent.

* * *

Josef Kieler sat with Stephen, eating dinner and reminiscing. The men shared pitchers of beer. One led to two, and two to three. It neared nine o'clock and they were both well on their way to needing aspirin in the morning. Josef developed a slight slur. "You really liked Laiken, didn't you, Stephen?" The tone was almost accusatory.

"What do you mean?"

Josef shrugged. "I don't know, it's just my gut feeling," he said. "I think you liked her more than you're saying."

Stephen smiled. "Here's to friends, Josef, here's to friends."

Josef raised his beer mug. Stephen raised his and the glasses touched.

The party was broken up suddenly. Milton Glavin, Devon Patterson, and Melanie Leary pulled chairs up to the table. Stephen looked at Melanie but she wouldn't make eye contact. "No, by all means fellas, don't be shy. Pull up a chair and join us. Can I offer you a beer?" Stephen asked sarcastically. Devon Patterson sighed.

"Pardon the intrusion," Milton said with genuine respect. "I'm Milton Glavin and this is Devon Patterson. I'm a special agent with the FBI and Mr. Patterson is a retired SAC with The Bureau. He's now working as a paid consultant. You obviously know Detective Leary." Stephen smiled at Melanie but she still wouldn't look at him.

"Pleasure to meet you guys. I'm Stephen Nicholson and this is my friend," he said theatrically. He had a few beers in him and everyone knew it. "This is my old boss, Josef Kieler. I used to work for him during my tenure at State." Milton and Devon gave Josef a nod.

"Stephen, you were advised to stay on the periphery of this case and not to interfere with our official investigation," Milton said.

"And?"

"And I'm afraid you violated that deal." Stephen surveyed Glavin. If first impressions meant anything, he didn't seem to be a pompous ass like the older guy. He spoke respectfully. "You visited James Petrilli today at the Berkshire County House of Correction. You should have at least conferred with Melanie before doing so." Stephen stared them down; there was tension at the table.

"What happened to your eye, Nicholson? Was it a bar fight with one of your guard friends?" Devon Patterson asked.

"No, *Devon*," Stephen replied. "I head-butted the fist of a guy who was fucking with one of my boys. But you wouldn't know anything about that type of thing, would you, *Devon*?"

Patterson was a true professional, but he was arrogant, having an ego to defend. "I've seen more in two months than you've seen in a lifetime, young man." Patterson was quiet for a moment, and he looked around the table. By rights, Glavin and Patterson should have asked Josef to leave, but they didn't. He listened intently. Melanie was unusually quiet, and Stephen was suspicious.

"We want you off the case," Devon said. "You're an impediment—too risky."

Stephen laughed, knowing now why Melanie wouldn't look at him. "You've absolutely got to be shitting me," Stephen said. "I don't work for you bozos, I work as a private investigator for a client. You can't dictate shit to me if I don't break the law; that's a fact and you two know it. Melanie...are you serious?" It wasn't her fault, Stephen knew, but he was angered. She was guilty by association and finally gave him a sheepish look. Patterson made a sour face before replying.

"Let me be more direct, Mr. Nicholson, as I gather you don't respond well to subtleties or suggestions. If, in our professional opinion, your meddling compromises our investigation in any way whatsoever, the Bureau shall charge you with obstructing a federal investigation. You are hereby instructed not to interfere with our investigation."

Stephen intentionally drained his mug and refilled it. "I'm gonna do the job I was hired to do. Don't worry about me stealing your collar, gentlemen."

Patterson said, "We will report any of your inappropriate actions to the higher authorities at your sheriff's office."

"Snitch," Stephen said.

"Excuse me?" Patterson replied.

Stephen smirked and pulled out a twenty-dollar bill. He placed the bill in front of Devon Patterson. "Those bullshit charges won't hold an ounce of water and you know it." Devon Patterson sighed, his silence indicating that Stephen should continue. "First of all, I have broken no laws. Secondly, you clowns never gave me any set of instructions. And thirdly, have you jurisprudence barristers ever heard of Separation of church and state?"

"Of course," Devon responded. "What does that have to do with this case?"

Again, the buzzed Stephen smirked. "I'm a Roman Catholic, Devon. When I visited Jimmy today I exercised my religious beliefs," Stephen said. "Do the corporal works of mercy ring a bell? Glavin, you look like a nice Irish boy so I'm sure you can follow me." Everyone at the table was puzzled. "You know...thou shalt feed the hungry, clothe the poor, visit the imprisoned, et cetera. Today I was following the dogma of my church." The Feds were awestruck. No one knew if Stephen's point was valid, but it didn't matter. Stephen wasn't their target; he was only a nuisance. Patterson's eyes homed in on the twenty-dollar bill.

"What's that for?" Patterson asked.

"That's partial repayment for the lunch money shaken from your trousers during your elementary school years." Patterson's face turned sour, but even Milton Glavin and Melanie had to look away because they wanted to laugh. Milton was a bit straitlaced but he thought Stephen was a character—and had balls. Josef didn't have to conceal his laughter; it was his restaurant. Patterson pushed the bill back toward Stephen with disgust. "Seriously now, Mr. Patterson, I have a question for you," he said.

"What?"

"What did your father do for a living?" No one knew where Stephen was leading, but Melanie knew it wasn't good. Patterson wasn't impressed with Stephen so he answered the question.

"My father was a political analyst. He was a mover and a shaker, so to speak, playing an intricate role in the election of two United States presidents. He finished his career as a high-ranking member of the Internal Revenue Service. Why do you ask?"

"So it's fair to surmise that he spent the large majority of his life fucking people—so to speak. As the saying goes, Devon, the apple doesn't fall far from the tree."

Patterson rose from the table, irate. "How dare you insult the good name of Wilford Patterson."

Milton Glavin had heard enough. He rose and took Patterson by the arm. Patterson leaned in toward Stephen, inches from his face. "You listen here, Nicholson," he whispered. "You're an ant and we can squash you. We're FBI agents and basically we do what we want. One wrong move and you're all done."

Stephen raised his beer mug and winked at him. "I thought you were retired, Devon. Why don't you go swing a seven-iron? The back nine at George Wright is a bitch."

The two FBI men left the bar but Melanie stayed, staring at Stephen with a blank look. "You look like shit, Stephen. You're drunk, obnoxious, and somebody punched you out. What happened?"

"I'll tell you later. Want a mug?"

Melanie looked at Josef disapprovingly. "I'll pass on the beer, thank you," Melanie said. "There's a funeral service tomorrow at eleven for Kenny if you're interested in going; it's at Saint Brendan's. After that I'm catching a plane to South Carolina to speak with Renee Gleeson. I'll keep in touch, and I strongly suggest you do the same." She walked away from the table, only to return a moment later. "And Stephen, don't disregard the warning from Patterson, because he will sink your battleship. By the way, that was real cute how you handled him. You might consider brushing up on the interpersonal skills." She looked at the other two. "Goodbye, Josef, nice seeing you.

Both men were quiet. Finally Josef raised his mug again. "I think she's mad at us."

* * *

Breakfast hit the spot. Stephen dined at The Indian, a popular breakfast joint on Main Street. Scrambled eggs, complemented by real hash browns and marble toast, rolled down his throat. He thought about Melanie, and how his idiocy the previous night had hampered their professional relationship.

And perhaps more.

Stephen didn't want to attend the funeral services for Kenny Rocek. It just wasn't his place. Instead he decided to pursue old leads; it was only quarter to nine. He visited four addresses of Hoosac Mills men who had dated Laiken Barnes at one time or another, including P.J. McClaren. It was a wild goose chase, however, and Stephen again drew blanks. P.J. McClaren wasn't happy with the visit; in fact, he warned Stephen of physical harm. Stephen laughed. He'd just fought the prison tough guy and now everyone was out to get him: McClaren, Patterson, Glavin, and Melanie.

No, Melanie didn't belong on that list, but his mind wandered. He looked in his rearview mirror and a red Jeep Cherokee was two cars behind him. The windshield was tinted.

He had noticed the Cherokee before but never paid it any mind. Why would anyone tail him? Paranoia was a correction officer affliction. The running acronym joke at the Boston House was ACP, or Acute Correctional Paranoia.

Stephen was an ACP patient.

A familiar saying was also prevalent: "Just because I'm paranoid doesn't mean that someone's not out to get me." The mentality came with the job, and now Stephen was convinced there was a conspiracy against him. He proceeded down Main Street and hooked a right onto Railroad, and the

Cherokee followed. He abruptly pulled to the right. The Cherokee passed him, but not before he copied down the Massachusetts license plate number.

One phone call and five minutes later he knew the vehicle was registered to Hoosac Electric.

Barnes.

Hence, if it was registered to Barnes, reasonable logic dictated that Simeon was driving. It seemed surreal. Stephen just couldn't fathom the whole scenario. If Stephen was theoretically chasing the bad guy, then who was chasing him? He immediately called William Jonathan Barnes. Stephen interrupted a staff meeting in New York but didn't care. He wanted to know why his client was having him followed.

Barnes was cool in demeanor, denying nothing. "You see, Stephen, Simeon is my most trusted and fierce ally. He and Bernard are the only family I have left. He has been with me for a number of years. Should I die, he receives a substantial amount of my fortune. He means that much to me."

"You failed to answer my question, sir. Why was he following me?"

"I instructed him to oversee this investigation, but at a distance. Laiken was a special girl to Simeon, too, so he is rather intent on the progress of your investigation."

"Do you not trust me, Mr. Barnes?"

"Quite the contrary, young man. But I do suggest you spend less time in the barrooms and fighting the battles of your correctional brethren, and concentrate more on finding the slayer of my child." Stephen was shocked. He was, in fact, offended at the insinuation that he prioritized this case as secondary or tertiary. That was anything but the truth. But how did Barnes know about his fight with Renzo DiLorenzo, and more importantly, why the fight took place? Money was a powerful tool, Stephen knew, and people like Barnes sustained themselves by transferring money into power and knowledge. He seemed so mighty, so powerful—omniscient.

Barnes had flexed.

The millionaire gave words of encouragement to Stephen before hanging up, assuring him of his unequivocal support. Stephen sat in his Jeep, both vehicle and mind idling. Things were getting weird.

23.

The Heat Room was aptly named. It was the interrogation room of IPS, the Inner Perimeter Security Unit at the Boston House. IPS was synonymous with internal affairs, and any trip to IPS by inmate or staff member garnered immediate attention from the rank and file. Ironically, the Heat Room owed its moniker to faulty duct work and an imbalanced heating system. At times temperatures exceeded eighty degrees; inmates gave up information just to flee the room.

IPS had undergone a major overhaul in the last two years. Sheriff Lindehan reduced the number of IPS investigators from seven to two. Five investigators were either fired or reassigned. The sharp reduction in the investigative workforce caught the attention of some political heavyweights. Questions were asked, but Lindehan's IPS division still—though barely—met all correctional code requirements.

The small IPS unit was led by Chief Inspector Frederick Charlemagne, age sixty-four. Charlemagne—a pompous ass on everyone's scorecard—had been a security supervisor at Boston City Hall for over thirty years. He'd recently completed his fourth year at the Boston House.

The assistant chief was fifty-nine-year-old Marie Tosconaro. Marie had served as an administrative assistant in the IPS office for over twenty years. When Sheriff Lindehan dropped the hammer on his IPS staff, Marie survived the fallout. She wasn't really an investigator; mostly she witnessed interviews conducted by Charlemagne. She simply changed titles, and gained a twenty-thousand-dollars-per-year pay raise overnight. Not bad.

The primary duty of IPS was to investigate criminal matters pertaining to inmates, particularly violent assaults on each other or staff. Investigators visited crime scenes, collected evidence, interviewed witnesses or suspects, and read reports. Historically, many inmate reports led investigators on wild goose chases; savvy investigators learned to cull pertinent leads which resulted in criminal convictions. Frederick Charlemagne was a politically connected gentleman approaching a lucrative pension. He was not a savvy investigator.

Officer misconduct was typically handled at the deputy superintendent level, but there were exceptions. First and foremost, IPS was to uphold commonwealth law and department policy. Optimum results generally necessitated the vast use of informants of low moral character. It was just how the business worked.

Beads of sweat fell from Squeaky Tubbs' face as he sat before Frederick Charlemagne. He was a short, black, portly repeat offender from Mission Hill. Squeaky rarely drank and never did drugs. He was thirty-two and serving his sixth county bid. All his convictions were for uttering—that is, forgery and processing stolen credit cards and checks. No one knew his real first name. No one cared. Inmates and C.O.'s called him Squeaky. Cops called him the Fraudulator. Squeaky was a regular contributor of information in the IPS office. Lately his popularity rating had plummeted. A false tip of a prison clergyman lugging drugs turned into a political nightmare for the right-wing sheriff. It nearly cost him reelection.

Charlemagne stared contemptuously at Squeaky. "This better be good."

"Come on, Charlemagne, you know I'm the man who loves the game and got the goods to produce my 411," Squeaky said.

Charlemagne leaned forward. "Your hot tip about the preacher nearly cost me a demotion."

"Fuck that, Charlemagne," Squeaky said. "That dude got tipped off. He was a lugging mofo and you know it. Ain't seen him back here since though, have you, if he so innocent? Listen, man, that dude got tipped off. I'm telling you straight up, Charlemagne, that preacher was lugging. Someone tipped him."

Charlemagne waved Squeaky off. "Never mind with that. That's ancient history. What've you got?"

Squeaky had recently been given an ultimatum by his wife, strictly of the sexual nature. He had to find a way to get on the street. His wife needed love; celibacy wasn't an option anymore. Otherwise Juanita was leaving. They had no kids, which hampered his position. Squeaky grew desperate.

His information was accurate but he felt uneasy. He was ratting on a decent correction officer, not one of the Cro-Magnons who strutted into work every day wearing a wife-beater tank top. He had no choice. "It's hot, man. It's smoldering, like red hot," Squeaky said. Charlemagne was bored already. "I mean it's blistering hot. Fuck that, it's white hot. Should punch my ticket out of this rat trap, man."

"I'll be the judge of that," Charlemagne said.

"Caesar from 6-Block went to the infirmary the other morning. Said he was decline-benching four plates and the bar gave way to his chest." Squeaky paused; Charlemagne said nothing. "That ain't what happened. One of your C.O.'s booted him in the ribs like a mule."

"And you are referring to whom as Caesar?" Charlemagne asked.

"Don't dick with me Charlemagne," Squeaky said. "I'm talking about Renzo and you know it."

Charlemagne perked. "Sounds like good stuff, Squeaky. Who's the officer?"

"Same dude walking around the joint with half his face caved in."

"I asked for the name of the officer."

"White dude works 3-11," Squeaky said. "Name's Nicholson."

"Private investigator," Charlemagne noted. "How good is your information?"

Squeaky smiled and shrugged. "Come on, man. I wouldn't steer you wrong."

"What was the fight over?" Charlemagne asked.

Squeaky put his hand up. "I need to know what's in it for me, man. Got to protect my own interests. You understand, Charlemagne."

"Okay, okay," Charlemagne said. "This pans out and I'll give you the halfway house."

"Now we talkin', baby," Squeaky said. "This story is off the hook, Charlemagne."

"Let's have it."

"Caesar from 6-Block is squeezing a fat white C.O. to bring in heroin and Nicholson intervened on the kid's behalf."

Charlemagne's eyes bulged. "You better not be jerking me off, Squeaky."

"Wouldn't jerk you on something like this, man. Stakes are too high."

"And who again is the Caesar of 6-Block?"

"Now you jerking me off, man," Squeaky said. "Just told you—Renzo. You just making sure your tape recorder get it twice. You top dog of IPS, Charlemagne. Shouldn't need no check forger to tell you who the 6-Block Caesar is."

Charlemagne nodded. "Okay, okay. What's the officer's name?"

"Sullivan," Squeaky said. "No, man, I think it might be O'Sullivan—same kid who got capped in the South End. Where the hell you been, Charlemagne? Can't you figure nothing out?"

"Never mind," Charlemagne said. "How the hell is Nicholson involved in this thing? Is he part of the drug dealing?"

"No, man. This is where it gets good," Squeaky said. "Dude Nicholson is off the hook. He's some kind of white knight from White Roxbury. A real do-gooder. Knows O'Sullivan from the street and he's bailing the fat bastard's ass out. Nicholson ain't a bad C.O. But prison ain't no place for sentimental dudes. Someone ought to tell him that. Renzo the real deal, baby. He laid dude out."

Retirement loomed around the corner. Charlemagne wanted to go out with a bang. "Who's backing Renzo?"

"Aw shit, Charlemagne," Squeaky laughed, "seems you're starting to figure this place out before you turn your papers in. You know what they say…C.O.'s eat their own."

"What's that mean?"

"It means Renzo answers to a 3-11 C.O. from the South End named Lucky."

A recent phone call from state police clicked in Charlemagne's head. He slowly pieced things together. Lucky Giannessimo's indiscretions were well known to the IPS office. Knowing about corruption and proving corruption were two different things, though. "Good job, Squeaky," he said. "You'll be in the halfway house tomorrow."

24.

Melanie was teary-eyed when she returned from Saint Brendan's. The official ruling was accidental death, caused by an unintentional release of the trigger while the retired detective was cleaning his gun. The church was packed with three hundred police officers from various departments all over New England and New York. No one in attendance believed Rocek's death to be an accident. Stephen had changed his mind about attending the services. He carefully slipped out of the church as anonymously as he'd entered. Melanie never saw him.

When Melanie returned home, she discovered that an envelope containing one thousand dollars in cash had been dropped through her mail slot. A small note indicated that the money was from the William Jonathan Barnes slush fund. It was for airfare, lodging, and any other travel expense she may incur. Stephen had signed the note. Melanie smiled.

The flight to Columbia, South Carolina, departed Bradley International Airport in Hartford at four o'clock. She unwound on the ninety-minute flight with a couple of gin and tonics. No rest for the weary, and no grace period for the bereaved. Kenny Rocek had been close to her and she felt betrayed, justifiably so. He had intentionally botched a murder investigation, an egregious law enforcement sin that could never be pardoned. Why, Kenny, why? She could understand a man protecting the son of a fallen comrade, but certainly not to that extent. Cops would bend over backward to hush up officer misdemeanors.

But not felonies.

And then Kenny took the easy way out instead of facing the music.

Melanie disregarded her new material for the case file. The drinks relaxed her. Instead of hypothesizing suspects, she revisited her failed marriage. In retrospect she knew it took two people to make a relationship work. Melanie considered her role. Had she done everything in her power to keep the marriage bountiful? What the hell had Stephen said?

You ran out of wine.

Yes, perhaps Stephen was right. But fretting over failed relationships served no purpose now. The plane touched down. Within thirty minutes she sped off in a taxi; within sixty minutes she slept soundly in a hotel room. It would be a good night's sleep.

Melanie learned quickly that spring mornings could be hot down South. It was mid-April, but the thermometer bragged eighty-four degrees. With the purchase of a map, she found herself sitting in a rental car across from Renee Gleeson's split-level ranch. It was eight o'clock. An iced coffee perked her up. She needed it.

The door to the home opened and Renee kissed her husband goodbye. In typical Americana fashion, three children draped themselves over Dad's legs and waist with genuine affection. His name was Troy, a tallish and fit man, and Melanie wondered if he possessed the famous Southern hospitality she had always read about. He looked like the guy next door.

When Troy left Melanie approached the home and rang the doorbell. Renee answered quickly, holding a young girl no older than three. "Good morning, Miss, how may I help you?" she offered with a hint of a Southern accent. Renee was prettier than the dated photograph suggested, and motherhood had not taken an adverse toll on her physical appearance. Actually, she was stunning—a beautiful brunette with green eyes and a Barbie doll figure.

"Good morning, Renee," she said. "I'm Melanie Leary. I've spoken with you on the telephone a couple of times. Could I please have a few moments of your time?" Renee was quiet. "I've traveled from Hoosac Mills to speak with you in person. I think you may be able to help Laiken."

Renee wavered. She certainly wanted closure to the macabre death of her best friend, but she didn't want her involvement to compromise her quiet and peaceful life. After a short delay she said, "Come in, Melanie, please do come in. Can I offer you something to drink?"

"Ice water would be fine, thank you."

Renee brought her daughter to the kids' room with her two boys, ages seven and eight, giving specific instructions not to be disturbed. She was a loving and fair mother; she was also stern, and the boys understood her message. In a few minutes Renee reappeared in the sitting room with a tray of ice water, coffee, and banana bread. She was a hospitable host.

"I notice you don't have a Mills accent, Melanie. You're about my age, and I would definitely remember a pretty gal like you. Where are you from?" Renee asked.

"Springfield. I've been with the Hoosac Mills Police Department for a while. I was a Wilbraham officer before that. Now here I am, talking to you, trying to make sense out of what happened twelve years ago." Melanie sipped on the cold water and nibbled on banana bread. "It's my understanding that you and Laiken were pretty good friends," Melanie baited.

"Best friends," Renee corrected. "Laiken was a character, believe me. She had everything—looks, smarts, charm, sexuality. She lived on the edge; she was quite a girl." Renee was saddened by this sudden trip down memory lane. Tears welled in her eyes. "Mr. Barnes is a wonderful man, I love him. I visit him every time I go home. And her mother—what a woman she was. She would have lived longer if Laiken hadn't died, I know it."

The conversation fluctuated. Renee spoke of the wild years—the times in high school and summers between college when the days and nights rolled into one. More than once laughter stopped a story in its tracks. Laiken had certainly been Renee's best friend. It was evident.

Renee also was curious about Melanie. She asked current events questions about Hoosac Mills and what it was like to be a female police officer. Melanie flowed with the conversation. She told Renee that Kenny Rocek had committed suicide. Renee couldn't have cared less.

"He's a creep." Before Melanie could ask the question, Renee answered. "I must have called him four times right after Laiken died. He refused to speak with me. I got him on the phone once, and all he said was, 'We have some solid leads.' And that was it, he hung up on me. Nothing else, nothing." Melanie sympathized but said nothing concerning Rocek. They talked for sixty minutes. They called each other by their first names and were comfortable in conversation. In fact, a good rapport had been established. It wasn't accidental. It was police work.

Melanie changed the tone of the meeting. She locked eyes with Renee. "Will you look at something for me?"

"Of course," Renee said.

Melanie handed Renee a copy of the letter she had written Laiken one month before her death. Renee took her time, carefully reading the letter. Tears again saturated her eyes. She looked at Melanie sadly.

"Times were different then. We were party girls, hard-core party girls." She was quiet for a moment. "We were young…kids, actually. And there were no rules. If there were, Laiken and I definitely broke them." Melanie thought of her own college experience, the many nights she'd partied in Boston, occasionally having a romantic encounter with a strange boy. "And before you ask me, Melanie, the answer is yes. We did threesomes on occasion."

Melanie nodded. "Renee, there's something I need to know, something pertinent. How *close* were you and Laiken?" Melanie was a learned woman. She buttressed her intelligent word choice with a soft tone inflection and guarded body language. The insinuation had been made; Renee understood.

"Take a look at my home, Melanie." She no longer spoke with a Southern twang. She was just Renee Gleeson, and her indigenous Hoosac Mills accent resurfaced. "I have a handsome and successful husband and three beautiful children. I love them and they love me. It's a genuine love. For Christ's sake, Melanie, we even have two dogs and a cat. It doesn't get any better than this." Ironically one of the dogs came flying into the room, followed by her two sons. Renee admonished her boys and the dog, but the interruption was needed. Renee collected her thoughts.

"What I say to you right now shall not be repeated. I believe you people call it *off the record*. Agreed?" Melanie nodded. "Like I said earlier, Laiken and I were the best of friends. There's nothing we didn't share. At times we even shared each other, if you know what I mean." Melanie was quiet, intently listening. "It's not like we were girlfriend-girlfriend, that wasn't it. I can't really describe it. It was spontaneous. We were young, pretty, and foolish." Melanie sympathized with Renee; she now understood her reluctance to speak on the telephone. Renee didn't want to rehash her past. "Too bad I couldn't let dead dogs lie. Now you know." Melanie was quiet but gave an approving nod. "Melanie, when you called me on the phone and asked me if I remembered a student Laiken called Boston Boy, I skirted the issue."

"What's his real name?"

"I can't remember. It was a long time ago, but Laiken liked him a lot. She used to go with him all the time. We were kids. My memory is faulty, and sometimes I think it's intentional."

"You can't remember his name? Was it Jimmy Petrilli?" Renee shook her head.

"I know Jimmy. He used to live in the Mills when he was a little kid. Had a different last name, though. It was Spillane. You're a cop so you've heard the story about his dad getting killed. No, Boston Boy wasn't Jimmy, though I do believe Laiken had something going on with him."

"What did Laiken tell you about her abortion?"

Renee's mouth went agape. "What abortion?" she asked in all sincerity.

"You didn't know Jimmy Petrilli got Laiken pregnant? We recently confirmed it. To make a long story short, that's why Detective Rocek killed himself. He knew about the abortion and didn't act on it."

Melanie elaborated on the abortion element of the case and Renee was startled. She was upset that Laiken hadn't told her about the pregnancy. She felt a bit betrayed by Laiken for not sharing her pain, but it was too late to brood. Melanie moved on.

"How about Billy Munsing? Does that ring a bell?"

Renee ingested the name. "Now that name I know. He's a looker if I've ever seen one. I only met him a couple of times, and even then I was partying at the time. He was a Boston kid, or a Boston area kid, I know that much. That might have been the name, I'm not sure. It was back in 1986 or so, I can't remember exactly when. I do know that Laiken had hooked up with Munsing before."

Melanie made a mental note: Billy Munsing had downplayed his romantic link to Laiken Barnes. She pulled out photographs of all the Kappa Chi Omicron fraternity brothers from the academic year 1987–1988. The array of pictures included a group photograph and individual stills of certain brothers. She handed all photographs to Renee.

It was a flashback to the 1980s. The haircuts were longer and dress styles had changed dramatically. Renee slowly sifted through the old faces. After a minute she picked up a photograph. It was a small group photo of young fraternity boys, teeth white in smiles and beer cups held high for the photographer. She turned to Melanie. "Is this what you came a thousand miles for? Only for me to identify a kid that I remember as Boston Boy?"

Melanie was getting anxious and sweat clung to her clothing. "The truth," Melanie said, "is that it's the only reason why I'm here." Renee Gleeson, mother of three and New England emigrant, stared at one of the boys in the picture. She looked at Melanie.

"It's been a long time, but I'm pretty sure it's him." Melanie simply waited and Renee pointed to one of the fraternity brothers. "If it makes any difference, there's your Boston Boy."

* * *

The young fraternity brother swayed on Stephen's shoulders. They were high on the ledge, two hundred feet. The extension on the paint roller worked well, and the final Greek letter, signifying Omicron, came out in sparkling gold. The task had taken two hours but it was done.

It was tradition at Taconic State for fraternities to paint the ledge. No one knew the ledge's official name, but its high elevation served as Mother Nature's billboard for the city of Hoosac Mills. Stephen hadn't been there in ten years, and his intricate role rekindled some of his lost fraternal spirit. It also relieved stress.

Smothered in paint, Stephen parked his Jeep in The Library's parking lot. Stephen promised the younger boys some celebratory drinks, but he first headed to the nearby fraternity house to get his cell phone. When he turned the corner onto Mohawk Street he almost plowed into an elderly gentleman. "Better watch where you're going, Stephen, or you'll get somebody hurt."

Stephen looked into Johnny Malfkoski's eyes, almost too stunned to speak. Johnny was a senior citizen who lived among the students on Mohawk Street. Stephen hadn't seen him in years and, truth be told, had thought he was dead. "How have you been, Johnny? Damn good to see you!" Stephen's face was electric and he shook Johnny's hand and arm firmly.

"Been good, Stephen, been good. You still drink the Budweisers? If you do, I'm buying." Stephen was stunned. He couldn't believe that the old-timer still imbibed. Within three minutes they occupied a table at The Library, away from everyone else.

Johnny was eighty-two years old. He had spent forty-five years laboring for the railroad and had been a widower since 1984. His needs were simple and his spirits were up. He was excited to see Stephen. "Heard you were in town last month, but every time I looked for you the kids said you were back in Boston. Good to see you, son." They clanged beer bottles in a toast. "I understand you're working with the pretty gal from Springfield, eh?"

"That's correct. I see you're still plugged in to the goings-on around town, Johnny."

"You two would make a damn fine-looking couple, you know."

Stephen laughed—but quietly agreed with him. He assessed Johnny. His once tight and sinewy frame had gained a little weight, but other than that he looked much the same. Johnny was an octogenarian, but managed to go beer for beer with Stephen through four rounds. The clock read one in the morning. It was a late night for Johnny.

"Stephen, I saw the Barnes girl leave your fraternity house on the night she was murdered."

Stephen didn't overreact. In fact, his face was blank. During their conversation Stephen had mentioned little about his state of affairs in Hoosac Mills. It was understood.

"Go on, Johnny."

"She was dressed up like the cat lady. You know, Stephen, like from the old Adam West series. Damn, I used to love Burgess Meredith when he played the Penguin. What a show that was."

"No digressions, Johnny. Keep going, my friend, please." Stephen was all business.

"I'm sorry, Stephen. It happens to me all the time now. The older I get the more I forget things and the more I tend to ramble." Stephen was quiet and Johnny realized that he again was drifting from the subject. "Well, anyway, she come out of the house by herself and got into a sedan that was driven by a guy with a sickle."

"A sickle," Stephen repeated, but it wasn't a question.

"Yeah, there's a name for the outfit, but I can't remember it. It's a scary mask and the guy carries a sickle."

"The Grim Reaper," Stephen responded flatly.

"Yeah, it's the Grim Reaper. Anyway, I saw the Grim Reaper leave the party before the girl and get into his car. Then he waited for her."

"Are you sure it was Laiken?"

"Didn't know what the girl's name was, Stephen, I just know she was dressed like the cat lady. And I know it was the cat lady that got murdered that night after being at your party."

"Why didn't you say anything to Detective Rocek?"

Johnny made a face and semi-shrugged his shoulders. "He never asked me, Stephen, that's why."

Stephen sensed he was not being completely honest. "Johnny?" The waitress came by and dropped off two more beers, courtesy of two young Kappa brothers.

"William Barnes done a lot of good around here in the last ten years or so, since his girl died. Wasn't always the case, you know. People around here put him on a pedestal on account of his donating money to different charities in the Mills. Didn't donate much more than a hundred bucks till his kid died. But I remember him years before…years before his daughter died."

Johnny was an old man. He spoke from the heart—he had no agenda. "He hurt a lot of people, Stephen. Closed a wing of his plant in the Mills and moved it to New York because it would be more energy efficient and he'd make more money. Didn't have to do that and everyone knew it. Four hundred townsfolk lost their jobs, but no one ever talks about that no more. I don't forget, though."

"There's a fine line between a philanthropist and an altruist, Johnny."

"What do you mean by that?"

"Never mind. But now we have to cut through the bullshit, my friend. Why didn't you insist on telling Rocek what you saw? It was a murder, Johnny."

"Because the only thing more stubborn than an Irishman or an Italian is a Polark, that's why." They both laughed. Johnny was searching for a segue, but Stephen wouldn't give it to him. He now looked sad. It had been more than fifteen years since he'd kissed his wife, and he knew that he too was near life's end.

"I find it kinda funny that you're up here snooping around looking for the girl's killer, Stephen," Johnny said. "Like a dog chasing his tail."

"Why is that?" Stephen asked.

"Didn't you just ask me why I didn't go talk to that no-good bastard Rocek?"

"Yes."

"Because the boy in the sickle outfit, Stephen…he walked like you. He walked just like you, son. That's why I never said nothing to no one."

Stephen was speechless and Johnny spoke on. "I hear rumors, Stephen. I hear most of my stuff from you kids. That girl—she was no good. She slept around with practically every guy on campus. And her old man—well, you know what I think of him.

"But you kids were always good to me, Stephen." Tears welled in Johnny's eyes. "Especially you, Stephen, especially you. Every time the snow came or I needed something, you boys shoveled me out or ran an errand for me. I never asked you guys for nothing; you boys just took it upon yourselves to help me."

Stephen was flabbergasted. Johnny Malfkoski had seen the Olympian, fully disguised, leave the party with his prey. He was overwhelmed, and even more so by the fact that Johnny thought he was the guilty party.

And had seemingly covered for him.

"It don't matter nothing to me if you did it, Stephen. You always were a gentleman to me and I never treated you any different. You probably did everyone a service." The two men drank the remainder of their beer in silence. Johnny looked deep into Stephen's eyes, but the young man seemed to be in a daze, in a dream of sorts. Johnny shook Stephen's arm until he became conscious, awake from his fugue. "So tell me, Stephen…are you the dog chasing his own tail?"

Stephen stood. He came to the old man and put his left hand on his shoulder. He leaned down and kissed Johnny on the forehead. "You're quite a man, Johnny."

Stephen headed to the fraternity house. He sat in the attic and flipped through old albums and yearbooks for the year 1987–88. Quickly he found photographs taken at the October Green Machine, the costume party. He found two interesting photographs. The first was of two young men, masks in place, crossing their sickles for the fraternity chaplain/historian. It was a good photograph. The second photograph was more telling. In the back row was Stephen's blood brother—the visiting Matthew—sporting a bare chest and a funky wig. He was a professional wrestler. Kneeling down in the front row were the two Grim Reapers, but this time they held their masks in hand.

The party had been wild—and sexually rewarding. He remembered. He, along with many of the brothers, had found temporary love that evening. It was so long ago, such a blur. He thought about the fraternity fundraiser he'd attended two months earlier, and he recalled speaking to one brother in particular. He thought about Wellfleet. Stephen looked back down at the photograph and quivered. At the bottom of the photograph were he and Billy Munsing.

* * *

J. Michael Kenneally, Esquire, sauntered out of Hoosac Mills District Court smiling. Dressed in spit-polished Perry Ellis shoes, his hair pristine, the power defense attorney from Boston needed only one hour to free his client. It was easy, actually, and any second-year law student could have gotten Jimmy Petrilli released from the county lockup. Other than circumstantial evidence surrounding the *accidental* death of retired detective Rocek, neither the FBI nor the local authorities had anything substantial to detain him for the death of Laiken Barnes. Kenneally was slick, and neither Glavin nor Patterson was in Hoosac Mills to stage protest. They had been canvassing Massachusetts, making stops in Amherst and Wellfleet. The FBI men were thorough. Along with Bobbie Thomas and Marcus Torres, they tried valiantly to draw connections to the three murders. Their efforts had given some rewards but they wanted more.

Milton Glavin remained calm when he received the news. Petrilli's release struck him as a bit ironic, though. A preceding phone call from the state police lab in Sudbury had confirmed a DNA match taken from hair samples found on Laiken Barnes and saliva fluids taken from Jimmy Petrilli's can of soda in the Berkshire County House of Correction. The broken fingernail recovered at Laiken's graveside was still being tested; the technicians would need more time. And the partial left-hand palm print taken from Laiken's headstone proved inconclusive to Petrilli's prints.

But it still appeared that Petrilli was their man, though the evidence was not gathered legally. That was okay, though; Glavin didn't panic. He conferred with Patterson; they would assign an agent to monitor Petrilli until they could gather enough substantial evidence to warrant a court mandate for testing. It might take time, but they were focused on one suspect. He was satisfied.

Jimmy Petrilli strolled out of the House of Correction and was met by his attorney. They both grinned. In three hours the Lexus arrived in Weymouth. Petrilli was a free man, for the time being. Alone in his condominium he examined the mess. Someone had been inside his home, though no search warrant had been issued. In a panic he went to his bookshelf, eyes locked on his set of *Encyclopedia Americana.* He extracted the B volume from the top shelf and opened it.

Petrilli breathed easy when he found the clipping. He had been foolish to keep such an incriminating article, but he had…just because. The newspaper article was dated November 2, 1987, and it told of the horrific murder of millionaire William Jonathan Barnes' daughter. Jimmy inserted the newspaper into his mouth like tobacco and chewed. After a minute he went into the bathroom, spit it into the toilet and flushed. He peered out his window and saw a van with tinted windows across the street. He closed his blinds and returned to the living room.

They were watching him.

* * *

Melanie was in shock. The drive to the airport in Colombia had been difficult, and at one point she was forced to the side of the road. When the car door opened, she regurgitated onto the pavement. She wouldn't fare any better on the flight.

Renee Gleeson had rocked Melanie's world. Without hesitation she had pointed out the Kappa Chi Omicron brother known to her as Boston Boy. And Renee had pointed directly at a nineteen-year-old boy named Stephen Nicholson. Disbelief supplanted anger in Melanie's body.

Say it isn't so, Stephen.

How could it be? If Stephen really was Boston Boy, and there was no reason for Renee to lie, then maybe it was just incidental. Maybe the Boston Boy character—Stephen Nicholson—had nothing to do with the murder of Laiken Barnes. Maybe Stephen had remained quiet about the Boston Boy theme because he didn't want to bring any unneeded suspicion his way.

But why would Stephen take the case? Real simple: to cover up his own guilt and channel it elsewhere. Stephen might have known that if he hadn't taken the case, then some other private detective would have. And that detective would have eventually tied Stephen to the murder.

But it couldn't be Stephen, not *her* Stephen. No way. He was too nice—a little rough around the edges at times, yet charming. He had already done so much for the case that it just didn't make sense. There had to be an explanation, a glitch. Melanie would talk to him when she returned.

On the plane, Melanie tended to new paperwork she had received. Kenny Rocek had been remiss—no, Kenny had been negligent—in his duties. It had taken a couple of weeks, but Bell Atlantic finally produced old phone bill records for Melanie. This list was a comprehensive one, though, unlike Rocek's. Melanie sifted through various phone bills connected to the case. They included a high volume of phone lines: Laiken's townhouse; Laiken's home number; Mr. and Mrs. Barnes' home number; Jimmy Petrilli's Weymouth home; Billy Munsing's Dorchester home; and the Kappa Chi Omicron pay phone, the college home of Stephen Nicholson, Jimmy Petrilli, and Billy Munsing in the fall of 1987.

Her eyes became hazy and the numbers seemed to blend together. The airplane flew over Block Island, and then Melanie saw it. She froze in the seat, the man next to her sensing tension of some sort. The phone number jumped off the page like a frog, hitting Melanie square in the eyes. Two calls had been placed on Saturday, October 24, 1987, to a number in Boston. Melanie recognized the first three digits of the number, and she knew what Boston neighborhood they were assigned to. But she wanted to be certain. She dialed out on the air phone to confirm the number with an operator. The information operator was businesslike, impersonal, and within one minute she confirmed Melanie's worst dream.

The outgoing calls had been dialed from a number listed to W.J Barnes. It made sense; Laiken didn't discriminate which phone in her parents' house she used. But these particular phone calls had gone to the Nicholson residence in West Roxbury.

Stephen.

Melanie hung up the air phone and put her head down. She didn't want to get emotional next to a stranger. Melanie was a strong woman and kept her mind clear—for a while. The descent into Hartford was smooth, but her emotional state changed. Too much time and effort had gone into this case. And there was something else, wasn't there? It was Stephen—yes, it was Stephen. She had lied to herself many times during the past couple of months, swearing she wouldn't get attached to him. But it was too late. The passenger next to Melanie asked her if she was all right. The answer was no.

She was crying.

The tears flowed only briefly, though. She pulled herself together and made it out of the airport. She would go directly to the source; there would be no conferring with Milton Glavin or Devon Patterson, or anyone for that matter. Melanie drove quickly toward Boston. This time it was personal. She needed to speak with Stephen, and she needed to do it alone.

It didn't make sense. Stephen just didn't seem the type, period. Melanie pondered; she had graduated magna cum laude with a degree in criminal justice, and had applied those principles to practice in almost ten years of police service. Something just didn't fit here.

Homicide is not a simple concept. One accepted belief, though, is that on any given night, any person could be capable of homicide. But every murder is a homicide, yet not every homicide is a murder. They can differ.

Some homicides, such as self-defense, are justifiable. Murder is the most wretched crime, but yet society *accepts* certain types of murder. The nightly news, ever redundant, repeats the same tales of wickedness: drug deals gone awry, jealous husbands, drug-induced and drunken rages, emotional fits of anger, and more. Although the end results of these heinous acts are the same, the nightly viewer has grown immune to them. That is, of course, until it happens to one of their own.

This case was different, though. This was a serial murderer, a relatively new animal in the world of law enforcement. The suspect's code name was the Olympian, and he was no ordinary man, no ordinary killer.

There are multiple categories to which serial murderers can be assigned. The two most basic types are *organized* versus *disorganized*. A disorganized serial killer is not calculating. He acts randomly and without much premeditation. He is typically undereducated and physically unkempt. His lack of planning makes him susceptible to error. Therefore, he is more prone to being caught.

The Olympian was organized. He was not a thug off the street; he acted with malice and forethought. He planned his crimes well, disguise and all, and executed with precision. He was a true professional, and if he intended to follow his sequential order, then some unknown woman was in imminent danger. Melanie recalled some of the things Devon Patterson said about organized killers at the seminar. They kill with a cause, and their actions are deliberate. Patterson's parting line hung inside her. It was one of his strongest opinions, a view not shared by everyone in the law enforcement community. He said that serial killers weren't necessarily bred by society; serial killers were born.

25.

The meeting was happenstance. Stephen was reporting to the visiting floor, Marcellus was returning from a parole board meeting. "Catch a word with you, Stephen?" he asked.

"Yeah, what's up, Marcellus?" Stephen said.

Marcellus Alexander was a freak—six-eight and 305 pounds of 8 percent body fat. Marcellus had shiny black skin, a precision 1980s high and tight haircut, and, inexplicably, the bluest eyes at the Boston House. Marcellus' disposition was second to none. He was dangerous, yes, but only when deemed absolutely necessary.

They stood in the hallway annexing the visiting floor. Marcellus waited until two staff members and an inmate passed. "Just got some good news. And I wanted to thank you in person anyway," Marcellus said.

Stephen was confused. "What's up?"

"The word you put in for me," Marcellus said. "Parole officer just said it put me over the top and got me into the halfway house. I'm out of here next week."

Stephen laughed. "You got that, Marcellus. Just don't bring the heat on me by stampeding a sorority house while you're out there sniffing around."

"You got that, babe," he answered. Marcellus scanned the area again. He knew the Boston House's walls had big ears. "Heard you had a rough outing in the gym with Renzo," he said.

Stephen chuckled. Marcellus lived in 6-Block—of course he knew. Then again, three-quarters of the inmates probably knew about the fight in the gym. "You heard correctly."

"Want me to straighten that?" Marcellus asked. "On the QT, of course."

Stephen was speechless. He'd met Marcellus four years ago when he came to Boston House on what was called an on-and-after sentence for battery with intent to kill, giving him a total of five years to serve. Marcellus was the cousin of Stephen's college friend. Stephen took the phone call when Marcellus arrived in the booking dock. He educated Marcellus on Boston House policy and got him a cushy job in the laundry room.

Last year Marcellus was granted furlough for his mother's wake. Stephen and Frankie Kohan were the escort officers. They broke department protocol when they permitted him an additional twenty minutes of privacy as he grieved his mother. It was an egregious violation of policy. It was also an act of kindness that correction officers showed on occasion yet would never admit—that would discredit stereotypes. What Stephen and Frankie did for Marcellus was merely a sign of respect. Discourteous and uncooperative inmates didn't get courtesies. Marcellus was neither—he was a man who always treated staff with respect. He earned it.

Stephen was confident the situation with Renzo was contained. He didn't want it to snowball. He reached high and gave Marcellus a quick slap on the shoulder. "I'm all set, Marcellus," Stephen said. "But thanks anyway."

"You sure, man?"

"Yeah, I'm sure." Stephen was called on the radio. He answered, heard the message, and looked back at Marcellus. He laughed. "Gotta fly, my man. Be good."

Marcellus winked and kept stepping. He thought about Stephen's plight on his return to 6-Block. He was pissed. Stephen had conducted himself like a man. Renzo had not. It had nothing to do with the fight in the gymnasium—that was a fair one. But it shouldn't have come to that. Marcellus never liked Renzo anyway, the "Caesar" of the white boys. He wasn't a true leader, a man who led inmates by example. He was a glorified schoolyard bully—not Marcellus' type of guy. Marcellus was bigger than almost everybody, but rarely used his immense size and strength inside the walls to obtain anything. He'd rather use his intellect. Yeah, his mind was made up. Renzo's days of bullying people around were definitely coming to a close. Someday Renzo would understand the meaning of reciprocity.

* * *

254

In 1976, a young Stephen Nicholson, abetted by best pal Kevin Shea, willfully placed a dead bird inside Maria Santofita's desk at Holy Name School. They achieved their desired result, a high, piercing scream which could have shattered windows in neighboring Roslindale. The "crime" was solved within minutes, and to this day Stephen remembered the chilling thirty-minute wait outside the principal's office. On the door was a sign of the cross and foreign words which all English-speaking students understood well: Vaya Con Dios.

The principal's office signified more than a central point of authority. Students called it the Penitent Room. Virtues such as honesty, righteousness, and discipline were force-fed to mischievous students. Nasty handwritten notes for Mom and Dad, implicating guilt, of course, always accompanied the children home.

Twenty-two years later, Stephen Nicholson waited outside the IPS office. Its message was embossed on the door and resonated throughout the hallways: *Integrity, Perseverance, Strength*. Lt. Paul Cullen waited with Stephen; he was Stephen's union representative. Unlike most law enforcement agencies, the Boston House included sergeants and lieutenants in their collective bargaining unit.

Paul Cullen was the Man among the rank and file. He was a Dorchester guy with common sense and street smarts, complemented of course with a master's degree from Boston University. What really separated Paul from others, though, was possession of a set of stones that couldn't be bought in a store, and a thinking man's acumen that intimidated most administrators. He was twenty-nine years old with a bright future. Now he huddled with his contemporary, his friend. Stephen knew damn well why IPS had summoned him. He relayed the entire scenario to Paul.

Paul was disturbed by the suddenness of his involvement. "Why didn't you come to me when this kicked off? I could have helped."

"Because I figured I could handle things without risking your LT bar. I was wrong."

"Okay, let's not worry about it now. Who called you down?" Paul asked.

"I'm not sure," Stephen said. "The captain just told me to report here ASAP. That's when I called you. I bet it'll be Charlemagne."

"That's beyond our control," Paul said. "What matters is that you don't let your sewer trap run loose." Stephen laughed. "I'm not kidding, Stephen.

Be brief with your answers; one or two words, if possible. If you aren't sure, look at me. I'll coach you."

"I read you loud and clear, Mr. Lieutenant."

"One last thing," Paul said with a smile. "Remember the Deer Island mantra."

"What's that?"

"Deny everything, admit to nothing, and demand proof."

The door opened. Chief Inspector Charlemagne quickly led Stephen and Paul into the Heat Room. Assistant Chief Inspector Marie Tosconaro remained at her desk, doodling with meaningless paperwork.

Everyone sat. Charlemagne conspicuously placed a tape recorder on the table and pressed Record. Paul smiled, pulled a miniature tape recorder from his pocket, and did the same. "For the record," Charlemagne said loudly, "today is April twenty-first and it is 4:10 p.m. We are in the interview room in the IPS office. Present is myself—Chief Inspector Frederick P. Charlemagne—Deputy Lieutenant Paul Cullen, and Deputy Sheriff Stephen Nicholson. A line of questioning shall now follow."

Stephen smirked. Had Charlemagne thought up that little intro himself, or had he plagiarized it from one of his disgruntled cop wannabe magazines? Paul secured a notebook and pen, ready to jot down any discrepancies by the IPS chief. Charlemagne looked to Stephen. "Deputy Nicholson, I just want to ask you a few simple questions."

"No problem, Chief. Go right ahead."

"How's your eye feeling?"

"Better, thank you."

"I have it on credible account that Caesar punched you with his fist in the gymnasium."

Stephen looked to Paul, then back to Charlemagne. He couldn't resist. It was like a juicy slow-pitch softball in the middle of the strike zone. Paul saw it coming but couldn't stop him. "Not quite, Chief," Stephen answered. "It was Marc Anthony with a candlestick in the billiards room." The three men shared a fake laugh.

"Okay, okay, I walked into that one," Charlemagne noted. "The inmate in question is Renzo DiLorenzo. And I also understand that you injured him with a kick to the ribs."

"Neither accusation is true," Stephen replied.

Charlemagne continued. "The cause of the fight was a rather noble one on your part, Deputy Nicholson."

"Is that right?"

"Yes. It seems that correction officer Mickey O'Sullivan owes a considerable sum of money and is being pressured to bring contraband—namely heroin—into the Boston House. You, playing the part of guardian angel, are intervening on his behalf," Charlemagne said. "Inmate DiLorenzo is a notorious thug and drug dealer. He currently works in conjunction with another correction officer whom this office is well aware of. I also intend on speaking with O'Sullivan when he returns to work."

"I don't know what you're talking about, Chief," Stephen said.

"How do you explain your black eye?"

"I was kickboxing. We were using ten-ounce gloves, which are light. I dropped my right. Shame on me."

"I don't suppose you'll tell me the name of your formidable opponent?"

"I thought you'd never ask," Stephen said, "You're very familiar with him. His name is Jamie Reegan."

Charlemagne rolled his eyes. "Jesus Christ," he said. "I'll be sure to speak with that human ball of fire later today for corroboration."

"Anything else?"

"Yes, there is," Charlemagne said. "State police called me a while back. A trooper's wife witnessed a peculiar assault in the alleyway behind Mc-Grath's tavern."

"What's that got to do with me?"

"She described three men intimidating and assaulting a tall, lanky guy with a ponytail. One of the assailants was short with curly hair, one was tall and muscular, and the other matches your description."

"Chief, I'm still not following you."

Charlemagne smiled condescendingly. "One of the men—I'm not sure whom—held a gun to the victim's head. Another punched him in the face. Oddly, the assailants handed the victim an envelope before they fled in a black Jeep."

"Lots of black Jeeps in Boston, Chief."

"The trooper ran a partial plate number. He came back with fifteen vehicles. He called me by process of elimination. And I pretty much dismissed the whole thing…until recently."

Stephen shrugged. "Don't know what you're talking about, sir."

"Of course you don't," replied Charlemagne. "The way I see it is this… you're using intimidation to free Mickey from the grasp of Lucky Giannessimo. I don't know who the other assailants were, but I'll find out."

"Can I go now?" Stephen asked.

"No, there's one other matter to tend to," Charlemagne said. "I received a phone call from a retired FBI supervisor currently working as a consultant in an FBI matter. His name is Devon Patterson. I know you're familiar with him."

Stephen wasn't shocked, of course, but he was trying to keep the Barnes case out of his head. It was difficult.

Besides, it seems you can't swing a dead octopus in Boston without hitting at least three tattletales.

Cullen interjected. "One moment, before you start…"

"I got it, Paul," Stephen said. "Don't worry about it." The room was quiet for five seconds. "What did Dr. Emeritus Patterson have to say?"

"He simply wanted me to remind you of professional ethics," Charlemagne said. "Obviously I'm aware of your investigation business. But you also represent Sheriff Lindehan every time you walk out the front door."

Stephen stared at Charlemagne. *My father played CYO baseball with Lindehan, you jackass.*

"I read you loud and clear, Chief," Stephen said. "Any more questions?"

Charlemagne motioned with his right hand and dismissively waved Stephen off. "I'm through with you."

Stephen cringed. Charlemagne was a patronizing bastard. Anxiety set upon him; all walls were closing in. Stephen's mind raced. He tried to maintain his calm but couldn't. Thoughts of the last two months attacked without mercy.

Who killed Laiken? Alicia Rivera and Darlene Hughes left crowded barrooms with their murderer, yet no one can identify him. Why? What is the common denominator between all these girls, or were they randomly selected? Who's Boston

Boy? What's the real deal with Petrilli and Munsing? How does Melanie really feel about me? Why the fuck does Can Man mock me? Why did David get in the car with that filthy bitch, Mandy McMasters? What would he be doing in his life right now?

"Stephen…Stephen…Stephen, snap out of it, buddy," Paul said.

It was a short fugue. Stephen looked at Chief Inspector Charlemagne. Restraint went out the window. "You're sure you have nothing else for me?" Stephen asked loudly.

"No, Deputy Nicholson, I'm…I mean, I'm all set," Charlemagne answered. Stephen's short daydream had clearly unnerved Charlemagne.

"No, I don't think you are, sir. There must be more dastardly deeds attributed to my blatant disregard for law, policy, and goodwill to mankind," Stephen said. "I'm quite known for social upheaval. Perhaps my fingerprints were discovered at a schoolbook depository in Dallas?"

"Stephen…" Paul tried. It was to no avail. The sewer trap was running loose.

He was in full animation. "Where was I when McKinley got shot? Or Garfield? For that matter, I may have been on a field trip to Washington D.C. when Reagan got capped!"

"Deputy Nicholson…" Charlemagne said.

"Did you know that hours before his death, President Lincoln gave authorization for the formation of the Secret Service? Pretty ironic, isn't it, Chief? I wonder if I was at Ford's Theatre on April 14, 1865. *Our American Cousin* was playing."

Paul's head was in his hands. Charlemagne was horrified. "Even better, Chief. I'd bet that my great-great-great-great-grandfather was conscripted into the British Army from Ireland and shipped to Boston to help enforce tax collection. And, while responding to an insolent mob, he fired the shot that killed Mr. Crispus Attucks."

No one spoke. The temperature in the Heat Room was eighty-two degrees. Stephen was sweating. Paul acted quickly. "Chief, I think it'd be best if Stephen stepped out of the room while we have a few words."

"I agree," Charlemagne said.

Paul escorted Stephen into the hallway. "Wait for me, pal." He returned to Charlemagne. "Sorry about that, Chief. He's got a lot going through his mind."

"I can only imagine," he said. "He's a bit impetuous, wouldn't you agree, Lieutenant?"

"This business will do it to you, Chief."

"I see. Anyway, I want to thank you for being so professional and understanding in there, Paul. I have a job to do, you understand."

"Yes, sir," Paul replied, flipping open his notebook. "Just a couple of items I'll need from you and then I'll be on my way."

"Certainly," Charlemagne said. "What do you need?"

"A copy of the eyewitness report naming Stephen in the alleged gymnasium fight."

Charlemagne was perplexed. "Excuse me, Lieutenant?"

"The eyewitness, Chief. I'd like a copy of the report from your source who witnessed the alleged fight between Deputy Nicholson and inmate DiLorenzo."

"I don't have one."

"Sir?"

"My source didn't actually see the fight."

"Then it was hearsay," Paul said. He calmly recorded information in his notebook. "Moving along then, Chief. Could I please have a copy of the nurse's report detailing inmate DiLorenzo's injuries?"

Charlemagne's face was now pale. "I don't have a nurse's report."

"How about a copy of the criminal complaint you filed in Roxbury District Court on Renzo DiLorenzo for assault and battery on a correction officer?"

"What are you talking about, Lieutenant?"

Paul rubbed his chin, feigning confusion. "Chief, you just said about five minutes ago that inmate DiLorenzo was responsible for Stephen's black eye. We both have your comments on tape. Did you not make that statement, Chief?"

"I did, but…"

"With all due respect, but nothing, sir," Paul said. "These are some pretty damning accusations, yet you seem to have nothing to substantiate your claims."

"Trust me, Paul. Everything will come out in due time."

"This guy's career is on the line and you take us on a fishing expedition. No wonder the kid lost his head in here."

Charlemagne soured. "Anything else you need, Lieutenant?" he asked sarcastically.

"Yes, a copy of the state police report filed from the incident with the trooper's wife."

"I only received a phone call. No report."

Paul was rolling. He wasn't about to let a big tuna like Charlemagne off the hook. "Chief, you alleged gunplay in The McGrath Principle tavern alleyway. Do you have a copy of Stephen Nicholson's permit to carry a firearm in Massachusetts?" Charlemagne raised his hands in surrender. "Let me help you, Chief. Stephen does not have a license to carry a firearm off duty in Massachusetts."

"Paul, you have to understand…"

"Chief, what commonwealth or federal laws has Stephen violated regarding his private investigation business?"

Charlemagne couldn't believe it. The shoe was on the other foot for the first time in his sheriff's department career. "No laws, to the best of my knowledge."

Paul leaned toward Charlemagne. "Then why, sir, are you harassing my union member?"

"Lieutenant Cullen, I take umbrage at the notion that you're questioning my integrity."

Stephen could hear the elevated voices from the hallway.

"And I, sir, take offense to the fact you label inmate Renzo DiLorenzo a notorious thug and drug dealer, yet you seemingly allow him to operate in general population with impunity when we both know he should be housed in administrative segregation."

"That's none on your damn business!" stammered Charlemagne.

"And last but certainly not least, Chief, is that you call down my union member under the guise of 'simple questions,'" Paul said. "Then your line of questioning quickly shifts to an area which could incriminate him in a criminal capacity. You did all of this, Chief, without ever reading Stephen his Miranda rights." Paul pressed Stop on his tape recorder. "Any judge will get a tickle out of this."

Charlemagne smiled. He reached into his breast pocket and handed Paul a sealed envelope. "It doesn't matter much anyway," he said.

"What's this?" Paul asked.

"Nicholson's suspended with pay until further notice."

Paul returned the smile. "Frederick, when you retire you should apply for some part-time work with Stephen. I'm sure he could help you fight off the boredom."

Charlemagne turned beet red. "Get the fuck out of my office."

In the hallway Paul apprised Stephen of the suspension. Stephen wasn't shocked and didn't care. He'd be cleared in good time. The two men walked to the lobby of the Boston House. Paul extended his hand. "You reached deep into the well to pull out the name Crispus Attucks, you smartass."

26.

Brooklyn was still Brooklyn. Some changes were evident. Everyone bought the newest cars and clothes, listened to the hottest music, and played with state-of-the-art electronic gadgets. But the heart of Brooklyn—its cultural diversity—remained intact. All the phonies had moved to Manhattan or Jersey. Good—they weren't missed and were never wanted.

Frankie Kohan was invigorated. He drank the Brooklyn air; it was his nectar. He returned home about twice a year. Frankie's heart was in Boston but his soul belonged to Brooklyn. This visit was special; it wasn't for pleasure or business. It was personal.

Carlita's Diner was a popular eatery on the West Side. Customers were immune to the brackish scent of the East River. Frankie smelled it. In Boston the Charles River had appeal. It was aristocratic, romantic, and beautiful. Those words didn't describe the East River. Instead it had something else: toughness, character, and grit. Yes, the East was a blue-collar river—just how Frankie loved it.

Alexia Martinez entered Carlita's effortlessly. Frankie watched—he could watch her forever. Alexia was striking at five-nine with long brown hair and brown eyes. She had a classic face—distinctly Puerto Rican, and distinctly beautiful. Her given name was Alexandra. It had been shortened in the first grade by her best friend, Frankie Kohan. Alexia and Frankie loved each other unconditionally. Platonic love. They were best friends for life.

Alexia was unusually tall for a Puerto Rican woman. She took advantage of her gifted physique by earning a track scholarship to Auburn University with her long, swift legs. But she wasn't just a jock. Alexia was the rare mixture of beauty and brains. A near-perfect grade point average was followed by a master's degree in business at Yale University. Alexia's thirty-one years had witnessed much. She grew up in a broken home with only a mom and friends like Frankie to nurture her. Now things were different. She'd earned $500,000 last year and hadn't earned less than $250,000 in four years. Alexia was moderately wealthy but retained her street smarts. Actually, she cherished her street smarts. It separated her from the other investors and high-powered stockbrokers on Wall Street. Alexia would always be a Brooklyn girl.

They ate bad food and talked about each other for an hour. Alexia got quiet. "How's my Stephen?"

Frankie stared into Alexia's eyes, analyzing a simple yet complicated question. Summer 1995 had been a passionate time. Stephen and Alexia alternated weekends together in Boston and Brooklyn. It was ecstasy, it was even love. The distance, coupled with Stephen's chaotic lifestyle, disintegrated the relationship. It ended quickly, oddly. The two had remained friends and Frankie correctly surmised they had rendezvoused more than twice since 1995. Stephen and Alexia shared a chemistry that didn't come along often. There were regrets.

Now Stephen was in trouble—real trouble. Frankie treasured his acceptance inside the Nicholson family home. He inventoried the various relationships. Stephen. Just his name made him laugh sometimes. He was trustworthy, dependable, witty, resourceful, and simply put—his brother. Matthew was complex. Yet Frankie was endeared to him. Matthew was introverted and extroverted at the same time. Frankie always appreciated his razor wit and incisive life analysis. Most importantly, their friendship wasn't bound by Stephen's existence.

Eamon was a man's man. Frankie enjoyed his company, his perspective of Boston life, and his Charlestown *edge*. Frankie was never inhibited from seeking Eamon's paternal guidance. He always delivered. Peachy was aptly nicknamed. True to form, she possessed all that a mother should: wisdom, passion, organization, discipline, sensitivity, and palpable selflessness which placed others first. Always. Peachy was Frankie's guidance counselor. She was the stabilizing influence who validated his self-esteem by quietly assuring him that manhood was defined by life's actions. Frankie had predilections—like all people—yet his involved infrequent, covert road trips to roadside motels in western Massachusetts where he would engage amorously with a Franklin County correction officer. It was Peachy Nicholson who looked him in the eye and said, "Son, it's okay."

Yes, the Nicholsons were his surrogate family. Thanksgiving and Christmas were spent on Meredith Street. He was Jewish. No one cared. Frankie exchanged Christmas gifts with the entire family.

Now Lucky Giannessimo the Lowlife presented a threat to Stephen, member of the Nicholson family. His family. Lucky was belligerent, thinking his immorality would go unpunished. Not on Frankie's watch. Never. Frankie's stare spoke volumes. Alexia was concerned. "Stephen ain't good," he said. "I think he's falling down."

Alexia nodded. "Explain." Frankie did, omitting nothing. Alexia was intelligent; she knew Frankie wasn't looking for a sympathetic ear. "What can I do to help?"

"I have a wild idea," he said, "But I need to know if you're game."

Alexia smiled, a wonderful smile. "Anything for my Stephen."

* * *

Lucky Giannessimo was rich in character flaws. In fact he owned stock in prefix words: dishonest, unscrupulous, unethical, and immoral. He dabbled in drugs, dealt drugs, played bookmaker, and mistreated women. He was a regular connoisseur of sin. Lucky had been hired two years earlier at the Boston House. How he'd passed the background check was to this day a great mystery. Lucky was a needle in a haystack, one of the few lifetime derelicts who were never arrested. It was incredible but true.

On the surface Lucky was a regular guy. He exercised regularly, dressed neatly, never smelled of booze, and was a model of routine. At approximately 2:00 p.m. every day Lucky picked up his evening dinner at the Middle Eastern Café on Harrison Avenue, located across from Boston City Hospital. All the employees liked him; he was courteous, consistent, and tipped three dollars every time. This was fact; it was monitored.

Lucky pulled his dated El Dorado to the curb at 1:58 p.m. He quickly spotted a new face in the Middle Eastern, a tall Spanish beauty who must have been an administrator at BCH. She wore a tight, knee-length beige skirt with a white blouse. She had incredible hips. A pair of flats gave her the right touch. The woman spoke quietly but clearly on her cellular phone. She was upset.

Lucky paid for his chicken and rice dinner. Something slowed him from leaving. It was her voice, a different yet sexy accent. She wasn't a local—maybe New York, maybe New Jersey. Her words stuck in his ear. "…But the taxi cab has already left…I don't know how to get to New Market Square…No, Ronald. It was your responsibility to meet me here!" She hung up, composed herself.

Lucky the gentleman caller wouldn't miss a golden opportunity. "Pardon the interruption, Miss, but is everything okay?"

The lady stared at the tall, mysterious man in police pants and a windbreaker. A gold tooth sparkled. "I think so, Officer," she said. "I'm here from Philadelphia on business and was supposed to meet a colleague, but he can't make it."

"I hate to appear an eavesdropper," Lucky said, "but I'd be more than happy to give you a lift to New Market Square. It's less than a mile away."

The lady was embarrassed. "Are you sure?" she asked. "Don't you have to report to the station?"

Lucky held up his hand. She thought he was a cop. He didn't deny it. Lucky smiled—the same phony smile that had actually won the lust of many. "I always have time for a beautiful woman."

The lady blushed. "Only if it's not a problem." Lucky opened the passenger door. What a gentleman. Thank God he'd just vacuumed. He slid coolly into the driver's seat. "Could you please wait one minute?" she asked as she calmly massaged her temples. The tinted windows were up.

"Sure," Lucky said, "whatever you need."

Across the street was a short man in disguise. He wore thick glasses, an authentic-looking mustache, and a baseball cap. He stood at a payphone with his back to the Middle Eastern Café. He dialed 911. A female voice answered in a fluent run-on sentence. "Boston Police this line's recorded my name's Mary Beth what's the nature of your problem?"

The short guy peeked across the street. The lady was now on the sidewalk, waving her hands and screaming loudly. Lucky was half out of the car, trying to placate the woman while making a futile appeal to onlookers. The short guy gave his best Boston accent. "Lady just jumped from some dude's car across from BCH on Harrison. She's screaming about a knife."

"Is the woman injured?" the dispatcher asked.

"Not that I can see. Lady's going off," the man said. "Wait…dude's getting back in his car."

"Can I have a car description and license plate?" the dispatcher asked.

"Gimme a sec," he said, pretending to put down the receiver. In five seconds he said, "Blue El Dorado. Massachusetts plate number…"

Lucky was shocked. The bitch was crazy—definitely looking for a lawsuit. He shut his door and sped off, barely making the light at the intersection of Harrison and Massachusetts Avenue. He drove toward the Boston House. Lucky saw flashing blue lights in his rearview mirror as he crossed Melnea Cass Boulevard. Damn, he thought the light was yellow, not red.

A young cop pulled his Glock as he slowly approached the side of the vehicle. "Hands on the steering wheel," he yelled. "Let me see your hands." Lucky complied and the cop looked in the driver side window.

Lucky tried to deescalate the situation. "I'm a deputy sheriff at the Boston House, Officer," he said. "I'm on my way to work."

The cop disregarded the statement. "Out of the vehicle…slowly." Lucky stepped out and the cop immediately handcuffed him behind the back, leaning him face first on the car. "Where's the knife?" the cop asked.

"Ain't no knife," Lucky answered. The cop kept an eye on Lucky as he carefully reached under the driver's seat. He pulled out a buck knife with a six-inch blade. A single thread of white fabric hung from the tip, the type of material that could have come from a blouse. Lucky lost his cool. "Fuck that, fuck that! Bitch just set me up! Bitch planted that and just set me up in front of the Middle Eastern! I got witnesses."

"Shut up," the cop said, continuing his search. To Lucky's dismay the cop pulled out a rectangular package wrapped in plastic. Lucky's face turned pale. He knew exactly what it was: a brick of heroin. The cop got in Lucky's face. "You're in deep shit, Mister."

The short man was again across the street, this time in an unmarked vehicle in a McDonald's parking lot. He laughed. Ten hours earlier he'd brandished a Slim Jim outside Lucky Giannessimo's apartment. Lucky was ignorant. He'd never experience true friendship or camaraderie. Lucky was incapable of feelings, friendships and love.

He was a degenerate; it would always be so.

* * *

Three friends sat at Frankie Kohan's dining room table. Alexia and Frankie drank expensive wine. Stephen sipped bottled beer. They listened to '70s music, swapped childhood stories, reminisced about shared times, and forgot about life's mundane problems. They were an odd trio but were tight nonetheless.

Frankie disappeared to his bedroom. Alexia and Stephen went quiet. Their eyes met. A small tear signifying happiness and sadness rolled down her cheek. Stephen wiped it away. Her eyes were a trap. He tried to look away but couldn't. "Too bad Boston doesn't have a stock market like New York," he said.

Alexia squeezed his hand. "Too bad the Yankees aren't your hometown team."

Stephen instinctively kissed Alexia on the lips. He couldn't help himself. It was a passionate kiss that didn't want to end. It was the forever kiss.

Frankie was returning. Stephen sat back. "You'll never know how damn beautiful you are," he said. She smiled. Stephen's feelings for Alexia were real; they had always been. But something bothered him. He didn't want to admit it, but someone else was in his heart. Yes, he and Alexia were friends—very dear friends.

27.

A campsite in Massachusetts
Summer, 1974

Mugginess permeated the sky, as it did every August in the Bay State. The scenic Massachusetts coastline provided a gentle breeze of relief, but inland tended to maintain an air of stickiness. The campsite was a popular haven for vacationing families. It was in relative proximity to Boston, yet offered woods and a lake to give a bucolic environment to the vacationing urbanites. Its weekly rates were reasonable, thus making the total package irresistible for moderate-income families. This particular Friday was no different from the others.

Children of different families fraternized, creating temporary friendships that were authentic, but would most certainly end as abruptly as they began. The kids played all day: king of the hill, lord of the raft, cowboys and Indians, and tug-of-war. Mothers passed the time in their own ways. They mostly relaxed on chairs at the lake, smoking Winstons and engaging in gossip.

The boy wandered through the woods, alone, in search of his makeshift contraption. He had left his siblings and the other kids behind at the lake. He was disinterested in the stupid game, lord of the raft. It was boring, and he was tired listening to the mothers rave about the Republican named Milhous. So he'd visited China and now was quitting his job—big deal.

He traversed a short hill, creeping deeper into the forest. He had other plans. A book of matches burned a hole in his shorts. He yearned for the sight of flames and smell of smoke, but he just couldn't do it. Last summer he and another boy had torched a Dumpster, and they got caught. Having been grounded for one month, he learned his lesson. Now he had a new fascination, a good one.

He found his trap and scurried to it. He placed two apples atop a bed of leaves, hooked his line and took cover behind a tree, anxiously awaiting a visitor. The bait was visible, and it was only a matter of time before the mouthwatering fruit tempted the palate of a hungry rodent.

An odd wheezing noise caught the boy's attention. It was only four o'clock and the boy knew that the rodent shouldn't have been out during the daytime. The raccoon appeared quickly from a burrow at the base of a moribund pine tree. It was swift, but not fast enough. Ever so dexterous, it nibbled away at the apples without fear. His courage was not equaled by wisdom, though, and the young boy pulled the fish line, jailing the animal inside.

The boy was overjoyed. All week he had tried valiantly to capture a critter, and finally his perseverance had paid off. This time the thief didn't flee with the bait; he was captured. He double-stepped to the cage, grinning ear to ear. He negotiated his small fingers into the cell, wanting to caress his new friend. The raccoon would be his pet—not his siblings', but his very own. He would call it Bruin, after his favorite sports team, and he would take care of it. Mom and Dad wouldn't mind. He would allow his siblings to play with Bruin, of course, but only if they sought his permission first.

Within minutes he was the talk of camp among the children, the cock of the walk. He proudly displayed Bruin—his pet, his new friend, his trophy. The other kids were jealous and quickly scattered around the camp in attempts to rig their own traps.

Bruin fidgeted inside the cage. To appease Bruin the boy fetched a piece of fruit from the family tent, a surefire way of sedating him. The boy's brother, in adulation, accompanied him for the feeding process. With approval, the sibling dropped the pear into the cage and Bruin again devoured it voraciously. It was as if the coon hadn't eaten in days; it was obvious that its adrenaline was pumping. And then the sibling made a mistake. Without permission he reached into the cage to pet Bruin. But the raccoon was not domesticated. He lashed at his jailers by sinking his teeth into the young boy's hand, drawing blood from his thumb.

The young boy writhed in pain, tears welling in his eyes. He began to cry but quickly regrouped, gaining his composure like a big boy would, like his brother would. The older boy sealed the cage and tended to the boy, taking him to the tent for a Band-Aid. His brother would be okay, but he would now have to tell his parents what happened. He frowned, knowing that he wouldn't be allowed to keep Bruin.

He took the matter into his own hands, picking up the cage and heading back into the woods, stopping near a brook. The coon made a funny noise, almost a hissing sound, and brazenly stared at him. The boy was incredulous. Bruin was acting defiant. First it had bitten his brother and now it openly challenged him. A new emotion suddenly introduced itself, something he had never experienced. Rage consumed him. He looked into the cage and cursed the rodent. With his rage came a feeling—no, a demand—for retribution.

Time seemingly slowed for the young lad. He couldn't feel his right hand retrieve a Swiss Army knife from the back pocket of his corduroy shorts. He had been whittling wood all week, but now the blade would serve a different purpose. He fixed the blade; the stupid animal would pay for its sin.

The raccoon, although in a dangerous predicament, maintained a cool demeanor, if such a thing were possible for an animal. It was not yet an adult but there were no signs of a protective mother looming nearby. The boy knelt as the coon dug into the ground in search of more food. Blood from his brother's wound had gotten on his wrist, and a droplet had landed in the cage. But Bruin wasn't a carnivore, so the scent didn't produce an aggressive charge by the animal.

The cage was lifted and the boy pinned Bruin to the ground with his right hand. In a deft display of force and accuracy the boy wielded the Swiss Army knife like a soldier. Bruin screeched but managed to cling onto a found berry as the boy stabbed him multiple times in the torso. After thirty seconds and forty entry wounds, the animal went limp.

The sun still shone and it cast a gleam of light through the trees onto his arms. Red speckles were everywhere. The boy walked around the woods, adrenaline still pumping, trying to calm down. He picked up the carcass by the nape and threw it in the brook. The water trickled, taking the fresh scent of blood downstream. The odor had already taken a pervasive effect on the landscape, though. Birds circled the burial spot, waiting for the boy to leave so they could fulfill their role in nature's food chain.

He looked down at his T-shirt. The emblem of his favorite rock band, the Bay City Rollers, was bloodied. His corduroy shorts were also spattered with blood. He was proud of his accomplishment. But he was worried about his brother's wound, and he would have some explaining to do to Mom and Dad, but it would be okay.

The boy had a strange feeling inside him. It was new, odd. Guilt and shame suddenly enveloped him. But these emotions were not predicated on remorse for what he had done. A portentous feeling invaded him. He felt shame because he realized that he had enjoyed his encounter with Bruin, and he feared that someday he might do it again.

28.

Peachy Nicholson sat on the veranda wearing a pair of shorts and a tank top, crossword puzzle in hand. It was eighty degrees; such temperatures were a rarity at this time of year, so she seized the moment. A smile came to her face when Melanie Leary approached the walkway. "Good to see you, Melanie. I wasn't expecting you. You missed Stephen by twenty minutes." Melanie had just come from Stephen's condo; he wasn't there, either. She couldn't conceal her frown. "What's wrong, dear? Can I help you with something? Sit down while I get you a drink." Before Melanie could object, Peachy disappeared past the screen door.

The women made small talk. Peachy Nicholson was a wonderful woman—caring, giving, motherly. She definitely reminded Melanie of her own mom. "So, where's Stephen?" Melanie finally asked.

"He's down in Scituate. He and Frankie…do you know his partner, Frankie?" Melanie nodded. "Wonderful young man, isn't he? Anyway, he and Frankie are working a case at a bar down on Scituate Harbor. Name of the place is the Gill Net. I'm surprised he hasn't called you. If you want I'll give you directions, or you can use the phone to page him. He usually carries his cell phone with him."

"Directions would be fine, Peachy. I don't want to startle him right now if he's doing a job." Melanie wasn't herself, and Peachy's maternal instincts picked up on it.

"What's the matter, dear? You seem so quiet. Is everything okay?"

Melanie couldn't lie to Peachy, but she could be delicate with her word choice. "It's this case, Peachy. It's taken too many twists and turns for my liking."

Peachy eagerly agreed. "I know, dear. Stephen was disenchanted today. Matthew and I talked to him this morning and he wasn't happy. He spoke only in spurts, and that's not like him because he's a talker. He thinks that one of his friends from school may be responsible for that poor girl's death."

Melanie was curious. "Did he say which one?"

"No, but I also think he's in some sort of denial. He's thinking about quitting the case." Peachy looked around. "Please don't repeat anything I tell you back to Stephen." Melanie nodded. "You should go see him; figure out what else is going on inside his head. He'll only tell his family so much."

"Did he tell you something I should know?"

"Yes, as a matter of fact, he did." Peachy was quiet until Melanie asked for more. "He's concerned about you and him." The statement landed like a punch, and Stephen certainly wouldn't have condoned his mother's next line. "He cares about you very much, Melanie. I know that because he told me. He thinks that this case will injure any chance he might have with you because he's overly involved."

A wave of ambivalence crashed in Melanie's mind. She'd suspected Stephen's amorous feelings for her; the feeling was mutual. But the visit with Renee Gleeson had shattered her image of him, seemingly putting him on the hook for Laiken's murder. Yet if that were really the case, then why hadn't she reported her findings to Milton Glavin immediately? It was because her feelings for Stephen were deep, and she *needed* to speak with him. "Did he elaborate, Peachy, on his over-involvement?"

"He didn't have to. I know him like a book; he's my son. The problem is that his fraternal bonds have been compromised with this investigation. It's become too personal for his liking."

"Fraternal bonds?"

"Yes," Peachy said. "You don't have any brothers, do you?" Melanie shook her head. "Men are funny creatures—a different animal, Melanie, and don't ever forget that. They live by certain rules…by certain codes. If those codes are broken or compromised, things are never the same. Friendships are lost, and that is a crippling price to pay, especially to a guy like Stephen." Peachy imparted an interesting perception of men. Melanie offered her analysis.

"Virility," she said.

"Yes, my dear," Peachy responded. "Virility is a dangerous thing. The male ego knows no boundary."

Melanie's affection for Peachy grew the more they spoke. She didn't have the heart to tell her that Stephen was now a main suspect. And she still couldn't explain Stephen's committing such barbaric acts, at least not the Stephen she knew. Melanie reached for anything that might lend credence to Stephen's involvement.

"Peachy, I've seen Stephen go into a blackout before. He told me it happens once in a while. It seemed pretty weird, but he didn't tell me what it was all about."

"They're called fugues," Peachy said. "Stephen's a dreamer, and he gets them sometimes when his mind is aflutter. It's happened to him since 1987. It also happens when he's stressed. He has prescribed medication for it, but he stopped taking it. I think…I think impotence is one of its nasty side effects."

"Can't say I blame him for not taking it," Melanie said.

Peachy grinned. "I don't disagree. Any particular reason you asked?"

"Just curious, that's all." Melanie looked at her watch and picked up the written directions to Scituate Harbor; Melanie could find the bar on her own. "Thanks for talking to me, Peachy. You've been enlightening."

"Glad I could help."

Melanie gave Peachy a hug and departed.

The directions were precise. In forty-five minutes Melanie walked into the Gill Net. Scituate was on the south shore of Boston, and for obvious reasons of ethnic composition it was often referred to as the Irish Riviera. Famous for its coastal storms that invaded beachfront properties, Scituate was a predominantly working-class suburb. New homes were now built on stilts or with the protection of stone seawalls, and the familiar sight of exterior walls covered in Tyvek wrap served as an indicator of ongoing home improvements. Scituate was on the upswing, as the real estate brokers say, and although there was an influx of new money, it would always be considered a fisherman's town. The Gill Net jammed five nights a week, mostly townsfolk, with the exception of a few stragglers.

Stephen and Frankie sat at opposite ends of the rectangular bar, and it was evident to Melanie that they worked surreptitiously. Stephen was nursing a beer. He spotted Melanie and asked her to join him.

The owner of the Gill Net had suspected his bartender—and lifetime friend—of embezzlement. He didn't want to make a direct accusation because it might sever a thirty-year friendship, so he hired Boston Investigations. It was really simple, and it took Stephen and Frankie only thirty minutes to figure out how the bartender operated.

The bar wasn't yet computerized, so all drinks were rung in manually. The barkeep worked the scam with a waitress. She would take all drink orders on a pad and take it to the bar. He would give her the drinks, and she would deliver them to the patrons and collect the money. Then the waitress gave the money to the bartender and he gave her back the change, which she would return to the customer. An original order slip was then tallied next to the register and punctured through a metal rod. The philosophy was that only one person should handle money transactions at the register.

What Stephen picked up on was that the girl had *two* order pads—a real one and a phony one. If a group ordered a big round for say, forty dollars, she would never overcharge them. She would charge them the correct price and give them the appropriate change. But then, without anyone noticing, she would write up another bill for fifteen dollars on the second pad. She handed in the phony bill for fifteen dollars to the bartender, and voila, they just made twenty-five dollars.

Stephen and Melanie watched the television, saying little. Neither knew what to say. The owner walked by Stephen, motioning him to the bathroom. Stephen waited thirty seconds before going in and apprising him of the scam. The owner was thankful. He decided to use tact and wait until night's end before firing him; it would be best not to cause a scene.

Stephen returned to Melanie and whispered in her ear, giving a brief summary of what had just happened. Frankie winked at Melanie and departed—his job was done. Melanie couldn't help but laugh. "So this is what you guys in the private sector make the big bucks for?"

"It's a tough gig, baby, but someone's got to do it." They laughed; it was a nice icebreaker. She looked deep into Stephen's eyes. He still looked like hell.

"What else is going on, Stephen??"

"Where do you want me to begin?"

"Start with today."

"Okay—my union rep called me today and projected I'll be suspended—with pay—for a while. He spoke with the dude in charge, Charlemagne, and the inmate I got a problem with has two broken ribs."

Melanie knew the ordeal—in detail. Stephen had fed her the story, piecemeal, over the last two months. Only now was the gravity of the matter so clear. "You gonna get through this?"

"Don't have a choice," he said. "I'll be okay in the end. DiLorenzo won't rat because he'll incriminate himself and his reputation will be tarnished forever."

"How'd IPS find out?"

Stephen shrugged. "Presumably some other inmate. Probably found out about it through the inmate gossip line and figured he could cut himself some sort of deal. This shit happens all the time at the Boston House."

"I'm sorry to hear this. Did you tell your family?"

"I told Matthew."

They ordered sodas and watched pro basketball. Melanie almost forgot the nature of her call. No, that was untrue. Melanie wanted to forget the nature of her call. "Stephen…I just got back from seeing Renee Gleeson."

"I know." He reached for the popcorn bowl, failing to elaborate on her statement.

"Aren't you going to ask me about it? Aren't you curious as to what she may have said, Stephen? After all, you're the one who financed the trip."

"First of all, Barnes financed the trip. Secondly, I don't know if I want anything to do with this fucking case anymore…pardon my French." Stephen couldn't keep anything from Melanie; he'd feel too guilty. He explained his encounter with Johnny Malfkoski, omitting no detail. He didn't know who the bad guy was. Was it Jimmy or Billy? He was confused, but he believed one of them guilty. Frustrated and suspended from work, he felt alone, and believed he had nowhere to turn. Melanie was a bright light for him. He forgot about suspects and prisoners and murders and FBI agents. He looked directly at Melanie. His mind adrift, he spoke his thoughts, not caring that Melanie sat next to him. He cared about her.

"My uncle used to work down at the Harvard Club years ago. Great guy, my uncle. His name was Harold Nicholson; they called him Nick. He'd give us boys advice all the time—flip us a quarter every time we walked into the family home in Jamaica Plain."

"You and your brothers ever listen to his advice?"

"Of course not," Stephen chuckled. "We were kids. But one time he said something that really got my attention. He said, 'Stevie Boy, there's only two things in God's world that are beautiful. There's the sun rising over the Atlantic, and the twinkle in the eye of a woman you love.' I'll never forget that."

Melanie was speechless, looking through the large window, staring at the ocean. Stephen looked at the television—quiet. What was he trying to say? Stephen was acting strange, as if he was reaching out to her. Melanie was torn. She *wanted* to grab him right now and hug him—tell him everything would be all right. But she couldn't. She came here for business and she wouldn't allow personal feelings to interfere with her duty.

"I talked to Renee." That was all she said. Stephen finally turned to her, knowing that she couldn't respond to his last statement, and motioned her to continue. "I showed her photographs of all the Kappa Chi Omicron brothers and I asked her to point out which kid was Boston Boy."

"What did Renee say?"

"She pointed directly at you, Stephen, she pointed right at you. It broke my heart. Tell me right now you're not the kid Laiken called Boston Boy."

He shook his head. "Is that what this surprise visit is all about?" Stephen was perplexed. "I've worked hand in hand with you for more than two months and now you think I'm the kid she called Boston Boy? Who told you to go down there to speak with Renee? You think I'm falling on my sword? You think that I'm a sociopathic serial killer?" Stephen's tone was loud, attracting the attention of bar patrons. "Obviously you've made the wrong read on me, Detective." She tried to maintain her composure, but her hand shook as she produced a copy of the phone bills. The Nicholson home phone number was highlighted with a yellow marker.

"I just want you to know that I haven't gone to Milton Glavin about this...yet."

Stephen examined the old phone bill; he couldn't believe what he read. "I already told you that I fooled around with Laiken before. Now, I'm amazed at the phone number thing, Melanie. I'll admit that this sure as shit looks incriminating, but you're just going to have to take my word. I'm a smartass, and a train wreck at times. But I ain't a killer."

Melanie could no longer face him; she rose from her stool. "I hope to God you're telling the truth, Stephen." He tried to call her back but it was too late. She was gone.

Stephen knew. The pretty girl from Springfield was set in her ways and he had no plausible explanation, no alibi. It was as if he was already convicted by the kangaroo court, the Honorable Melanie Leary presiding. His life had been turned upside down so quickly. He looked to the barkeep and motioned him with his hand.

He thought about it, but this time he used his head. No, the wheat, hops, and barley wouldn't solve anything. In his Jeep he sought refuge with the stereo, but the pounding decibels couldn't assuage the hurt. After all, things between him and Melanie might never be the same.

29.

Pedestrian. That was the most fitting description of the Olympian's bedroom. If asked to create an image of a serial killer's room, a typical criminal justice student would probably paint images of Gothic statuettes, dreary-colored walls, shelves of vampire books, and drawers filled with pornography.

Such décor did not befit the Olympian. He considered himself a regular guy, and ostensibly he had that right. He sat at his mahogany desk slowly rolling the computer mouse . His king-sized bed was neatly made, covered by a down comforter. The hardwood floor was spotless and the clothes in his closet were fastidiously separated, first by season, then by color. The only mount on the walls was a painting of a clipper ship, valiantly fighting an invading sea in its attempt to stay afloat, though certain doom appeared imminent. His small library was divided equally for his three tastes: sports, finance, and literature.

Curtains drawn, rain pounded down on the streets without the slightest hint of a coming sun. He read the two Boston dailies online, as always. The story was on page one of both newspapers; they were nearly identical. He would later find the same story in the major newspapers for Pittsfield, Hoosac Mills, Brockton, Lawrence, Fall River, and other Bay State cities. FBI Special Agent Milton Glavin was appealing to the people of Massachusetts for help in the search for a serial killer.

Special Agent Glavin commented only on the 1987 murder of Taconic State College student Laiken Barnes, stating that "new witnesses" had come forward, and that the investigation was "making progress." The vast majority of Taconic State College students were from the Boston area, so he was reaching out to the appropriate target audience. Other unsolved murders were also being investigated in connection with the Barnes murder, but Glavin declined to specify, noting "the irregularities of the murders." An FBI hotline number was provided, encouraging any telephone calls and assuring anonymity. Glavin announced that in honor of Laiken Barnes' recent birthday, a candlelight vigil would be held this coming Friday night at the Hoosac Mills Boys and Girls Club, of which Laiken had been a member. All were welcome.

The Olympian went to the window, watching droplets streak inches from his face. He couldn't control his laughter, thinking of Milton Glavin's appeal to the people.

I was born at night, Milton…but not last night.

No, the Olympian would not be attending the candlelight vigil. His focus was hours away, and his greatest fantasy was about to come to fruition. Today he had a date, and no word of emotion could justly capture how he felt inside.

Yes, today he had a date, though no one told the poor woman to prepare.

* * *

The spring rain soothed Stephen. He slept soundly on the recliner. At times in his life he suffered from insomnia, and even worse, sleepwalking. The rhythmic patter of raindrops was his sleeping pill. Two hours passed before he awakened. WXKS FM radio played in the background, pushing out the lyrics to "Wishing on a Star." It was noontime.

He was at the family home—his comfort zone. His dad and Matthew had spoken quietly in the living room, unaffected by the stereo or Stephen's snore. "Glad to see you're up, sleepyhead, been meaning to speak with you." Mr. Nicholson turned off the stereo, a visible sign that a paternal lecture loomed ahead. Matthew recognized his cue.

"Time for me to depart, gentlemen," Matty said with a curious grin while noting the time. "I have to take care of some family business." Mr. Nicholson handed Stephen a cold can of diet soda. Stephen rubbed his eyes and stared at his father.

"What's up, Eamon?" he asked with a yawn.

"You," Eamon replied. "How about apprising your old man about the craziness you're engulfed in? I've been talking to your mother and your brother. It seems as though you can't see the forest through the trees." At times the Nicholson family was close—too close. Secrets were an anomaly; they all knew each other's business, so it was only fitting that the patriarch was well informed of Stephen's movements. "Now then, let's start with that shiner you're sporting. Whose fist did you catch with your face?" It had been almost a week, but the effects of Renzo DiLorenzo's left hand were still prominent. Stephen sighed.

He was straightforward with Eamon, telling him the truth about his suspension from work and his inner struggle with the murder investigation. He was scrupulous in detail, even considering quitting the Laiken Barnes case, cold turkey. This time the father-son talk was different. Feedback wasn't unsolicited—he sought his father's advice.

"Stephen, listen to yourself," Eamon said. "This isn't the damn movies. You're fighting a two-front war right now."

"It's tough," Stephen answered. "I feel like walking away from it all right now, but the truth is I can't. Too much is at stake. It's a pretty difficult thing to deal with when you think that one of your friends might actually be capable of calculating and devious murders, and now Melanie thinks that I may have done it." Eamon's eyebrows jumped. "Don't worry; your son isn't a killer. The last two months have been imaginary for me, and it's as if I'm waiting for a movie director to yell 'cut,' but it isn't happening. It's real and I don't like it."

Eamon gave a fatherly nod. "I need to ask you a few questions."

"Okay, shoot."

"Why would Melanie look at you as a suspect?"

Stephen wanted to avoid detail, so he simplified his answer. "I hooked up with Laiken a few times before she was murdered, but like I said, you've got nothing to worry about."

"So you think that one of your frat brothers may be responsible for these murders?"

"I just told you that."

"Just answer my questions."

Stephen involuntarily dipped his chin, admonished. "Okay, sorry, go ahead."

"Do these boys know that you're suspicious of them?"

"Jimmy does but Billy doesn't…I don't think."

"Is Billy the same Billy Munsing kid from Neponset?"

"Yes it is. Jimmy's last name is Petrilli. You've met him probably once or twice; he's from East Weymouth." Stephen was momentarily lost in thought. "Neither one of them have the right tatties."

"Excuse me?"

"Tattoos. They both have tattoos, but not a Celtics tattoo. The killer in one of the murders had a Celtics tattoo on his arm, but neither of those guys have one. Melanie cross-referenced laser surgery places and their names never came up."

"Okay, so maybe they're not guilty," Eamon suggested. "How about this prison thing? Are some Mafioso goons gonna come looking to break your legs now? Will you have to worry every time you leave your condo?"

Stephen shrugged. "Probably not. But then again, I thought I solved the problem two months ago, so it shows how much I know."

Eamon was quiet. He pitied Mickey O'Sullivan, once a fixture in his living room, the best friend of his youngest son, David. Mickey was a good kid; he'd simply drifted astray. Now Stephen was looking out for Mickey, protecting him—an act that seemed only natural. Eamon understood; it was the right thing to do. But Stephen was in a mess. His son's problems were his problems. It was the price of fatherhood.

"Well?" Stephen finally queried.

"I'll tell you what I think." Eamon paused as he organized his thoughts. "I think I'm too damn old to be playing in golf tournaments dedicated to you."

"What?"

"Do I have to spell it out for you, Stephen? You've been chasing killers and guys connected to organized crime, son. You're a nickel-and-dime gumshoe. Don't you get it? You're gonna get yourself killed. Stephen, listen to me. The FBI is working on your case, not to mention other agencies, right?" The question was rhetorical. "Stop with the bullshit and go back to finding truant schoolchildren. I've got news for you, it's much safer." Eamon paced the room; Stephen remained silent. "Stephen…your mother and I already buried one of our boys. We don't want anything to happen to you." His words were biting. Eamon's hand rested on his son's shoulder. "And another thing—you're thirty years old. Stop chasing girls around the saloon. Find a woman and settle down, will you? It'll add years to your mother's life."

"Eam—Dad?"

"Yes, Stephen."

"Thank you."

Eamon Nicholson nodded, staring at his boy. "Sometimes you have to be pulled from the water when you don't know you're wet."

"I understand," Stephen answered.

The tension softened. They looked at one another—both relieved, as if the white elephant in the room had been vanquished. The quiet was interrupted: the doorbell rang. Stephen motioned from the chair, but Mr. Nicholson—Eamon—stopped him. "Let me get this one," he said.

Stephen heard the door open. Small chatter ensued but Stephen couldn't quite place the voice of the visitor, though it sounded oddly familiar.

It was a thick Boston accent, sort of like Eamon's. No, on second thought, it was exactly like Eamon's. Boston accents, though sounding one-size-fits-all to outsiders, actually have distinct neighborhood signatures. The footsteps grew closer. Eamon, smirking, entered the parlor with a man who, ostensibly, was his guest. The guest was tall, well over six feet, with long appendages and a confident gait. He was lean—maybe two hundred pounds. The gentleman was in his early sixties. He wore casual khaki pants, black leather shoes, and a blue-and-white striped button-down shirt. No tie. The stately yet handsome Irish American's face was complemented by salt-and-pepper hair. Eye color was difficult to determine. Stephen's best guess was blue—whatever. Stephen knew the man's exact identity. He rose from the recliner and walked across the room to shake hands with Michael Lindehan.

Sheriff Michael Lindehan.

Stephen stared at Eamon—Eamon the Townie, that is. Eamon smiled, knowing that his son was forming a reasonable form of betrayal. Stephen now looked at Sheriff Lindehan.

Jesus, Eamon, I know you said you knew Lindehan from growing up in Charlestown, but you never said that you KNEW HIM knew him.

Both Eamon and Lindehan read Stephen's thoughts. The young West Roxbury man didn't understand the depths or value of the Charlestown Code of Honor. It was often misinterpreted as the Code of Silence, which dealt specifically with a *no witness sees anything* attitude of reporting criminal activity. The Code of Honor was different. It was a deeper, richer, and more fulfilling neighborhood stamp by which native Townies strived to honor and protect the name of one of its sons or daughters. In this case, the provider was Michael Lindehan. Stephen Nicholson—by virtue of being the son of a Townie—was the name in question. Stephen instantaneously knew that Eamon and Sheriff Lindehan were far more than "childhood acquaintances," as implied years before.

Lindehan strolled to the trophy case. He softly yet deliberately placed his hands on the bottom shelf. Various-sized sports trophies, many covered with a light layer of dust, occupied four shelves of the built-in bookcase. Lindehan read a sampling: Matthew Nicholson, South Side Gym Boxing 1979; Matthew Nicholson, Parkway Little League Mike Melling Team 1976; David Nicholson, Holy Name CYO Basketball Under 15 Champions 1985; Stephen Nicholson, Parkway Youth Hockey Midget A's Greater Boston League runner-up. No year was listed.

"You played Parkway Midget A's?" Lindehan asked.

Stephen realized he was now alone in his parents' parlor with the Shawmut County sheriff. Eamon had slipped out uncontested. It was no mistake. "Yes, I did, sir," Stephen said. "Played JV for CM but I wasn't good enough to make varsity."

"No shame in that," Lindehan said. "CM's had a hell of a hockey program for years."

Something was different—no, something was peculiar about this already-weird conversation. Stephen stared at Sheriff Lindehan's hands. They had yet to move from the bottom shelf, which of course could be substituted—theoretically—as a table. The conversation, of course, was about sports. The gravity of the moment hit Stephen like a freight train. Stephen walked across the room and assumed a seat on the sofa. He needed to be sure. He placed his two hands on the glass of a newly purchased coffee table. "Yeah, CM hockey still kicks ass," he said. Lindehan locked eyes with Stephen. "It's kind of like Xaverian's football team, but only better." Lindehan smiled. Stephen's instincts were accurate.

He was actually engaging in correction officer table talk with Sheriff Michael Lindehan in his boyhood home. Lindehan read Stephen's body language. He knew that Stephen knew.

Wow.

Lindehan freed his hands and faced Stephen. They both now stood in the center of the parlor. The sheriff smiled, disarming the tension.

"People forget I was a block officer for three years when I was in my early twenties—long before I went to law school."

"The difference," Stephen said, "is that any other politician would cram that fact down your throat." Lindehan smiled again. "You don't even mention your correction officer days in your department biography."

Lindehan opened his hands in a placating gesture. "I am comfortable with my resume."

Stephen observed that Sheriff Lindehan wasn't holding a beverage. Eamon hadn't offered. There was a reason; it wasn't a social visit to talk about Parkway Youth Hockey. Both men knew this.

"Young Mickey O'Sullivan never brought drugs into the Boston House," the sheriff said.

Stephen was in a precarious situation. Sheriff Lindehan was Eamon's friend. He'd also declared the conversation off the record with the sanctity of the table talk gesture. Yet he still had to be careful. He had to be precise. He had to be delicate.

"Fuck Renzo DiLorenzo," Stephen said. "And double-fuck Lucky Giannessimo."

Lindehan laughed. Stephen made some bold statements yet admitted to nothing at the same time. "The initial reason he didn't mule drugs is because you paid a multiple-thousand-dollar debt to Officer Giannessimo," the sheriff said. "When your efforts failed, you had a fair one with Inmate DiLorenzo in the gymnasium. Officer Shaughnessy was your backup. Inmate Shawn Blighe was also present."

Stephen gave the sheriff a genuine smile.

Damn, Lindehan, you have some quality snitches. It may even be Renzo for that matter.

"You've got some balls," Lindehan said. "DiLorenzo's a badass."

"This here is table talk, Sheriff, is it not?" Stephen asked.

"Yes," Lindehan replied.

"I ask because on a scale of one to ten, my ACP is a ten."

Sheriff Lindehan was a cerebral yet cool man. He entered the three-letter acronym into his internal search engine but couldn't decipher it. Stephen sensed Lindehan's reluctance to question the statement.

"It means Acute Correctional Paranoia," Stephen said. "After all, sir, you are in fact standing in my parents' parlor talking about fair ones and lugging while I'm currently on suspension. With all due respect, Sheriff, I'd like to know where this conversation is leading."

Lindehan nodded. "Of course, it's a reasonable request," he said. "A dear friend of mine—a classmate at Suffolk University Law—is a high-ranking official with the DEA."

"Okay," Stephen said.

"With my cooperation he has made some high-profile arrests—and subsequent convictions—in the last two years. Many of these cases have made a media splash."

"I still don't know how this concerns me, sir."

Lindehan gestured with his left hand. "Our communications unit—not the IPS unit—has been monitoring the phone activity of Giannessimo on the street, and Renzo DiLorenzo inside the facility."

Stephen nodded. "Shooting fish in a barrel," he said.

"Precisely," the sheriff replied. "But now the end has come. Giannessimo was recently arrested by BPD, which will cause some embarrassment for my office. I will defuse it with my media contacts."

"What about Renzo?" Stephen asked. "Can you ship his ass to Berkshire County?"

"I'm afraid not," Lindehan said. "I can't compromise the integrity of my internal resources." Stephen made the quick translation: If Lindehan transferred Renzo, he would jeopardize the safety of his white inmate informants inside the Boston House.

Damn again…no wonder Lindehan has been sheriff since the early '80s.

There was a pregnant pause, broken by the sheriff. "I understand you have good feet," he said.

"I do okay," Stephen said. "One Step Beyond is a quality dojo."

"Pretty risky kicking high against a guy like Renzo," Lindehan said. "And so is throwing a right-handed lead punch." Both men enjoyed a staged laugh. "On a separate note, Deputy Francis Kohan should not be jeopardizing his job and criminal charges by holding a gun to Giannessimo's head outside of The McGrath Principle Tavern."

Stephen eyed Lindehan. He sized him up, from polished shoe to the finely combed salt-and-pepper hair. "Chief Inspector Charlemagne did not tell you that," Stephen said.

Lindehan smiled. "Freddy is a good enough guy," he said. "He is married to my sister, Margaret, and is the father to my four nieces."

Boston politics.

"Charlemagne didn't tell you that," Stephen repeated.

Lindehan didn't speak. Instead, he raised his eyebrows in a suggestive manner that indicated agreement. Yet he did not verbally acknowledge it. Lindehan thought about the overhaul he'd implemented two years earlier to the IPS division. On paper—and to the casual eye—the division had been eviscerated.

What had actually happened was Lindehan's philosophy change in regard to information collection. The old system was broken. Too many investigations were compromised because the investigators either had a good relationship with the officers or, in some cases, the inmates. So Lindehan had taken drastic steps. He maintained his skeleton crew of Charlemagne and Mrs. Tosconaro in IPS, but their duties were limited.

Lindehan's real sources of information came from the streets. For years he had a private investigation firm, Johns, Jacobs, & Johns, on his payroll. They had been used, at times, for background checks on prospective employees. Now Johns, Jacobs, & Johns served a much greater role.

Private investigators had the luxury of anonymity and, more importantly, were held to a much lower level of accountability in terms of public responsibility. Johns, Jacobs, & Johns had more than ninety investigators on its payroll. Some were squared-away college types who only chased white-collar activity. Others were street guys who sat on city barstools, speaking to ex-inmates—and correction officers—without fear.

It was a recent ex-inmate from 6-Block, Chico Pires, who drank with an investigator at the Hunan Pagoda and detailed the full story of the Nicholson-O'Sullivan-Giannessimo-DiLorenzo ordeal. Pires was from Roslindale; he'd graduated from Catholic Memorial. He was three years younger than Stephen. More notably, he had been a classmate of David Nicholson's.

Why target Pires? It was simple; Pires was the longtime cellmate of Shawn Blighe. Pires accumulated all his information over the course of two months. Blighe, on occasion, would make mention of the situation. Yet being near Blighe and DiLorenzo—along with quietly knowing the

Nicholson brothers and Mickey O'Sullivan—allowed Pires to form a crystal-clear snapshot of the drama.

The investigator paid Chico's bar tab and slipped him three hundred dollars. Just like that, presto—the data was collected and delivered to Sheriff Michael Lindehan. There is a paradox, in a sense, to solving crimes. Sometimes the best information from a street felony comes from inside the walls of a penal institution; other times a drunk on a barstool tells the real reasons why good correction officers are fighting inmates.

Lindehan paid Johns, Jacobs, & Johns a handsome yearly stipend. Yet he was not responsible for the conduct of its investigators. He did not have their investigators on his payroll. He did not pay for their health insurance or vacation time. There were no worker's compensation issues. They were merely contractors who saved the department thousands of dollars in salary reduction, yet paid immense dividends in terms of useful information.

Charlemagne was good enough to learn the *what* of a story by making penniless deals with guys like Squeaky Tubbs. But Johns, Jacobs, & Johns possessed the street savvy to learn the *why* of a story by plying guys like Chico Pires.

Lindehan was brilliant.

"Here's the deal," the sheriff said. "We don't fight inmates in this business. Perhaps there was a time when that was the case…but not anymore."

"Agreed," Stephen said.

"But," Lindehan said, "seeing this is table talk, you did a hell of a job preventing drugs from entering my facility. That is commendable."

Stephen considered the sheriff's words. "I wasn't going to let that happen, sir."

"As far as the future of young Mr. O'Sullivan," Sheriff Lindehan said, "that is yet to be determined."

"Fair enough."

The sheriff stepped toward Stephen and took his hand. "You return to work next Monday. The investigation is over. You have been officially cleared."

Stephen squeezed the sheriff's oversized hand. "Thank you, sir."

"No, Stephen," Lindehan said, "thank you."

Sheriff Lindehan released his grip and in a swift motion disappeared from the room.

Like he was never there.

Conversely, Eamon quickly entered. "Listen," Eamon said, "your mother has the SUV and I have to pick up a table saw at Home Depot. If I put the backseats down, will it fit in your Jeep?" Stephen nodded and tossed him a set of keys. Eamon left the room.

"Dad?" Stephen called.

Eamon reappeared. His face showed no emotion. He dangled the Jeep keys and acted as if he were in a rush. Better yet, he acted if everything was normal. "Forget it," Stephen said. Eamon pretended it was just a typical early afternoon on Meredith Street.

Like Sheriff Michael Lindehan was never in the house.

Stephen's head hurt. He sat back on the recliner. "Townies," he said. No one else was in the room. He accepted and appreciated the sheriff's visit. A burden had been lifted. But now, as he leaned back in the chair, Eamon's earlier words formed a searing impression. His father was right. If Jimmy or Billy were responsible for those deaths, then the FBI could catch them. Why should he be involved in that mess? He would call the case quits on Monday.

Stephen flicked on the television. Raindrops still bounced outside the window. He channel-surfed. It was Saturday afternoon—nothing good on. He came across a classic movie and paused. It was a screen adaption of *Oliver Twist*, a good movie but he had already seen it twice. He continued to peruse the television and found a baseball game. The new season was underway, and with the help of cable television, he watched a fresh John Smoltz hurl at the St. Louis Cardinals.

He fought to keep his eyes open. Big Mac took a young pitcher for a four-bagger, deep into the upper decks at Busch Stadium, but Stephen didn't see it. He slept, and more importantly, he dreamed.

It was 1987, the night of the first murder. The Green Machine parties had always been the favorite of the Kappa Chi Omicron brothers. They provided spirits, camaraderie, girls…and stealth, if one so chose.

Stephen appeared as the Grim Reaper, and he remembered entering the basement. It was exhilarating, walking the Kappa dungeon in secret, sipping the delicious libation and chartering a course through the crowd.

He awoke as McGwire touched home plate. Semiconscious would best describe Stephen's lethargic state on the recliner. His focus returned to that infamous party. He remembered having a blackout of some sort that evening, but he couldn't recall when it happened. The fugues had been a new thing. He arose from the chair and walked around the house. At the front door he gazed into the rainy afternoon. It was barren on the side street—no traffic, no kids, no dogs. He turned and looked at the family photograph hanging on the wall—a complete family photograph—taken in the fall of 1986. It had been a Christmas gift for Mom and Dad, and they treasured it. Young David Nicholson smiled at the photographer. Stephen reached out, touching his brother's cheek.

There was nothing on Stephen's agenda. He returned to the comfort of the recliner, thinking of his brother. The rain didn't subside, and as he entered into another sleep, neither did his dreams.

* * *

"He's being cute," Milton Glavin said. The poem written to Melanie had been read, reread, turned upside down, and scrutinized again until the two agents were exhausted. They concluded that the Olympian was simply being sly, mocking them. Verse, word selection, overall content, and style weren't weighed heavily. It was Devon Patterson's assertion that the Olympian wanted to rattle them, force them to overanalyze the poem's message. He could have written anything; that part didn't matter. And it wasn't perceived as a direct threat to Melanie, though they advised her to keep her weapon nearby at all times.

What did matter was that the Olympian had made contact. The poem was no hoax—they all agreed—and it was obvious that he was an attention seeker. He was vain. And he made it abundantly clear that there would be another victim. Milton knew that immediate action was necessary; he opened a bag and passed out copies of various newspapers from around the state—today's editions. "Remember I talked about a proactive approach. Well, there you have it." Unbeknownst to the others, Milton had made an official FBI press release to the major media publications in Massachusetts. He detailed certain aspects—some false, as to weed out false confessions—of the 1987 Laiken Barnes murder. He admitted that there were other unsolved murders around the "New York and New England area," but he couldn't further comment due to extenuating circumstances.

Milton was smart. Anonymity of the Hughes and Rivera victims precluded nosy reporters from drawing their own conclusions of a quadrennial killer. If they had, women in Massachusetts would be panic-stricken, knowing they were living in 1999—year of the next kill. But Milton did send out his own special messages to the Olympian, hoping to draw him in. Ten minutes was allotted for everyone to read. "Will he take the bait?" Marcus Torres asked.

Milton shrugged. "We'll know soon enough."

"Something's been on my mind that I have to ask you," Melanie said to Patterson. "It's about your lecture from the other night. Did you find something odd about that man who was challenging you? Something about him bothered me."

"I thought the same thing," Patterson answered. "His name was Carlos. He seemed witty and intelligent—very confrontational. Chances are that he was just some lunatic getting his cheap thrills. He was at the back of the auditorium so I couldn't get a good look at him, and the student in charge of taping the lecture screwed the film up. We'll never know."

The task force sat together, brainstorming. The meeting was in Melanie's home court, Hoosac Mills. Milton, careful with his word choice, indicated that James Petrilli was still a suspect in the death of Laiken Barnes. He and Patterson had yet to disclose their illegal finding of Petrilli's DNA. More importantly, they'd received the DNA results from the fingernail recovered at Laiken's graveside. Its DNA composition didn't match Jimmy Petrilli, but it did match the DNA from blood recovered at the Darlene Hughes crime scene. Milton had a conundrum: there were three sets of DNA samples, one positively linked to Jimmy Petrilli and two sets linked to an un-sub. And Petrilli had admitted to Nicholson that he'd had sex with Laiken Barnes on the day of her death. Yes, Petrilli was still a suspect, but evidence against him was starting to go the other way. Admitting to having sex with Laiken was now working in his favor. But the question lingered: who was the unknown man?

Milton addressed the group, speaking only on what was proven. The Olympian had worked diligently in the Alicia Ana Rivera murder. He left his genetic fingerprints, hair, and blood, at the Barnes and Hughes crime scenes, respectively. It was the Rivera murder in which he had been flawless. If not for the gold chain pattern, no connection would have been made. Patterson thought—the gold chain. The gold chains were the Olympian's

Achilles heel. "Are any of you familiar with the Totem Phase of serial murder?"

Bobbie Thomas and Melanie looked at one another. Marcus Torres, the book-smart detective, spoke. "It's when he takes a trophy or souvenir from the victim. He does it so he can relish his kill, to prolong it."

Patterson smiled. "Good. Now we seem to be dealing with the opposite. We're not sure if our Olympian *takes* things. We don't know that yet. What we do know is that he *leaves* things, specifically the gold chains. Why?" Patterson spoke as if he were in a classroom at Quantico.

"To bait the police, make us wonder, think…maybe to tease us, like the poem," Melanie offered.

"True. Another example of that took place in 1888. Jack the Ripper, or a man purporting to be Jack the Ripper, sent letters to Scotland Yard in a teasing fashion. What else?" Everyone simultaneously looked toward Marcus Torres, as if he were the prized student. He did not disappoint.

"It's his signature, his own brand. So we know it's him, and no one else can take credit for the kill. And it may also tell us *why* he kills, as opposed to his modus operandi, which tells us *how* he kills."

"Excellent, Marcus. Very perceptive, but what else?" They were quiet. "The unknown, ladies and gentleman, the unknown. It's the intangible—a nasty word in law enforcement. He may also be leaving these chains for a personal reason, something unknown to us. Our Olympian may have ghosts or demons to exorcise, and the gold chains may play a role in his healing." They all stared at Patterson. "Remember, a serial killer is a different animal; I can't state that enough. Sanity and rational thinking, as we understand those words, don't enter into play. You have to think like a killer to catch a killer." Milton had been quiet. He and Patterson had been working long hours, balancing their workload across Massachusetts.

"How about your profile, gentlemen? When will you complete it?" Bobbie blurted out. Milton and Patterson glared at one another.

"It's an inexact science, Bobbie, you have to understand that," Patterson said. "No two cases are the same, so we'll have to wait and·see." He wasn't being forthright and it showed. They had recently completed their profile of the Olympian, but their results were a bit surprising. Because a profile is merely a tool, and it is indeed inexact, they now minimized the significance of the profile. Bobbie had been a cagey police officer, and she had taken her feistiness to the district attorney's office. She spoke her mind.

"No bullshitting us, guys. Everyone here has time invested in this case, so please don't have it both ways. You can't expect us to give you all of our information if you're not willing to reciprocate. If you've completed the profile, we'd like to hear it." Milton and Patterson looked at each other and smiled. Bobbie had balls; they liked that. Milton caught himself looking at Bobbie's ring finger, making a mental note that it was naked. An interesting woman, he thought. He wouldn't mind knowing her intimately, wondering if she carried the same moxie in her personal life as she exhibited professionally. Milton was an introvert, conservative by nature, but he liked women with zeal.

He liked Bobbie Thomas.

Melanie was quiet. She respected Bobbie for speaking up because she could not; she hadn't been forthright with all of her information, and she knew it was wrong. It was Milton's case, so he made all decisions on the dispensation of facts. But this profile wasn't a fact, was it? No, it was more of a hypothesis. Milton looked to Patterson, and his mentor gave him the nod of approval.

"Okay. The truth is that Petrilli doesn't really match our profile, as you've all figured out by now." They all nodded, and Milton took inventory of the small conference room. He saw cops, street cops, the men and women who put their lives on the line every time they left the station. And they cared. They cared too much at times, working hours that would prove them indefatigable, sacrificing from their personal lives for even the smallest results. He read it in their faces; they badly wanted to slam the door on the Olympian. And like himself—but not necessarily his mentor—they weren't concerned with the publicity of the collar. They were cops, and words such as *public safety* actually meant something. It was the life they had chosen.

Milton remembered his college days in New York. He had been an apt student—top 10 percent of his class, always giving an honest effort. "There's no substitution for honesty, dear," his grandmother used to say. And he remembered the sign on the wall of his ethics classroom: Veracity Breeds Justice.

But was that saying true? Was it practical? The bad guys never played by the rules; they had no accountability whatsoever. He reminded himself—*the good guys are the good guys because of who we are*. We're held to higher standards and should never stoop or compromise. Milton's mind decelerated, questioning the ethical nature of his most recent tactic. At times subterfuge could be your best ally, but he wondered—did the ends justify the means?

He would let the others decide. "We got Petrilli's DNA from a soda can that was brought to him by a visitor, Stephen Nicholson." Marcus and Bobbie looked at Melanie. "Nicholson had nothing to do with it, actually. We knew that he'd visit Petrilli because he's his fraternity brother. Berkshire County IAD cooperated, and we also bugged the room."

Melanie glared at Milton Glavin. "You guys set him up. He's been busting his balls on this case and you set him up anyway, didn't you?" she challenged. "Yeah, you definitely did. You could have held Petrilli at the federal courthouse lockup or Norfolk County Jail. You could've held him anywhere, but you didn't. Instead you drove him out to Pittsfield because you knew Stephen would go see him. No, correction—you *wanted* Stephen to see him." The room went quiet.

"It's business, Melanie. Don't look any deeper than that; it's business," Patterson said. Milton made eye contact with Melanie, not speaking but acknowledging her point.

Patterson still had the floor. "Petrilli admitted to Nicholson that he slept with Laiken Barnes on the day of her death, but he denies killing her."

Melanie understood why Milton Glavin and Devon Patterson wanted Stephen off the case. They used him and spit him out. Law enforcement was a cutthroat business.

Milton wasn't finished. He explained the contradictory DNA sample, the fingernail found at Laiken's grave. "So now you're implying that maybe Jimmy Petrilli isn't our man?" Marcus asked.

"He hasn't been excluded," Milton said. "But truth be told, I think that's the route it may be going. Right now we have an un-sub out there, someone's who's been scientifically linked to Laiken's graveside and the murder site of Darlene Hughes. And before anyone asks, none of the murders, in our opinion, were committed by more than one perpetrator. Our guy operates solo."

Milton looked at Bobbie Thomas. "We examined all three murder sites. We looked over crime scene photographs, autopsy reports, depositions, and everything else you all know about." He hesitated, searching for his next words. "We try to get a feel for our man, and this Olympian is a strange fellow. He's certainly organized and progressively improves, which is a bad thing. He's a mission-oriented type. According to all statements we've received, his victims were all promiscuous."

Milton suddenly preached. "Law enforcement is a tricky business. You have to let go of your ego at times—you folks all know that—and at times it's not easy. I didn't want to listen to any facts on Jimmy Petrilli until after our profile was complete. I compromised that process when Melanie learned of the connection to Detective Rocek and the plausibility of a police cover-up. If I hadn't acted at that time I would have been negligent in my duties to the citizens of the United States. That may sound corny, but it's the truth. Now the irony is that Petrilli is slipping as a suspect."

The agent returned to his desk and picked up a folder, extracting a piece of paper. He sipped his water, then made eye contact with Bobbie. "You asked for the profile, here it is…"

The profile was an inexact, objective analysis, and nothing more. Both Milton Glavin and Devon Patterson conducted separate profiles and their findings were strikingly—almost eerily—similar. They were looking for a white male aged thirty to thirty-five, with a higher likelihood on thirty-five. He would be single, heterosexual, and live at home with one parent, his mother. A churchgoer, he would be socially functional and possess an above-average IQ. He was strong, athletic, a sports fan, and left-handed. He had a white-collar job, most likely in banking or finance. He would have a license, driving a well-kept, dark-colored SUV or Jeep. It would be no older than three years and a stick shift. And if he had a criminal record, if would be limited to his juvenile years.

"Why a standard and not automatic?" Bobbie asked.

"Control. He'd have more control, and that's indicative of his type," Patterson said.

"There's one other thing we've considered," Milton said. "We're leaning in the white-collar direction for occupation. But there is something else we may want to consider." All eyes were on Milton. "Devon and I feel kind of foolish, being avid readers. Our man the Olympian is literary.

The pseudonyms he chose—Dawkins, Sikes, and Cruncher—they all have something in common. We speculate the Olympian may be a..."

The words rolled smoothly off Milton's tongue, not knowing the effect they'd have. Melanie felt a small knot form in her stomach. She had absorbed all of the FBI agent's words, and the knot snowballed into a large mass, occluding her from speaking. They all looked to Melanie, curious. In thirty seconds she regained her composure, breathing steadily as Bobbie Thomas rubbed her back. Finally she said, "I know the Olympian."

* * *

The immense Catholic church was an amazing sight. The nasty inclement weather, to its chagrin, couldn't conceal its beauty. The Olympian stopped, disregarding the rain, and marveled at the magnificent holy place. He then entered the side door quietly and took a seat in the pews, his face in his hands.

The church was empty and dark—very dark. He looked up at the Gothic ceiling in amazement and marveled. The red light was lit on the confessional booth; within two minutes a fiftyish woman, hair up in a bun, scurried to the side tabernacle. She repeated her Act of Contrition, and the Olympian could not help but chuckle, for he knew that her transgressions were probably no greater than profanity. She finished her prayers quickly and departed.

With stealth and quickness he affixed something to the middle door of the booth and entered the side compartment. The slide panel opened. "Forgive me, Father, for I have sinned. It has been twelve years since my last confession, and these are my sins..."

"Twelve years is a long time, my son," the priest said in a Spanish accent. "For what reasons have you waited so long?"

"I have my reasons, Father. I should have you know that I have never missed a weekly Mass or a day of obligation since penance." It was dark in the booth, each man only able to see the profile silhouette of the other.

"These days younger persons are more concerned with avarice, with fulfilling their own selfish needs. I note your attendance, son, but why have you waited so long to fulfill the never-ending sacrament of penance?" The Olympian stirred in the booth. He had known for the last several days that his identity would be uncovered. He also knew it had been his own fault. He had made necessary monetary provisions for his disappearance, and today would be his greatest moment. Today he would finally gain revenge on the tramps of the world. Today justice would be served.

"With all due respect, Father, I have come to air my sins. Will you listen to them, and will you hear my Act of Contrition?"

The priest was set back by the man's response. He hesitated, then said, "Okay, my son, tell me your sins."

"I have taken the Lord's name in vain; I have coveted; I have engaged in premarital carnal activity; I have sinned. I have sinned terribly, Father, and even though compunction is absent for some of my deeds, I performed those deeds for good purpose. Yet I still seek forgiveness."

"What are these terrible sins of which you speak, my son?"

The Olympian was restless. It was a revealing moment. "I have serviced society by vanquishing three disease-spreading wretches from God's soil. I have not committed these acts in the name of God, Father, so do not mistake me for a delirious religious fanatic. I am sane and rational. My actions have been premeditated, and while they were committed without regret, I have violated God's creed. I sit across from you today and ask for absolution nonetheless."

Father Asturias was a visiting priest from Venezuela. He was highly educated, fluent in French, Portuguese, and English. It took a moment to absorb the totality of the man's words.

"My son, you say that you have taken the lives of three innocent children of God?" he asked.

"Innocent? Father, these 'children of God' were anything but innocent. They were wretches of society; they perpetuated all that was and is wrong with today's world. They were whores—baneful wolves outfitted in sheep's clothing." The priest was silent, not knowing what to say. "Please do not misread me, Father. I am no threat to society. I am friend, not foe, to the law-abiding people of this world."

Father Asturias turned and looked directly through the mesh panel. It was too dark. "My son, what you have done is wrong," he said quietly. "Although such women do exist, it is not for you to pass judgment. God is almighty, and it is he who shall judge all things made. I say to you, my son, go to the police and turn yourself in. It is what God wants you to do." The priest played the role of psychologist, hoping the Olympian would heed.

"Father, I have been a good Christian, and I am asking for your forgiveness. Help me."

Sweat escaped the priest's pores. He had seen much in his twenty-three years of service, but never had he encountered a true psychopath. His will was strong, and he wouldn't acquiesce to a murderer. "God cannot forgive those who are not repentant."

"Please, Father." The Olympian truly believed his plight in danger, and although his quest was not yet complete, he needed this pardon in the event that his life should end soon.

"No! You must express sorrow for your sins!" he stammered.

The Olympian shook his head; it was evident his effort was futile. "*Yo entiendo, Padre, vaya con Dios.*"

Father Asturias couldn't listen any more. He was a follower of Christ, a true ambassador of God, spreading goodwill throughout the Americas during his years of the cloth. He would stop this savage killer, stop him in his tracks before more blood was shed. He arose from the chair, ready to confront the monster nearby. Sensing sudden movement, the Olympian slid from the booth and out of the church, undetected.

His full body weight against the door, Father Asturias pushed in vain to exit his compartment. But a two-dollar doorstopper jailed the visiting priest. As the Olympian crossed the rainy street, shouts and obscenities spoken in a foreign tongue echoed off the ceiling, falling on deaf ears.

* * *

The dreams continued. Stephen's head involuntarily craned on the chair while beads of sweat saturated his shirt. Most dreams are fanciful occasions where the mind is a roller coaster, granted carte blanche, and takes its passenger on a twisting track anywhere in the world. They are usually adventurous; vicarious times that spare no expense and come without risk of injury, no matter how real they seem.

But not this time. These images were real. They were neither fictional nor pleasant. This time the dream was biographical. It told no lies. Again the setting was 1987, but no college students filled the streets. The summer swelter was in session. Stephen's dream was a recount, and it was personal. The images were vivid.

The bare-chested boys loitered on the corner, dunking the basketball over the street sign. The game on television had just ended, and the tall point guard for the

Lakers sank an improbable hook shot over two Boston Celtic Hall of Famers. It was a devastating loss for the hometown team, and the Lakers would go on to win the series.

The distinct sound of a woman's heels on pavement neared the boys—click, clack, click, clack, click, clack. They looked up and drew deep breaths. It was Mandy Mc-Masters—stunning, sexual, flirtatious. She was older—twenty-three. "Hi, boys," she said in a seductive voice. "How about giving me a ride down to the square?" The boys couldn't believe she was talking to them. Mandy was a local girl. But her life had taken a wrong turn. She reeked of booze and looked high. The boys were speechless. "Come now, boys, I won't bite you," she whispered. "As a matter of fact, if you give me a ride I'll make it worth your while, if you know what I mean." Mandy rolled her tongue around her lips.

"We…we don't have a car," Mickey O'Sullivan said before David Nicholson pulled him aside. They conferred the matter. It was the opportunity of a lifetime, complete bragging rights all the way to graduation. The Nicholson boy disappeared into his family home. His siblings and neighborhood friends partied in the basement. Without detection young David Nicholson grabbed a set of keys from the kitchen and went back outside.

Mandy smiled.

A learner's permit stuck out of the Nicholson boy's pocket; neither boy had a license. The blue Oldsmobile soon crossed the West Roxbury Parkway, finding Beech Street. Mandy inched closer to David, intending to meet her end of the bargain.

The car moved safely at thirty miles per hour, and it truly wasn't David Nicholson's fault when a drunken driver ran a stop sign, crunching into the driver's side door at a forty-five degree angle. The sedan spun, rotating two-and-a-half turns before dismantling a manicured row of hedges on a residential lawn.

Mandy's head connected with the windshield, spraying blood everywhere. The windshield cracked, and she sustained a concussion. Other than some blood loss and small bruises, she was all right. Mickey O'Sullivan was lucky, very lucky. He climbed out of the rear door virtually unmarked. His best friend was not so fortunate.

The steering wheel had jammed David's torso; blood oozed from his mouth. Mandy and the O'Sullivan boy dragged him out of the car and laid him on the lawn. Sirens interrupted the quiet neighborhood. The Nicholson boy was lucid and Mickey held his hand. David was most concerned about the condition of his brother Stephen's car, which was totaled. After a minute David's eyes rolled back and he stopped breathing.

Mandy screamed. Unsure of himself, Mickey performed mouth-to-mouth resuscitation on his friend, blood and all. It worked, and young David gasped aloud. He stared into Mickey's eyes, thankful. The first ambulance arrived and strapped young David to the stretcher. Before the EMTs closed the doors, the O'Sullivan boy offered a gift, placing his silver medal of the Holy Mother in David's hand. Mandy—suddenly sober—felt compelled to give something. She leaned down and kissed him on the forehead, and as a token of good luck she unclasped the glitter around her neck and affixed it to David.

It was a gold chain.

The ambulance sped off. Three hours later the resident doctor entered the waiting room, a sober look on his face. He conferred privately with Mr. and Mrs. Nicholson, who had just arrived. Within one minute hysterics rang loud. Aunts, uncles, cousins, and family friends held each other tightly. The thirty-nine-year-old drunken driver lay in stable condition three rooms down. Vigilante cries rang out. Mr. Nicholson quelled those thoughts.

Enough blood had been shed.

The Nicholson boys were traumatized, having failed in their duty to protect their youngest while Mom and Dad were down the Cape. The drunken driver would have his day in court, though many wanted to mete out their own brand of justice. But there was one member of the family who did not dwell on the drunken driver. He focused his attention elsewhere, to the girl who was crying incessantly in the corner. He had yet to speak in detail with young Mickey O'Sullivan, but he already knew who was responsible for his little brother's death.

Stephen spooked himself awake. The dream—no, the nightmare—was all too real. He wiped his forehead. In an inexorable fashion he picked up the clicker and returned to the movie classic. Two young boys conversed on the cobblestone streets of London. Stephen had been called to the movie, but he wasn't sure why. He thought about the dream, now remembering that David had died while wearing a gold chain. And the chain had been a gift. Before he could scream aloud, one of the English boys spoke. "My name's Jack Dawkins…but my nearest and dearest friends call me the Artful Dodger."

"Jack Dawkins," Stephen said aloud. "Oh my God…John Dawkins." He slid from the chair and ran upstairs, reporting to the library in the rear bedroom. And there it was. In the literary script of *Oliver Twist* Stephen found the name Bill Sikes. Bill was short for William—William Sikes, a pseudonym used by the Olympian. He scanned more classic English literature but found nothing. Later he would connect the name Jerry Cruncher to a character from *A Tale of Two Cities*, Jeremiah Cruncher. Considering the circumstances Stephen maintained his composure; he was on the right track. He needed his case files.

Mr. Nicholson had borrowed his Jeep, but had removed Stephen's case files to clear more space. The files sat in the hallway. Stephen sorted through different material until he found Laiken's high school yearbook. Something had always bothered him about the caption, but he could never figure it out. He looked down at her beautiful picture again.

Laiken Anne Barnes

24 Cheshire Street, Hoosac Mills
Cheerleading, Key Club, Honor Society, Drama Club
Thanks: PJ, RG, TW, AW, CW, NC, SS, LP, WR, AT, MC, etc.
Remember when: Bermuda '84, Jr. Prom hangover,
spelunking the tunnel with the crew, Congrats BB—good luck
with Scrooge, chemistry experiments, babysitting for Mr.
Fisch, Fenway Park trip, "Do you really have a butler?",
partying on Mohawk Street
Here I come Taconic State! Watch out!
Thanks Mom and Dad! I love you!
Ciao!......................L.A.B.

Finally Stephen saw it. In the middle of Laiken's "Remember When" section, she'd written, "Congrats BB—good luck with Scrooge!" BB was a two-letter acronym for Boston Boy.

The simple facts were settled. Boston Boy was in Hoosac Mills for the academic year 1984–85, the year of Laiken's high school yearbook. Boston Boy was a scholarly fellow, and a young Laiken had bid him prosperity. He had been an enigma, this Boston Boy character, until now.

His affinity for English literature was more than a hobby. He had dedicated his senior year in college to the collective works of the English master, Charles Dickens. He continued his passion by pursuing a master's degree in the same field, and now even instilled that very passion into the minds of young students.

Stephen gasped. He knew that Boston Boy was no longer fictitious, that Boston Boy had attended the infamous Green Machine party, and that Boston Boy could easily have gone unnoticed in Amherst and Wellfleet. He was handsome, he was slick, and he was intelligent. Boston Boy was the Olympian, and he was no longer an unknown variable.

The Olympian was Matthew Nicholson.

30.

The white van slid down Centre Street at a moderate clip. The driver relaxed behind the wheel. The mustache looked authentic, as did the curly wig. A well-positioned pillow, taped about his midriff, sealed his disguise. He looked at his watch and knew he was punctual. He double-checked inventory for his impending mission, as well as his supplies for the aftermath, and breathed easy when all was accounted for. He prepared well, as the Olympian always had. He hooked a left, following the SUV into the health club parking lot adjacent to Billings Field. A tall, muscular man stepped from his vehicle and walked into the health club. He would be picking up his children from their swimming lessons, as he did every Saturday afternoon. But the Olympian knew this, of course.

When the man was out of eyesight the Olympian slid out of his van and quickly punctured the left front tire of the SUV. The air gushed out, and surely the man would take notice of his flat. It would be at least a half-hour delay. The Olympian smiled and drove away.

* * *

A half-mile away Stephen Nicholson fidgeted in the family home. He didn't know what to do or where to begin. He paced the house, again staring at the old family photograph. He thought of the dream. What had Matthew said before he left the house? Stephen relaxed as Matthew's words came to him: *I have to take care of some family business.*

Mandy McMasters immediately came to mind. The name came to Stephen quickly and without notice. Yes, Mandy McMasters—she who had coaxed David and Mickey O'Sullivan into giving her a ride, proffering sex. What a costly ride it had been for the Nicholson family. It was a tragedy, one that Stephen was just coming to terms with. But apparently David's death had triggered an unknown evil in his brother, a disguised hatred he apparently couldn't cope with. Stephen couldn't believe this sudden turn of events. He needed to act quickly. The reality was simple: Mandy Mc-Master's life was in danger.

Stephen bolted out the door, running up Meredith Street as fast as he could, the falling rain not deterring. Mandy McMasters lived on Bellevue Street, less than a mile away. Stephen understood his need for action. No call to the police was made. It would be too time-consuming and, truthfully, no one would believe him.

His mind aflutter, he thought about his cause with each step. Mom and Dad immediately sprang to mind. He wouldn't contemplate his next conversation with them; it wouldn't bode well. They were great parents—excellent role models—and the maniacal Matthew was no reflection of their rearing. Matthew was the errant child gone astray, his mind infected with disease. No, it was not the fault of his beloved parents. They would be crushed. Stephen thought of Mom and Dad, the two whose unconditional love for their children—alive or dead—was on display every day. He loved his parents, coveted them. Stephen exhaled noisily in rhythm as he ran fast, prioritizing his objective. He ran for Eamon and Peachy.

Right on Kenneth Street.

Jimmy Petrilli had been unjustly maligned and arrested for these grisly crimes. He was the prime suspect in the eyes of the FBI and his life would never be the same. It could never be the same. Billy Munsing's reputation was also sullied. Guilt enveloped Stephen for his inaccurate assessment of his fraternal brethren. He hoped that one day they would forgive him. He ran for his fraternity brothers.

Left on Stratford Street.

Soaked from the rain, his determination did not wane. An oncoming SUV didn't have properly functioning windshield wipers and barreled toward Stephen. He twisted his entire body on the slick pavement and ran onto the sidewalk, averting a fall. He didn't stop moving; more importantly, he *couldn't* stop moving. He found the street again, pushing harder.

Right on Anawan Avenue.

Stephen thought about the victims: Laiken Barnes, Darlene Hughes, and Alicia Rivera. What unnecessary and senseless deaths they had been.

How could he repay them? Who would speak for the vanquished? He weighed the tardiness of his actions, the gravity of his ignorance. Yes, his thoughts were morbid. But he soon realized the answer. The onus was now on him—not Devon Patterson, not Milton Glavin, and not even Melanie. He could stop the killings; he could stop the Olympian. He was invigorated. He ran for the dead.

Left on Park Street.

Stephen didn't know if he hated her. She never meant for David to die—he knew that. West Roxbury was still a close-knit neighborhood where the Irish whisper could be heard five blocks away. He silently followed her phases of life after the accident. She had changed, and changed for the better. She was married and had three beautiful children who loved her, and called her Mom. He ran for Mandy McMasters.

Right on Oriole Street.

Halfway there, he wondered if he was too late. Images of his baby brother appeared. Big brother had gone mad—flipped his lid, as they like to say. And big brother's actions were predicated on baby brother's death. It was funny how each year he somehow grew younger. He used to be little brother—or even younger brother—but on this day he was baby brother. It made his death sound more innocent, more senseless. The ugly pieces of the puzzle now fit. The case had come full circle. Stephen ran faster, thinking of his childhood playmate. He ran for David.

Left on Bellevue Street.

Breathing labored, he continued up the street, nearing his destination. Now was his chance to make a contribution to the world, to take a risk, to walk like a man. It was his time to do what was right. He could see Mandy's house, and he ran as hard as he possibly could. He ran for honor. He ran for justice. Most of all, he ran for himself.

It was his duty.

There was no visible sign of activity—good. He leapt up the concrete stairs, banging the screen door and ringing the doorbell. Controlling his breathing was nearly impossible; he managed. He arrived at Mandy's house in remarkable time, a testament to the treadmill. The inner door opened. It was Mandy, but her new last name wasn't McMasters, it was Mahoney. She looked at him, perplexed. "May I help you...Stephen?" They hadn't spoken in years, but Mandy knew who he was; the Nicholson brothers looked alike.

"Mandy…Mandy…you have to get out of this house. Now!" She looked at Stephen oddly, as she should have, but she opened the screen door nonetheless.

"Are you okay, Stephen? Would you like me to call an ambulance?" Stephen shook his head. He bent over, hands on his knees, trying to catch his breath. He raised his finger to indicate he'd need a few moments. After five seconds of hyperventilating he looked her in the eye.

"Mandy, you've got to leave here with me right now. I know I look like a lunatic, but your life is in immediate danger."

She was shocked. "What are you talking about? Are you nuts? Stephen, my husband should be home any second now." He knew she wouldn't understand. Why would she?

"Let me spell it out for you then…Amanda!" Calling her by her given name made her think. "My brother Matthew hasn't forgiven you for the accident, and he has all intentions on knifing you to death! Come with me—now!"

There was something in Stephen's eyes, a certain passion that told Mandy he spoke the truth. She hesitantly took his hand and went down the steps toward the driveway.

Stephen watched a man carefully getting out of a van seventy-five yards away, and there was something familiar about him. He pushed Mandy deep into the driveway. The stairwell provided cover, and the approaching man couldn't see them. He carried a package, appearing to be a deliveryman. But Stephen knew the modus operandi of the Olympian; he wasn't fooled with the disguise. It was no deliveryman. And as far as Stephen was concerned, it wasn't the Olympian either. It was his brother—Matthew.

Matthew turned onto the walkway. Stephen seized his opportunity. He blitzed around the stairwell, driving a shoulder into Matthew's chest, knocking them both onto the pavement and sending the package in the air. They wrestled on the ground but neither man could gain an advantage. Instinctively they rose, blood flowing freely from Stephen's knee. Mandy was screaming, and soon neighbors came out of their homes. The rain continued to pour.

Stephen unleashed a hard left hook, crushing into Matthew's head. It jolted him, but he was a gamer. He was three inches taller and thirty pounds heavier than Stephen, but more importantly, he was a better fighter. Matthew absorbed the punch and grabbed Stephen by the shoulders, headbutting him in his face. Stephen backed off and Matthew continued his offense with a right hook to Stephen's head and a short left to the jaw. His fighting stance was unorthodox. He was a lefty. Both punches found their mark, sending Stephen to the lawn. In truth Stephen wasn't a bad fighter; he was just picking the wrong opponents lately. Mandy continued her screams.

Stephen rose quickly, but before he could square off again two male neighbors intervened, tackling Stephen back onto the grass. The two men were hefty, giving Stephen no chance of breaking their grasp. They detained him, despite his urgent pleas to stop the other man. Perception was a funny thing, though. The neighbors thought Stephen was trying to rob a deliveryman. Oh, how wrong they were. Stephen capitulated, and the men finally listened to a frantic Mandy's explanation.

Stephen jumped to his feet. His brother was gone. Nestled in the middle of the bush adjacent the stairwell was the contents of the package intended for Mandy. It was a nine-millimeter automatic with shiny stainless steel and an affixed silencer. Matthew had obviously deviated from his signature choice of weapon.

Mandy went to Stephen. She didn't know what to say. She was hysterical, and tried to regain her composure. Stephen looked and felt like he had been in a car accident. His black eye was cut open, courtesy of Matthew's head, and his left hand hung limp. It was a boxer's fracture; again, courtesy of Matthew's head. The knee gash continued to bleed. Mandy strained for words. Finally, "Thank you, Stephen, I can't believe this." He stared at her, too tired to reply. After one minute he knew he had to leave. The neighbors called the police.

"Stay with your neighbors," Stephen said. "Get hold of your husband immediately, and please don't tell the cops where I went."

"Where are you going?" Mandy asked.

Running awkwardly in the rain, Stephen turned a last time to Mandy. "To find a brother I used to know."

Melanie's hypothesis had been derived merely on circumstantial evidence. She actually felt a bit foolish, fearing the others would deem her crazy. But it was quite the contrary. Her description of Matthew Nicholson matched the profile to a tee, and Devon Patterson and Milton Glavin proudly glared at one another. It was more than the fact that he met the ingredients of the profile. Logistically, he could be culpable. He had attended Taconic State College. He partied at the Kappa Chi Omicron fraternity house on the night of Laiken's murder. The sticking point was motive, but that could be explored. The FBI men didn't flinch. Milton picked up the phone and called the Boston Branch. He walked around the room speaking to a special agent, his speech muffled. The only words Melanie could decipher were Meredith Street, West Roxbury, and immediately. Milton hung up the telephone. He faced the task force. Silence became the room. Finally, "Kudos to Melanie for having a detective's mind. Boston Branch should have him within the hour."

Manhunt.

* * *

Matthew drove to Daley Field in Brighton. The field abutted the scenic Charles River, a popular haven for residents and tourists alike. The park was equipped with a public boat ramp. Matthew parked his vehicle in its spacious parking lot. Twenty-five minutes later he emerged from the van, a new man.

He was precise with his razors and scissors. The top of his head was bald while he'd symmetrically shaved down his sides. He even managed to leave a little clump of hair on top, the last vestiges of a man's vanity as he neared total baldness. The hair dye, now making him blond, was credible. To complete the package he sported new wire-rimmed glasses and a dazzling set of green eyes, thanks to colored contact lenses. He loaded two suitcases into the trunk of a 1998 Ford Taurus and drove off.

In preparation for this scenario, Matthew had made provisions after the Alicia Rivera murder in 1995. In ghoulish fashion he went to Forest Hills Cemetery in Jamaica Plain to rob from the dead. He copied down the names of two deceased boys who were approximately his age. After a couple of trips to City Hall for birth certificates, and to some local parishes for Baptismal certificates, he had begun his quest for two new identities.

It worked, and now he had two new driver's licenses, Social Security cards, and even sets of credit cards. He used the credit cards somewhat frequently, always sure to pay them off in time. His addresses for the phony names were separate post office boxes in downtown Boston.

Living at home, Matthew had been a shrewd investor, proving his intelligence wasn't limited to the classroom. As the FBI would soon find out, his large investments in the Internet in the early 1990s had paid huge dividends. Having liquidated all of his assets, his net worth was more than one and a half million dollars. Matthew's new identities and money would protect him well, as would his ability to change appearances like a chameleon. He pulled out his new license, the one whose photograph mirrored his current disguise. His stratagem for anonymity was complete. No longer would he answer to the name Matthew Nicholson. His name was now Daniel Quentin McCafferty, but to friends he was simply DQ.

The man purporting to be Daniel Quentin McCafferty drove from the parking lot. He was leaving Boston, heading west on the Mass Pike, en route to California. As he drove he thought of his brother Stephen, and for the first time in years he felt a smidgen of remorse. But the remorse was unrelated to the deaths of the filthy whores; he felt for Stephen. David's death had been difficult for Stephen, and Matthew knew that he was only now beginning to heal. "I'm sorry, little brother," Matthew said aloud in the car. "But in time you may understand." Matthew continued his conversation, speaking next to his parents, justifying his actions. He was a bright man, but his mind had changed progressively over the last twelve years, and the change was not for the better.

He thought about old times, about family vacations. He recalled the summer camping trips, and how much fun they were. His mind eased backward into the annals of time. He reflected on an old pet; it was a raccoon that he'd named Bruin. In his dream Bruin was alive and unharmed, playing with him and his siblings. Matthew envisioned picking up Bruin and setting him in the lap of his kid brother Stephen. The younger Nicholson boy was small, so Matthew watched carefully as Stephen stroked the pet raccoon. Bruin licked the boy's small fingers, igniting a bright smile to his face. The young boy was happy; all was well.

And now it was Matthew who smiled as he drove calmly on the highway. In his dream Bruin didn't bite Stephen. Bruin was a good pet: friendly, affectionate, and obedient. Matthew granted his memory carte blanche, a revisionist history that provided only happy endings. All was well in his life; everyone was safe. He was the big brother, and he would never let anything happen to Bruin or his little brother. He was the big brother, and he was supposed to protect.

It was his duty.

* * *

Stephen dragged himself to his parents' house. His father had returned but was in the basement setting up his new table saw. Good, he would be preoccupied. He went upstairs and got into the hot shower. He cleansed. His whole body ached, especially his left hand. Ironically he went to Matthew's room for fresh clothes before sneaking out of the house.

While Stephen drove away in his Jeep, two Boston cops pounded on his Washington Street front door. A gun having been found on Bellevue Street, the cops demanded Stephen's name from Mandy. She, along with neighbors, explained the story in detail. An all-points bulletin was immediately called throughout Metropolitan Boston for Matthew Nicholson.

Simultaneously, unaware of the current events and not working in conjunction with Boston Police, two FBI agents fought traffic on the Jamaica Way. One plotted the map, hoping to find Meredith Street without difficulty. Their assignment was simple: locate Matthew Nicholson and detain him. They were five minutes from their destination, but their trip would be for naught. Matthew was already on the highway.

* * *

The five-speed was tricky for Stephen. He could shift with his right hand, but maneuvering with his left was difficult. When possible, he held his injured hand on an ice pack that rested between his legs. The swelling was alleviated. Three aspirin helped the pain in his head, but he still ached. The hurt was internal, something no medicine could cure. He drove, his mind racing everywhere. It wasn't until thirty-five minutes later, when he got on Route 2 West, that he realized where he was going: Hoosac Mills. He called Melanie on his cell phone, catching her just before she left the station. "Stephen...I think we need to talk about something very serious," she said.

"Let me speak first, Melanie."

"Okay. Shoot," she said.

Speaking in fragments, thoughts clouded by emotion and physical pain, Stephen somehow explained the events of the last hour. Melanie was excited and, much to Stephen's dismay, put Milton Glavin on the phone. Stephen reluctantly gave him an abridged version of the events. Milton asked few questions. He was cool, as usual. He quietly instructed Stephen to return to Boston.

Stephen didn't listen. To hell with the FBI, he thought, and besides, it was his brother. He hung up and drove westward. Matthew could be anywhere right now, and they probably wouldn't catch him for some time. But there was something that lured Stephen to the Mills; he just couldn't place it. He simply drove, listening to the CD player and remembering all of the good times he and his siblings had had growing up. He couldn't dwell, there was no use. Not until his descent into the valley did he realize why he'd come.

It was the Hoosac Tunnel.

There was always something about Laiken's murder site that had bothered Stephen. Now he knew. Many years before, when Stephen was in high school, Matthew had frequently boasted about having sex inside the Hoosac Tunnel with a local girl. Stephen never knew the girl's name. He never asked because it wasn't relevant. The prurient tale, though, had mesmerized his teenage imagination. It was now obvious that the young local girl could only have been Laiken Barnes.

As Stephen walked into the Hoosac Mills police station, a small Cessna aircraft flew overhead. In fifty minutes it would land in Norwood Airport, fifteen minutes away from the Nicholson family home. Milton Glavin and Devon Patterson were aboard, but not Melanie. She knew Stephen was coming—and opted to wait. She needed to see him.

He walked into Melanie's office. She looked up from her desk. Time seemingly froze. He stared at her. The physical pain would not go away, but Melanie's presence somehow soothed it. She looked at the dried blood under his eye and went for a wet paper towel, ministering to it. She was at close range, smelling the blood and dried sweat mixed together. "Are you okay?" she asked hesitantly.

"No, but I'm gonna have to deal with it."

"I'm so sorry, Stephen, I really am."

"I know you are." They looked at each other. Melanie buried her head into his chest and he wrapped his arms around her, rocking gently as they stood in the middle of her office, door ajar. Sergeant Petrowski came to the office to check on Melanie. He saw the embrace and spun away, unnoticed. "Feel like taking a walk into the Hoosac Tunnel? I think we might be able to find something if my memory serves correct." Melanie looked up at him; he explained.

At the local Kmart they purchased two sets of headlamps, two small flashlights that attached to a belt, a small shovel, a spade, two sets of work gloves, and a large nylon gym bag for storage. He also brought matches and extra batteries.

Stephen knew that Matthew had attended the infamous Green Machine party. He also knew that because he'd stayed in Hoosac Mills on the night of the murder, he must have disposed of the murder weapon and other incriminating evidence. Because Laiken's body was found in such close proximity to the entrance of the Hoosac Tunnel, Stephen now theorized that Matthew had buried the evidence at his old romantic spot inside.

Stephen knew the spot.

* * *

Matthew's illness manifested to its worst stages. His mind abuzz, he decided to delay his road trip with a quick stopover in his favorite city. His head told him to proceed west through New York, but his heart told him otherwise. Why not? He might never again have the chance to walk on the sacred soil. And besides, he thought of a souvenir that he could unearth. After all, he was the Olympian, and he would never be caught.

Matthew turned north on Route 7. He was aiming at Hoosac Mills.

* * *

The entrance to the tunnel was ominous, holding dark secrets and tales of the nearly two hundred men it had devoured during its construction. It was gloomy, a spooky enough place to venture on a friendly walk-through, let alone a murder investigation. The April showers began to wane as they entered. The sun gave a final peek, but was ready to set.

The tunnel was dark. It was always midnight black in the long cylindrical passage. It was also home to thousands of nocturnal creatures.

Rats abounded.

Melanie stayed close to Stephen. The headlamps, similar to miner's hats, cast a long stream of light. They moved quickly, hoping that an oncoming train wouldn't force them to the gravelly ground. Trickles of water dropped on Melanie's head. She stopped, looking up into the ceiling of the tunnel. Millions of bricks formed an arch that kept the tunnel intact. The construction was an engineering marvel. "Water's falling on us, Stephen," she remarked nervously.

Stephen mollified her. "Don't worry, Melanie, Hoosac Mountain is probably saturated with a couple million gallons of water." She looked bewildered and suddenly felt claustrophobic, as if the walls of the tunnel could close in on them.

Something echoed. Stephen spun around but saw nothing. It sounded like footsteps, but they ceased. They continued down the single track and soon arrived at their destination after half a mile. It was the west portal airshaft, the spot Matthew had alluded to many years earlier. He shone the light on a rusted ladder on the wall of the tunnel, the exact location where Matthew and Laiken had allegedly fooled around. Melanie looked to the ground. "Oh my God, Stephen, someone's been here."

A small hole was at the base of the ladder, fresh gravel and dirt shoveled off to the side. Stephen immediately looked toward the east portal of the tunnel, his headlamp following the path of his eyes. Twenty feet away stood a man, holding a burlap bag and what appeared to be a rusted buck knife. It was a stranger. The man was bald and had the look of death in his eyes.

"Good to see you again, Stephen. We've been running into each other quite a bit lately. I hope Mom knows where you are." His voice was distant, unattached. A curious smile formed at Matthew's lips. "Good evening, Melanie. I apologize for the circumstances surrounding our second meeting. Please forgive me."

Both headlamps shone on Matthew. He was holding a bag with tattered clothing and a mask. Stephen looked closely—it was a Grim Reaper outfit, and it had been buried along with the knife in a burlap bag for the last twelve years.

The night of Laiken's murder flashed through Stephen's mind. He finally pieced everything together. Matthew had known the popular costume of choice on that night in 1987, so he showed up early for the party. No one remembered that Matthew planned on driving up alone that weekend;

it hadn't been a big deal. He easily slid into the party, met up with Laiken, and left with her. And Johnny Malfkoski had seen him go. He took her to the parking lot adjacent the tunnel entrance, killed her, and disposed of the evidence inside. Then he returned to the costume party dressed as a professional wrestler, acting as if he'd just arrived.

Brilliant.

Stephen didn't speak while Melanie coolly unholstered her Glock automatic. "Drop the knife, Matthew," she said. "Do it now!" She hadn't screamed but her instructions were clear. Matthew disregarded Melanie's directive, instead focusing his attention toward his younger brother. Melanie's gun steadied on the still Matthew.

"It was all quite necessary. I'm sorry it's caused such an inconvenience to you, Stephen, but it really has been for the best. I know in due time you will agree." Stephen stared at Matthew, still quiet.

"Drop the knife, Matthew!" Melanie now screamed. Matthew gave her a vacant stare.

"I've taken a fancy to the name the Olympian, Melanie. It's an honor." Matthew was calm—eerily calm. His voice lowered and he assumed his natural role of teacher. "Are you aware of the grand history of the name you've bestowed upon me?" Melanie wasn't sure if the question was rhetorical. She remained quiet, his instability now speaking volumes. "The first Olympic Games were known as the Pan-Hellenic festival, but they were not limited to the hyped and exploited sporting events that we know today. No, not at all. True art—such as poetry, art, and theater—they too were part of the games. And now I have been dubbed with such an honorary sobriquet. I am blessed."

Stephen was in disbelief. This wasn't *his* brother speaking, was it? Matthew never spoke in such syntax around the house. Melanie attempted to placate him.

"It's okay, Matthew, it's okay. Everything's going to be all right. Just drop the knife, lie on the ground, and place your hands on top of your head." She focused her gun on her target—center mass—not wishing to squeeze the trigger.

"You seem like a truly remarkable woman, Melanie, you really do. But right now I'm trying to have a private conversation with my brother. It's rather personal. I must cordially request that you either remain quiet or leave the premises at once. Thank you." Melanie went quiet, unsure of a response. "Now then, Stephen, do you remember your romantic encounter with that beautiful woman on the evening of my Miss Barnes' demise?" Stephen flashed back to the party, fully remembering his sexual encounter with the most beautiful woman he'd ever kissed. She had been a sexual woman—one whose name he didn't know and face he'd never seen again.

"Yes, why?"

"Almost too good to be true, wouldn't you say?"

"What do you mean?

Matthew laughed—deeply. Stephen then realized that the woman had been hired flesh, a simple safeguard by Matthew to ensure his absence. "Give it up, Matthew," Stephen said. "Let's end the madness. No more deaths."

"Fear not, young one," Matthew snickered. "Neither fratricide nor police homicide is on my itinerary. I have made my true intentions, as the Olympian, all too clear."

"Stop believing the hype. You're not the Olympian," Stephen said. "You're my brother and your name is Matthew Nicholson. Now put down the knife." Stephen waited, thinking of something else to say. Finally, "David was a great kid, Matthew. He wouldn't want you doing this. Think of him."

"I have thought of him," Matthew said. "Now I speak for him."

Footsteps approached and they all turned. It was Simeon. In his hand was an unidentifiable handgun pointed at Matthew. Simeon's eyes were blank. Matthew smiled when he saw the gun—fearless of death—yet death became his eyes. The two had never met, but Matthew Nicholson, associate professor, knew the intruder's exact identity—and intent.

Stephen unconsciously reached for his weapon. It was instinctive, just as the instructors at the sheriff's department had trained him. But it would be for naught. His draw was quick, but he grabbed at air. The city had denied his application for a gun permit. Melanie now leveled her Glock at Simeon.

"Police, don't move!" she screamed. "Drop the weapon!" Simeon hadn't known Melanie was present. He'd only observed Stephen's Jeep when he was driving toward the tunnel. And her presence drastically altered his plans. Stephen thought about William Jonathan Barnes' careful wording only two months earlier: *If you provide me with the name of my daughter's slayer, I will give you an additional fifty thousand dollars, cash.* Provide me with the name, Stephen repeated to himself. And what Barnes did with the name would be up to his discretion.

Hence, Simeon now stood with a gun in hand, ready to mete out the justice Barnes had always sought. The irony was that Stephen didn't blame Barnes; he would have done the same. But not today, not while he had some say. Matthew was a vicious murderer, but he was also his brother.

Matthew turned to Simeon, taking note of his ape-like features.

"Aptly named, Simeon, aptly named. Your proboscis runs wider than the banks of the Old Miss." Matthew laughed aloud and the three others gazed at one another. The four bodies formed an oblong rectangle with Matthew and Simeon on one side of the tracks, and Stephen and Melanie on the other. Nobody seemed to make a move. Matthew would change that.

"Hey, Simeon, catch," Matthew said as he gently lobbed his flashlight toward him. Matthew utilized the full twenty feet of height in the tunnel with his toss, and Simeon's natural reflexes made him look up to the falling flashlight. The slight distraction worked and Matthew rushed at Simeon with a fury, leading with the rusted buck knife in his left hand.

Shots rang out as Matthew crashed into Simeon. Matthew was atop him; his intentions were never questioned. Stephen and Melanie didn't hesitate, diving into the fray. The gun roared twice more, and the rumble and tumble of the scrum ripped off both of their headlamps, turning them off. Groans and shrieks echoed in the tunnel but no one could see. The wrestling fight desisted after thirty seconds. It was quiet and dark—painfully dark. Matthew's discarded flashlight pointed toward an aged wall.

Stephen stood, limping. His knee was injured earlier, but now he felt a burning sensation in his thigh. He reached down and felt warm blood. He walked toward the errant flashlight and picked it up. "Melanie? Melanie, where are you?" There was no answer. He cast the light around the tracks and saw Simeon. His shirt was ripped open and blood splashed about, painting his chest and the side of his face red. He had been butchered, but still managed to keep his eyes open. His breathing was steady—for now. "Melanie, where are you, honey?" he screamed. Stephen was disoriented, his equilibrium clearly affected. He heard a groan, but it came from the other side of the tracks, opposite Simeon. He shone the light and there she was, lying on the gravel parallel with the tracks. He went to her.

Melanie was on her back, semiconscious. Blood soaked her windbreaker. Stephen recovered his headlamp, steadied it. He unzipped Melanie's windbreaker and saw a blood-soaked shirt. He breathed easy, reminding himself never to panic.

Stephen quickly removed his own jacket and T-shirt. He ripped his shirt into pieces and put his jacket back on. He applied direct pressure to the gunshot wound next to her navel, trying to clot the bleeding. He gently rolled her on her side, recognizing an exit wound in her back. It was even worse than he thought. Melanie groaned while Stephen whispered words of encouragement.

His cell phone wouldn't work—he accepted that. He had to act quickly in order to save her. There was no time for second guesses; he had to carry her, bad leg and all. He quickly tied a strip of his T-shirt around the knife wound in his leg, tight enough to stop the bleeding without affecting circulation. Stephen picked up Melanie, cradling her in his arms.

He completed a slow 360-degree turn, the headlamp covering all directions. Matthew was gone, like a thief in the night. Stephen surmised he went east, toward the other portal entrance located in Stockholm, four miles away. It would have made sense for Matthew to enter the tunnel from the isolated east portal, a safe distance from Hoosac Mills. He focused on the other fallen victim. "Simeon, I'll send for help, I promise." Stephen tossed his small flashlight to Simeon, not wanting to leave him in the dark. Simeon merely grunted in acknowledgment.

One hundred thirty pounds or so had never felt so heavy. Sweat poured from Stephen's face as he limped down the track, the light flashing in every direction that his twisting neck turned. Melanie was still disoriented, but she managed to wrap her hands around his neck. "How's...how's my wound, Stephen?" she barely got out.

"You're fine, Melanie, you're just fine," he lied. "Just hang onto me real tight and I'll get you out of here. Only another quarter of a mile." His leg throbbed, but he willed away the pain. It was time for sacrifice, great sacrifice, and he knew that although he couldn't guarantee survival, her life would definitely be lost if his pain got the best of him. He did not want to be her pallbearer.

He trudged along, thrice stopping to boost her up into his arms. Melanie's loss of blood was taking its toll, and she intermittently slipped in and out of consciousness. "Stephen?" she said.

"Yes, Melanie?"

"Do we have wine?"

"Excuse me?"

"You and I," she said, "Do we have any wine between us?"

He was astounded. "Don't be ridiculous, Melanie. Please be quiet, honey, and save your energy. I want to see you in one piece again." She faded into unconsciousness before responding, her head drooping. Stephen was nervous, but he was relieved upon feeling her breath on his neck.

Stephen's eyes were locked on the glowing end of the tunnel. The relief was short-lived, though, when he stepped into a pothole next to the track. Stephen fell to one knee—his good one—and summoned all the power in his body not to drop Melanie. Before he could gather his thoughts, a strong hand pulled him up. Stephen rose with Melanie still cradled in his arms. Stephen looked at the unexpected helper. It was the Hoosac Mills legend, the Hoosac Mills hobo who wore his custom trench coat and fedora.

It was the Can Man.

They looked at one another for the longest three seconds of recorded time. Then Can Man, in character, grunted. He quickly slid next to Stephen, dropped his walking stick, and supported Melanie's legs. This relieved a substantial weight for Stephen, and allowed the two men, awkwardly, to carry Melanie the last one hundred yards into daylight.

Stephen and Can Man set Melanie on the ground slowly. Her eyes remained shut but she moaned gently. Stephen retrieved his cell phone from his jacket and called 911. He coolly and deliberately gave the dispatcher instructions and information. Next, he re-dressed Melanie's entry wound while awaiting the ambulance and, more importantly, held her hand. Soon the distant sirens neared.

The young emergency medical technicians wasted no time securing her in the stretcher. A paramedic appeared, seemingly from nowhere. An I.V. was inserted. Her blood pressure was eighty over fifty. She was in trouble. The white sheet that covered her was stained with blood. Stephen squeezed her hand tight, praying. He looked at the EMTs. They quickly lifted Melanie onto the ambulance. He scanned the immediate area before boarding. The Can Man had vanished as mysteriously as he had appeared.

The truck moved quickly toward the hospital. Stephen sat close to Melanie, staring at her. Dumbfounded. As they eased into the hospital bay, Melanie raised her right arm, just a fraction. She suddenly opened her eyes, looking at Stephen. No words came out. They didn't have to; her expression said it all.

Thank you, Stephen.

He was frightened. The last few months had been tumultuous and harrowing. His life had been shattered. There was one thing, however, that had been a godsend. She was engaging, she was beautiful, and she was remarkable in every way. Above all, she seemed to understand him the way no other woman ever had. Stephen stared at her as she was whisked away.

"No, thank *you*, Melanie," he said.

31.

July, 1999

The view was breathtaking; it was everything he'd ever imagined and more. Stephen stood behind the statue of General Robert Edward Lee, a man once vilified in the North but forever a hero in the South. Stephen's binoculars stretched across the green pasture, homing in on a copse of trees that was protected by a wrought-iron gate. Confederate soldiers had marched from this very spot 136 years before, crossing undulating fields in an attempt to break Union lines at Cemetery Ridge. It was Gettysburg, Pennsylvania, the place Stephen had always wanted to experience. The Laiken Barnes case had denied him his visit, but now he was here.

He began the almost one-mile trek. It was early, five-forty-five, and Stephen had the famous battlefield all to himself, just as he'd always envisioned. It may have been the bravest march in any battle, in any war. What was once known as Longstreet's Assault would forever be known as Pickett's Charge.

Stephen crossed the field, walking the path where twelve thousand men had marched into the eyes of death. He couldn't imagine what had raced through their minds. Fear—it must have been fear. But fear could be the greatest motivator, and it was on this very soil where so much blood was sacrificed. Shrapnel didn't discriminate; each second, young boys were felled by canister, cannon, and a fusillade of bullets that pierced proud uniforms, transforming their colors from battle gray to blood red.

It had been a macabre day, that third day of July in 1863. Young Confederate boys fought with spirit and pride, and although their cause may have been immoral, they sacrificed their lives for it anyway. They were believers, and they had looked to a higher mortal power, to Robert E. Lee, to give them the belief they needed. And he made them believe, though they would not prevail. Lee had promised them victory, and he intended to bring the war northward.

It did not happen.

Stephen had driven to Gettysburg to escape the guilt—and the fear. His world was turned upside down, and for the first time in his life he truly did not know what to do. Yes, he came to this hallowed ground to find peace, but soon learned that emotions didn't honor geographical boundaries. His guilt and fear had not abated.

He tried clearing his head as he moved to Little Round Top, standing tall on Vincent's Spur, the extreme left flank of yet another special place. It was here on July second that Colonel Joshua Lawrence Chamberlain and the brave men of the 20th Maine fixed bayonets and raced down the hill, repelling the Rebel Yell and onslaught of the Texans and Alabamians. The men from Maine saved the day for the Union.

Proud men had died on these hills—men who died for ideals; who died for principle; who died for the future; who died for fellow man; who died for freedom. They died, and they died in droves. But the great Abraham had spoken eloquently, and they did not die in vain.

They died for cause.

Stephen could feel the pain. Matthew had killed, but he hadn't killed for cause—not true cause. Unlike the great soldiers, he had killed in retribution, killed the innocent, and killed in disgrace. Why, Matthew, why? Stephen looked out into the Wheatfield, into Devil's Den, into the Peach Orchard and into the Bloody Stream. But these places where the brave had perished didn't speak. They were silent, and Stephen was left alone in search of an answer. Maybe he would never understand his brother, and shouldn't be comparing his actions to the great soldiers'. They had killed and died for the inalienable right of freedom; Matthew had killed out of hate.

Where was he now? Was he out in the hills, watching his brother grind with pain? No, he was anywhere and everywhere he wanted to be. And while he was alive and well, the streets wouldn't be safe. He was not the brother Stephen had known; he was a psychopath, and he had to be stopped.

Some blood had been found in the tunnel—blood belonging to Matthew—but he had disappeared from the face of the earth, yet to be seen. The story had been big—national headlines. And the story would never go away, not until Matthew, the Olympian, was behind bars. Contrary to what the FBI said, apprehending him would be an arduous task.

A gentle morning wind came across the hill. He looked out into the town, his eyes stopping at the cupola atop the seminary. At the seminary there was peace, an intangible ally Stephen needed to find. It could only help.

His time at this place was done; he could only hope. Yes, Little Round Top serviced Stephen well, listening to his thoughts and absorbing his pain. It couldn't, however, solve the puzzle. No vane on the hill pointed Stephen in the right direction; he would have to figure it out on his own. He held his head high, admiring the surrounding beauty. He was happy with his visit; it had been long overdue. He was still a proud American, and that would never change.

Stephen saluted the dead men of Gettysburg.

32.

Officer Malley looked the part—clean shaven, spit-polished shoes, and a pressed uniform with crisp creases. Mickey O'Sullivan was still out of commission. No one knew his return status. At age twenty-five Malley was the new Lead Dog in 6-Block. He was proud of himself; friends and family would soon learn of his new title. The 6-Block ran more efficiently. Malley was firm, fair, and consistent, just like a good correction officer was supposed to be. The inmates respected him.

Malley conducted rounds during evening recreation. He strolled past Renzo DiLorenzo and his crew. Pleasant hellos were exchanged. When Malley was out of sight, the unit Caesar nodded. It was back to business as usual. Inmate Roscoe McFarland—professional victim—tentatively approached Renzo and handed him a brown bag of goods.

Rent money.

Renzo slapped him on the back. "Nice doing business with ya, Roscoe." Everyone laughed. Roscoe scurried away.

Marconi Beach seethed as he watched Renzo enforce the nightly shakedowns. He wasn't impressed; in fact he was never impressed with Renzo DiLorenzo.

All hail mighty Caesar.

Marconi Beach sat at the card table with friends. They weren't professional thugs. They were a lot like Marconi Beach—grown men who'd made mistakes. "Where you eating first—Joe Tecce's or Il Panino?" one guy asked. Marconi Beach was leaving soon. Inmates customarily talked about initial plans upon release. Sex and food usually came first. Marconi Beach wasn't talking. For that matter, he wasn't paying attention to his cards, either. He stared at the end of the unit. "Yo, Beach, you all right, man?" another asked.

"Yeah, Beach, what's eating you, man?"

Marconi Beach had a laser lock on the almighty Renzo DiLorenzo. His mind was filled with emotion. Hatred—a strong word—lingered. Marconi Beach hated everything about Renzo: his looks, his posturing, his philosophies, his actions, and most of all, his acceptance. Inmates followed villains like Renzo not because of admiration but rather fear. Being a follower was safer. Besides, the unwritten inmate judiciary system called for a sovereign; Renzo DiLorenzo merely answered the calling. The whole process was a tradition that was rarely questioned or challenged.

Marconi Beach was frustrated. Why didn't anyone challenge this backward-ass tradition of idiocy? Real men stood for ideals, principles, and the prudent application of democracy, not elected tyranny. Marconi Beach was just one man. He couldn't be alone in his thinking, could he? In order to effect change there must be cause. The cause was undoubtedly there. It was simply a matter of courage. No one wanted to slay the king. The danger was too great.

"Beach...what's going through your mind, buddy?"

In a greater sense Marconi Beach knew that the impending moment was unavoidable. Stephen Nicholson's face had paid dearly for throwing a lead right against Renzo. The unit Caesar gleefully absorbed the compliments of his now-famous prison knockout punch of a correction officer. Now, however, Renzo must be willing accept its consequences. It was comeuppance time.

You shouldn't have fucked with my boy, Renzo.

Marconi Beach stood, squared his shoulders. What began as a brisk walk developed into a jog. His actions—ever so slight—deviated from the norm. Nosy inmate peripheral vision matured into blatant stares. Marconi Beach's jog graduated to a run. Telephone lines dropped. Trivial conversations stopped abruptly. All inmates rose from their tables. Something big was going down in 6-Block.

Renzo saw Marconi Beach coming fast. It was a short distance. He turned, looking for Marconi Beach's intended target. Only the unit Caesar could okay a white-boy hit in the block. Oddly, he saw no nearby victim.

Renzo's face changed. A human freight train of kinetic energy closed on him. It was in that nanosecond Renzo arrived at the inevitable conclusion: someone was trying to usurp his power. He tried to drop into a fighting stance but it was too late. Marconi Beach clothes-lined Renzo's neck at full speed. It was an incredible sight. The thumping sound of Renzo's muscular body penetrated the unit. Renzo was no sissy. He was too damn tough to stay down with one hit. Dazed and shocked, he stood up. All great leaders overcome adversity. It was all part of the image he created; it was all part of being Caesar.

Marconi Beach was no longer the mild-mannered giant, the friendly big guy who helped underprivileged inmates in pursuit of a GED. Marconi Beach had changed masks. He was a predator. It took a wolf to kill a wolf. The inmates were awed by his assault. He dealt a wicked combination, a right elbow to the jaw and a left uppercut to the chin. Renzo fell. Marconi Beach adhered to prison protocol, kicking Renzo in the face when he was down. Renzo rolled on his back.

This was a real prison fight. The gymnasium fight between Renzo and Stephen was real, but different. That fight was arranged; it was fought with honor, like a throwback to the Dempsey and Tunney days. Prison fights weren't measured by ring generalship; they were measured by who stood last. Blitz attacks, gang beatings, and merciless weapon assaults were always at a premium. Chivalry didn't exist at the Boston House.

Malley called for help on the radio. Dozens of inmates formed a circle around the combatants. Neither Malley nor his partners attempted to break it up. It was too risky. They screamed repeated orders for all inmates to return to their cells. Nobody listened. The unit Caesar was being attacked and all eyes would watch until reinforcement officers arrived. Besides, prison by nature was a sadistic place. Malley and his partners not so secretly wanted to see Renzo get his ass kicked.

Top inmate "Lieutenant" Shawn Blighe rushed from the shower, bare-chested and soaking wet. Blighe instinctively went toward Marconi Beach's blind side. A big surprise befell him. Inmate Marcellus Alexander, supporter of Stephen Nicholson, intervened. He met Blighe with a short right to the jaw—the same punch George Foreman hit Michael Moorer with. It produced the same result. Blighe lay on the unit floor, seeing proverbial stars and spitting out blood.

The scent of a kill was in the air. Inmates cheered. Everyone sensed a change in leadership. Ever the warrior, Renzo rose. He could barely see straight; he wobbled. He somehow managed to throw a left, right combination. He missed by three feet. Marconi Beach head-butted Renzo in the nose and kneed his balls. Renzo buckled over and Marconi Beach scooped him over his shoulder in one motion.

A wall of inmates parted as Marconi Beach walked toward the officer's panel. The unit fell silent. Blood gushed from Renzo's nose, leaving a dotted line that would later be remembered as the Red Trail of Caesar.

Marconi Beach eyed his target—an industrial trash bin near the unit exit. Renzo moaned. With great strength Marconi Beach heaved Renzo above his head. Blood rained on Marconi Beach's head. He faced the crowd of inmates. They screamed relentlessly; this was a blood sport, their most exhilarating form of entertainment. It was prison—they were carnivores.

Marconi Beach wanted to send a message, his own editorial opposing dictators like Renzo. He dumped Renzo face first into the loaded bin. Bags exploded on impact; Renzo oozed deeper into the malodorous trash. Correction officer response teams flooded the unit. There was no resistance. Sated inmates returned to their cells while Marconi Beach compliantly dropped to his knees and put his hands behind his back.

The show was over. Lt. Paul Cullen entered the unit and assumed control. Sgt. DuBane and the nurse tended to the unconscious Shawn Blighe. Cullen and Malley walked to the trash bin. Renzo squirmed and moaned. Cullen looked at Malley. "Any officers hurt?"

"No, sir," Malley said.

A nearby response team awaited instructions from Cullen. Finally, one asked, "What do you want us to do with Renzo?"

Cullen couldn't contain his smile. He understood the depths of Renzo's defeat. The bad man was vanquished. He looked at Malley, then to the response team. "Wheel his ass out of here, handcuff him, and take him to booking. Have a nurse waiting for him."

In a stroke of irony, Frankie Kohan was working the segregation unit where the response team led Marconi Beach. The response officers performed their procedural task of searching Marconi Beach for weapons or contraband. None was found. His handcuffs were removed and the door was secured.

Ten minutes later a staff nurse reported to the unit to medically evaluate inmate Marconi. The young nurse gave him a bag of ice for his left hand. All was fine.

The clock ticked. Thirty minutes later, while conducting a unit security check on all inmates, Frankie Kohan stopped in front of cell sixteen where Marconi Beach was now being housed. Marconi Beach and Frankie had never spoken much, but both understood the other's direct connection to Stephen Nicholson. Marconi Beach approached the door. He motioned with his hands for a pen and paper. Frankie obliged.

News of 6-Block's purported change in leadership would race about the prison like a forest fire. Marconi Beach scribbled and held the pad up. It read: "Peachy and Eamon?"

Frankie shook his head. "Not good," he said.

Marconi Beach nodded, then dropped his head—dejected. He scribbled again: "Tell Peachy and Eamon I love them."

Frankie nodded. He understood the meaningfulness of Marconi Beach's words. Lastly, Marconi Beach scribbled: "Stephen?"

Frankie considered the question. Maybe his best friend would recover. Perhaps not. He looked at Marconi. "Not good."

Marconi again began to scribble. He crossed out whatever was on the yellow-lined sheet. He tore the page and began anew. He raised the paper with his right hand. With his injured left hand, Marconi Beach made a fist and pounded his heart. Tears were in his eyes. After all, he had once witnessed young David Nicholson win a Parkway Babe Ruth baseball game with a towering homerun at Billings Field. He continued to pound his heart. The tears streamed. The paper read: "Just tell him…"

* * *

The 6-Block was now quiet. All cell doors were locked. A family of house mice paraded near the back of the unit, feasting on a cinnamon bun. The smell of blood and Wexcide disinfectant filled the air. Malley and his partners wrote reports. Conflicting emotions and thoughts of life swirled through the minds of 173 inmates. In theory, Marconi Beach would most certainly be elected Caesar upon return from segregation. But inmates—like correction officers—have a sixth sense. Marconi Beach was unique, different from others. If elected he would abdicate; it just wasn't his style. One thing was certain in 6-Block: Renzo Caesar was slain.

33.

The black Jeep purred across from Mandy's house. It idled, music quietly playing while Stephen witnessed innocence in motion. Mandy's kids laughed as they raced through a water sprinkler. The kids were oblivious to their innocence. But that was okay—ignorance is bliss. Stephen stared at the sprinkler, lost in thought, reminiscing about the 1970s—his time of innocence. It was a time of gas lines, eight-track tapes, presidential turmoil, post-Vietnam hate, the bicentennial celebration, disco fever, the death of Elvis, and Bucky Dent's homerun. It seemed so long ago. Kevin from Heaven was mayor, busing divided the city, and a new show called *Saturday Night Live* was the rage. Every pitcher in the American League feared Jim Ed Rice, and the ovation at the Boston Garden never seemed to stop when Bobby Orr's jersey was retired to the rafters. There were tears; there was joy.

Stephen snapped his head when the door swung open. Mandy gracefully made her way out with a tray of lemonade. The kids scooped their drinks and ran back toward the sprinkler. The children were neglectful in thanking Mom, but that was okay. She smiled, knowing she was lucky to have them, lucky to be alive. The smile showcased her beauty—but then again, Mandy McMasters was always a beautiful girl. She was no longer a troublesome girl. She was a woman, a successful and loving one.

Stephen couldn't guarantee that Matthew wouldn't return to this place, but that was out of his control. He dropped the clutch and drove away, feeling a bit of satisfaction, a confidence boost he desperately needed.

Mandy was safe for now.

The commiseration continued. Peachy cried—cried a lot. Time supposedly heals all wounds. Only time would tell. Eamon was stoic. He stayed strong, trying his best to shield the pain. He was anguished, but his weaker moments remained unseen by the family eye.

The trip to Pennsylvania helped Stephen, but it was no panacea. He would need time. The FBI would be presenting him with a civilian meritorious award for his actions that saved the life of Amanda Mahoney, known best as Mandy McMasters. The Boston Police would cite him as well, but considering the circumstances, both awards would be given discreetly.

William Jonathan Barnes was ambivalent. He'd gotten what he'd asked for. Now he knew the name of his daughter's slayer, but it had been costly. Simeon Kolotov was a loyal, lifetime friend. Matthew's aged knife had severed one of his arteries. He never left the Hoosac Tunnel alive. But Barnes was true to his word.

Four weeks after Matthew's disappearance, a man in a business suit unexpectedly arrived at Stephen's condo unit. When Stephen opened the door the man handed him an envelope and suitcase before walking away. The envelope contained a check for Stephen's hourly rate of service. It was a substantial sum of money, but the true windfall was inside the suitcase. It was fifty thousand dollars—cash—just as Barnes had promised. Stephen was shocked, not knowing how to react. The money sat under his bed for a week. It was blood money. Keeping it was never an option. After careful thought and consultation with Eamon, he knew what was best.

Stephen sat at his desk and wrote. The letters were lengthy, probably longer than they should have been. But he needed closure, and he wrote with clarity so that there would be no doubt as to his emotions and intentions. Stephen was devastated by the sinister actions of his brother.

He mailed all the letters except one. It was his turn to play deliveryman. Stephen taped the letter to the top of a sealed shoebox and drove, reaching the Lower Cape in ninety minutes. He rang the bell and a tired woman answered. "May I help you, sir?" She looked at Stephen but he didn't speak. He couldn't speak. The woman had a vacuous stare. She sensed his apprehension.

Finally, "Ma'am, please take this." He handed Mrs. Rivera the box of fifty thousand dollars, then walked away. She called to him but he moved quickly, climbing into the Jeep and racing away, never looking back. Alicia Rivera's mother was poor, still having children to support while subsisting on a marginal income.

It was the right thing to do, the only thing to do. One of Stephen's friends was a lawyer, and he had contacted the parents of Darlene Hughes. Their beloved daughter too had fallen at the will of evil Matthew. The lawyer explained Stephen's intentions and they wholeheartedly agreed. They were wealthy people; they didn't need the money. Stephen's letter to the Hugheses sat on the mantle, and every time Mrs. Hughes looked at it she cried. She telephoned Stephen, an awkward thing for him to handle, but he felt relieved afterward. The Hugheses were proud of what Stephen—the good brother, they called him—did with the money.

Goodwill was not limited to the Rivera family. Barnes gave Stephen five thousand dollars in slush money. It was for any purpose. Barnes made it clear that expense receipts weren't necessary. Stephen now retained over three thousand dollars of the slush money. He had initially intended to return it to Barnes; after all, it was his money. But then he remembered a particular house in Hoosac Mills on the corner of Mohawk Street. The old home was weathered; the back porch and stairway were dilapidated. They needed replacement. The old home belonged to Johnny Malfkoski—a true friend and one of the world's last stand-up guys. Stephen would help.

Stephen's relationship with his fraternity brothers was fractured but not beyond repair. Billy Munsing visited Stephen after receiving his letter, trying to help him cope. He embraced Billy, giving him a hug he desperately needed. They would always be friends.

Jimmy Petrilli called Stephen. The conversation was uneasy for both. Things were different now; things would always be different. Stephen couldn't shake the guilt. His brother's sins seemed to have affected all parts of his life. In the coming weeks Stephen would see Jimmy. Maybe then things could change.

All was normal and routine at the Boston House. Cleared of all allegations, Stephen returned with an unblemished record. The Boston House was a funny place—an oxymoron. It epitomized chaos and monotony at the same time, depending on the day. Mickey O'Sullivan survived his plight. An undercurrent of his predicament—and Stephen's cover-up—whispered around the institution. Nothing was ever proven. But in prison, perception and supposition outweigh reality. Stephen wouldn't be putting in for promotion anytime soon.

Stephen's attention finally turned to Melanie, the topic he tried to repress. He would have to deal with her sooner or later; it was inevitable. Melanie was everything he ever imagined in a woman, even more than Alexia. Melanie was his dream girl. There was nothing she didn't have: charm, intelligence, wit, beauty, and a big heart. Oh, how beautiful his Melanie was. He thought of her every day. The decision was made.

It was time to see her.

* * *

Stephen turned violently in bed. He was beginning to heal but the dreams continued. They evolved into nightmares, and this one was more horrific than most…

The Jeep cruised into Springfield late in the afternoon. Stephen stopped in front of Sampson's Funeral Home—then gave it a menacing glare. He moved along, begrudgingly. In minutes, the Jeep, seemingly on autopilot, rolled into the Gate of Heaven—Melanie's new neighborhood. He was hesitant to see her. He was scared because he didn't know what to say. She was staying in an area the locals called Ireland's Row. Names like O'Connor, Dunleavy, McDonald, Smith, O'Brien, Flaherty, and Leary abounded.

He squirmed in the rental bed.

He tentatively walked Ireland's Row, suddenly stopping. Melanie appeared before him. She was beautiful, more beautiful than ever. She was wearing cutoff jeans and a tank top, her long hair swinging freely below her shoulders. Her green eyes lit up the sky, her dimples accentuated her smile.

"Hello, Melanie."

"Good afternoon, Stephen, it's a pleasure to see your handsome face. Where have you been? How come you haven't visited me sooner?"

"I don't know. I guess it's been fear…and shame."

"Shame? Why do you say such a crazy thing? You did the best you could. There's no reason for you to feel shame. That's ridiculous, Stephen."

"Is it? Look at the buckets of blood spilled at the hand of my brother, my flesh and blood. I should have figured it out sooner."

"Don't beat yourself up, Stephen. You couldn't have done anything to prevent it. What's meant to be is meant to be."

Stephen tossed and turned, trying to awaken. But the dream captured him; it wouldn't surrender.

A hummingbird invited itself into the dream, perching on the limb of a magnificent oak tree. Stephen adored the bird. It represented all that was beautiful; it represented

Melanie. When he turned back to Melanie her appearance had changed. She now wore a lavender dress and her hair was drawn back in a bun. Melanie's image was quite real. Her watery green eyes changed to ocean blue. Stunning, he thought, absolutely stunning.

"I never told you how beautiful you are, Melanie. You don't know how much you mean to me."

"You and I were meant for each other, Stephen, you know that."

"Yes, I do. And it's unfair. You and I, we never had our chance—yet I feel for you like I've never felt for any woman in the world before."

"I love you, Stephen Patrick Nicholson. I love you very much."

"The feeling is mutual."

"Come now, Stephen, you can do better than that. Say what it is that you came here to tell me."

Stephen's eyes drifted to the headstone. The cutter was a fine craftsman who wielded the chisel with precision. A three-leafed shamrock stared him in the face. Fumbling for the right words, he finally spoke.

"I came here today, Melanie, to tell you I love you more than anything in the world, and I'd die a thousand deaths just to touch you right now."

"Oh Stephen, but you can. Come to me and let me feel your soft lips."

Stephen walked toward the image of Melanie and dropped to one knee. He extended his arms, reaching out and finding her face. He kissed her, and when he pulled back his mouth, chalk residue from the engraved shamrock clung to his lips. He rose and took a step back, gazing at her beautiful visage with all the will and imagination he had left.

"I need you in my life, Melanie. I can't manage without you. My feelings for you are that strong."

"I'm anywhere and everywhere you want me to be. Just close your eyes and open up your heart and soul. There you will find me."

"We had a future, Melanie, but what never was shall now never be."

"Stephen?"

"Yes, Melanie?"

"Don't search for me in the bottom of a glass because you won't find me there."

Stephen ingested her words, hesitated. "I know that."

"You never answered my question, Stephen."

"Excuse me?"

"The question I asked you inside the tunnel—you never answered it, Stephen. Have you forgotten?"

Melanie's beautiful image began to fade. He reached out again and caressed the side of her face. He was trying to stay strong, but for only the second time in twelve years his dam was breaking.

"Of course I remember, Melanie."

"Well, then?"

Stephen woke from the nightmare in a furor, his body saturated in sweat. His face was soaked, tears in his eyes. It was a dream—a bad dream. He reached over, feeling the space next to him. It was warm; it was empty. He panicked.

He jumped from the bed. He fled from the cabin wearing only a pair of boxer shorts. He ran down a winding trail. He found her at the dock, standing alone on the banks of the Penobscot River. It was a cool summer night in Maine. A trace of fog filled the air yet the moon shined bright in the sky, resting on the peaks of Mount Katahdin. Stephen looked up—the constellations were witnesses to his panic. Orion, Perseus, Hercules, and Gemini owned the night. In a short moment he found the Big Dipper and his eye quickly guided him to Ursa Minor, his favorite. He smiled, thinking of something his uncle told him many years before.

Stephen approached the woman. He stopped fifteen feet away. She wore a pair of his charcoal-colored boxer briefs and a loose T-shirt. She turned, faced him. When the woman smiled, he froze. Stephen was in awe of Melanie Leary.

I love you more than you'll ever know.

"The answer to your question is yes, my dear," he said.

Melanie shot him a quizzical look.

"There will always be beautiful wine between us," he said.

Five seconds of comfortable silence ensued. A tear crawled down Melanie's cheek. "Come to me, Stephen," she said.

He obliged.

Stephen slid his hands carefully around Melanie's waist. He didn't want to aggravate her healing wound. Melanie placed her hands on Stephen's cheeks. She leaned in close, inches away from his face. Melanie's gaze was intense. He could barely breathe.

"I love you the world," she said.

Then he kissed her.

ABOUT THE AUTHOR

Thomas Donahue is a lifelong resident of Massachusetts who earned his degree from North Adams State College in western Massachusetts. He has completed twenty-one years with the Suffolk County Sheriff's Department in Boston where he holds the rank of lieutenant. During his tenure he has worked as a line officer, sergeant, and training instructor. He developed a broad view of the prison world and has used this knowledge and viewpoint to craft an authentic subplot that will appear very real to anyone who has worked behind the walls of a correctional facility.

Made in the USA
Lexington, KY
14 December 2012